THE SOJOURN

BOOKS BY ALAN CUMYN

FICTION
Waiting for Li Ming (1993)
Between Families and the Sky (1995)
Man of Bone (1998)
Burridge Unbound (2000)
Losing It (2001)
The Sojourn (2003)

FICTION FOR CHILDREN
The Secret Life of Owen Skye (2002)

NON-FICTION
What in the World Is Going On? (1998)

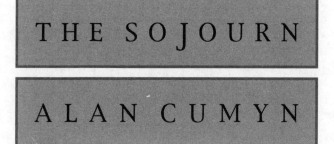

THE SOJOURN

ALAN CUMYN

M&S

National Library of Canada Cataloguing in Publication

Cumyn, Alan, 1960-
The sojourn / Alan Cumyn.

ISBN 0-7710-2492-4

I. Title.

PS8555.U489S64 2003   C813'.54   C2002-905909-7
PR9199.3.C775S64 2003

We acknowledge the financial support of the Government of Canada through the Book Publishing Industry Development Program and that of the Government of Ontario through the Ontario Media Development Corporation's Ontario Book Initiative. We further acknowledge the support of the Canada Council for the Arts and the Ontario Arts Council for our publishing program.

The quotations on pages 140-42 are from the play *A Little Bit of Fluff* by Walter W. Ellis. Copyright © 1922 Samuel French Ltd. Reprinted by permission of Samuel French, Inc., 45 West 25th Street, New York, NY 10010.

Typeset in Minion by M&S, Toronto
Printed and bound in Canada

This book is printed on acid-free paper that is 100% ancient forest friendly (100% post-consumer recycled).

McClelland & Stewart Ltd.
The Canadian Publishers
481 University Avenue
Toronto, Ontario
M5G 2E9
www.mcclelland.com

1 2 3 4 5   07 06 05 04 03

For George and Adam and Claude,
who were soldiers of the Great War

ONE

I t's nighttime, endless night, and I can't walk four steps without Johnson treading on my heels. The first eight or ten times I say, "Shit, Johnson!" without turning around – *shit* like steam escaping from a pipe, but not too loud, nothing that would carry, and then *Johnson* full of hopelessness. I have iron pig's tails on my shoulders, stacks of a dozen on each, which weigh the earth. Johnson has two sheets of corrugated iron but can't figure out how to carry them. I like to sling them on my back with rope and tried to show him, but he doesn't want to be a bloody Egyptian slave – his words, *bloody Egyptian slave* – so he's got them spread across his long skinny arms and every time the wind puffs he swings around like a sail. He's almost running.

Slow down, I mean to tell him, take it step by step. Eyes large, ears aquiver, follow the blur of the back ahead of you: haversack and tin hat, the mud-squelch of one foot after another, and there's no use running, we'll just get there sooner.

"*Shit, Johnson!*" I say one more time, and as I turn, the pig's tails smash against the corrugated iron and we're like horseless medieval knights clambering around in armour.

"Quiet down!" the corporal hisses, and someone else in the murk says, "Shut up, arse-heads!" and when I turn around again we go clang one more time and Johnson slips off the duckboards.

"He's down," I say, feeling nothing, and I wonder vaguely, as if from a distance, what's wrong with me. He's down in a mudhole and might die and it's my fault.

Miller ploughs into me carrying a load of lumber, looks up finally with the eyes of one awakening from an awful dream into an even more awful reality. We can hear Johnson sloshing in the dark. "Fuck my arse in a shell-hole!" he says, too loud, and I let my picquets drop, hit the deck expecting the worst. Almost everyone else does too, but the hurricane light show is left, right, ahead of us, not here for some reason, not yet.

"What are you people doing?" the corporal asks. The clomp-clomp of investigative feet. "Why don't you send up some flares and start playing the bagpipes while you're at it?"

"I'm stuck," Johnson says, somewhere in the dark. "Crome knocked me over."

"He walked right into me!" I say.

"How deep is it?" the corporal asks.

From far down the line someone growls, "What buggered shit is holding us up now?" and the corporal, taking a risk, turns on his electric torch, scans the dark quickly. Johnson is mired to his chest, the iron sheets oddly floating in the mud beside him. Then the light flicks off and I think, that's it, we're all dead. But again there's nothing.

"Crome, stay behind, get him out," the corporal says curtly.

"The rest, let's go." Then, his face in mine, all moustache and fear: "I expect you to catch us up!"

I work on my knees, shove the two stacks of pig's tails to the side of the boards so the passing men won't trip over them. We're in what passes for a wood these days, shattered stumps of exploded trees, and the moon is obscured, the shadows are deeper than caves.

"Johnson! Where are you?"

"Here!" he replies, sounding yards away, even farther than a moment ago when the corporal shone his torch.

"Try to reach." I plant my foot, keep most of my weight back on safe territory. No sense having two of us lost in the muck. Men loaded like pack mules pass inches away. They are carrying bundles of empty sandbags, trenching tools, boxes of ammunition, spools of barbed wire, loads of lumber and iron stakes, crates of tools, more corrugated sheets and bundles of pig's tails, all these things along with their haversacks and rifles slung on their shoulders, and the new steel hats that produce such awful headaches, with gas masks packed on their chests, boots clogged with mud, eyes dull as sleepwalkers', so that half of them wouldn't worry if they happened to knock me into the slop. The other half say things like "What some buggers will do for a break," and "How's the fishin'?"

"Where are you?" Johnson whispers, and I tell him, "Here. Over here!" I reach out but he's still too far.

I take my rifle off my shoulder, double-check to make sure the safety is on, and extend it. I have one foot wedged in the muck, am holding on to the slimy boards for dear life. "Come on, Johnson. I haven't got all night." A shell lands near enough that the boards lift and fall, slurping, into the mire. "Come on!"

He grabs my barrel suddenly and nearly pulls me in. I almost lose my grip on the stock. He pulls and pulls. The barrel dips into the mud and I curse him under my breath.

"Hey, careful!" some idiot says as he steps on my calf. He has a beam on his shoulders and staggers. An end crashes down a foot from my head, cracks some of the boards. The bugger stays quiet, but trips again over one of the stacks of pig's tails and the beam goes splashing overboard. I cringe, keep hold of the rifle and Johnson.

"What in God's name is going on here?" someone asks in an officer tone of voice.

"This man is lying on the track," someone else says.

"Pull, Johnson!" I say.

"You there! Stand up!" the officer says. He starts kicking at my foot.

"I'm pulling someone in," I snap back.

"Stand up, Private!" he whispers harshly. "The boards are too narrow for this. If a man has fallen in he's to be left to his own devices. What battalion are you from?"

Without getting up I tell him and he says, "Bloody green-horns! On your feet at once!"

"Steady on!" I say. "I've almost got the major."

"The major?" he says, and in a second is kneeling beside me. "Who's there? Give a hand here. A major has fallen in!"

For ten, fifteen minutes – a lifetime for me and Johnson – we become a struggling mass of mud-soaked humanity, grappling for "the major," trying to get the earth to loose its vacuum hold. Eventually ropes are procured and he is hauled out like a horse caught in a drinking hole – though no horse is ever hauled out of one of these slime-pits – and for a few moments is allowed to writhe and wriggle on the duckboards while men crowd around. He's unrecognizable, mud-slimed from head to foot.

"Are you all right, Major?" asks the officer who helped us. He dribbles water from his canteen into Johnson's blubbering lips. Johnson has lost his pack and rifle, thank God. He has been transformed by the slime into . . . well, in this darkness, why not a major?

"He's not himself," I say quickly. "But perhaps I could get your name. I'm sure the major would be happy to write you up."

"Lieutenant Benson," the man says, dribbling some more water. "Of the 42nd. And I was helped by Sergeant Brown, Corporal Rawlings, and Higgins, Private Higgins."

"Very good, then," I say, and I repeat the names.

"It's T.H. Benson," the lieutenant says. He has narrow, intense eyes, a horsey nose. "There's a T.F. Benson as well, that's not me." And in a moment he has taken out his notebook, is scratching the names for me in pencil.

"Would the major like an escort back to the rear?" Benson asks, and I say no. I take the paper quickly and fold it once, stick it in my pocket. "We'll rest here a few minutes, then carry on."

Johnson, finally coming to his senses, nods his head once, major-like, then reaches out a muddy hand. "Thank you, Lieutenant," he says gravely. "I am in your debt."

"Right. Very well," Benson says, snapping to his feet. "Carry on," he orders to the darkness and soon the line is moving past us once again. Johnson beside me holds his head, smells of the ooze of creation.

"Bugger me," he says. "I've shit my pants."

◈

There is no sense trying to retrieve the lost articles: the haversack, Johnson's rifle, the sheets of corrugated iron. We let the passing 42nders go by until there's no more talk of "the major" and bloody greenhorns fouling up the supply lines. A weary group straggles back from some forward trench and for a while two lines are passing on the narrow boards, with me and Johnson perched on the edge, sitting on the pig's tails. Then we get to our feet and hoist up the bundles – he takes one of mine now but my burden feels no lighter. With loads on both shoulders there was a balance; with just one weighted side now we weave drunkenly on the slippery boards, especially with our boots so muddy and slick. For days this spring it has rained but tonight it's clear; there's no way to wash our boots. At least I'm only slimed to the knees, not head to toe like Johnson. Soon enough I switch the pig's tails to my arms, carry them bundled like a bunch of long-stemmed flowers you'd bring to a girl in an awful play. It's an odd thought and sticks with me a good long while: a girl onstage in a bonnet, with long ringlets and a ruddy face and everyone in the audience yelling, "Kiss her! Kiss her!"

Johnson steps on my heels again and I nearly smash into him once more. He says, "I'm sorry! I can't see a thing! Some mud has slipped into my eyes." So we stop and I wash his eyes with canteen water. Then we're on our way again, and within a few dozen strides my arms feel welded stiff, heavy as the iron in the bundle I'm carrying.

A shell lands behind us and the duckboards throw us forward like clods of dirt being whip-snapped off a rug. Johnson ploughs into me from behind and then we're rolling, pig's tails and all. I lie dazed in a heap on top of something hard and irregular – a shard of a tree trunk that might have sliced my body into spaghetti but somehow spared me. The next shell lands a little farther away, then the next farther still, so we are lucky. Just the smoke and mess and the groaning of some poor buggers back there, whoever they are. I swear I can hear a horse agonizing in the gloom, but no horse could've made it this far up the slippery boards.

In time I regain my feet, hoist my load again, and find Johnson sitting cross-legged on a dry spot off the trail. He's staring towards the lights of the big show.

"Come on, get up!" I say. "Where's your helmet?"

"It isn't right," he says.

"Damn right it isn't. Corporal said we were to catch up. God knows what he's going to have us do to make up lost time."

Boom! Boom! Boom! Johnson keeps staring at the agony of shellbursts on the horizon.

"Come on!" I say again and kick him in the thigh. "It's this way. We have to keep going!"

"Why?" he says, stupid, watching the lights.

"For King and bloody country!" I say and kick him again, too hard, and right on the knee: I astonish myself. I'm an instant from leaving him. Shells start landing closer again. Bugger it, I think, and start along, hugging my pig's tails. There's no duck-walk now. The ground is slime and shattered wood and strange, destroyed artifacts of war: wagon wheels, planks, odd bits of iron, unexploded shells, shrapnel, parts of corpses. A severed hand on a mess tin, and a soft blur in the muck underfoot that could be a dead rat or a bit of internal organ or even an abandoned pair of boots.

I don't know where the hell I am.

There was a guide at the front of our column but I was near the rear, and all that changed anyway when Johnson fell in. I lurch forward an uncertain amount of time, catch myself breathing like a crazed man, then stop to wait, to listen, to give sense a chance to reassert itself.

Mud-soaked Johnson scuttles to me. The six feet of him have somehow been compressed into a bent and cringing animal. "Ram. Ram," he says. "I think we should go back."

"We can't go back. The trenches are up there somewhere. Do you remember from the map?"

He doesn't look at where I'm pointing but fondly back into the darkness, where there's a terrible commotion, now that I listen – some other company has been hit and the stretcher-bearers haven't arrived yet.

"Weren't the trenches supposed to be just out of this wood?" I say.

"I wasn't paying attention," he says.

It's not so bad where we are. The shells are hitting to our rear, and we aren't getting run over by different units going up and down the paths, and it dawns on me slowly that we must be off the path now.

"I lost the picquets," Johnson says. "I lost my helmet and pack and rifle."

"Just pick up someone else's. Come on. We'll keep our eyes peeled. There must be other rifles and helmets around here. Maybe even some picquets." I say it but I don't move. It's as if my body knows I'm blustering, a bloody coward, a windy voice.

"Yeah," Johnson says. "I'll keep an eye out." He looks around as if those things might be right here, at hand, and I turn to look too, happy enough to pretend this is reasonable. We are both leaning into the shelter of an uprooted tree, looking, looking. The night is full of unnatural shapes, strange shadows, earth thrown up, roots exposed, what could be a weapon, a helmet, a bayonet, a limb. The noise now is continuous, makes me think suddenly that the Front has come to us and if we stay where we are it will pass over like a storm and be on to somewhere else.

And we'll be shot for desertion or taken prisoner, I think.

"Follow me!" I say, moving forward in an awkward crouch. My limbs rebel, are clenched solid. "This way." I say it in a firm, reasonable manner, as if saying it could make it so. It's better to act, to do something, anything almost, rather than wait to be pulverized into wormfood.

Through a horrible stretch of scrapland now, the shell-holes water-filled pocks upon the earth, our boots slipping in glue. The pig's tails are on my right shoulder again, and I leave my left arm for guiding me along the ground, like a third leg, to help me slip and tumble forward. Johnson heaves and grunts, happy to not be left behind. I think it's this way, honestly I do. I need to believe it, and must be right, too, because the shellfire increases, the clattering of the machine guns, the buzzing whine of the bullets is suddenly all around us, and we are on our bellies dragging the pig's tails together over rocks, clods, clumps of destroyed field. On and on, all uphill somehow, although the ground is flat on the aerial photographs they showed us back in the broken cellars of civilization. We heave and pause, heave and pause, with Johnson saying, "Jesus! mother, Jesus! mother," in a strange rhythm, our boots struggling for purchase in the squelch, my mouth now full of mud, I spit it out in shock and anger.

The pig's tails plough deeper and deeper into the ground. It feels like I'm trying to pull a dreadnought through this field.

We rest on the edge of three shell-holes, the iron bundle so deep in the muck we could easily lose it if we don't keep our hands on the rods. "Ram," Johnson says, catching his breath, "I think you broke my knee when you kicked me back there."

"You're doing very well for a bloody invalid," I say.

"I don't think I can stand up any more."

"Maybe you've caught a Blighty."

"No. No," he says.

"A nice piece of shrapnel. Could be your ticket."

"I'm not lucky enough."

"You already made it out of the Slough of Despond," I say. "*Major.*" It seems so suddenly funny, we're both giddy with it for a moment.

"What was his name? That bugger of a lieutenant?"

I feel for the piece of paper in my pocket, pull it out with some tenderness, try to read the printing.

"Benson." Johnson remembers it for me, and as he says it I can faintly see the letters.

"T.H." I say. "Not T.F." And we both erupt in laughter. A shell lands with an impotent thud somewhere in front of us, not far at all, and then another smashes into a pile of stones beside us, winging fragments everywhere. Johnson's body humps up suddenly beside me and a hot mist of blood seems to rain down for a moment, clogs my nostrils, makes me blink and wipe my eyes.

"Are you all right?" I say. "Johnson, are you all right?"

"A-1," he says after a time.

"Really? You weren't hit?"

"I'm too muddy for the shrapnel to reach me."

He lurches forward, pulling on the near-buried pig's tails. I come alongside and in a moment he resumes his, "Jesus! mother, *Jesus!* mother," grunting. I keep thinking he's going to collapse. He must have been hit back there – where else was the blood from? But there are bodies strewn all through this land, and perhaps the blood was simply in the air.

I think I know where I'm going. It's over this rise here, this sickeningly slight, two-foot Mt. McKinley that takes all our will and strength to crawl up and over. It suddenly seems the right direction, and when we reach the lip of the parados the pig's tails slide down into the gloom and we follow like bags of rock dumped down a slippery ravine, then lie on the bottom in the muck catching our breath.

"Are you sure this is the right trench?" Johnson says after a time. We can't see very far in either direction. The trench zigzags after a half-dozen paces either way.

"Shhh," I say. If it isn't the right trench, who's to say it's not a German one? We didn't cross any wire, but still, weirder things have happened, even in the short time we've been in this bloody dance. I motion to Johnson to go right while I go left. I rise carefully, wipe off the muzzle of my muddy Ross, slip the safety, fix my bayonet quietly, then take a couple of sloshing steps, realize Johnson is right behind me still.

"I haven't got a rifle," he whispers.

Step, wait, step, hugging the muddy corrugated-iron walls of the trench. Strangely, under the thunder of explosions from all sides, I can still hear the trickle of water in the trenchbed underfoot, the ragged, nervous breathing of Johnson at my shoulder.

I peer around the corner, panic when I catch sight of the bucket-shaped outline of a German helmet. But in front of my eyes it turns back into a friendly saucer. Another moment and I might have murdered a man in a fit of hallucination. Then just as I am thinking that, the soldier catches sight of us, raises his rifle and aims it straight at my shattering heart.

"Friend! Friend!" I say, but realize too late that I'm still aiming my rifle straight at him. I hear him fighting with the bolt – thank God for the Maggie Ross – then I drop my own rifle into the muck. "Seventh Canadian Pioneers!" I say. "What trench is this?"

We've fallen in with the RCRs, not too far, it turns out, from the reserve-line trenches we're supposed to be working on. The RCR corporal sends a guide to bring us round the right way, a shuffling, slope-shouldered hedgehog of a man who seems to smell his way along the labyrinth of passages, and who's almost too nimble and fast to keep up with. Johnson, afraid of being left behind, treads on my heels twice more before I finally think to send him ahead, and then I'm happy enough to concentrate on his soggy, dark form.

When we get to the right place at last, our corporal says, "Crome, where have you been, on bloody vacation?"

"We got turned around, Corporal," I say as briefly as possible.

He looks for a moment like he wants to pursue the issue, but says instead, "Put the picquets down over here. We've been waiting for you two." We follow him until the trench is a minor slit in the ground. "Shovels, gentlemen. But keep your nut low. We already lost Reese and Snug at this end."

I feel the bottom fall out of my stomach, have a hard time finding my breath for a moment.

"Are they dead?" I manage to ask.

"We were clobbered by coal-boxes coming in and a couple

of the lads saw them smeared out on the edge of it all," the corporal says, his voice lined with tin, as if he were telling us what was in the new rations.

I crouch a little lower. Reese was our clown, our farm boy from Ontario. I remember him spreading biscuit crumbs on Bill Frampton's chest that time we were sleeping in the barn outside Poperinghe, and in minutes Frampton had rats crawling on his face. Reese! Who organized the swimming down by the river where the Belgian girls went to bathe naked just at a certain time. And Snug was like a father. Like no father I ever had.

Johnson has already started to dig.

I get on my knees beside him, twist from the shoulders and waist, try to keep my head down. Why those two? I remember the Belgian girls with their dark hair down to their knees, looking up at us, at where we were near the bend in the river. Not caring, not turning away or scattering like flustered geese. Bare breasts, black triangles – we all got to see because of Reese and Snug. "Calmly, gents," Snug said, shucking off his own clothes, as we stood dumbstruck. "Do as the Belgians do!"

Snug and Reese wading into the water, wiry white muscles, pendulous manhood hanging in the open air. The both of them looking at the ladies looking at them. "Come on, lads!" Reese said. "You don't want them thinking we're a bunch of Englishmen!"

That look on Snug's face: free from his wife and family, walking in the world like a man should walk.

Johnson and I work on our knees, keep our heads as low as we can, shovel the mud into bags then tie them off, heave the bags up onto the sides. It is quiet, sweating, slavish work that drives the clock around with a slow, relentless grind, work that is measured in feet gained, rearranging the earth in such a minor but backbreaking way – this third reserve trench in the darkness of God's own Salient, which in just a few months has wiped out everything else in my life. Nothing exists except this shovel, this muck, this cutting, twisting motion.

This channel in the ground, which we extend so slowly, the sides rising with the sandbags. Every few feet we hammer in stakes to keep in place the boards and corrugated-iron sheets that someone else managed to wrestle this far. They seem so flimsy now that they have to hold back the earth, keep it from shrugging its shoulders and burying us. We're fortunate, though – most of the action is happening elsewhere tonight, and the shells that do land close by are swallowed by mud, barely disturb us in our burrowing.

"Where am I going to get another rifle?" Johnson asks in a break. We are leaning against the trench walls, stupid with fatigue.

"I told you, you have to pick one up. Try to get a Lee-Enfield."

"Maybe somebody picked up Reese's or Snug's rifle?" Johnson asks hopefully.

I look at him. The sweat has cleared some of the mud from his face, and he's taken off his shirt with the work. His body looks like a skinny, wind-bent tree. It's cold enough, this hour, that despite the work he's shivering.

"Stand-to pretty soon, and I don't have a rifle," he says.

"Well, go tell the corporal."

"The corporal's an arse-wipe." Johnson slams his shovel down and a rat scurries away.

"Ask someone else then," I say. "You go ahead and I'll keep chipping away at this."

He nods thankfully, pulls on his shirt, clambers off – the

slouching-crouch of the successful trench soldier – and I sit still, not moving a muscle, air barely entering and leaving my lungs. What time is it? It's endless time, Eternity, never-get-past-it time. I am stuck on Reese and Snug, gone just like that. I remember Snug coming up to me in training. I was polishing my buttons, couldn't for the life of me get them to gleam the way that was required. I didn't even notice him at first, standing in front of me with two heaping plates of food. Finally I looked up, and realized that I was starving.

"Let me give you a tip, son," he said. "The King is not going to keep you from battle just because of the state of your buttons. So feed your belly first, all right?"

He handed me one of the plates and sat beside me on the cot. We talked about fly fishing till the food had disappeared.

Now Snug is gone.

For a moment I am insanely aware that if I just stood up and stretched my arms in a normal, human sort of way, if I lit a cigarette and had a look around, I'd be shot through the brain. Or maybe not. Maybe the throat, maybe the chest, if my chest were high enough to show above the trench wall. It would be agony for a second or two – or maybe much longer if Fritz was a bad shot, if I got run through the jaw, say, like MacDonald last week. But if I was lucky and pegged out in an instant, as all the letters home say: *shot through the heart . . . died painlessly while urging the men onwards . . .* if I caught that sort of end, then I wouldn't have to finish this trench.

It's probably how Reese and Snug went. They probably didn't feel a thing.

I start to work again. The point of my trench shovel bounces off something hard, and then when I turn to empty the gains into a bag I notice a piece of bone, of cheekbone – there is old Frenchie staring out at me, or, rather, not staring. His eye cavity is vacant, partially covered by bits of hair, by mud and shadows, his cheek is dented where the shovel blade cut, and his peaked *képi* cap is squashed down the other side of his face. Nothing else of him can be seen – the rest of the body is buried in the ground still. Possibly he's lying stretched out in exactly the direction I'm digging.

I try to go around, to avoid him somehow, but he's an insistent ghost. With every shovelful a new section of him is uncovered: a bit of shoulder, wrist, hand, sleeve, a flap of haversack, a soiled scarf around his neck. Some flesh remains, but parts of him are simply skeleton, like the barrel-stave ribs that come out in twos and threes. The smell is overpowering, a gas attack of its own kind.

Where is bloody Johnson?

I don't want to handle this alone. I glance back impatiently, listen for his shuffled walk up the line.

There's no way to keep the body intact. The longer it takes the more angry I get, until I'm slashing at the damn thing, hacking out the skull, sections of backbone, the remaining bits of pelvis and guts. Several shovelfuls are no more than oozing soil and I can't help it – I vomit suddenly.

Bloody Johnson!

There are letters in the haversack, and what look like ration and pay books. His name, which I can just make out in the gloom – daylight coming soon, I think, Johnson must have fallen asleep in some dugout – his name is Gastonville. I tie a soiled pouch of papers to the neck of the sandbag holding most of the remains. Then I lean back against the wall of the trench and feel an arrowpoint of pain, a headache burning into a tiny section between my eyes, two or three inches into the matter of my brain.

I don't know how long I stay like that. When I open my eyes again it's because Johnson has come back, finally. "Stand-to!" he says.

I look at him dully.

"I found a rifle. Lear, MacMillan, and Dobbins were all wounded on the way in – they were standing with Reese and Snug. We were lucky I fell in when I did!"

"Bloody charmed life," I say to him.

I spend some time on my rifle. I bang off the remaining mud, pull the barrel through several times, oil the bolt and breech. Maybe it'll fire. The Maggie Ross. It's made for the range, of course, for target practice, sharpshooting in perfect conditions, and everyone knows it except for our great minister of militia, Sam Hughes, who must be mad to continue to insist on it when it has jammed up by the thousands, cost so many lives. They knew it at Second Ypres, and just a few months ago at St. Eloi, the tail end of which we caught coming in. Even our commander, General Alderson, has complained publicly. And yet here we are, still using the Maggie Ross, when we could have Lee-Enfields, which fire fifteen rounds a minute, on and on, reliable as a locomotive.

Put Sam Hughes in a trench for five minutes, I think, five minutes with a Ross rifle in the mud, then see what he thinks.

I keep expecting to look over and see Reese with an amused glint in his eye, captivated by something a rat is doing. I expect to see Snug leaning on his shovel in the gloom, asleep on his feet. That man could fade off anywhere.

Sergeant Williams, with the curving, hangdog moustache, the shoulders up to his ears, the broken front tooth, comes by a little later with the rum. It's almost light now; the sky is an unforgettable bruised purple, as if bleeding beneath its skin, but strangely peaceful too. I toss down my cupful, close my eyes, wait to feel it burn. In a moment I look up, disappointed – I am still shivering from the pre-dawn, am ravenously hungry.

"Somebody rum-sick here in the night?" Williams asks, sniffing at the spot where I vomited. At the word *rum-sick*, I think of off-duty nights under canvas with men staggering in, collapsing on their cots, sometimes making it out again to void themselves, sometimes not.

"I found a Frenchie in the path of our trench," I say. "Had to dig him out of there."

"And this is him here?" Williams asks, indicating the bag with the pouch of papers tied on top.

"So far," I say.

"Poor bugger," Williams says. Then, sentimentality over: "Lime him down, Crome."

At dawn, word comes down the line in a series of whispers, fast as the wind. Reese and Snug have wandered in! They weren't killed in the blast at all, but were blown back behind a bunch of old tree stumps, and then were stuck in a shell-hole all night under some zealous machine-gunner's eye. They finally slipped out when Reese realized he might miss breakfast. Binks grins in the dying darkness as he tells the story.

And if I were a better teller, I think, then "Major" Johnson floundering in the slime would have been just as good. But I'm the same as Snug, happy to pal around in quiet with a character like Reese.

We stand-to for an hour and I can't stop smiling to think of it – Snug and Reese walking back from obliteration, and telling it all like a tall tale. Then just as the sun is clearing some of the tree fragments in the distance, the morning hate erupts: a horizontal hail of bullets smashes into the parados behind us, some ricocheting off wood and iron, off rocks and helmets and, down the line, off loophole shields. It's a time for crouching into the soil, for shrinking, for jamming fingers into earholes and keeping one's head down. Our new sandbags have caught someone's attention: in a few minutes they're cut to pieces, and Johnson and I have to crouch lower and lower, until we're flat on our stomachs hugging the muck.

At the end, when the sun has risen just enough to push us through the morning hate, I have a hard time releasing my hand from the grip of my rifle. The muscles have locked, my whole right side is rigid from strain.

"Fritz must be in a bad mood today," Johnson says, finally, when it's quiet enough to be heard.

◈

After a hard night's work we are graced with breakfast that has been brought up from the rear. Campbell has the gluey porridge pot, Jenkins is ladling coffee from a cauldron, and the lineup is ragged, disorderly, impatient. We are in a well-dug section of the reserve trench now, tall enough that a short man like me can stretch to his full height, stand with almost dry boards under his boots, digest a good deal of breakfast just from smelling the air. And a good thing, too, because there's never enough actual food to satisfy the gnawing hunger that is our constant companion out here.

I catch sight of the two of them, our prodigals, at the head of the line. Snug with his stolid, chiselled face, and young Reese looking like he's posing for a poster, his helmet cocked back, that blond hair, the sculpted cheekbones, almost Teutonic, those blue eyes in this sunshine. Despite their adventures they hardly look any mouldier and muck-bound than the rest of us trench rats after this long night.

And except for the buzz around those two, the lads are quiet, exhausted. After working hours in the night with shirts off we are now buttoned to the neck and bundled against the cool morning air. May! When we arrived in March there were mornings with snow, midnights when we wondered if our bodies would be frozen into a mudbank, when we thought with amazement of the veterans who'd made it through the raw killing days of February, January, December.

But this is sweet May. The dawn sky is a childhood blue, there are white puffs of clouds, and already aeroplanes are carving noisy paths above our heads. A friendly Belgian flyer passes over our lines two, three times, only a hundred feet up, and waves as we lift our mugs. I spoon down the oatmeal hungrily, gratefully. Could anything taste better than this? It's almost warm still. Sitting on a firestep, I scrape the porridge from the edges of my mess tin, my coffee resting on my lap, warming my abdomen. *Dear Mother*, I compose in my head. *Last night was something of a trial, but we made it through all right. A bit dicey, sometimes, this getting to and from the front lines. But once in things settle down and so far . . .*

I hear a pop and my coffee spills. Then I am pressed against the wall of the trench, scanning the sky. There it is, far overhead, the *minenwerfer*, trench mortar, going *zung-zung*, end over end like a rugby football. I watch its sickening descent, at first something slow and unreal, then faster, faster, not here, thank God, but fifty yards over. But there are more pops, of course there are, in a while too many to keep track of, men start to run pell-mell, scramble for shelter.

Unbearable noise, sudden, choking smoke, the terrible shock of concussion. Fielding staggers by holding his arm, yelling, "He was German. A bloody German!" until I understand that the pilot from a few minutes ago was not Belgian at all: he was flying a captured aeroplane. Soon the mortars, fired from the German lines just a few hundred yards away, are joined by screaming shells from farther off, and I crawl on my belly along the trembling floor of the trench until I reach a crowded dugout and pull myself in. We are a mass of men, some wounded, some crying, all of us covering our heads with our hands, huddled.

"Stop it! Stop it!" someone cries out, and another yells, "Bloody shut up!" at the top of his lungs, but among the explosions around us these voices sound frail, terribly small.

For a moment I'm certain this is it – the roof timbers are going to collapse, we will soon be joining the Frenchman in the mud. It seems insane to stay inside but I can't move either. One, two, three explosions scramble us, and mud falls from above, but not the huge slide I expect. I can't move anyway, am welded rigid with fear and anticipation.

Sooner than I expect the hate passes. As the explosions turn into rumbles sounding farther and farther away, we blink in the darkness, become men once more.

"Smells like a bloody sewer in here!" Reese says, and he monkeys around, sniffing trousers. "Eew, Johnson, is that you?" Down the line. "Snug! Have you been bathing in the latrine? My God, Peterson, what's your mother going to say?"

We spill out of the dugout, dazed at the light and the change in scenery. The trench has caved in just a few feet from the entrance, a direct hit; farther along the line in the opposite direction, where Johnson and I were working before, there is no trench left at all, only a series of holes in the ground. The bag with the Frenchman in it has either been obliterated or buried again.

We have surprisingly few casualties of our own. You'd think such explosive power would destroy us all, and yet the toll is slight: Fielding's arm has been cut from shrapnel, a skinny boy named Franklin twisted his knee running for cover, and Jones with the crossed-anchor tattoo on his forearm – he didn't want to join the navy because of the U-boats, but still he liked the tattoo – bumped his nose against an overhead beam as he ran into a dugout down the way.

We fared worse last night just coming up the line.

When the excitement dies down we sit in the sunshine, in the less-battered lengths of our trench, and smoke, write letters, chat, doze. The bombardment has been an isolated event – in the wake of the chaos no Huns are marching across to take us on. Repairs to the damage will be for tonight. There's no point showing ourselves now to receive more bloody attention. Besides, we're exhausted. We lie like corpses, hugging the walls of our refuge, are within an hour a fly-swarmed troop of oblivious, snoring men. I blessedly dream of nothing at all, then open my eyes slowly and see Gryphon and Partridge back to back, cradling their rifles, heads slumped forward, hands limp and open. Gryphon has a bad cut on one finger. I can see it oozing from where I sit, some feet away. A trio of flies worries the wound incessantly. I'm surprised the sergeant hasn't ordered him to clean and bandage it. We've been told over and again it's the sort of thing that kills a man out here.

Three, four, five rats amble down the floor of the trench, sniffing the muddy puddles that are forming and reforming now that the shape of our little world has changed with the bombardment. They are large, fat, prosperous creatures with glossy hides, and are having a very good war. When I flick my boot at them they turn insolently, look at me with their beady rat eyes as if fixing my identity for some future feast. Then they waddle off, tails slithering in the muck.

Some men have been pissing in the trench, or what's left of it. With the walls blown apart in so many places, it isn't safe to try to make it to the latrine – too many yards of exposure. No order is given, as far as I know, and so men make up their own minds, avert their faces, relieve themselves, then turn over the soil with their shovels. It's what I do myself. By midday the smell of ammonia is awful, but no worse, in a way, than the stench of unwashed bodies, of chemicals from explosives, of rotting flesh laced through this soil, of putrid water dripping relentlessly down to the lowest, filthiest level at which men can live.

I look down the line at Reese at the exact moment he looks at me. It's a strange thing. I haven't asked him about his night in the shell-hole, he hasn't asked me about my adventures with

Johnson. They are over with now, done hours ago, and we'd both rather think about other things.

He smiles, begins to sing softly in the tune of "Auld Lang Syne":

We're here because we're here because
we're here because we're here . . .

It's taken up along the line. Soon the tune comes from ragged voices in the distance, some so far away, so faint, I imagine the song travelling like a telegraph signal all the way to Switzerland through this network of muddy ditches.

"Cut it out! Cut the crap! No singing!" Sergeant Williams says, stamping his boot, splattering us into silence. He turns as if ready to bayonet us for insubordination, but the men are smiling; we're lazing here in the sun on a perfect day, in God's perfect world.

◈

"So how is our Ram?" Reese asks, sometime in the afternoon.

I tell him my belly is full, and try to think of the phrase in Chinese. Father taught me once, but it's gone from my mind. For just a moment I am seized with a sense of the strangeness of life. Somewhere in Hong Kong is a cable car that he helped build up a mountain as a young man, and here I am in a hole in Belgium struggling with a phrase from that time.

"Full of bully beef and biscuit?" Reese asks, easing himself beside me.

"Full of fruitcake from my aunt in London," I say. "Nearly mouldless, and completely gone."

"You laughing bugger!" I think he's talking about the fruit-cake, but says instead, "What wouldn't I give to have an aunt in London?" His eyes have a misty sheen. "I can't get enough of London. I have a girl in London."

"Only one?"

"One main one. That's a principle right there. A girl in every port, but *just* one. Two is much worse than one."

I ask Reese about his girl in London and he fishes out a letter. "*Dear Jeremy,*" he reads, his voice slightly raised, like a girl, a silly one. "*I hope that this finds you in all ways safe and comfortable. My mother and I –*" Reese looks up. "She lives with her mother," he says, "the father's a captain somewhere – *were very concerned to read about your hand-to-hand combat with the German thugs who were spraying your trench with poison gas.*"

"Hand-to-hand combat?"

He grins sheepishly.

"Spraying poison gas? How did you get that horse manure past the censor?"

"Those clerks don't care if you tell a few tales," Reese says. "As long as you stay away from the truth!" He turns his attention again to the letter. "She's asking about the size of my feet. She's been knitting socks like a woollen factory. Do you want some?"

It seems like weeks since my feet were last out of these boots, though it was only yesterday that we left billets. They feel like they'd swell to melon size as soon as I tried to loosen the laces.

"Why not?" I say.

"I'll put you down for two pairs." He reads again. "*I cannot tell you how proud I am to be able to do my bit in the patriotic effort, small as it is compared to what you and your gallant comrades are accomplishing in the battlefields of Honour!*"

It seems, suddenly, hilariously funny. "The battlefields of Honour!" I say, and gesture with my hand at the oozing mud, the dripping sandbags, rusting iron, the flies at our faces.

"Of Honour! Of Honour!" Reese says, giddy with it, with all this Honour, and his foot slips, he loses his perch on the firestep beside me, wallows exaggeratedly in the mud. Men look at us from up and down this pitiful, wounded ditch and start to laugh as well, not knowing what the hell we're laughing at. But it's Reese, of course it's funny.

Later I make a quick sketch, on a precious piece of writing paper, of Reese on his back in the mud, his helmet askew, boots in the air, holding the letter safe from harm, and print at the bottom, BATTLEFIELDS OF HONOUR. "You must send it to your London paramour," I tell him gravely. "What's her name?"

"Cynthia Elaine Whyte," he says, accepting the sketch. "Whyte with a *y*."

I try out the name. "Cynthia Elaine Whyte."

"If you say it often enough –" he says, pausing, as if in deep thought.

"Yes?"

"You get to fuck her," he says. When he sees my look of surprise, he adds, "In your mind. Over and over, there she is, raising her petticoats, spreading her long, white, luscious . . ." He stops because of the whine of a shell, the first hint of close action in a while. The shell hits and explodes a couple of hundred yards off; neither of us looks away. "Cynthia Elaine Whyte," he says slowly, as if feeding me medicine.

◈

The sun turns cheerless by mid-afternoon, and then we are drenched in another cold, pitiless rain. Greatcoats appear, and rain capes, mackintoshes, and makeshift covers. The rain drips off the rims of our helmets, drums dolefully against any surface open to it: rubber, canvas, metal, mud. As luck would have it, I am on sentry while most of the platoon retreats to the relative shelter of dugouts. I survey the surroundings in snatches from the field periscope that has been set up close to the trench wall that collapsed in this morning's attack: tangles of barbed wire scratched across an ungodly expanse of blown-up field, the mud yellow in places, soupy, saucered with rain-filled ponds. The jagged folds of the forward trenches crease the earth ahead. Now and again I catch a glimpse of the top of a helmet gliding by, a bit of mud-spattered khaki. Farther along, up a slow rise, is No-Man's Land: some poor bugger is twisted still on the wire, too far away to make out clearly. Past him, surrounded by shattered tree stumps, more jagged folds in the earth – the German lines, in which there are no signs of life.

Sleep, Fritz, I think. Stay quiet for three more days, until I am back in billets.

With the night comes more labour, troglodyte sweat. At first it's difficult to rouse ourselves from the day's lethargy, the bone-numbing task of staying warm and sane while exposed to the elements, the bosom of Mother Mud. "Get stuck into it, you lazy slugs!" Sergeant Williams says. "What do you think this is, a bloody paid vacation?"

When the sergeant has gone Reese says, "Enjoy the bucolic splendour," bending, grunting, the soil on the end of his trenching tool as much water as dirt.

"The alcoholic splendour?" Snug says. He looks around for Williams, then takes his helmet off. His grey hair shines in the dull darkness.

"The bucolic, alcoholic, frivolic splendour of the Belgian countryside!" Reese says. Johnson holds a sandbag open and Reese pours the guck into it. Snug follows with his contribution, then me. Our blades make a funny, squelching noise when we carve into the soup. "Enjoy the natural, healthy rhythms of the land."

Drive with the legs, straighten the back as much as you dare, turn, dump.

"Sweat like a horse!" Snug says.

"*Be* a horse!" Reese counters.

Drive with the legs, straighten . . .

"Come on, Johnson!" Reese says impatiently. "If you're going to be bag man, you have to keep up!" Johnson is wrestling with the twine to tie off the sandbag – the mudbag. The pile of dirt we are combating is showing no signs of reduction, but seems able to regenerate from an inexhaustible source.

Johnson finishes with the twine, hoists the bag to his shoulder, and then the tied end bursts, dumping mud all down his back.

He swears under his breath, and we are choking back laughter.

"I won't fill a bag more than once," Reese declares, stepping back from the mudslide.

"Sorry, union rules," says Snug. "Rates go up. Time and a half in the middle of the bloody night."

There is a light show all across the lens of the Salient. Flares –

green, yellow, brilliant white – signalling their silent messages. Fiery explosions, lit semi-arcs of strange, unknown shells, like stars racing to oblivion across the sky, sudden flashes of purple and red, then the startling, brief return to blackest night. If it weren't for the noise, the choking smoke, the upheaval of earth and bone, it would be a fine show, a wonder.

"Double time when they're shooting at you," says Reese.

"Triple time when the beds are made of mud."

"When the *food* is made of mud."

"When the *mud* is made of mud," says Johnson.

"That's it," says Reese. "This mud-made mud. This bloody man-made –"

"Mud-made –"

"*Blood*-made!"

"Mud."

We leave the aborted sandbag for now, fill another, another, another. We become blubbering, grunting, farting, digging machines. Drive with the legs, straighten the back, turn, dump. Tie off the end, hoist, place, pack. This black slurp of soil, these strained lungs, tight muscles, ridiculous effort, our own war in miniature. Extend this slash in the soil, fortify, fit in the fire-steps, the shielded loopholes, the beginnings of a dugout for shelter. We have heard the stories of the reinforced-iron-and-concrete palaces over on the other side, where the tender meats, jellied fruits, dark bread, bottles of German wine and beer are brought by rail to the Kaiser's spoiled, indulged soldiers, who sing every night (but we're too far away, we can't hear them from here), who play cards and chat about the weather in their bunkers underground whenever our artillery tries to bother them, whose scientists are month after month inventing weapons for them to try on us. Like the new gas that someone in an *estaminet* told Reese about that gums up rifles and machine guns. We've yet to see that. Chlorine we've had, but there's another one too, a colourless, odourless killer that does nothing for twenty-four hours and then you can't breathe, start to choke and wheeze, die slowly in agony. We might be breathing some of it now and not even know.

"Shhhh!" Snug says and we stop, even Johnson. I sniff the air, listen for the sound of a gas gong. Hard to know in the trench, but there seems to be a steady wind heading our way, a perfect night for an attack.

We stand still for an endless minute while Snug cocks his ear: rumbles of explosions, diverse late-night wartime carnival sounds, the grunts and groans of the other crews working up and down the line.

"What is it?" I ask finally.

"I hear a tapping," Snug says. And he beats two fingers on his forearm in time.

"Miners?"

Snug nods his head. "Could be," he says.

We all try to hear what Snug is hearing. When I watch his fingers I can just make it out, I think – a methodical, thud-thud-thudding that I feel so slightly in my feet as much as hear it.

"Should we tell the sergeant?" Johnson asks.

"No, I think we should just stay here and get blown up!" Reese says. "Try to find the lieutenant," he says, and Johnson scampers away like a puppy. Snug puts his helmet back on, kneels down in the mud, blocks up one ear with his hand and listens some more.

Word travels and soon almost all our own sounds of digging

stop. Ferguson slouches over to listen beside Snug. "I used to work in the coal mines," he says. He lays both palms on the walls of the trench and presses his ear flat between them. "Hell of a long way for Heinie to be digging," he says after a while.

"It's not getting stronger," Snug whispers. "But it's not going away either."

Sergeant Williams sloshes towards us like a moose walking along a creek bed. "What are you arseholes doing?" he says.

"It's hard to hear," Snug says quietly.

"Damn right it's hard to hear!" the sergeant says.

"Shhhh!"

Williams looks ready to horsewhip him, but stands still instead, seething.

"It's faint, but I hear something."

"Could be digging," Ferguson says quietly.

"And it could be a bloody bugger of a fly buzzing around in a puddle!" Williams says. He is referring, of course, to C Company, which fell into a near-panic the first night in the trenches over exactly that, the buzzing of a fly in a puddle. "Get back to work!" Williams barks. "Everybody, get back to bloody work!"

Snug looks at him with slow contempt, sighs heavily, straightens up. "I don't hear any flies in puddles," he mutters.

"What was that, soldier?" Williams shoots back.

"Nothing, Sergeant," Snug says with murderous calm.

Back to the mud-shovelling. Evidently Williams decides that we need a great deal of supervision, and so we work in silence and endure his steady sarcasm. "What is this, the Daughters of the Empire tea party? Put your backs into it. I want to see some effort. Or do you hear more flies buzzing? You're the slowest bunch of buggered sissies I've ever –" And on and on, in a lashing voice. Snug works steadily, not hurrying a fraction. I am thinking, *one turn, I could smash his face with the shovel.* I am thinking, *it's dark here, who would know but us?*

Stupid thoughts.

Drive with the legs, straighten the back, turn, dump. Body into machine. Lungs and legs, shoulders and arms. Williams's voice recedes in the night, just another irritation, one of so many in this crawl of time.

◈

At two-thirty in the morning we get a break, sit on sandbags, sweat carving down our muddy bodies. Tea has come up the line – bitter, old, lukewarm, greasy. But perfect for the likes of us. I feel drunkenly tired, sodden in the head. Muddy sweat drips from my face into my cup. "What day is it?" I ask blankly, keeping my voice low. When were we in billets – only yesterday? It seems like a month or more ago.

No one answers. There's a terrific explosion to our right, miles away, but it seems to throw flame hundreds of feet in the air, blanks out all other sights, sounds, thoughts for a time.

"I'm trying to remember why I agreed to come out here," Reese says.

"For the fresh air and healthy living," Snug says dully.

"I think it's Tuesday," Johnson chips in.

"I think I came out to ride horses," Reese says.

Idle machine-gun fire, someone groaning in the darkness, rats splashing by in the mud. We are all scratching our chatts. The warm work has brought them out from their safe spots in the seams of our clothing.

"They said they wanted men who were good with horses," Reese says. "I never would have joined up if I thought I was going to be turned into a workhorse myself. A whole bunch of us would have stayed home."

"Headed for the hills," Snug grunts.

"Yesterday was Monday," Johnson says. "So today must be Tuesday."

"But Tuesday the what?" I ask.

"That's it," Reese says, scratching his head, his armpits, his elbows. "Tuesday the what of May?"

"Year of Our Lord," I say with fatigue, for no particular reason except that I like the sound of the words, and Johnson chimes in, "Nineteen-sixteen," as if I needed help with that as well.

Reese repeats, "The what of May." Then he says, "I was reading the newspaper in billets, I should know. It was all about bloody Ireland. Who gives a damn about Ireland?"

"Maybe we should be fighting this war in Ireland," Snug says. "They have some nice horses there."

"Do they?" Reese asks.

"How the bugger would I know?" Snug says. "But I saw a picture once." Then, after a pause, "I came to teach the Kaiser a lesson. And if the minister of munitions could pull his head out of his arse for a moment he'd fix it so we'd have the right rifles and enough artillery to finish this work and all go home. I've heard enough twaddle about fighting to the bitter end and all the further sacrifices we have to make."

"Our great sacrifice," Reese says. "Someone told me Hughes is trying to throw Alderson out for criticizing the Ross rifle. You know what else I heard? There's a move afoot to send us all to Verdun to shore up Frenchie there. Wouldn't that be a nice step into the meat-grinder?" We are silent for a while, and I feel I have heard too many rumours about Hughes, Alderson, the Maggie Ross, the killing at Verdun, and everything else for that matter.

"As much as possible," I say quietly, "I try not to think about ministers and generals. It just gives me a headache." I'm trying to remember how important certain things were – honour, valour, the call of one's king. These seem claptrap now, in such surroundings, hardly worth mentioning to the likes of Snug and Reese. So I say what we all still know. "The truth is that Fritz won't back down till we've fed him enough iron. It's all the Germans believe in, and if we don't give it to them, they'll give it to us. I came to paint signs, but since I'm here I'll do what it takes. We'll win despite the generals and politicians."

"You came to paint signs?" Reese says.

"I was told a pioneer painted signs and did a few other things, and that sounded all right. I had no idea what the few other things might be, and I've yet to paint a sign, much less anything more interesting." I think for a moment of that simple pleasure of sitting still and looking deeply, and pouring everything from the eye into the hand, and how long it has been since I could give myself over to it in the old, carefree way. They are looking at me, expecting me to finish my thought, so I say, "Even my father accepted the decision, and he's no admirer of this war." There is much more to say, of course, about Father, about painting, about this blasted, necessary war. But I find myself weighing my words so much that I lapse into silence.

Then Snug says softly, "I can still hear it." We all look at him. "The bloody digging," he says. "If anything it's stronger." We strain to listen. It's hard not to imagine that Fritz is right underneath us, packing the mine with explosives, getting ready to blow us up the moment he can scramble back to his own side and plug up his end of the tunnel.

We hear Williams's moose-clomping boots and make a show of getting back to work.

"The first was a Monday," Johnson says, gripping the edges of the latest bag. "So today is either the ninth or the sixteenth."

"What?" Snug says.

"I said the first was a Monday –"

"And who cares?" Snug snaps, and his shovel blade overshoots the bag, dumps a load of mud and slime on Johnson's boots.

"Hey! What the –"

"Doesn't bloody matter," Snug says.

"Well, you don't have to dump shit all down my –"

"Why don't you guys yell a little louder so we can all get blown to pieces?" the sergeant says. "Johnson, can't you keep yourself clean?"

Johnson mumbles something, wipes his muddy hand on the least-soiled part of his uniform.

"Just muck it through," the sergeant mutters, shaking his head at all of us.

◈

Once again we get cold in the early-morning hours. Clothes soaked, not enough to eat, the sun still weak, we shiver like wretches. Not even the exercise can warm me up. I start to shake involuntarily, small tremors at first, then more violent spasms that make me think of what's-his-name – Davidson? – who lost his senses that first time in the trenches, who reeled spastically, threw himself at the sandbag walls, shook like the devil was bothering his bones. Williams wasn't there then; it was Perdue who grabbed him by the shoulders, slapped his face, and Lieutenant Fox who yelled at him to settle down. But he couldn't, wouldn't – he was mad with panic, ran crazed straight into a wall and knocked himself out. So Reese and Ferguson had to carry him out later, and then he was quietly sent out of the unit. Reese said he saw him working as an orderly in Arras and he looked fine, perfectly normal. Maybe saner than anyone else here.

"Tell me," I say to Reese, "about Cynthia Elaine Whyte." We are digging still, every movement slow, methodical, mindless, as if we were camels plodding across endless desert. "Where did you meet her?" I ask.

Reese continues working as if I haven't spoken.

"You said she was from London?"

"Who?" Reese says without looking up.

"Your girlfriend there. Cynthia Elaine Whyte."

"We met in *The Times*," he says curtly. "'London woman willing to correspond with lonely soldiers.'" He continues to stab with his shovel, turn, load the bag, which Snug is handling now – Johnson has joined us on the shovels.

"So you just write to her?"

Reese grunts in the affirmative.

"Have you actually met her?"

Another grunt, apparently a no. "I have a picture," he says.

"What does she look like?" I press. The talking helps to take some of the frozen feeling out of the meat of my jaw.

"She's a mademoiselle," Reese says, finally with some semblance of his usual élan. "The picture I have is a bit blurry, and she dresses like most women, you know."

"Like what?" Johnson asks, as if he has just woken up.

"In too many clothes," Reese says. "But when I go to see her I'm going to take her walking in Hyde Park, and we're going to find a nice private spot in the bushes . . ."

"In the middle of Hyde Park?" Johnson says.

"Everybody's doing it there these days," Reese says. "I was talking to some Australians just up from Egypt, they said it was like a public brothel, and nobody minded, as long as you waited till after dark."

"What does Cynthia Elaine Whyte say about Hyde Park?" I ask.

"She wrote to me exactly: 'When you come to London we shall go for a walk in Hyde Park.' Now everybody knows what she means by that. I figure I just have to show up. You know, all the women in London are in a sweat about a man in uniform. There are no men left in London under fifty."

"Except cowards and shirkers," Snug says.

"Skrim-shanking windy types," Reese says.

"Mama's boys," Johnson adds.

"Bloody geniuses," I chip in and the others pause before laughing.

"Bloody brilliant geniuses," Reese says.

The rain settles in after dawn and we eat cold, dismal rations in a dugout while the war rumbles around us, seemingly far away. I doze and have a brief dream of walking on a misty lane somewhere on the coast, it seems, near Victoria. The Brown House is there, not where it should be but by the side of a hill, and Mother is sweeping the walk, in a bad mood, muttering something. I mean to tell her it's all right, I am here, but slip past

ALAN CUMYN

instead. I'll show myself to her on the way back, I think. It will be more of a surprise.

She curses the mud on the walkway. I twist myself round to see her face before she looks up, but she doesn't look up. She's wearing a pretty yellow dress, the wrong thing for cleaning, but usual for her – her skin shines so darkly against it.

I follow the lane down to the harbour, see Father sitting in his shirt sleeves, peering out to sea, his eyebrows twisted like wire, his nose so hawklike in its arc. "Father," I say, but he doesn't turn towards me. "Father, it's me."

He motions brusquely, swats at something on his head.

"Father –"

"Shhhh!" he whispers. Then – "*There she goes!*" I peer into the gloom, try to see what he's referring to. There's nothing out there, steely grey water, the growing black of the night sky.

He lights and raises a candle, shields the flame from the breeze with his hand. "That's Ramsay's ship," he says, more to himself than to me. I look out to see the stern lights, so faint they're almost a hallucination.

◆

In the latrine dug in a sap off the main trench I see Gryphon slumped over, his chest ripped open. I push his body back, straighten him up in a stupid fit of inquiry, and a bullet smashes against my helmet, knocks me back against the wall. Then I'm down on my face and belly, my helmet spinning like a drunken saucer before it comes to rest by my hand. I wait a terrible, blood-boiling moment for the next bullet to hit home, my muscles seized, unable to move. Finally I force myself to

· 40 ·

yell, "Sniper! Sniper!" and "Gryphon's down! Stay back!" and manage to grab my helmet and crawl on muddy boards back to safety.

"There's a sniper shooting from behind," I gasp to the lieutenant, heaving as if I've just run full-pack up a half-mile hill. He scratches his moustache, peers with annoyance in the direction of the latrine. He's a new man with the unit, Lentworth, soft-looking, as if he'd be hard-pressed to accomplish a push-up or shoulder his own pack. So far this tour he's been off somewhere most of the time, in a dugout perhaps, something of a common officer practice.

"Any idea how far away he is?" he asks.

I get control of my breathing, will myself to speak in a normal voice. "He sure crowned me. He might be within a few hundred feet. Back there somewhere," I say, pointing behind our lines. "He must be at a height too, to be able to see in like he did."

"Right then," the lieutenant says, and bites his lip – *of all the rotten luck*, he seems to be thinking.

"There's a bit of farmhouse wall still standing back there, if I remember," I say. "He must be perched there. We could fire a few bombs in his direction, sir."

"When I want your opinion, Private," he snaps, "I will bloody well ask for it."

"Yes, sir." Mistake, mistake, I'm thinking. Now he's going to –

"I'd like you to take two other men and go around behind, flush out that sniper. Ferguson and Jackwell. Understood?"

"Yes, sir," I say, my heart ragged, a ripped shirt flying in the breeze.

"What are you waiting for?" he barks, as if completely oblivious to what he has asked.

"Begging your pardon, sir," I stammer, "but it might be more useful to get him at nightfall. In broad daylight he'll be able to see us coming out of the trench and –"

"Well, if you're going to saunter out like a civilian. Is that your plan, Private?"

"No, sir."

"I don't want a murdering German clogging up the latrine all day. And one more word from you I'll have you shot for either insubordination or cowardice. Do you understand me?"

I stand stock-still, looking past him at the dull mud-splattered walls of our sorry refuge.

"Right, then," he says. "You'd best get to it."

I slouch down the duckboards to the dugout where Ferguson and Jackwell – Snug – are lying low. Ferguson is writing a letter, cramping tiny jagged words onto a soggy sheet of paper with a pencil "shorter than a seaman's dick," as Snug would say. Snug is squatting in a position of silent thought. For a moment I think he's dead – he has the same aura of stillness, of almost-peace, as many of the corpses I've seen in the last few months. But then I realize he is still listening for that tap-tapping of miners.

I tell them that Gryphon pegged out, show them the fist-sized dent in my helmet from the sniper. "The lieutenant wants the three of us to get him," I say.

"What, now?" Ferguson asks, disgust and incredulity on his face. We are all unshaven, look like men who have crawled back in time to live in mud.

"Why don't we wait till dark?" Snug asks.

I tell them what the lieutenant said about not wanting the latrine plugged all day by a murdering German sniper.

"Did you send some bombs in the arse-head's way?" Snug asks.

"The lieutenant wants us to go over the top. He specifically named the three of us," I say.

The two look at me in silence, beyond swearing.

"You go back there," Snug says finally. "You tell that bugger of a lieutenant he should go over the top first and show us the bloody way. You tell him from me." He looks for all the world as if he means it, as if it will take bombs and bayonets to get him to move.

"Snug," Ferguson says.

"Shut up! If Lentworth thinks he can just waste my life in an arse-headed –" And he's scared, I see it in his eyes, the first time I've recognized it in Snug. He looks cornered, trapped, damned both ways and in between.

"He told me one more word from me and he'd have me shot," I say.

Snug looks at his filthy hands – puffed up from abuse, like all of our hands – and I know he's still hearing it too, the tapping. For all we know we might be blown up any second. His nostrils flare out for a moment; he holds his grey head in his hands, then straightens up.

"Right then," he says. "Everybody written their mother?"

◆

At the break in the trench wall a few hundred feet down from the latrine, Snug insists on going first. I tell him no. "If we build up this side a bit, put in a loophole, we could fire rifle grenades and hit him from here." We have a good angle, would probably be able to see part of the wall when we poke our heads up.

"That's not what the lieutenant ordered," Snug says. He's in a strange, calm, ornery state.

"He said to flush him out," I say. "That's what we'll do. Let the rifle grenade do the work."

"He said we had to go over the top. He said he'd have us shot if we didn't."

"No, no, I think we could do it this way –"

But Snug won't listen, is already hauling himself up. "You follow right behind me," he hisses. "As soon as he fires I want you to nail him. All right. One, two –"

"Wait!" I say, hanging on to his belt. "We don't have to –"

"Get your bloody hands off me!" he snarls. "The lieutenant wants dead soldiers," he says and shakes my hand off, then slithers over the side.

Crack! goes the shot. Jesus – Snug is hit! I force myself to look, not at Snug falling, but at the crumbling wall in the distance. Was that a flash? I try to aim, to squeeze off a round, but my own head snaps and the world spins. I'm slammed back and fall, bounce off something, feel my face in muck with my brains ringing.

"Ram! Ram, are you hit?" Like a voice in a theatre saying something made-up, from out of a story.

Am I hit? I suppose I am. I suppose my head is wide open, I think, calm as an old rock, not the way I thought I would be if I were hit. This sudden unreality. There is the sky, grey, unrelenting. My last view of it. There is Ferguson shaking my shoulders. As if that will do anything. He smells like he's halfway to wormfood himself.

An odd thought to be the last one.

"I don't see any blood," he says, shouting almost, right in my ear (I see from his face that he's shouting; he sounds like he's at the other end of a corridor).

I close my eyes, can't bear to look at anything more.

◈

The wall of the dugout shines in lamplight, greasy with water. The ringing in my ears pulses with my heartbeat, an annoying siren. I lie for a time on a chicken-wire bed normally reserved for officers, with a dampish grey blanket over me until it seems silly to stay here. Twice in one day I've been hit by the same sniper. I sit up on the bed, turn my head slowly from side to side, listen as the ringing whines higher when I turn to the left than when I turn to the right.

A body is on a stretcher on the floor a few feet away, his chest bloodied, mouth and eyes wide open. At first I think it's Snug – it takes a moment to recognize Gryphon. Someone got him in from the latrine, pulled up his trousers. But he doesn't look at peace. I pick up my rifle, fiddle with my helmet, which fits badly now because of the two deep dents. Then I step over Gryphon towards the entrance of the dugout, come up unsteadily into the light of day. Part of me longs for the cot, of course, for rest and sleep and withdrawal. But not with a corpse in the room.

I make my way back to the broken-walled area where five men are now busy building up the trench and installing a shielded iron loophole as I had originally suggested. Ferguson turns to look at me, says, "Back from the dead?" in a tired, almost accusatory tone.

"How is he?" I ask.

"Snug!" Reese says, calling almost directly into a sandbag. "How is you?"

After a pause Snug's voice comes on the other side. "Bloody brilliant."

"He's bloody brilliant," Ferguson says to me. He hoists a sandbag on top of the shield – quickly, gingerly, careful not to expose any more of his flesh than is necessary.

"Is he still there?" I call out to Snug.

"Who?" comes a tired voice.

"Who do you think?"

A moment later, as if in answer, a shot rings off the iron shield, knocks it partially back into the trench while the rico- cheting bullet buries itself in a sandbag between me and one of the other men who was bending down to dig more mud.

They fill another bag and hoist it up, poke the shield back in place with a shovel tip. A second shot knocks it off again and we scramble back, press our bodies against the trench walls.

The ringing in my head is gone.

"Go down that way and distract him so we can get this loop- hole in properly." The voice comes from Williams – I am just now realizing he is here. He has been strangely quiet, out of focus. And he's talking to me. I pause, jolted by the unreality of all of this, and then I head off. Around two corners, quickly to yet another damaged section of trench. I wedge myself into a jumbled pile of sandbags, mud, broken timber, clods of dead grass, hoping I'm not exposing myself to fire on both sides. With my head pressed down into the ground, eyes straining up to see through the slit between my helmet brim and the roots of the dead grass, I can just make out bits of the offending wall.

I gaze through my sight at a blurry, crumbling section of brick, feel the uncomfortable lumps in my helmet, which will not hold a third time, I know. I have seen helmets full of bullet holes, of blood and bits of brain.

I ease my bolt back, squeeze, feel the shock of the recoil against my shoulder, watch a puff of dust jump on the wall.

Can I see him?

I press into the earth, will myself smaller and smaller, invisible. Then I bolt and fire again, count two, three, four, five, bolt and fire once more, and retreat back down until I am behind the safety of a couple of sandbags.

I count out two minutes, creep my way up again. *Crack!* A bullet lodges in the mud two feet away, freezing me, but there's no follow-up. I have even less of a shot from here, but fire anyway, miss everything – God knows where that bullet will come to rest. He's going to get me any second, I know it, but I force myself to wait, to aim properly, to find the shattered hole in the wall where he probably is. I fire again and don't wait, but crawl back down to safety, realize after a time that I have forgotten to count, am holding my breath instead.

Finally I hear the distinctive pop of a rifle grenade. After a second there is an explosion, but I restrain myself from looking, wait for another grenade to be fired. Then I push back into position, fire, look as I'm heading back down – the wall is mostly gone, a crumble of dust and smoke.

There is no return fire. A third grenade goes off, I allow myself to scan the area. I can see Snug – it must be him, but he's so still. I watch the wall, the rubble of former-wall, for anything, a trace of movement, a glint off a rifle barrel. The sniper might be buried in brick, might be a paste of flesh and bone, might have already relocated, be looking at us from a different angle.

Ferguson starts out towards Snug, moving in a slouching crawl, without a rifle, is bending over him when he suddenly straightens, twists weirdly, and as he's falling on top of Snug I hear the sound – too late.

Oh shit. Oh shit oh shit.

◈

For the rest of the day we listen to Ferguson's wailing blasphemies, to Snug's rattling moans, to the cold rasp of death breathing down our necks. The sniper will not finish them off, not as long as they can serve so well as bait, and we can't bring them in until darkness affords some sort of cover. So we're left with an agony of time, slower than mud, than life leaking out of a wounded body. Nothing seems right – I have no appetite, cannot write a letter, concentrate on any small task. Snug and Ferguson are just feet away, and now we have orders from Lentworth to let them rot, and we are all coward enough to do it, to crouch here safe in our slit in the ground, to listen and do nothing.

It's enough to stop the blood in the heart, to freeze the breath.

And yet it doesn't. This is the horrible thing: the blood and breath continue. We cling to our fragments of life and let our friends fail, do nothing to help.

◈

They are dead by nightfall. The sounds slowly stop. Near the end Snug's voice suddenly sounds clear and strong. He says, "Ram, will you write to my mother?"

I tell him yes, of course I will. "What do you want me to say?"

"Tell her I died . . . you know."

"Instantly," I say.

"Yes. And it was . . ."

I wait for him to finish, but he drifts off.

"Snug?"

No answer.

"Ferguson, is he still there?" I call.

"Don't call for Ferguson." Snug's voice, feeble. "He's pegged out. He weighs a bloody ton."

"He always did eat a lot," I say, and despite himself Snug laughs. I can hear him wheezing, chortling on the other side.

"He slurped from his mess tin," Snug says. "He –"

Again, a long pause. "Snug?" I say.

A cold rasp of wind. A trickle of water. The usual teeth-grating explosions.

"Snug? Tell me something to say to your mother."

Silence. Awful silence.

I work through the night at a savage pace, seething with anger, guilt, frustration. Reese, too, beside me, is a muttering, cursing, earth-moving machine. I feel like charging out of the trench with my shovel, launching myself at the German line, smashing a dozen bodies to a pulp before they tear me off. Why didn't I just race out and drag his body back in? He wasn't more than a few steps away. Why didn't I force him to stay back in the first place? He would've calmed down in another minute.

Lentworth shows his face and I feel like running him through the gullet.

"Crome, Reese," he says, not looking at either of us, "bring those two in."

Those two.

I feel the words rise to my throat. *No, you shit. They had names. I will not bring them in until you realize.*

"Yes, sir," Reese says, and gives me a look and then an elbow. His face is a grim, frozen mask. We drive our shovels into the muck, leave the lieutenant standing in the shadows, still not looking at us.

It's a bright, clear, murderous night, a full moon, no night for above-ground extracurricular activities. For all we know the sniper might still be there, fixed up with his bratwurst, some heavy German bread, a stiffening drink to keep his eyes open. I remember a sniper from the 42nd telling us about his set-up, how he waited a day and a half in the remains of a pig trough, and finally at dawn a new section of German recruits came into the line. One by one they mounted the firestep, had a look, were shot down. Four, five, six in a row wondering what the war looked like.

At the section of trench closest to Snug and Ferguson I slither over the wall, crawl quickly, head down, almost ploughing into the mud. The moon is so bright, the German star shells are so frequent, it feels as though the world can't decide between day and night. Reese follows and there is no shot, thank God. I glance over quickly. The wall where we thought the sniper was, where he must have been, is a ghostly, shadowed pile. He could easily be there still. Or farther back, amongst those shattered tree stumps, or in any of a thousand shell-holes. Perhaps he doesn't have the vantage he had this morning. Or maybe he's back in billets, drinking himself into oblivion.

I reach the two bodies, Ferguson slumped over Snug, whose face is up, hands open, but eyes closed, as if asleep. I can't help myself, nudge his shoulder stupidly, say, "Snug! Snug!"

Reese gets to Ferguson and starts to pull at his arm to disentangle the bodies. "They're dead!" he snaps bitterly, and I know, I know – we'll join them if we take too long. Ferguson's body starts to slide and roll. I see at a glance he was hit in the upper chest, his whole front is black with blood. Reese loses his balance, slips in the mud trying to handle the moving body.

"Jesus, he's heavy!" he whispers. "Take his legs. I'll grab under his arms."

I grab the dangling limbs under the knee and straighten up slightly. I have a hard time getting the legs off the ground, and Reese, who's no weakling, flounders badly trying to raise Ferguson's shoulders.

A particularly bright shell lights the sky and we fall to the ground an instant before machine-gun fire – *sss, sss, sss* – rakes the dirt all around us. Ferguson's corpse takes several hits, and I burrow deeper and deeper beneath his flesh.

When the shooting halts it is some time before I can find my voice.

"Reese?" I say. "Are you all right?"

He doesn't answer.

The hissing moves farther down the line, making me think that no one actually saw us, but they're firing at randomly chosen targets in unpredictable intervals, just as our gunners do, blasting unseen points on the map. I don't wait for it to stop. I say, "Reese!" but he doesn't answer.

I push my way out from under Ferguson, crawl around to where Reese is lying splay-legged like a horse hit by the shock of a bomb. I feel for a pulse in his neck, turn his head towards me. He opens his eyes. "I'm hit, Ram," he says weakly, his eyes so sad I almost don't want to look.

"Hang on. Hang on!" I say and shove him awkwardly, trying to keep low but still find some power.

"Just go. Just go," he murmurs. "I'll be all right."

I stand, to hell with it, let the gods take me down if they must. I clasp round his chest from behind, drag him the few steps back to the parados. There are no shots, or if there are any I don't hear them. I stumble over the wall, try to brace myself, soften the fall for Reese but he lands on top of me; we both crash onto boards and muck.

"Reese is hit! Reese is hit!" I cry – and when the others get to me I'm still screaming it over and over, as if I want the shells to come find me, to bring silence.

"Shhhhh! Damn it, get a hold of yourself!" Williams says, looking like he's ready to bust my teeth to shut me up. I slump like a coward, like a piece of wet laundry, and sit shivering, bawling, while the stretcher men do Reese up, carry him off in the shadows.

"Crome! Get on your feet, soldier!" Williams orders. "You have an assignment, you complete it. Do you understand me?"

I look at him from my slumped position, wonder for a moment if I will just stay where I am, limp, pitiful, to be hauled off and shot. For a moment I feel like I don't know.

"Get up!" Williams barks, his hands on his hips now to make himself larger. A shell screams into the line not too far away and we are shaken, lit up, then plunged back into darkness. He doesn't flinch or move.

"Johnson, you help him," Williams says. Then – "For Christ's sake, Crome, on your feet," and I realize it's a matter of sanity. I either rise now or they'll send me home drooling, smashing my head into walls.

But I don't know if I can get up.

It's a sliding, sickening moment, this horrible feeling – I don't care. One way or the other, what does it matter? I sit waiting, while Williams glares.

He turns finally, spits in the trench. "Johnson," he says. "Get him on his feet."

And then it's done. Of course I get up, follow his shambling form back over the top. We wrestle the bodies in mud and filth, slip, flounder, flop about like Charlie Chaplin without the laughter. The corpses are insanely heavy. Ferguson especially is a monster to move, a liquid piano, slippery as a pig. But even Snug is next to impossible. We heave and strain and fall over, rise again as if advertising our lives for the taking, hapless soldiers silhouetted against the moon. Where are the bullets now? I expect to be cut in two at any moment. But nothing.

We get the bodies back into the trench, collapse in gasping sweat and filth. When Williams returns to check on us we are puddled together. I see from his face that we all look the same, like four corpses, not two, Johnson and I are so limp. A second glance reassures him – Johnson lolls his eyes over to look at him – and he says, with a surprising gentleness, "Come on, lads."

We barely move, so he stiffens his jaw. "Up! Now! Don't be so bloody lazy!" and I see from his eyes – when I am standing again, walking past him to return to trench work – I see that he has saved my life.

◈

Through the night and into the day and on and again, time blurs in an awful greyness of effort and fatigue. In the middle of some afternoon, the sun shines in the most insolent, insane manner, aeroplanes happily roar overhead, shooting at one another and sometimes at us, and bombs burst in a carnival of death. Under endless, grunting labour the trench stretches and winds, with a fine screen of barbed wire strung in front, screwed to the earth with iron pig's tails, some of which I vaguely remember hauling here myself.

Snug and Ferguson are brought back of the line to be with Gryphon, three dead from one platoon in one tour in third-reserve trenches, what was supposed to be "light duty," just slave work, no fighting. And Reese is wounded, also sent back down the line to be with Lear, MacMillan, and Dobbins. It's our worst stretch yet and we are dizzy with it, staggering through the next minute and the next. When the Princess Pats finally come to relieve us – bloody late, almost two o'clock in the morning before they shuffle in – the trenches are bully and strong, as A-1 as they will ever get, but we are brittle, angry, exhausted men. No time for more than a few words of briefing – *bit of sniper trouble, watch the latrine, thought we heard digging* – and then we're off, back to billets for a few days' rest before the next dreadful turn.

Not a dawdler among us, not on the way back, out of the mouth of hell. The moon is still nearly full, a terrible night to be on the move, and so we go in a desperate, jagged single file, nearly running in the beginning to be out of there.

Down the slimy sewer of a communications trench, onto the duckboards, across ruined fields, cratered forests, remnants of houses, like a pack of weary wolves. The farther we get from the worst of the night's madness the more anxious we start to feel, all of us thinking, *not now, not here, I've almost made it back*. We dive for cover when a coal-box smashes into the blackness ahead of us, nearly suffocating us with smoke. Then later we flatten for machine-gun fire a hundred and fifty yards away, for the snap of a sniper shot in the distance – maybe a Princess Pat trying to take a shit – for a green flare that illuminates us piteously but brings no hate directed our way.

We've had our hate already, are fleeing from it now, crazed men staggering for home.

Along a short stretch of the Menin Road the columns of traffic build, a slogging, dark, two-way river of mules, horses, limbers, transports, mud, and men. A wounded soldier, uniform hanging from his body in strips, limps along with the help of another whose head is wrapped in white bandages, both eyes covered. A listing motor-ambulance spins its wheels in a soupy rut while weary men push from the rear; we are too fatigued to help. Stretcher-bearers pass us in the darkness; a bicycle courier gives up and walks, his wheels so clogged with mud they have a hard time turning between the forks. And the shells come thicker, with nerve-shattering regularity. One smashes into a group of horses ahead of us. When we get there they are a shrieking agony of sinew, bone, and blood, thrashing on their backs and sides in the darkness. The gun team that should have been in charge of them is nowhere to be seen. Blown to molecules, perhaps. Four of us are ordered to shoot the horses down and we fire away into the writhing darkness. Johnson continues well after the others have stopped, until Williams has to shout in his ear, "Enough, God damn you! Do you want to waste ammunition?"

When Johnson turns to him his face is that of a dog caught in a frenzied fight, of looking now at its master from the old, old place of blood-fire and rage, of claws and teeth set to kill.

We turn in towards Zillebeke and slog through the dark ruins of the village, then to Shrapnel Corner, a sorry crossroads lined with ghostly trees, some skeleton silhouettes, others in leaf with an only partial shattering of limbs. But the junction is a magnet for enemy hate, and it's hard to time the crossing, to wait long enough for darkness to return following a blast or flare, but not so long as to be caught in the next sweep of fire. We practise the peculiar soldier's hunched sprint, try our luck in groups of two or three. I cross in my turn, Johnson's ragged breath behind me every step, shadowy forms ahead, think nothing of it – or rather, resolutely think nothing, for to think it through would be to go mad. It's not the time for that but for muscles, bone, blood, wind, for throwing your hand in with God, for the wrenchingly silent elation of men who pass through shrapnel storms without registering a scratch.

Another slogging half-mile and we are at the Lille Gate, where the remnants of its battered arch span the pillars, and the ramparts of the old town, pocked but still formidable, provide the illusion at least of safety. Here, where the strafe can be dis-astrous for moving troops, we pass in blessed peace over the bridged moat. Dugouts riddle the insides of the city walls, but they are not our billets. Instead we must cross the ruins of the old town: jumbles of broken stone and dust, smouldering rubbish, splintered half-walls jutting into blackness or standing ominously against the bright moon. I watch a section of wall tremble in the roar and flash of a shell, forget to put my head down as bits of rock and glass spray around us. I am too tired now to take much care, and it seems to me as well, in some demented part of my brain, that it would be all right perhaps to catch a suitable Blighty, now that we're not too far from rest – some good wound to an arm or leg. Not enough to take it off, of course, but to necessitate a spell in hospital with nurses to wipe my brow, bring hot tea with sugar in the afternoon.

We trip over broken bricks, slashed beams, the scattered remnants of evacuated lives: a dresser split and leaking clothing like entrails from a belly wound; a cockeyed perambulator with wheels wedged inwards, half buried under fallen stones; a woman's black boot, the toe curled by the rain, curving in upon itself; an endless warren of cobblestone streets. Nothing is right. If it were raining we would at least have cloud cover, I think. Every shell that hits the blackened, shattered town, no matter how far from our group, is a personal insult, a splinter in the shattered nerves of weary soldiers.

We pass by the old Cloth Hall and I barely look: fingers of darkened towers battered into grotesque shapes that appear as if they will crash upon us with the next slight breath of wind.

This is enough, I think for the thousandth time tonight. Get me through this. Get me back to a bed and rest, to closed eyes, to any other nightmare than this one.

◆

It is nearly dawn when we stagger into the reserve camp, a hunching collection of farm buildings and sandbag huts huddled behind a vague ridge in the relative safety to the rear of Ypres. I am ready to collapse anywhere, to ditch my kit and rifle on the ground and slump the weight of my body against anything that will hold me. We are all too aware that if we stand around someone will order us off to shower parade, to de-lousing, probably even to kit-and-dress inspection before breakfast. So we head for our old billet, a large, mostly intact wooden barn tucked behind shivering trees that seem to know they cannot stand much longer, not in Flanders, not with the war just a few miles away. Bloody Tommies have taken it over, and they seem ready to fight for it, are not bone-tired and asleep on their feet the way that we are. It is precisely the type of situation where Reese would recognize someone from an *estaminet*, and they would make room, and we would be asleep like babies – like filthy, lice-infested, snoring babies – in a matter of minutes.

Instead we wander haplessly until we stumble on the administrative hut by a cluster of ancient buildings on the next farm over. The duty corporal there has no idea where we're supposed to billet, seems irritated that we have made it back in breathing bodily form and need to be fed and housed. *Go to hell*, his expression seems to be saying, *go back and fight until you are proper corpses buried where you fell, and not such a bother as you are now.*

Johnson sights the bag behind the corporal's table and asks if the mail is for us. The corporal says that he can't release the mail until it's signed off by the lieutenant, and where is he? He has disappeared, off somewhere in officers' quarters, I think, probably already asleep.

"It's all right," I say. "You can release it. We've done this before. Nobody minds."

"I don't know," the corporal says. "This is my first week. And Captain Sutherland ..."

"Oh, we know Captain Sutherland. Don't worry about him," I say. "He wants the men to see their mail without delay."

Johnson nods grimly; four or five others are crowded around the corporal's table. We look like hounds of hell, scraggle-faced, mud-soaked, dangerous men. The corporal can't move, he is frozen with indecision, so Johnson reaches in behind him, picks up the sack, and in seconds we are rummaging through it. Binks has his usual packet from his wife in Nanaimo; Hunter and Coles have parcels from their mothers in Vancouver; Johnson something from his father in Esquimalt. There is a letter from my father, which I tear open, am partway through when the corporal says, "Is one of you Crome?"

Dear Ramsay, my father writes. *I hope you are well and keeping your head down. Though the progress of the war has been frustrating for us all* ... My eye skims to see immediately if there is black news about Thomas or Will. But they're fine, thank God. Near the end my eye catches something strange.

"Is one of you Crome?" the corporal repeats, and when someone elbows me I grunt without looking up. *At your very next chance*, my father has written, *you must visit your Aunt Harriet. She was extremely disappointed when you were in Shorncliffe all those months and did not* ...

"Are you Crome?" the corporal asks, standing now, his big nose right in my face.

"Yes."

"Crome, R.H.?"

"Yes."

"430776?"

"Right again."

He hands me a thin slip of blue paper and I look at it, then back at the letter, at the letter and the order sheet.

"What is it?" Johnson asks.

"I've been granted leave," I say in shock. "Annual leave. Ten days."

"Fuck and wonder," Johnson says. "Starting when?"

I ask the corporal what day it is and he says the nineteenth, May the nineteenth.

"It's today!" I say.

"Where are you going to go?"

I look at the letter, at the slip of blue paper. "London, I suppose."

"The Big Smoke!" Johnson declares, and then he pushes me towards the door. "Hurry up!" he says. "Get signed out! Run! Before they change their bloody minds!"

I stagger out of the tent and there is the first glimpse of sun. A few miles away the morning hate is going to start at any moment, but I don't have to be a part of it. It can bloody well go on without me for a while.

No breakfast for me. I sprint to the bathing tent where I strip off my filthy uniform and leave it to rot on a pile of others, the stinking, muddy clothes of some other unit who've already been through and collected their new duds. Then it's into the next tent for a minute and a half – as long as I can stand – under a dribbling, cold-water shower, soaping like a fiend.

London! I think. *I'm going to London!*

Fresh underwear from the orderly clerk. Not new, precisely, but different, and much cleaner, boiled free of chatts. But the trousers he has for me are a bit too long, the tunic short and tight. "Sorry," he says, his face scrunched up like a baseball mitt, like it's been punched in by too many soldiers. His hands tremble, and his eyes look squarely at my neck. I imagine him whimpering and yowling in the trenches till they found a proper place for him.

Lucky bugger. All his limbs intact.

From a bin in the corner of the changing tent I extract a splendid pair of new woollen socks. But I have to return my feet to my tired, muddy, hopeless boots. I ask the orderly if there are any new boots to be had but he shakes his head at my shoulder. "Impossible. Can't be done!" he says. "Can't can't can't can't can't!" His head wobbles when he talks, as if something has come loose.

Just before I leave, a section of new recruits comes through for their showers. I know they're new because of how clean, bright-eyed, undamaged they look. They stand too straight, laugh too loud, take over the place as if it's their private party. Not their fault, I guess – they'll find out soon enough. But I hate them immediately. How cocky and stupid they seem, too muscled, fresh out of training. What we all must have looked like just a few months ago. I remember our train into Poperinghe, passing so slowly by a scraggly group of *Poilus* smoking, lounging on a grassy hillside. As soon as they saw us they broke into a chorus of *baaaaa*s.

And now I see what they saw. These sheep strip down too friskily, and I can hear them japing and laughing in the shower, the whole group of them at once. Leaving me with this nice pair of boots right here, barely broken in. The only mud from the walk here.

They look like they'll do just fine.

◈

I stand at attention in front of the duty lieutenant, a tall, weedy, pale-faced man in his mid-thirties with a brown mouse of a moustache on his upper lip. He looks at my boots and puttees, my trousers, belt, buttons, at my sloppy collar and worn sleeves. His own uniform is gleaming, kept that way by the lucky stiff who looks after him.

"Ill-fitting sort of rags," the lieutenant mutters, as much to himself as to me.

"It's what I was given from de-lousing, sir," I say, unsure whether he expects me to speak or not. He makes a dismissive sort of blowing noise with his lips.

"Do you feel you're fit for civilized company, Private, what-is-your-name?" he says. He looks at his chart. "Crome?"

"Yes, sir."

"You just got to the trenches in March, and already you have annual leave?" he says, looking too closely at my papers. "How the devil did you manage that?"

Officers get leave every four months. I nearly say it. Instead I say, "I enlisted last year, sir. With training and everything, my leave is actually overdue."

"You didn't take any at Shorncliffe?"

"No, sir. I was saving it."

"Yes, of course you were," he says with irritation, flipping through my papers. "All right, then, Private. Drop your trousers."

"Pardon, sir?"

"You heard me!" he barks. "Short-arms inspection!"

One more word from me, I know, and he'll send me back to my outfit to spend my leave polishing rifle butts. I strip down and he bends to within a few inches of me, looks left and right, sniffs briefly.

"Lift the tackle," he says, and when I do he snorts, "All right," and turns his back. I continue to stand at attention until he says, impatiently, "Get dressed, man!"

I rearrange my uniform.

"You know, I assume, about particular diseases," he says, pacing in front of me. I stay silent, look straight ahead. "Answer me!" he barks.

"Yes, sir!" I say. "Particular diseases, sir."

"You know what a scourge they are to the common soldier. You know that they rot your flesh and mind. That you can carry them for weeks and months without symptoms. That you can transmit them to others unknowingly. That a certain kind of woman can disable not only yourself, but hundreds of fighting men, and far more effectively than the Boche ever will be able to. Whoever comes in contact with her . . . You look at me when I'm speaking to you!"

"Yes, sir," I say, and shift my eyes onto him.

"You know how these diseases are contracted, do you, Private Crome?"

"Yes, sir. No, sir," I say. "I mean, I know, but I've never –"

"Through morally degenerate behaviour," he says. "Through conduct unbecoming a soldier of His Majesty's Canadian Expeditionary Force. Do you know what the rate of infection is among our Canadian soldiers?"

"No, sir."

"Twenty-eight per cent! That's a bloody disgrace. Especially when the Brits are at only *five* per cent. There's a move in Ottawa – don't be surprised to find you've been docked half your pay if you get infected. Do you understand me?"

"Yes, sir."

"I am instructed to offer every man going on leave a preventive kit. Do you think you're going to need one, soldier?"

"A preventive kit?"   "It has a bottle of potassium permanganate and a tube of calomel for application after suspected exposure. Are you planning to require such a kit?"

"No, sir."

"Good. While you are on leave you represent the hopes and aspirations of your battalion, your nation, your King, of the British Empire itself. Drunkenness will not be tolerated, nor will lewd and indecent and unseemly behaviour. You will be held to the highest moral standards and I will not let you out this door unless you swear to uphold them. Break your word to me, Crowder –"

"Crome, sir," I say.

"Crome, damn it! Are you following what I'm saying?"

"Yes, sir."

"Then conduct yourself like a soldier of the King's Empire, or there will be hell to pay."

"Yes, sir. Thank you, sir," I say.

◈

The right boot begins to split my heel on the long walk to Poperinghe. At first it's just a niggling ache, like a twinge of conscience, and then it's the stab of an awl with every step. I sit down on the side of the road to investigate, and find the slightest nib of leather – it seems impossible that such a tiny flaw could cause such pain, after everything I've been through. I rub at it, take out my penknife to bring it down, but make a bit of a gouge instead. And it's worse – of course it's worse – so I grit my teeth and blunder on. About halfway there a motor-ambulance gives me a lift. I ride next to a poor bugger on a stretcher whose hand has been blown off. His head jerks up with every pothole and I tell him, stupidly, it's all right. Everything will be fine.

In the old town, the fighting is a forgettable rumble in the background, although I do catch sight of a few buildings stove in from long-range shells. But it's khaki everywhere, in marching columns, in transports, in the masses of men on leave or light duty, milling around, laughing, crowding the local shops and the main square. I catch a lucky break with the RTO: he barely looks at my papers before he sends me off to the leave train, which is just pulling out when I arrive. An open-topped cattle car for the men. I'm almost in full stride – damn the wretched boots! – when I heave my pack and rifle to waiting hands and get pulled aboard.

A mile out of town, the Belgian countryside streaming past, blue skies above, and the full extent of my hunger starts to hit. "Hey, anybody got a bite to eat?" I ask. There are about twenty of us on board, mostly Brits, with a few other Canadians, stragglers on leave. Not everyone has cleaned up. The car didn't get completely mopped out either after the last shipment of horses.

And the smoke too from the engine is pouring back on us. "I was in the line till early this morning," I explain. "Then my leave came through. I didn't get a chance to eat."

We scrounge up somebody's hard-boiled egg and a bit of time-toughened Belgian bread, and then the whisky bottle comes out. The owner is a dough-faced Brit named Hopkinson, a digger. "No sense going underground without lubrication," he says. (It's awful stuff, raw on the throat, edged like glass and whiffing slightly of gasoline.)

"No sense going into the bloody war without lubrication!" another says. I can't tell if they're friends. A handlebar moustache and droopy expression; worry lines on one side of the face but not the other.

"I heard of one man," Hopkinson says, "who indulged himself one night and got a little lost, and wandered right into the German trenches. Captured twenty-five of them, and then couldn't remember how to get back. Ended up marching them to their own headquarters!"

So how did you ever hear about it? I wonder, but stay silent, stand instead to get a bit of air. Stone houses by the side of the tracks. Poorer-than-poor peasants, tiny, old, withered people, staring at the men in the cattle car going by. Not waving, but no raised fists either. Dull, cold fatigue.

"We had a man named Peterson," someone else is saying. I close my eyes for a moment, hold my sleeve over my nose to lessen the stench. "He kept shooting other men in the foot. He did it four times in all before the brass started to figure out what was going on. But he always claimed it was an accident. Every time he just took off a few of the least important toes." The car starts swaying badly and I slump to my knees. "They shot him back there in Poperinghe. Thank God I wasn't on the firing line." I fight to my feet again, try to get to the fresh air.

"He's looking green!" someone says.

"Stand clear! Stand clear!"

"Hey!"

"Shit, there he goes!"

Wild cheering. Stupid, stupid, stupid thing.

An old farmer looks up from his hop field. Poles and strings and such. His quizzical expression. As if we were beasts, trying to talk like men.

◈

Somewhere in France, in the middle of nothing – ploughed fields, far to the left a stone building that looks like it's been rundown for hundreds of years, a church spire in the distant haze (the war now a low growl, innocent as thunder in some other valley) – our train stands idle and stopped. The bottle is gone, and so is the second, which was allegedly wine, and the third, even more allegedly, and the men are singing. I'm leaning over the rail still, resting.

The squire had a daughter, so fair and so tall,
She lived in her satins and silks in the hall,
But she married a man who had no artillery at all
*   No artillery at all,*
*   No artillery at all,*
But she married a man who had no artillery at all.

I'd sing too, but it's better if I close my eyes for a stretch.

From artillery to gunnery, to pokery to dear old Maggie Ross, then it's on to "Mademoiselle from Armenteers" (*she ain't been fucked for forty years*) and then a derisive, angry version of "Tipperary." Someone starts rocking the car, and the bunch of them are stamping their feet in a mock march (I shuffle mine, try to hang on, my head nodding in fatigue) that threatens to tear our transportation apart. The men from the other cars take it up as well, until whistles and shouts and angry orders up and down the track wrestle the song and men into silence.

Hopkinson takes off to visit the local farmhouse. I watch him pick his way across the field. It all feels a bit of a haze. I expect the train to start up again at any moment.

"Old Hopkinson, he'll find some mademoiselle back there in the dairy barn," his friend says, watching him. "He'll have two weeks of jig-jig before the mademoiselle's father shoots him in the arse."

More men spill out onto the fields. It's cigarettes and lounging in the sun. A stuffed sack turns into a football and the lads are kicking and yelling, running, booting one another in the shins. I sit with my legs dangled overside, watch with a sort of dreamy fatigue. It's an odd time to think of death, but what I think is: now would be all right. I have no quarrel with now, in the sunshine, with my limbs so heavy they seem to be full of water and sand. A big shell now in the middle of us and I wouldn't mind so much, if it was certain and instantaneous, and there was no pain.

The train starts suddenly, with a little lurch and some bumps and then walking pace forward. The men race back yelling, laughing, jumping aboard, some awkward, some athletic. My turn now to pull in the late ones. The football gets left behind, a forlorn little kicked-in bit of canvas. For a while some of the men shout and gesture, but no one goes after it. Then we spy Hopkinson, a black form in the distance, waving and running. Shouts and more shouts, to Hopkinson to hurry up, to the engineer to slow down the train.

"Come on! Run, you bastard! Run!"

We're all on our feet now, screaming at him. He has something in his hand slowing him down – a white sack.

"A chicken!" someone says. "He's brought a roast chicken!"

"No, a goose!"

"A side of beef!"

"Rack of lamb! Come on, you bugger, run, Hopkinson! Run!"

Hopkinson misses the last car by a hundred yards. For a time he keeps running, almost apace, then he stops and stands waving, calling. Finally he drops his arm and becomes a still, diminishing figure in the distance, alone with his white sack, whatever he managed to scrounge.

I sink to the floor of the train car, close my eyes, and soon in a dream I am on another train far away, one that clacks and rattles and sways much the same but has a roof and proper seats. The soldiers are gone, but there is Father in his suit, with his collar shoved up under his neck, his scarred hands resting on his thighs. The sun slants through the window, which is dirty from the smoke, as dull, endless, flat prairie passes by, the grasses waving in the wind. A book is propped open on his chest – something in Spanish – and I'm thinking: *he has chosen me.* Of all his sons, he has chosen me to go with him.

I smell soup cooking on the pot-bellied stove up front. Oh, what I'd give to have some! But I remember now that Mother has filled us each a sugar bag of food for the trip – cold chicken and boiled potatoes, with raw carrots and apples as well. They're up above our seats, stored with the rest of our luggage on the wooden bunks that become our beds at night. When did we eat last? When Father said we might.

Of all his sons, I am thinking, *he has chosen me*. But now he sits and stares out the window with railway-builder eyes. I know nothing of trusses and cantilevers, of rail beds and bridges and explosives and granite schist, of his whole world of lines and surveys and what a thousand men can do to rearrange the earth. I don't even know where we're going, if we'll be working rails, or if it's a canal project, a harbour, or gold mine.

I look at his hands again. They have guided mine on a fly rod, have shown me how to work a knife in wood and sharpen an axe and wield a saw, and have beaten me blistered at the slightest infraction. I have glimpsed them in private through a doorway tenderly touching my mother, and seen them shaking in the morning with Nicaraguan malaria. But I know them most for the hard edges of his writing, in pencil often on rough paper, little notes from far-flung jungles: *The men are treated as animals, I'm afraid, and I will leave soon, whether the money comes through or not. They can find someone else to manage the rest of the work.*

"Father," I say to him, but he doesn't turn, is rock-quiet as he looks out the window.

It has been days like this, of silence. I think of him in the roped-off patch of dirt in our backyard, when we were all gloved and stripped to the waist and he fought us, one by one, smacking us on the nose, on tear-stained cheeks, and taking the occasional blow himself with a resolute, dismissive little grunt: *Is that the best you have to offer?*

He pulls out his pocket watch now, turns to me finally as if it is time for bed. And it is – I realize it suddenly, for the windows have gone black and the other passengers have already rearranged their luggage for sleep. I expect him to bid me good-night, as usual, in his formal, stiff way. But instead he says, "I had to get you out from under your mother's skirts, or else you'd never stand on your own as a man."

I have trouble finding my voice. "No," I say, feebly. I mean to say that that's exactly what I want, to stand on my own. But he's looking at me in his withering way and the words die in my throat.

◆

At Boulogne, crowds of French girls sell cigarettes, coffee, bread. They are swarmed by the men from the train, but I find myself beyond hunger – it is somehow enough to be on solid ground, to wander the old streets in this strange sort of freedom. If not for my aching foot I would think it could not be real.

I follow the others down to the docks, manage, in most of a daze, to get my papers looked at and stamped by men who seem to know what they're doing. By the leave ship, waiting to board (ravenous, suddenly, again, and I think of Reese and Snug, who would never let an opportunity to eat go by), I'm nearly pulled over from behind. I whirl, almost smash the poor bugger. Then I see it's an officer, drunk and dishevelled.

"Take my bag, there, Private!" he says, pointing to an enormous case behind him. "I need to go to the hotel."

"I'm sorry, sir," I say. "I'm just about to board." And I point to the ship. He's even smaller than I am, looks all of seventeen, and about to pass out.

"Did you hear me? What's your name? I'll have you horse-whipped for in . . . for insub –"

A sudden blast from the ship's horn sends him staggering back a pace, then forward, almost into me.

"I'll get you a cab, sir," I say, holding him when he staggers too close. His case is full of cannonballs. I wonder where his batman has escaped to. "A hotel, is it? Yes, sir, right this way," I say, and lead him into the most crowded section of the harbour station, where men from every part of the Empire, it seems, are milling about. Then, when his back is turned I slip off, don't glance round until I'm safely on the gangplank. When we're pulling out I catch sight of him haranguing someone else to put his bags into a cab.

Later, a voice from somewhere. "Just my bloody luck. I finally get leave, now we'll probably be sunk by a U-boat." I'm slumped on the deck in a tiny, last patch of sunlight before the afternoon gives way to evening.

"Shut up, Carter," someone else says. The smell of cigarette smoke, of too many men – but not as bad as the train, which was just short of poison gas.

The rolling of the ship, but it's all right, I don't mind the motion. I'm too tired to really think about it. "I wrote my Jennie I was on my way," another voice says, from something of a distance. "I said, 'See all the shows and smell all the flowers you want now, 'cause the next five days you're going to be feet in the air staring at the ceiling.'"

This little snippet before I fall asleep.

TWO

I t's terribly quiet. I open my eyes, stretch – stiff, oh, especially my shoulder where the slats have dug in. My hands are cramped around the edges of my greatcoat, so cold and sore from clenching they hardly want to loosen. I see the trees, the overwhelming light, feel cold in the familiar way, the deep-bone, life-draining cold, and I think, *Snug is dead, so I must be too.*

Then I kick myself upright and awake. Water runs in a quick set of rivulets down my greatcoat, off my legs and boots, and I turn my face for a moment to the sun – the chilly, magnificent dawn – and close my eyes, allow my whole body to absorb this new whiff of paradise.

It's so quiet!

When I open my eyes again I'm overwhelmed with flowers: soaking, purplish. I have no idea what their names might be, but it doesn't matter, just the idea of it. Flowers!

I am in London. I giggle with the word, turn it around in my mouth, say it out loud, "London. London. London!"

Other soldiers are slumped on benches down the path, some under the bushes, quiet, breathing forms, with rain capes and greatcoats slung over them as blankets, haversacks for pillows. They are the happiest corpses I've ever seen. They're going to wake up soon, just like me, open their eyes and think, *I am in London.*

And there is the river. I get to my feet, walk stiffly across the path and under the trees to the bank, look out at the swollen grey water, at the magnificent bridge. Which is it? It doesn't look like London Bridge. It's one of the others – Waterloo Bridge, perhaps. I don't know my bridges. I don't know anything. Except I'm in London, and that's all that matters.

I relieve myself behind the thickest of the bushes, with the heavenly smell of those purple flowers – not lilacs, but something like it. Then I brush some of the mud off my puttees. It must have come from the filthy train to Boulogne.

But I'm in London. Snug is dead, and Ferguson, Reese too probably, and here I am in London.

I find some water in my canteen, splash it on my face, rinse out my mouth – it feels hairy – spit and then tip the canteen to the clouds. What a bloody world is this. And how strange to pull on this pack, to pick up my rifle in its canvas sacking, to take a dozen strides with my steel hat banging against my back and gas mask on my front. The digging in my heel is the only thing that feels true. I don't remember it bothering me last night as I wandered in the London fog, after the train ride in from the ferry landing at Folkestone. But now the pain is biting, and I have to stop and take off my boots. I try rubbing the offending spot with a bit of whale oil, which is so good against trench foot. Perhaps it will soothe my wound as well.

I think for a moment of the wormy-toothed woman with the tea and cake last night at Victoria Station, and of the others, offering different pleasures, to the swarms of us mud rats pouring out of the train. I could have just caught a cab, or stopped at any soldiers' rest. But I was happy to stretch my legs and get out on my own after all that time being cooped up. How difficult could it be to find my aunt and uncle's house in Chelsea? Just follow the King's Road, someone said. I figured I could walk and walk and eventually . . .

. . . the fog defeated me, and there I was by the water in a park of sorts, and how many nights have I slept out already, in conditions worse than this?

Besides, I was in no hurry.

I buy a muffin – splendid, greasy, life-giving! – from an old man who has a push-trolley business on a street corner and ask him for directions.

"King's Road?" he says, "It's nowhere near here." *Neer 'ear.* "And where might you be from, Major?"

"It's Private," I laugh. "I'm from Victoria."

"*Wha*, South Africa?"

"No, Canada," I say.

"They don't 'arf drink, those Canadians!" he says. And he shakes his head, grey-whiskered, some days' growth. "But you don't look Canadian."

"My father's a Scot. My mother's Spanish," I tell him. I don't mention the South American Indian side of her family.

"Spanish! Ah, you got the Latin blood in you, son." *Blud.* "A Scot and a Spaniard. What's the world coming to?"

"No good," I tell him and head off in the direction he's pointing.

I am surrounded by towering, solid, respectable buildings. Motor cars, carriages, trams, wagons, omnibuses stream by. The city is waking up gloriously. I walk like the dazed stranger I am, twist my neck, eyes gaping in amazement. Young women are everywhere, skirts dangling at mid-calf, for God's sake, smiling at me in my muddy boots, my wrinkled uniform. A captain passes on the arm of an exhausted, giddy-looking woman – either they've been out all night, I think, or are up rather early now – and it's only at the last second I remember to salute. Even then it seems like an absurdity, and he returns the gesture with a hint of annoyance, and as he moves she leans even more heavily into him. A drunken step? It's just a fleeting impression, and then they are past.

"KITCHENER CONFIDENT OF VICTORY," screams a headline at a newspaper stall, and I walk on past – don't want to have anything to do with it for now. The sweetness of the muffin is still in my mouth, the fullness of it still in my belly. I could walk all day, now that my boot feels better. A young boy in a school uniform asks me if I shot any Germans when I was at the Front. I tell him I had a chance but missed.

"You'll get him next time!" he says cheerfully. "I know you will."

Nods from gentlemen – older men, mostly, but some young shirkers, too – in bowler hats and civilian suits, carrying black umbrellas. Do I look like I've wandered in from the mouth of hell? I suppose not, because the Londoners stream by without much of a sense of it. I'm just part of the crowd on the sidewalk – the man with the haversack and rifle, the muddy puttees, that delirious gaze.

I don't even know what day of the week it is.

An omnibus, rattling and chugging, comes to a stop right at my feet, with a pretty conductress standing on the stair before me, so I ask her for directions.

"The King's Road? We're going there. Hop on!" she says cheerfully, in her little cap and tight-fitting blue uniform, with gaiters and boots, eyes like a dream of colour and softness. The stair beneath her reads "IRON 'JELLOIDS' for Anemia and Weakness."

"H . . . how much is it?" I fumble around for my wallet, try to think in shillings and pence.

"Free for men in service," she says. "Come on. I'll tell you when to get off." The bus is already moving again and I have to walk quickly, take a bit of a leap to catch the "Iron 'Jelloids'" stair. For a moment our bodies touch and I'm afraid of crushing her with my weight against the railing. But she wards me off with a fine, strong arm and I take a few steps farther up the stairs towards the second level.

"Have you come from the Front?" she asks, before I've drifted off too far.

"Yes," I say, turning on the stairs, stopping.

"We get quite a few these days. Not too horrible, I hope." *'Orrible.*

"No," I say.

"Nice to get a few days' leave. How long have you got, then?"

I tell her until the twenty-eighth, and she says that it passes quickly. "You should see them when we take them back to Victoria," she says. "But they have fun till then." The streets pass by, cut from my view by the side of the omnibus doorway. She has dark curly hair, skin like . . . like a woman's skin, like something you'd want to fall into.

I miss something she says and have to ask her to repeat it, which she does in a louder voice. "Do you have people to stay with?" she asks. "Or are you in one of the shelters downtown?"

"My cousins," I say. "In Chelsea."

"They'll be happy to see you," she says.

"Yes, I hope," I say, after too long a pause.

We make another stop and several people press on, squeeze by me on their way up to the viewing deck. I'm more conscious than ever of my rifle and pack, the smell of war still on my tired body.

"This is the King's Road here," the conductress says as we take a sudden, quick turn that throws me against the rail, then the vehicle shudders to a stop and I'm jolted against the other side of the stairs. "Bet them Germans didn't bomb you half as hard as that," she says, smiling wickedly. I step off somewhat clumsily under my burden, feel the edge of my helmet knock against the side of my neck, my cloth hat askew on my head.

"What's your name, then?" I call out to her as the bus starts on its way again.

"Miss Laughton!" she says.

"And I'm Private Crome!" I cry, somewhat stupidly, so a dozen people on our side of the bus turn their heads to examine me.

"Well, have a good stay, Private Crome!" she says. Then the omnibus rumbles on, taking some side street that is not the King's Road. I turn around in a circle, a dizzy man in full kit in the middle of London. I peer down to the right, to the left, try to remember which way we just came from. But my mind is dull from the travel, from the hard sleep and too little of it, from being here so suddenly, so unbelievably.

"Excuse me," I say to a fattish, balding man who is standing in front of his meat shop, a row of tired, fly-buzzed sausages hanging from hooks in the window. "Chelsea is which way?"

He nods to the right. "Are you just in, then?" he says.

"From the Front, yes," I say.

"Were you at Gallipoli last year?"

"No. No, not there."

"My son was at Gallipoli," he says. He looks down at his shoes a moment, as if unable to speak. Then he looks at me in too searching a manner.

"Pretty rough going, I guess," I say after a time. "It's this way, is it?"

"Have you had breakfast?" he asks, and pulls on the sleeve of my tunic before I can answer. "I have some things in the back," he says. And before I know it I am being led into the pungent darkness of his shop. Through the one room and into the back, a small table by a window looking out on a shaded square of garden – so deeply green, such a small splash of beauty and order. His wife is a tiny, fierce woman in a stained apron, her hair tied back with a red kerchief.

"He's been at the Front," the man says importantly. "He's staying for breakfast!" And within minutes I am being served hot sugared tea, buttered toast, steaming sausages, a plate of fried eggs with yolks impossibly yellow. I wolf it down, am nearly overwhelmed with the succulence of it, the luxury.

The shop owner brings me a hat box full of letters, photographs, badges. I see a young man with a close-cropped head, full moustache, military bearing, not quite looking at the camera, full of the moment of being observed. A private, from one of the pals' regiments. There he is with his friends in battle gear, but not a helmet among them.

The shop owner shows me one letter in particular, from last year.

No. 2 General Hospital
B.E.F. Lemnos
4 September 1915

Dear sir,

I deeply regret to tell you of the death of your son, Pte. C.H. Turner, yesterday in this hospital. His right leg was injured and, owing to the gangrene which is so frequent in this war, had to be amputated in order to try to save his life. Unfortunately his strength seemed unequal to the shock and he died peacefully yesterday afternoon, a day and a half (I think) after his operation. I saw him a couple of times the day before he died and was with him at night for a while. The nurse also sent me a message at 6 a.m. yesterday, at his request, and I went over and sat with him holding his hand for a while and talking to him. He was very weak but quite clear, brave, and peaceful, and talked about his home, about you, about his little sister to whom he wished his love sent. He asked me to write to you, and tell you anything I could. He was strangely alive at this time and was even smoking his pipe and apparently enjoying it – though of course I knew, and I think he did, that there was little chance of his pulling through. The only thing noticeable except pallor and weakness was that he said his head was full of fancies, and occasionally for a minute or two he drifted off to describe the old friends he had (he said) just met outside – and then he would realize that he was wandering and become perfectly clear again. We talked about his prayers too, and he seemed to be trusting God. I was very greatly attracted to him and so was his nurse, and I feel I should like to express my deepest sympathy for the loss of so gallant and fine a son. I saw him again about 9:30 a.m. and he was weaker but very cheerful. The next time (3 p.m.) he was unconscious, and just slipped away in the afternoon.

I only saw him during that one day and night and the next morning, but I really felt his death like a personal blow. He will be buried in the Military Cemetery here with a wooden cross to mark the spot. "In sure and certain hope of the resurrection to eternal life" – A few small possessions are being sent (according to rule) to you, through the official channels.

With much sympathy,
Yours faithfully,
W.A. Talbot
Chaplain

"Poor bugger," I say, and then when I realize what has escaped my lips I apologize. "It is quite a letter," I say. "A wonderful letter."

And I owe one just as wonderful to Snug's mother, I think.

The man and his wife ply me with more sausages until I have had my fill. The man tells me a great deal about the "bloody Asquith government" and their many connections to the Kaiser, about how German spies have infiltrated every important department, about the munitions scandals that have left the soldiers fighting without proper arms.

"I know, I know," I say, easing my way out the door. "Thank you. Thank you so much." I notice for the first time the small shrine in the window: Private Turner in a blurry photograph, looking very young, pudgy – before training, no doubt – with dried flowers at the base, and a syrupy poem I cannot finish reading.

They are both weeping as I leave, and my chest tightens dreadfully.

The pain returns to my foot as I walk down the King's Road, and that feels better somehow. My strategy is a simple one. I follow the King's Road and ask every four or five blocks if I am in Chelsea yet. And when I am finally told I am in Chelsea, by a prim set of ladies gusseted so tightly their eyes seem to bulge, I ask where Stokebridge Street is. Since they don't know – and the next four or five have no idea either – I continue on. Finally, a greengrocer tells me where to turn, what roads to follow, and then I am on a curving, quiet street of joined houses, quite new-looking, with black iron gates and tiny front gardens.

Number 30 is exactly halfway down the street. I pause for a moment, consider, absurdly, turning around, making my way back to the King's Road, finding a bus to return me to the woman with wormy teeth at Victoria Station who knew where soldiers were meant to stay.

Instead, I push through the gate, walk to the front door, handle the knocker with too much authority, as if I were some barbarian come to ransack the place. When the door opens, a tiny old woman in a maid's apron gives a jump. "Yes?" she says, with swimming blue eyes, not frightened so much as full of questions and surprise.

"Excuse me, ma'am," I say. "My name is Ramsay, Ramsay Crome. I'm a cousin of –" and I halt, tied up in the semantics of it. I try again. "My father is George Crome, who is the brother of –"

"Good Lord!" she says and takes a step back, then shuts the door in my face. I can hear her clucking down the hallway, and stand still, unsure of what to do, how long to wait until I knock again. I haven't moved a muscle, am standing as if on parade when the door is pulled open once more and a soft-eyed, pear-shaped version of my father – he looks like an illusion, a doughy parody of father's wiry toughness – is standing before me in shirt sleeves, suspenders, and stockinged feet.

"Are you George's boy?" he says in wonder – my Uncle Manfred, looking me up and down, not entirely with approval. "He did write that you might show your face sometime. Why the devil didn't you have the decency to wire ahead?" I stand stunned, trying to think through some kind of answer.

"Well," I stammer, "there was awfully short notice about my leave, and I –"

"Come in, come in, for God's sakes!" he blusters and pulls me through the doorway into a narrow entrance hall. "Harriet. Harriet!" he yells and walks ahead of me. "Put your bags here." He motions to the foot of the stairs. "You're staying, of course? How long have you got? HARRIET!" And he stamps up the stairs like an avalanche in reverse, disappears onto the second level. I am left to let my sack slump to the floor, to free myself from the gas-mask bag on my front, to stand my rifle in its canvas bag beside the rest of my things. I have just enough time to look at the small, fussy landscapes on the wall before a calm, willowy, silver-haired woman glides down the stairs and stands before me almost eye to eye.

"So you are Ramsay," she says. "I'm your Aunt Harriet. We are absolutely delighted to see you." She offers her hand, captures me in a moment with her large, bright eyes. "When did you get in? You must be starving," she says. "Miffy!" she calls down the hall in the direction of some back room, perhaps the kitchen. "We have one extra for breakfast."

"No, please, actually, I've eaten," I say.

"Nonsense!" she says, with a funny grin, as if I've made the most wonderful joke. "A growing boy like you. The last pictures we saw you were with your brothers, riding ponies, I believe. You couldn't have been more than eleven or twelve. And now look at you!"

She does look in some amazement at my sorry frame.

"Perhaps you would like a bath," she says after a pause that is so perfectly timed we both break into laughter. I have fallen in love with her, I think – this graceful, sunny-eyed aunt I am meeting for the first time. "Miffy. Miffy!" she says. "Could you draw young Mr. Crome a bath? And his clothes are going to need laundering." She turns to me. "Perhaps you would care to eat in the bath? I know, it's absolutely decadent, but why not? You're here, you've been in the horrors of the trenches – you have been in the trenches, haven't you? I sent those things off not knowing exactly –"

"Yes, ma'am. Thank you so much for the fruitcake."

"Auntie. Please call me Auntie. And you are my Ramsay, and I won't hear a moment's protest. You are here to be spoiled and pampered and fed to within an inch of your life, is that understood?"

My uncle blunders down the stairs, still in stockinged feet, his collar open, sleeves dangling. "How long is he staying?" he asks, and she shushes him with a single look – incredulous, dagger-eyed, punctuated with a dismissive sigh.

◆

In the bathroom I stand naked, contemplate my thin, battered body. A bruise on my ribs, shoulders so narrow they look like skate blades, my arms and hands more bone and bulging vein than muscle. A withered, ancient-looking sprig of manhood. A face all bone and nose, sprouting whiskers, dirt. Eyes too intent on seeing everything, and my hair so short it barely hides the many bumps on my head. Chest pale, unhaired, sunken-looking – probably wouldn't pass a physical now. A doctor would tap my chest and hear the rattle of broken tin, order me to a sanitarium for a month of country rest.

I place my toe in the steaming water, lower myself in. The water isn't scalding but hot enough to be uncomfortable at first, then is simply soothing, enveloping. I soap my aching feet, pull the toes apart, examine the ragged nails, then the red, blistered heel which aches just to look at. Again I think: Snug is dead now, and Ferguson, and Reese too probably, and I am here in a hot bath with soft, civilian soap, a door that closes, all the time in the world.

A knock on the door and Uncle Manfred comes in with a bowl of steaming porridge on a silver service, brown sugar piled high but melting quickly into the cream, with a plate of toast on the side, another of scrambled eggs with bacon, and even an orange sliced thinly. "Have me doing maid service next!" he mutters. "Shall I take these?" he asks, bending to gather up my clothes, scattered where I've dumped them on the floor.

"They're all right, I think. I put them on clean just a day ago –"

He dangles a puttee for a moment, bits of mud and dirt falling off it.

"I'll see what other clothes I can round up for you," he says. "Have to be civilian, I'm afraid. Unless you have a change?"

When I shake my head he says, "Didn't think so. Your pack weighs like lead anyway. The girls are very anxious to see your rifle. I told them to wait until you come back down. All right?"

"Yes," I say. "No one should be fiddling with –"

"Precisely," he says and takes his leave, flecks of mud now on the bathroom floor where my uniform used to be.

◈

I have a dream of standing on the platform at Victoria, looking. Soldiers are everywhere, surrounded by women and children – stout mothers in floral hats, and teary-eyed wives clutching their bosoms, and wailing children pulling at the fringes of their father's uniform. Soldiers and their women are kissing every-where, in plain view, right in the station, they are backed against lampposts and pillars, are hardly bothering to hide in the shadows. Everywhere I turn I see flashes of them. I don't know where to go, somehow can't find the big station clock to get my bearings. It's just in the corner of my eye, whichever way I turn. I can't quite glimpse it past the scenes of reunion and parting.

Then I'm back on board ship. It's rolling with the waves in a way I'll never get used to. I stagger from side to side, hold the walls of the chamber to try to keep them still. Snug comes down the stairs – clang, clang! – with a mop in his hands. He says, "Bloody Williams. Gave me sanitary duty." And mops at my feet until I move. "Did you see the candle?" he asks. "On the point?"

"No."

"He's standing there in the rain with a candle."

"Who is?"

"Bloody sanitary duty," he says, and mops viciously past me, the floor and the walls, making them dirtier with every swipe.

I need to get up the gangway, to stop the rolling of the world, make it steady for a moment. I reach the steps but have a hard time grasping the rail, which is thick and wet, too slippery to hold.

I groan and the water splashes over the side of the tub, the silver service on the tray across my lap is nearly upset. I catch it quickly and look around, rub my eyes – my fingers wrinkled like an old man's. The porridge is half-eaten, I can feel it lumping in my stomach with the rest of the food. *London*, I think, marvelling again at the strangeness of being here.

I let out the water, move the tray to the floor, stand up stiffly, take the towel from the door and dry myself, fit on Uncle Manfred's limp old robe. Then I pick up the tray, open the door, and nearly collide with a young woman coming down the hall.

"Oh, good heavens, don't bother with that!" she says, a crimson blush invading her white, white skin. She averts her eyes, but not right away. She has Father's light brown hair, and something of his gaze: stark, penetrating, too intense to be comfortable, and yet entirely, unsettlingly female. "Your room is that one," she says, pointing, and takes the tray from me, is halfway down the stairs with it before I can open my mouth.

"Thank you," I say to her receding back.

The room is small, fussy, stifling. I brush aside the curtains – a heavy brown material, with lace edging – and force open the window, which seems to have been shut for years. Down below is a patch of glorious green garden in the small square of back-yard belonging to the house. But also there's a view of several other gardens and private spaces, of clothing on the line, cluttered window boxes, mouldy bird baths, ivy-covered walls. It's all so gloriously, delightfully ordinary.

Below the window, what I'm leaning on to see out is a small, slanted writing desk, with, I now notice, a jar of ink on the ledge. How easily I could have upset it and blackened the desk, myself, the dainty lamp.

It's a girl's room. My visit has put someone out, and if I tromp around like a galoot I'm going to break something.

Some of Uncle Manfred's clothes have been laid out on the small bed, including a change of underwear, for which I'm grateful. The trousers of course are far too big at the waist, but suspenders help, and the shirt is baggy, the collar roomy at the neck, the sleeves a bit long. The jacket too is oversized; the whole outfit seems clown-like, and not just because of the poor fit. It's civilian clothing, which I haven't worn since last year, but it seems like a century ago, in someone else's lifetime. I put on fresh socks, and my stolen boots, which someone has already brushed clean. Then I fill my pockets with the essentials – a battered package of cigarettes, some matches, my wallet – and step out of the room feeling very much the charlatan.

They're waiting for me in the sitting room, Uncle Manfred in his proper jacket now, shirt sleeves done up, and Aunt Harriet and the two of them, the girls. The young women.

"I fell . . . I guess I fell asleep," I say. "In the bath."

Aunt Harriet makes the introductions. "Here are your cousins, Ramsay. This is Margaret," she says, and the brown-haired one from the stairs, the intense one, stands up. She does not proffer her hand, we both nod our heads somewhat awkwardly. "And my youngest daughter, Emily." I turn my gaze to a bit of a flower – soft reddish curls, peachy cheeks, seventeen perhaps, who does hold out her hand, and so I take it gently.

"We have been so looking forward to having a soldier in the house," she says.

"It's wonderful of you to welcome me," I reply. "I'm sorry I didn't wire ahead. This whole leave came as a huge surprise. I found I was running out of camp to try to catch the leave train . . ."

"Sit down, man!" my uncle says. "What can I get you? Would you like a whisky, or a glass of rum –"

"Manfred!" my aunt says. "It's ten o'clock in the morning!"

"And we're at war, my dear," he says. "Our young Ramsay might seem like a callow youth to you, but he has seen things that we will never see, and I am asking him –" He turns to me again. "Do you want a glass of whisky, man?"

"No. No thank you, sir," I say, and sit in a straight-backed chair by the dark fireplace, and look at them ranged before me on the chesterfield, my two female cousins, in short dresses at that, ankles, mid-calves clearly exposed. Uncle Manfred is standing by the window, Harriet is seated in a padded chair near the door.

"How do you feel about the progress of the war?" Manfred presses. "I was reading just this morning, late reports finally getting out about the fall of Kut in Mesopotamia. A shocking business, the capture of the whole 6th Division. What was it they were saying? The garrison was down to eating mules. And one fellow, the supply and transport butcher, simply refused to slaughter a particular animal, this mule who wore the ribbons from three Indian border campaigns. Can you imagine it? The men were so tired in the end they couldn't even carry their kit."

"I can believe it. I know that feeling," I say.

"Well," Manfred says, his face animated, hands shoved into his pockets restlessly. "Can you tell us anything about where you're posted? It's not Verdun, thank God, eh?"

"No, not Verdun."

"The Salient, I suppose?" he says knowledgeably.

I nod.

"What's that?" Harriet asks.

"Ypres! Ypres, dear woman!" Manfred thunders – he's caught up in the subject, alive with it. "The Ypres Salient. It's a bulge in the line. Where the first poison-gas attack was last year. My God, those Canadian troops held firm. You weren't part of that, were you?"

"No, no," I say.

"Bet that just got you rushing to sign up. You remember, Harriet, the Algerians were streaming away in wild panic. But the gallant Canadians refused to yield. What was it your chaps did? No, no, don't tell me – they urinated into their handkerchiefs and held them over their mouths. Oh, don't look at me that way, woman –" He turns back to me. "They can't handle the plainest details of warfare," he says. "They can drive omnibuses, they can build bombs, but just mention a man urinating into his handkerchief –"

"Manfred, would you please calm down. Have a seat, dear," Harriet says. "You're getting all wound up." She turns to me. "He's getting all wound up."

Manfred lowers his eyes meekly for a moment, walks to the only other empty chair, by the chesterfield, looks as though he will stay quiet, then bursts forth with, "Did you hear about this Canadian chap, what's-his-name?"

"The sergeant?" I say. "Who was crucified on the barn door by the Germans?"

"Oh, that fellow," Manfred says. "That's not who I meant. But did you see him?"

"No. Everyone knows someone who knows someone who saw him," I say. "Which makes me think it's just a latrine rumour."

"Really. Extraordinary!" Manfred says. "Still, I wouldn't put it past the Germans to do something like that. These stories don't just come out of thin air. Usually something to them. But I meant another Canadian. This Scobie fellow. It was in *The Times*. He'd been wounded, you see, was here convalescing. And he got in an accident, was run over by a tramway car, and the attendants refused to back it up, to get the wheels off his arm. So what did they do? They tried to raise the car with a jack, which broke, you see, and so he had to have his arm amputated after that. He just got five hundred pounds' damages from the court."

"And he's out of the war," I say.

"Yes! Out of the war effort. If it were me," Manfred says, "I'd want to hunt down those attendants. Snuffing out a man's chances like that. Probably of German extraction."

"Manfred!" Aunt Harriet says sharply. "You prattle on sometimes like a demented old man."

"Do you see? Do you see?" Manfred says to me, getting up, pacing agitatedly. "What I have to put up with in this henhouse?"

"Manfred desperately wanted to go to the Front," Harriet says. I look from one to the other – it's an old routine, I decide, her mock-shrewishness, his pretending to be upset.

"Well, I have bad feet," he says, and stands to show me. "Quite flat, I couldn't last a mile carrying a pack. But the officers are given horses, aren't they?"

"You're not much at riding horses either, dear," Harriet says, and she slips me a dazzling, cutting smile. "But perhaps our Ramsay does not want to think about the war while he's here. What would you like to do, Ramsay?"

"Oh," I say. "I think – stay in bed for a week."

They laugh, they have no idea. Then I suddenly see him – Snug – slumped across the floor in front of us, his chest blown open by the sniper's bullet. He *couldn't* be here, of course not, and yet the stench of body rot rises up. He has crawled out of the slime to die here at my feet. I look at my cousins in horror, then back at the body I'd swear is staining their fine, innocent rug. In confusion I lurch to my feet, open my mouth to somehow say what can't be said.

And they are looking at me like – well, like a madman.

"Ramsay, can I get you some tea?" my dear aunt asks me, in a voice of concern.

When I look again there is no corpse, no Snug, no stain or stench of rotten flesh.

"Perhaps a cigarette," I manage to say, easing back uncertainly into my chair.

She offers me one from Manfred's box, which I take, trying not to seem too anxious. They are a fine English brand, and I immerse myself in the calming smoke.

"We must go to the theatre," Emily says too brightly. "Some of wittiest things are playing now. Honestly, you forget yourself completely. We haven't been for ages. Do you remember, we used to go every week?"

Against my better judgement I look down again at the rug, which is still perfectly normal. Of course it is.

"The war has brought its changes," Harriet says abruptly. Then she says to me, "Your father was here in London last month. Did you know that?"

I look at her in added surprise.

"Manfred saw him in Green Park. Didn't you, Manfred?"

"That's right," he says. "I was walking along –"

"He was walking along," Harriet says, "and looked up, and there was a familiar face not seen since the honeymoon, yes – twenty-five years ago?"

"That's right. Since that famous honeymoon trip they took. Your father and his –"

"– bride," Harriet says. "You know all about that trip, I suppose?"

I nod but Uncle Manfred blusters on. "They carried her over the Andes on muleback! Oh, she was full of the story, a blazingly beautiful woman, one could certainly see why George would want to marry a –" He stops short of saying "native," tiptoes around the word. "At any rate," he says, "there I was in Green Park, spring flowering all around, and I looked up, and I see my long-lost little brother. 'Hullo, Manfred!' he says, striding by – well, you know how he strides, like he's got to walk the rest of the world by ten a.m."

"And what did you say?" Harriet asks. "You said –"

"I was in shock. I said, 'Hello, George!'"

"He said, 'Hello, George,'" Harriet says. "*And they just kept walking!*"

"We just kept walking!" Uncle Manfred blurts. "That was it after twenty-five years. 'Hullo, Manfred.' He was by me in a whisk, I barely had time to see him." He shakes his head. "But that time he brought your mother round, she was full of stories. Vampire bats, do you remember, Harriet? What was that?"

I take up the story before Harriet can jump in, grateful for the distraction. "She would wake up in the night in her tent in the mountains and her feet would be bloody from vampire bats," I say. "So Father posted guards outside her door to keep them away. He'd decided to go east over the mountains from Bogotá instead of the easy route west – he had some data still to check on a project he was completing. I think he wanted an adventure as well. His men carried my mother over the worst of the terrain, and there were alligators in the rivers, and all of Mother's jewellery was stolen in the steamer across the Atlantic. The story has been told, and told, and told around our table at home."

"I've never seen a wife more angry at her husband," Manfred says.

"Or two people more in love," Harriet adds. "The room would crackle when they were together."

"He was always an odd man," Manfred muses. Then, at a gaze from his wife, "What? I can't talk frankly about my brother?"

"Diplomacy was never a Crome strong suit," she says, to me rather than Manfred. "You must forgive your uncle –"

"No, no, I'm happy to hear people talk about my father," I say. "Sometimes I feel like I hardly know him. He's away so much –"

"Building railway bridges, digging canals, dredging harbours, sinking mines. Is there anything he hasn't done?" Manfred says.

"Or anywhere he hasn't been?" Margaret interjects. "We've had letters from him from the oddest places: Mexico, Siam, Hong Kong, India . . ."

"And they say nothing, practically, about what he's been

doing, or what's happening with the family," Harriet says. "I think your mother must be –"

"She's a saint," I say. Harried, overworked, exhausted, I think, Keeping us all together.

Emily digs out a photo from a drawer and we gather round. It's an old one from childhood, taken by a friend of Father's he'd met somehow coming in from San Francisco, a man we never saw again, although he did send copies of the family portrait. We are all looking out at eternity, the five boys and Mother and Father.

"Father had just come back from abroad," I explain. "He would line up the boys first thing, have us bend over and then whip us with a switch, for all the trouble he was certain we'd caused our mother while he'd been away. But for this photograph he'd also cut off all of the boys' hair. You see, our heads are almost shaven, and Mother was furious at him for that. You can see it in her face, there. Alex, the young one, had fine curls. She didn't speak to him for days."

"Is he really such a tyrant?" Margaret asks.

"Oh no, no. He's a scientist. You should see when he comes home, the whole front room in our house is taken over by his drafting table, which he sets up by the big picture window, and all of Mother's decorations are swept aside as the room is littered with pulleys and switches, strangely shaped pieces of rubber and tin, little wooden models of devices he's working on. For years he's been designing a shallow draft river steamer. And he has some ideas for train engines, to make them work better in tropical climates."

We are all close now by the chesterfield, looking at the old picture of my family, listening to the words that are flooding out of me in a way they haven't since . . . well, since who knows when. Since before the wretched war.

"There was one time," I say, "Father came home after a year in Colombia, trying to drain a lake that supposedly had sunken Inca gold at the bottom. But it was spring-fed, couldn't be drained. He just arrived one day, with no notice. And he took me aside, he said, 'Ramsay, how old are you?' 'Seventeen,' I replied. 'Well, son,' he said, 'when I was a year younger than you I crossed the Atlantic and went to New York and started to learn engineering. How would you like to come work for me?' How could I not? A chance like that, to be with my father. I told Mother that day, and the next we were off on the train. I hadn't the slightest idea where we were going. We would rise in the morning and Father would say, formally, 'Good morning, Ramsay.' And then most of the day we'd sit in silence looking out the window. Every so often he'd read out some place name: Hope, Penticton, Lethbridge, Regina. In the evening he would bow stiffly and say, 'Good night.' Day after day passed like this. I was nearly bursting with anticipation, wondering where we were going, what work we would do. Finally we got to Montreal. 'Here's where we get off,' he said. I followed him. I had just the one small suitcase. The crowd on the platform was enormous, swirling around us, and I was dazed from the travel, the strain of sitting in silence."

They are following with eagerness, and the words are pouring out, I can't keep them back.

"He turned to me and grasped my hand, looked me straight in the eye. He said, 'Here's fifty dollars. It's certainly more than I had when I landed in New York.' He put the money straight into my pocket. He said, 'You should find work. And write your mother, she'll want to hear from you. And one more thing. If you should ever get –'" I stop, suddenly realizing where the story is headed. "Well," I say hastily, "no need to repeat everything in mixed company. The upshot is that he turned and left, disappeared into the crowd."

I am clenching my jaw, remembering the stunning jolt of that moment.

"What else did he say?" Emily presses.

"No, I'd rather not. It's not fit for –"

"Oh, surely you can repeat it. We are all grown-ups here."

I look around for my aunt and uncle to intercede, but they too are nodding, pressing me onward.

"Well," I say. "Here it is. He said, 'If you ever find yourself with a certain disgraceful disease' – that's not exactly what he said, but you catch my meaning – 'do not hesitate to write to me, and I will send you the money for treatment.'"

I've never told anyone that story, am filled now with it so that my voice is almost choking.

"He's a monster!" Harriet says indignantly.

"No, no," I say, coming to his defence despite myself. "You can see at least what he was trying to do. He wanted me to stand on my own feet, to be a man." I glance from one set of eyes to the next: Manfred's incredulous, Margaret's guarded but curious, Emily's blazing. "Going to New York, leaving his home the way that he did as a young man – that was the most important thing in his life. And here he was sharing it with me."

"By abandoning you in a strange city when you were only seventeen?" Aunt Harriet says.

"What did you do?" Margaret pursues.

"Well, he hadn't completely abandoned me," I explain. "In the envelope with the fifty dollars was the address of a rooming house, and at the rooming house was a note from a Mr. Pollard, who ran a machine shop. My father had helped Mr. Pollard in some undisclosed way and so I was being offered an apprentice position, which I took. It was all much safer, I suppose, than it sounds. But Father had gotten me out from under my mother's skirts, you see, had given me a taste, at least, of the freedom of life. It was three good years."

"And then I suppose the war broke out," Margaret says. "So much for the freedom of life!"

"Yes, so much," I say, and look at her. "I headed for home then, and, eventually, signed up."

"You poor boy," Harriet says. "You've only just arrived on our doorstep and here we've pried out your story as if it were the price of admission. Please excuse the baldness of our interrogations. Sometimes I think we're the most shameless of families."

"Not at all," I say. "It's quite a relief, actually, to –"

"Come, come with me!" Manfred says, rising abruptly. "Enough of this suffocating female company. They will have the bones of your life spread out on the living-room rug before you know it. No, no, it's my duty to protect you, young man."

"Father," Margaret says. We're all standing now, and Manfred has me halfway out the room. "Please don't subject Ramsay to your invention. He has only just arrived."

"Shhhh, daughter!" he says. "Enough henpecking for now!"

"It's a Zeppelin-finder!" Margaret calls as we leave the room. "In case he asks you. And you aren't obliged to spend more than half an hour trying it out!"

"Pay no attention to them," Manfred says as he leads me down the narrow, irregular stairs to the dully lit cellar where, in the corner farthest from female eyes, his tools are ranged on a rough wooden table. The ceiling isn't high enough for us to stand, but once seated at a splintery bench we are all right. It's not so different from many dugouts I've been in. He pulls a flask from a dark canvas bag somewhat hidden in the shadows, uses his elbow to wipe out a dusty mug on the table, then pours a generous portion of whisky for me. "No time like the present," he says, and waits for me to down it, which I do with some discomfort. Then he takes the mug and pours even more for himself.

"A man needs a refuge," he says, after a gulp. "Too much civilization is unhinging, don't you think?" He drains the mug, then pours more and hands it to me. "The problem with the Zeppelins," he says, "is knowing when they're coming. You can't see them at night, not on a dark night, not in clouds or fog. If we could *hear* them better we'd have a better chance of getting our guns in position. Have you seen our so-called defences? Of course not, you've been at the Front. They roar around mounted on the back of these motor cars, careening through the city. I think more pedestrians are killed by them than are killed by Zep bombs. It's a shocking situation. But if we could *hear* the Zeppelins coming from farther out, then we'd have more time."

He gets up awkwardly, nearly bangs his head on the ceiling, then opens a long, narrow cupboard that seems to have been directly designed to house Manfred's masterpiece, a pole perhaps five feet in length, with a megaphone on each end attached to a stethoscope.

"You see," he explains, "when one first hears a Zeppelin, one invariably turns one's head in the correct direction from which it's coming, so that each ear is equidistant from the sound. This forms a triangle with the space between the ears as the base – a very narrow one, of course. But this device of mine allows one to increase the size of the base. Are you following? If you fit it over the head so that the middle of the pole is directly over the centre, and insert the listening tubes like this –" he is placing the ridiculous thing on my head as he speaks – "then all that remains is for a listener to turn to face the direction of the Zeppelin as soon as it is heard, and through triangulation –"

"You can figure out where the Zeppelin might be."

"Precisely!"

I adjust the tubes to make them more comfortable.

"Of course you wouldn't hear anything now," he says, his voice booming into my ears. "But if we bring it outside in the evening, when the Zeps are most likely to come round . . ."

"I don't think my ears are up to it," I say, taking the tubes away, pulling the pole from my head. "I think with all the constant noise of the Front I must be wearing out my eardrums."

"No, no, it wouldn't be you. Of course not. This is the really brilliant part of it. We'd use *blind* men, you see, to listen for the invaders. They desperately want to contribute anyway, poor chaps, and they have heightened hearing, so why not?" He takes the contraption from me, reinserts it carefully into the cupboard. "I've been trying to get to see the colonel of the home-defence outfit, want to have this thing perfected by then. You don't know how helpless we've come to feel, sitting here in the evenings waiting for those untouchable German machines to come floating over with their infernal bombs. Targeting civilians, can you imagine? What else will this Kaiser do? I think he must be related to the devil. Gas attacks, U-boats, this horrible business with the Irish. You don't think the Germans aren't mixed up in that too? Of course they are. There's no limit to what they'd stoop to. And we are completely riddled with spies here in England, I hate to tell you –"

"Father!" Margaret calls from the top of the stairs. "Please don't detain our cousin longer than necessary in the dungeon."

"There are spies in this neighbourhood. I've seen the cleaning lady for the Wandsworths four doors down signalling at night with her attic window blinds –"

"Ramsay, you don't have to stay down there if you don't want to. You've humoured him quite enough, I'm sure," Margaret calls down.

"*Damnation*," Uncle Manfred says, but quietly, under his breath. "Whatever you do, Ramsay, don't have daughters. You aren't planning to, are you?"

"I'm not even married, sir."

"Quite right. Quite right! And no need to be, either. Not with your whole life ahead of you. Oh, how I envy you. Everything ahead!" He rises as he says it, leans forward to avoid a beam. "You're a free man now, best enjoy it!" he says, leading the way out of the dungeon.

◈

Over luncheon, in the cramped dining room at the back of the house, we talk about food. Prices have been rising alarmingly, I am told, with quantities of many things in short supply, especially meat and fruit. I tell my story of encountering the butcher on my way in and Aunt Harriet assures me that I was uncommonly lucky to have been fed such a meal.

"What you were served came from his private stock, I'm sure," she says. "If he'd had much meat for sale there would have been a long queue for it. Poor Miffy has become expert at sniffing out shops with new supplies. And the prices! Bread has gone up to nine pence a quarter-loaf. Can you imagine? It was five pence or less before the war. And they want us all to eat wholewheat bread."

"In the Napoleonic Wars bread was almost two shillings," Manfred says. "I read that the other day. I think it's Asquith's way of telling us things could be worse."

We're eating something vaguely meaty in a greasy, brownish sauce, with cabbage and white bread. At the talk of high prices I slow myself, try to make the smallish portion last longer. What about that enormous breakfast they served me? I wonder. A fine show for a guest, no doubt.

"Not to mention the coal rationing," Harriet says. "We had a terrifically cold winter. Not as bad as being in battle, of course."

"It was difficult, with all the men gone," Margaret cuts in. "Delivery was drastically reduced, you could see serving women and boys lined up at depots with perambulators and soapboxes on wheels to get the coal. And the price went up two shillings a month. I just pity the poor people."

"The poor people. The poor people," Manfred intones in a mocking voice. Then, at Margaret's glare, he says, "The poor people have never had it so good. The poor people are now regularly employed assembling machines of war. They now have so much money they're drinking it up by the gallon, leaving our fighting men" – a nod to me – "high and dry, with munitions that lag far behind the Germans'. What about all those shells that fail to explode? The poor people – *the poor people* – are having a grand old time while the flower of England's youth is being ground into the soil of France and Belgium." He wipes the last traces of brown sauce from his plate with a crust of bread, leaving his plate shining clean.

"Vast numbers of sons of poor people are currently serving in the trenches," Margaret says with an almost exaggerated restraint. "What I was trying to say . . ."

"And the sons of bankers, the sons of lawyers and business-men and the upper classes are disproportionately represented, especially among the junior officers, who are being killed and wounded at an astonishing rate, which our young lieutenant here would know all about. While *others*, who shall remain nameless, stay at home in safe government positions . . ."

"Private," I say, scraping my own plate clean, then washing my last crust down with a glass of water.

"Pardon?"

"I'm a private, not a lieutenant," I explain. "No stripes or pips. A simple soldier."

Uncle Manfred looks at me for a moment in incredulity, then recovers and wipes his mouth with his napkin, pushes himself away from the table. "Extraordinary," he says finally. "Whyever would you do that?"

"Father!" Margaret says.

"Well, the boy has joined up below his station. I'm simply inquiring as to why he would do such a thing. Especially at a time when sons from the leadership classes are required to take their rightful positions."

"I knew nothing about waging war," I say, feeling the hair bristling on the back of my neck. "And if there's one thing all of us soldiers have learned, it's that officers should have a decent idea of what they're doing. When I joined up I had no pretensions about being better than anyone else. I simply wanted to do my bit and then go home."

"And your father allowed you to join as a simple soldier?"

"My father didn't have a say in it. I told him and he didn't disagree."

"Yes, I suppose not," Manfred says. "He abandoned you in the station, after all."

"I think it's marvellous what Ramsay has done," Harriet says. "I'm sure the Canadian army is much more egalitarian than ours anyway." Miffy is clearing the dishes now. "Of course, if he were British he would have *had* to become an officer. He would have been out of place otherwise."

"I suppose Canada might be different," Manfred says doubtfully. "A more classless sort of place," he adds, in such a tone that he might be talking about savages. "At any rate, the important thing is you joined up, while *others* have done nothing at all," he says archly, "despite the Military Service Act. They just hang on to their safe government jobs while civilization is imperilled . . ."

"Manfred!" Harriet says crossly, and he winces – evidently kicked under the table. Margaret's face has turned crimson and she is resolutely staring at her waterglass.

"What? *What?*" Manfred says. "I'm not mentioning anyone by name. I am talking generally of intelligent, healthy young men whose cowardice has been manifest to such a degree that one would hope –" He winces again and gives a little yelp, then turns to me. "You can see, Ramsay, that some subjects are not open to debate, even amongst the so-called freethinkers of the family."

I look in incomprehension from one face to another. Finally,

Emily says, "Margaret has a young admirer, of whom Father does not entirely approve."

"Emily!" Margaret says and rises abruptly, slams down her napkin. A fork spins off the table and clatters to the floor. "Why don't I just leave so you can all gossip behind my back?" And she turns, stalks out of the dining room, her feet hammering up the steps to the second floor.

We sit painfully, in a moment of disbelief, and then Manfred, who is locked in unspoken battle with his wife, says to her, "*What?*"

"Sometimes," Harriet says, "I wonder if *anything* can be going on inside your brain, sir," and she rises as well. "Excuse me, Ramsay. This has been a frightful display." And she too leaves the dining room, striding purposefully, the hem of her dress rustling against the floor.

When she has gone, Manfred says coolly, "Don't go after women who have stormed out of a room, Ramsay. There's a piece of advice for you." He deliberately drains his glass of water, waits patiently while Miffy clears the rest of the table and then returns in a minute with small bowls of tired, grey canned fruit in syrup for the three remaining diners. We spoon down the dessert, the sound of our cutlery discomfiting.

"If you ask me," Manfred says abruptly, "the Irish rebellion has its roots in fear of compulsory military service. I think there's a profound cowardice in much of Irish blood, which is why they would rebel now, when the Empire is battling for the soul of civilization. Simple cowards, that's all."

I sip the fruit syrup from my spoon. "I'm afraid I haven't been able to follow it as closely as I'd like," I say.

"No. No, I suppose not." Then after another silence, he ventures, "The Germans are conscripting young Belgians now, apparently. After raping their country." We all listen to the muffled sounds of heated discussion upstairs. "Not that the Belgians have turned out to be such great shakes after all. There were riots against them here just last week, Ramsay. They've been setting up their own shops, and taking British jobs, murdering policemen. It's a wonder we don't run them out and send them back to the Germans." Emily studies her fruit bowl while I nod at my uncle, try to decide what to say. Manfred says, "Terrific round of fighting in the southern Tirol, I hear. The Italians really taking strips out of the Austrians. Who would have thought it?"

Miffy brings tea in a silver service with cream and sugar, and the sound of argument turns to muffled weeping. Finally, Manfred sighs deeply and says, rising, "I suppose I'd better see what's up."

"Apologize, Papa. For me too, please," Emily says.

Manfred makes a huffing sound and shuffles out of the room. As his heavy steps mount the stairs, Emily says to me, "Margaret is very sensitive about some things."

"She has a young man?"

"Henry Boulton, yes. They're unofficially engaged. He works at the Ministry of Munitions for only three pounds a week, and doesn't even have a permanent position at that. He's an 'ordinary,' a clerk. And his family has no money to speak of, though they're very good people apparently." She pours tea for me, asks me what I would like in it, gracefully places two sugar cubes and a healthy slurp of cream, then pours her own straight. "Father of course wants him to go to the Front and get shot to pieces."

"But Margaret is in love with him?"

"I think she's in love with the idea of him. He is rather sickly, actually, and would never make a good soldier. I think she likes how crazy he makes Father. But she does tend to become very hurt whenever someone talks about it, so I should stop now," she says. She smiles at me like a very pretty, clever young woman safely on the sidelines, watching everything like a hawk.

We sip our tea quietly. No sounds now from upstairs. I expect yelling, stamping of feet, the hurricane that would ensue back home when Mama was furious with Father for things done or not done, said or unspoken. But here there is an unreal sort of calm.

"So," I say, "what do you and Margaret spend your time at? I know many women now are joining the war effort in some way."

"I would like to be a nurse. I would jump at the chance to go to the Front, to help out meaningfully, but both Mother and Father are opposed. So I find myself knitting a great deal, and I help out Mother with her charity work at Lady Templeton's Foundation. And I paint, of course."

"You do?"

"These are some of mine," she says, pointing to two oil paintings I've not noticed till now. They are in the same fussy, muddied style as the ones in the hall – a blurry hedgerow on a country lane, cows in a pasture under the canopy of a large tree.

"They're very nice," I say.

"Oh, you don't like them," she says immediately.

"No, no, not at all. I mean, I do like them! I like them very much!" I say, with too much enthusiasm.

"Don't apologize," she says with a studied amiability. "If you don't like them you don't like them."

"They're very . . . well, the craft is quite good," I stumble. "It's excellent. It's just that –"

"What?" she says with a tight sweetness, and I know I have blundered.

"It's just that I do some painting of my own," I say. "I have, at any rate. That's why I joined up as a pioneer. You see, I thought I was going to be a sign-painter, do odd jobs, instead of donkey work in the front lines. Though I'm happy, of course, to do it – I'm no shirker. Anyway, artists are often the worst judges of other people's –"

"I see," she cuts in. "Have some more tea?"

I've barely sipped from my cup as it is.

"I'm sorry. I've offended you," I say. "I do like the . . . sedateness of the scenes. There's an air of calm and –"

"Perhaps you could tell me about *your* work," she says.

"I've painted nothing since I signed on," I say, looking at my fingertips.

"Well, we'll have to paint together while you're here. You can tell me what I'm doing wrong," Emily says. She sips her tea, looks at her own fingertips, and I think of slogging through mud – the horrible effort of it, and how every step seems ridiculously wrong, liable only to make things worse and worse.

"I do . . . I did portraits, mainly," I say. "Faces. The human aspect. So, of course, I'm no judge of landscape painting."

"You must have seen many interesting faces lately," she says. I look at her and I think – blackened faces, charred faces, bloodied faces, grinning skeleton faces, grimacing, nervous-tic faces, faceless, obliterated faces.

"Margaret is our writer," Emily says, after I say nothing for too long. "She is bearing witness to the war on the home front. She writes for hours in her journal every night. Since we were little we've talked about doing books together as writer and illustrator. She used to show me her stories constantly, but everything she writes now is very secretive."

"We all need our privacy," I say. And it seems to me, suddenly, an overwhelming need – to get out of the house, be on my own for a time.

I make my excuses to Emily, walk down the hallway, have my hand on the door to freedom when Aunt Harriet spies me as she descends the stairs. "Oh, Ramsay," she says, "Not heading off so soon?"

"I thought I would just stretch my legs."

"A wonderful idea. Perhaps we should all go. It's such rare good weather." And she turns and calls up the stairs, "Margaret! We're going for a walk in the sunshine." Emily appears in the hall, gives me a you-can't-escape-us sort of look. "Emily, dear, will you come with us? We're going for a bit of a walk. Where shall we go?" Harriet asks of me.

"I'm afraid I –"

"Don't know London, of course, dear," she says. "That's why I'm wondering if we shouldn't take you to some of the sights. Westminster Abbey and Trafalgar Square, Piccadilly. You really must see them. I'm afraid that many of the museums and galleries are closed. Can you imagine that? Shut down to economize. Here we are trying to save civilization, and we're doing exactly what the Kaiser has been unable to do with all his Zeppelin bombs."

"You don't have to make a speech, Mother," Margaret says, coming down the stairs now. She has scrubbed her face: it looks too fresh, with her eyes still stormy. And she has put on a large flowered hat that makes her seem, on the staircase especially, quite tall. All possibility of escape drains away. So I wait in the hallway as Harriet and Emily gather their respective hats, lacy shawls, and handbags for going out.

Margaret stands in the narrow space quite close to me, in silence for a time, and then she says, in a low voice, "Now you can see why your father was in such a hurry to flee the family."

I don't know what to say, am saved by Harriet and Emily finally ready to depart.

"Your Uncle Manfred is not coming with us," Harriet says. "He has decided to read the newspaper again, in case there was something he missed the first time round." She hands me a straw hat of my uncle's, and when I pull open the door the day's sunshine floods in – a startling brightness. As I am passing through the doorway I am again seized by a feeling of unreality: here I am accompanying ladies into the radiance of London in May, with nothing more frightening than the sound of distant traffic. The street is lined with trees in purple bloom, with window boxes of delicate colour, with tiny, gentle gardens. The order and cleanliness are striking – how my eye has been trained to expect half-shattered walls and rubble, pocked roads, trees splintered and stumped, a cascade of disorder. It's like a fairy-land here, a trick of the imagination.

"We have a motor car," Harriet says, taking my arm, "but it's on loan to Lady Templeton's Foundation, and at any rate the government has asked us all to cut down on private motoring. So I hope you don't mind the omnibus." I tell her that I caught one on the way in.

As we walk Margaret starts to pepper me with questions about life in the trenches. Is it as muddy as the papers make out? How many days on duty, how many days off? What is the food like? Where do we sleep? How often do we go over the top, and have I ever endured hand-to-hand combat with a German? I find myself answering as curtly as possible: "No, no, not so bad"; "We all sleep anywhere"; "Hand-to-hand is rare. It's mostly long-distance shelling." I explain what a pioneer does, in simplest terms – building and repairing trenches, laying down rail lines, bridges, and such, supporting the engineers – and then change the subject. "Do you think we might see a show while I'm here? I'd like that," I say.

"We could see many shows," Margaret says. "*My Lady Frayle*. Somebody saw that and said it was very good. Who was that?" Emily shakes her head. "What else?" Margaret goes on. "*Kultur at Home*. I've heard it's very cutting about Germans. The supposed barbaric centre of the German soul. There are all sorts of revues and such –"

"And cinemas," Emily says. "Charlie Chaplin. And film from the Front –"

"Perhaps Ramsay does not want to see that," Harriet says.

"No. No film from the Front," I say.

"We could probably just camp in the City and frolic the whole time you're here," Margaret says. I have a sense of her working hard to recover from her previous embarrassment.

"Yes. Perfect," I say.

We catch an omnibus on the King's Road, climb to the top and find seats right at the front of the vehicle, so sit like monarchs in a slow parade. My head spins at the passing shop signs: Lechie's Sausage & Onion, the Rampant Lion pub, Boots Chemists, Lampert's Stationery and Dried Flowers, and myriad fashion stores for women, with window displays of dresses and hats, blouses, boots. A poster for Binnacle cigarettes: a lovely young woman eyeing the officer with the right brand, not the civilian slacker with the wrong one. "KRUSCHEN SALTS, ENTIRELY BRITISH FOR 160 YEARS: VICTORY! IS A MATTER OF DAILY HABIT." Another poster for Fry's cocoa: "IN ITSELF A PERFECT FOOD." And one for Golden Dawn cigarettes, showing clean, cheerful, relaxed Tommies in cloth hats with Lee-Enfields pointed lazily over the side of a trench, their sergeant standing in complete exposure, shading his eyes from the brilliant sunshine. "TIME FOR ONE MORE." What a pleasant sort of war that must be.

The passing street scene seems to me a miracle of ordinary civilian life: the bustle of motor cars and horse carriages, of hand-pulled carts, and pedestrians with not a worry in the world. No steel helmets, no hunched, exhausted men furtively dashing from one bit of cover to the next, no sea of sour-faced, miserable troops wishing to be anywhere else.

This is what I'm fighting for, I think. This gloriously mundane, orderly progress of men and women, with nothing more to mar the May skies than the usual pall of coal smoke hugging the rooftops, the taste of progress in our noses.

An aeroplane twists and twirls spectacularly in the distance, somewhere over the river, apparently. The girls especially become excited at its antics, exclaim at its sudden lunges and steep climbs, the high-speed, sparrow-like turns, the long low swoop upside down.

Margaret says, "A friend of mine is a VAD – Miss Liddell, you remember her, Mother. She has an airman who buzzes the hospital cafeteria every day around noon to say hello to her. The administration has spoken to her rather sharply about it. He's shattering everybody's nerves flying so close, and the occasional window too."

Was it just this morning that I arrived? Very little of the road seems familiar from this height. I check the street signs: Old Church, Square, Carlyle, and see a trio of wounded soldiers. A man on one leg, with a single crutch, the stump of his other straining against his pinned-up trouser leg, walks with a swinging, precarious progress. An armless young man leans against a lamppost, smoking a cigarette. Another in khaki helplessly holds the shoulder of a white-haired fellow, thick bandages across the eyes of the soldier, a rickety cane in the hand of his guide.

"There's nothing more entertaining than seeing a man in a kilt," Margaret says to me, and I look at where she's gazing: on the other side of the street, a group of Highlanders walking sloppily along. "They don't know what to do in a wind, and it's piercingly funny when they try to sit down and don't know how to arrange themselves. But it must be no fun at all in a cold, muddy trench."

"They're terrible for chatts," I say without thinking, and so I have to explain to them about the many pleats and seams in the kilts where the lice thrive. "I'm sorry," I say. "It's not a fit subject for polite conversation."

"Don't worry about being overly polite for our sake," Margaret says, though Aunt Harriet's gaze says otherwise. Then Margaret asks if it feels strange to be in civilian dress. When I reply that it seems strangely normal, she says, "We'll protect you from the white-feather ladies. Poor Mr. Boulton – he's a friend of ours – has had a difficult time with some of them."

Emily gives me a knowing look at the mention of Margaret's young man.

"Who are the white-feather ladies?" I ask.

"Indeed, who are they?" Margaret asks. "One never knows. But everyone knows someone who's been pinned as a coward. They seem to specialize in choosing off-duty servicemen who don't happen to be in uniform at the moment. In fact, I heard of one man who won the Victoria Cross and then was slapped with a white feather the same afternoon because he'd changed attire. He claimed to be equally proud of both."

A slow progress on a sunny day, like a pleasure boat touring the islands back home. We dismount at Westminster Abbey and I look in awe at the grand old building, so familiar from photographs. Inside, the Abbey looks like something of an armed camp or a tomb expecting the worst. It's crawling with men in khaki – they are tourists gawking, milling about, off from training mostly, loose in this extraordinary relic – and with workmen plying the sandbags that are rising around some of the monuments. Pitt the Elder, Lord Palmerston, several Cannings, Disraeli, Gladstone: even beyond the grave they do not seem safe from fear of German bombs. I stop and gaze at the ceiling arches, impossibly narrow, high, ornate.

"Is all this really necessary?" Aunt Harriet asks as we pass by sweating men erecting a barricade. I imagine the weight of the sandbags in my back and shoulders, and feel like a shirker not lending a hand. Before hoisting the bags, the workmen brace themselves, a pause before stiffening that I know too well.

"You should see the ancient Cloth Hall in Ypres," I say. "It's in complete ruins."

"The Zeppelins could bomb whatever they want here in London," Emily says. I look again at the ceiling, imagine it suddenly ripped open to the sky, with a rain of gargoyles and angels, stone bits, splintered wood, shrapnel made of centuries of remembrance. We turn down a grand aisle.

"So who were these famous people?" I ask, and then read one of the names memorialized: Jonas Hanway, 1786.

"I hardly know any of them," Margaret replies. "But Hanway introduced the umbrella to England, did he not?"

"He was a traveller," Aunt Harriet says. "He wrote about Persia, I believe."

Sir Isaac Newton I recognize on the ornate woodwork on the left, and Darwin and Kelvin, but who were Stephenson and Trevethick? We wander farther into politicians, apparently – Lord Holland, Sir J. Mackintosh, Earl Russell – and then by a door stand under a bronze bust of General Gordon, who put down the Taiping rebellion and died defending Khartoum. I think of my teacher Miss Smithson with her bark-scraping voice ringing out in music class: "We hold a vaster Empire than has been, / Nigh half the race of man is subject to our King. . . ."

I find myself plunging on, past statues or busts of Wordsworth, Kingsley, the Arnolds, and countless others I do not recognize. There is too much to comprehend, treasures everywhere, markers, carvings, paintings, inscriptions to the famous and the now unknown.

"At least they haven't touched the rose window," Margaret says. I turn to see where she's looking, a circular sunburst high above us. I can't seem to appreciate anything, but imagine the window exploding into a hail of rock and coloured glass. "That's Jesus in the centre," Margaret says. "And he's surrounded by . . ." She turns to her mother and Emily, who have just caught us up. "Who is he surrounded by?" Then to me: "We did have a wonderful tour once. But that was years ago. Before the war."

"Angels, I think," Aunt Harriet says. "Angels and others. I wonder why they haven't boarded it up?"

I look at it for a time, try to imagine the architects, artists, craftsmen, labourers whose hands, minds, backs, sweat, lives went into this vision. And I can't help it, I think of wretched Johnson and the lot of us hauling barbed wire and pig's tails up the line, of our hands bleeding raw from digging trenches, of the sheer medieval effort of it all.

We continue among the crowd, pass into the gloom and shadows of Poet's Corner, where Chaucer, Shakespeare, Tennyson, and the others are being outfitted with proper military protection. It seems ludicrous, in a way, this effort to protect the dead. I think of my Frenchman, imagine his grisly parts filling some of the bags now going to shield these shrines to old famous Englishmen. It could be my flesh, too, filling these bags, and there will be no monument to me, either.

On the floor I see the names of Abraham Cowley, Sir Robert Moray, Charles de Saint Denis. I have no idea who they were. And who was Sir William D'Avenant? And who is that looking down so glumly? Michael Drayton, it says. I gaze at someone else, Handel – not a poet at all, but certainly famous – looking over his shoulder as his sheet music gets out of hand. Even Shakespeare is disappearing behind sandbags.

Soldiers, sailors, gawkers, girl friends, mothers, tourists among the dead. There are too many ghosts here. I feel as if we are miles underground, trespassing in what should be the tranquil rest of these passed souls. My escorts pause and murmur among the crowds, lean in to read the carvings, consider small details of the artwork, the ceiling, the floor. I find myself plunging on.

Around a corner and then to a roped-off section with a sign indicating that tours for the Ambulatory and the Chapels are sixpence per person, except on Mondays and Tuesdays, which are free of charge. But I can't wait, feel vaguely trapped. So I head in a different direction, and soon find myself looking at more tombs being sandbagged.

"There you are!" Margaret says, approaching from behind. "You are a fast walker. I suppose all soldiers –" And she stops. "Are you well?" she says.

"Yes. Yes, I'm fine," I say, although a great deal of the air has gone out of the place, vaulted ceilings and all.

"You're sweating."

"It is very hot. It's nothing." I make a show of examining the tombs.

"These ones I know," Margaret says. "This, I believe, is Edmund Crouchback. He was the second son of Henry III. And Aveline over there" – she points to the smaller mass of boards and sandbags – "she was the money behind the House of Lancaster. The third tomb is Aymer de Valence, their cousin, the son of William de Valence, who's somewhere else in the Abbey. He was the Earl of –" She falters, says, "Oh, I should know this," and tightens her jaw in consternation. "Pembroke, I believe," she says finally. She looks at me in some surprise then and asks if I need to go outside. And damn if my legs don't suddenly buckle underneath me. Margaret is surprisingly quick, catches me as if she knew what was coming. It's just a moment of light-headedness, and then I'm all right. But she insists on holding me up for a step or two.

"Oh. Poor thing!" she says. But besides her disarming tenderness there is strength in her grip and something else, a sudden pulse heating my blood. I step back and look at her, unguarded, and just for a moment she returns the same naked, unbalanced gaze.

"I think you should get some air," she says finally, her voice very gentle and reassuring.

"Yes. Yes," I allow.

Now the dizziness is gone completely. My head feels clear again, as fresh and alert as it has been in months. But I let her lead me out of this tomb of tombs. At the door of the Abbey where we came in is a line of perhaps twenty poor gas victims in uniform, bandages over their eyes, arms reaching forward onto the shoulders of the next bugger ahead, the lot of them being led by a prim woman in blue with a tiny cap and the voice of a sergeant major.

"It's too much death," I say when we're outside, and I make a show of breathing deeply.

"Yes. I suppose you've seen altogether too much," she says, her eyes shifting, as if in conscious effort to remember what I've just said.

Stupidly I blurt out, "You have a young man, is that right?"

She flushes.

"Henry, yes. Henry Boulton. I suppose Emily has told you."

"She mentioned him," I say, and I pause, staring at my knuckles, wondering what in God's name made me say what I did.

"She's never been known for her discretion," Margaret says with a hint of anger. Then: "He's a friend. A dear friend. Perhaps you'll meet him during your stay."

"Yes. I'd like that," I say. And nothing else occurs to me to say, except that he couldn't possibly deserve her, that she'd be wasting her time with him. It's an irrational thought, and thankfully I'm able to hold my tongue. But undeniably I find myself drawn to her, to whatever she has – beauty and spirit, her quiet intelligence and grace.

"And you?" she says suddenly. "There must be some lovely girl back in Canada pining for you."

"No. Nobody. My mother." And then, absurdly, I say, "I don't go fainting on the battlefield. I'm afraid I've made a poor impression."

"No. Of course not."

"It's an odd thing, this . . . return to civilian life for a few days. It's very disorienting."

"I'm sure it must be."

"And I didn't eat at all yesterday. I was travelling from dawn, practically, when I came out of the trenches. And then on the train there was hardly anything to be had. They shipped us down in cattle cars."

"I think it's wonderful for a man to be vulnerable," she says. "Somewhat, at any rate."

"I've been through stretches of thirty-six hours sometimes without stopping for anything except the odd cigarette," I say. At the thought I reach for my pockets, pull out my ragged packet and light one quickly, draw the breath deep inside.

"My Henry – Henry Boulton," Margaret says, "doesn't have a heroic bone in him." She makes it sound like the rarest quality. "I'm afraid with the Military Service Act he's going to be compelled into khaki. You'll see when you meet him, it mustn't be allowed to happen. He'd last as long as a little reed in a flood. It would be a complete waste of his talents, his mind, his sensibilities."

I find myself almost instantly fed up with this Henry Boulton and his talents, mind, and sensibilities. I look around, hoping that Aunt Harriet and Emily might emerge from the door to spare me. "I joined up as a sign-painter," I say. Because I have my own talents and sensibilities, I fail to add. "And now I'm working like a slave."

"But you *can* do it. You have that iron in you," she says. "Anybody can see it. But Henry –"

Spare me Henry and his lack of spine, I think.

"At any rate," Margaret says, "it will be an awful thing if this war swallows up *all* the young men, all of you. What sort of life are we going to have afterwards, even in victory?"

"It is far from having swallowed all of us," I say. "It's amazing what we survive. Germans and us alike. The worst bombardments can go on for hours, for days, and then afterwards men crawl out of the earth like worms and rats, still very much alive."

"But when will it end?" she says. "When the last poor Henry, or Ramsay, has been buried in his trench?"

"It will end when the Germans have been taught a bloody lesson," I say. "Force is the only thing that penetrates their square, military skulls. It will end when they finally understand that the world will not sit idly by while they rape and pillage and swagger all over the rest of Europe."

"Yes. I suppose," she says in a small, retreating voice. She looks at me as if biting her tongue.

"Tell me you aren't for a negotiated peace," I say. "You couldn't be."

"Why not? There must somehow be a peaceful way to resolve things, even now. Especially now."

"I don't see it," I say. "Too many men have already been bombed into the soil! We can't let the Germans think they can get away with any of it! Look, *Westminster Abbey* is huddling here in sandbags. These people only understand one thing." Then, when I see her look away, I say, "You haven't seen what I've seen."

"No. No, I suppose not," she says carefully. Angrily, it seems to me, with a stubborn note in her voice. And she too looks to see if Harriet and Emily are joining us.

There they are, finally, not a moment too soon. I glance from them to Margaret – to strangely beautiful, wrong-headed Margaret – and find myself yearning, oddly, for the rough, simple, uncomplicated company of men.

We saunter a slow progress up Whitehall and Aunt Harriet points out the Foreign Office and the Ministry of Munitions. Many of the buildings here have frames and nets strung on top of them, a hopeless precaution against Zeppelin bombs, it seems to me, like the netting at Hell Fire Corner and elsewhere, which is supposed to reduce the accuracy of the enemy's fire but instead seems to draw constant attention. With too many others we stand and watch the red-coated horse guard in the silver-plumed helmet sit so quietly by the gate on his towering black horse. Besides the soldiers on leave, there are hordes of young women – difficult to keep my head from swivelling to follow them all in their bright spring dresses and hats. The swirl of traffic. At Trafalgar Square I crane my neck to see Nelson on top of his pedestal. "He's forever looking out at the enemy," Emily says. "The French, of course."

Margaret stays determinedly quiet, her eyes either down or looking away from me.

Soldiers and sailors pose for pictures by the huge, dark lions, with young women hanging all over them, and pigeons erupting in flight around the fountain.

"Here it is," Aunt Harriet says after a time, beaming at me now, "the centre of the Empire. Whenever I come here I think of all the people as tiny blood vessels pouring through the heart of the nation."

"You should write a poem about it, Mother," Margaret says dryly.

"Don't be cynical, dear," Harriet says. Then, to me: "How do you feel, Ramsay? After fighting for the Empire in far-off lands, here you are in the heart of the capital."

I have to think for a moment. Nelson is so high it is hard to see him against the sun. "It was a long, bitter struggle against Napoleon," I say finally. "I can see why the builders would have wanted to erect something that would last forever."

"And here we are in it again," Harriet says. "Only this time it's to defeat all war, to make certain that barbaric aggression can never win."

"Perhaps," I say, gazing around this clean, grand, famous spot. I look back down the road from which we came, see for a moment instead the Menin Road – the corpse-filled mud, the shell-holes brimmed with poisoned water, the ambulances forever stuck to the axles, horses bleeding, men trudging black-eyed, and stretchers lined back into the gloom, a never-ending parade. This road and that, worlds apart, but only a day's journey.

I am thumped on the back and turn to see a fellow from my hometown, now decked out in khaki with a trim moustache. A lieutenant at that.

"Ram!" he says. "What, were you wounded?" And then his roving eye meets Emily and Margaret, and Aunt Harriet, and I stammer to make the introductions. I can't for the life of me remember his name, though we went to school together for years, played rough and tumble through the back alleys of Victoria, his brothers and mine. But it's so strange to see him here.

"Bill Kelsie," he says finally. "Old Ram here must have been hit on the head. Or maybe it's too much dazzling female company. Did they run you out of the army?"

I explain about my uniform, that I'm on leave from the Front.

"No kidding," he says. "I've been on training forever, haven't been over yet. We're just busting to get at them."

"There's no hurry," I say.

"Are you kidding? It's all going to be over in a couple of months, after the big push."

"The big push?" I say, and Kelsie makes a sudden, secretive motion, his finger in front of his lips, then an exaggerated nod to the women. "Don't want it getting out to the Kaiser!" he says. "Not that I think that women can't be trusted." And he winks blatantly at Emily. "What are you folks up to anyway, this fine afternoon?" he says.

"Wandering aimlessly," Emily says, beaming at him. "We've been to see the Abbey, and were thinking that perhaps a show –"

"But Ramsay has not been feeling too well," Margaret cuts in. "It's his first day out of battle, really, and perhaps we should –"

"What's it like?" Bill Kelsie cuts in, staring at me starry-eyed. "You've been in the front lines? Stared across at the enemy?"

"It's much better here," I say. And then, quickly, "I'm fine. Thank you, Cousin Margaret, for your concern." And she takes the formality of my tone as a rebuke, though I didn't mean it that way. I don't think I did, at any rate.

"I'm crashing in on your party," Kelsie says. "Excuse me. I really don't mean to intrude. But it's lovely to meet you," he says to the ladies – to Emily – and then to me, "If you get a chance, we tend towards a pub called the Prospect of Whitby. It's in the East End, on the Thames. Any taxi driver could get you there."

"Yes. All right," I say. He isn't a handsome man, I think. But he could always talk. And there was a spit and polish about him even before the world went mad. "Though why you'd want to leave such dazzling company, I've no idea," he says, before heading off.

We have tea in some little place made for women – chairs quite dainty, tables squished in too close together, the biscuits, scones, jams, and cakes all fussy, delicate, ornamental in a way. I think of bully beef and baked beans, of sweat-soaked, grimy men forking down such brown sludge, of the grim satisfaction of a belly full of plain food. I think of hunger honestly won, of desperate effort, strained nerves, last meals for uncomplicated men who can joke about sharing their tins with rats, lice, and flies. And while I chew Margaret looks over at me archly.

"You haven't said a word in ages, Ramsay," she says. "Surely there must be etiquette courses and such for soldiers." She has a touch of marmalade on the corner of her mouth, removes it gently with the point of her tongue. And the line of her cheek and nose, the brim of her hat, the turn of her lips, that stray wisp of hair all become part of a sketch in my brain, something my fingers yearn to trace out.

"I'm sorry," I say, and take a sip of tea, my hand too big for the little cup. "The food is excellent."

"Your friend the lieutenant is very nice," Emily says. "Do you know him well?"

"I broke his brother's nose with a baseball bat," I say, and then smile – it is funny to see their reactions. "It was an accident. I overswung, went right round, and somehow his nose was there.

Blood everywhere." And then, when I realize what I'm saying: "I'm sorry. I'm not fit for proper company. Bill Kelsie used to cry a lot when his brothers beat him up, and he hated fishing for some reason. But it has been a few years since those days."

"And do you love fishing?" Margaret says. Again, I have another chance to look full at her.

"I used to live for it when I was a boy," I say. "Some years ago my brothers and I went on a sailing trip up the coast of Vancouver Island. We ended up in the Chemainus River, and I've never seen anything like it for steelhead, coho salmon, rainbow trout. And there were seals, sea lions, eagles, osprey, otters, hawks. It's God's country, stunningly beautiful. The water, the islands are constantly changing with the light, the tides, the turn of the days. We capsized on some white water at one point, I thought we were going to lose Rufus – my younger brother. He nearly killed himself going after his hat."

"So all your brothers are adventurers?" Margaret says.

"Father set it up," I say. "He got the sailboat, the supplies, the maps. He talked up the idea and told us where to go. I suppose he wanted Mother all to himself for a week. He didn't have to ask us twice, but Mother was uncertain. It took a lot of selling. He thought it would be good for us, and it was, though if we had lost Rufus we probably wouldn't have bothered coming home. Father would have skinned us, then turned us over to Mother for the roasting." I remember her on the shore as we pulled off, too angry to speak, to complain, to wave us off. "Father always hated the thought of us being mothered to death," I say. "But of course he went off fairly frequently and left us in our mother's care. So when he was home he'd think up these schemes to make men of us, counteract whatever pernicious effects might have set in."

"Every boy needs a mother's care," Aunt Harriet says. "But I'm so glad I had daughters." The three women exchange a look of some understanding.

"We were a pretty wild bunch," I say, feeling more comfortable now at this polite conversation, this tea and cake with refined ladies in the capital of the Empire. "I'm sure Mother has lost years of her life worrying about what's to become of us. In some ways Alex is the worst. Thomas and Will had taken off to do ranch work in the interior and Father had deposited me in Montreal, and there was Alex left alone with Mother and Rufus. So the morning after his graduation from grade ten, when he was sixteen, he slipped out his bedroom window, went down to the docks, and signed on with a salmon-fishing boat. Not a word to anyone. A couple of days later he stopped in at Vancouver and sent Mother a telegram: *Don't worry. Gone fishing for the summer. Gainfully employed.* He wrote to Mother a few times, heard nothing, got the odd letter from Father. It seems he hardened himself with the tough work. Then at the end of the summer he returned to the Brown House – that's what we call it, the Brown House – and found a different family living there! By sheer chance Will was back in town and had a letter from Mother for Alex. She'd gone down to Los Angeles with Rufus to live with her sisters while everyone was away. She'd left fare for Alex to join her, but, instead of that, he took the money and what he'd saved from the summer and bought a cross-continental ticket to Montreal. A week later, at midnight, rain slashing down, I heard a knocking on my door, and there was my younger brother, soaked, penniless, asking me if I could pay off the cab driver who'd brought him from the station, and could I put him up for a few days, and by the way, did I know of anywhere he could get a job?"

I laugh at the remembrance Alex's jug ears, his hair plastered to his forehead, that beaming look on his face, misplaced adolescent pride of achievement, but the ladies look at me in a sort of horror.

"Does *everyone* in your family run off like that?" Margaret says.

"Your mother is extraordinary to put up with it all," Aunt Harriet mutters. Then, to Margaret: "Would you like to run off, dear?"

"I would never leave the bosom of my family," Margaret says, fluttering her eyelashes. "Although now and again the wilds of Canada do seem like a romantic alternative." She turns to me: "Are all Canadian men as rough-hewn and as refined as you, Ramsay?"

For a moment I find it hard to respond, can't decide whether she's making fun of me. And before I can, the conversation is off in another direction – the colours of the season, some important flower show coming up, and whether women are wearing brighter colours now or not (some are, mostly from the working classes, because they have money and they want fine clothes, whereas those used to money are wearing shabbier things, to be patriotic). And on and on, this unpredictable, caroming play of frivolous discussion that I feel barely able to follow, much less contribute to. Margaret is driving it, but assisted ably by her mother and sister. These three nimble female minds, with lips as quick as their wits, and Margaret's eyes returning to mine, like sunlight playing through a crystal. Dazzling, deceptive, too sprightly to catch or hold. But she wants me watching. She wants me to notice.

I signal for the waiter and scrutinize the bill, finally realize through the scrawl that they're asking for eight shillings, eleven pence. It's no problem, I have nearly fifteen pounds that I converted in Folkestone.

"You shouldn't have to pay," Aunt Harriet says irritatedly. "How much is it? I'll have Manfred reimburse you when we get home."

"Not at all," I say gallantly. I fold my offering into the bill and hand it to the waiter as discreetly as I can manage. "Where are we off to next?" I venture, with a forced sort of cheerfulness.

"You look exhausted, poor boy!" Harriet says. "I think we should take you home in a smart cab and tuck you into bed with some warm milk." Margaret and Emily laugh and I gather my defences.

"I am on leave," I say grandly. "And this is London, and I am not going to bed early on my first day here. I want to see *everything*. Who knows when I'll get this chance again? If ever!" The *if ever* comes out too heavily and I regret it at once, though Margaret slides us past it.

"We talked about the theatre," she says quickly.

"By all means!"

"But we need to have Manfred here," Harriet says. "I don't want my young nephew paying for expensive theatre tickets for us all. But is there time to go back and get him?"

"We could telephone," Emily says, "and he could come meet us."

"Of course!" Harriet says.

Margaret uses the restaurant telephone, and returns several minutes later, once the call has been successful. "Father will secure the tickets and we are to meet him at the Criterion at a quarter past eight," she says. "I hope no one minds. Father really has a hankering to see *A Little Bit of Fluff*. It's outrageously funny, apparently, and there's a very pretty girl in it. You won't mind, Cousin Ramsay?"

"He won't mind," Emily answers for me.

"In the meantime," Margaret says, before I can open my mouth, "Father suggested that we take in the Raemaekers exhibit. It's on New Bond Street. I have the address. If we hurry we might just be able to make it."

"I was hoping we could stroll along the Embankment Gardens," Aunt Harriet says. "The flowers are so lovely this time of year. And our Ramsay doesn't want to see more about the war, surely?"

"Perhaps you've had too much walking already," I say, trying to sound gentlemanly. But, as well, my new boots have started to become uncomfortable again. "Or would that be the lesser of the two jaunts? How far is it to New Bond Street?"

"We'd take a cab," Margaret says.

"I don't think our Ramsay would be very comfortable among flowers," Emily says. "Although he is an artist. He likes faces and people. Perhaps Raemaekers would be best."

"*Are you?*" Margaret asks, and I look at her, tongue-tied, until she says, "An artist?"

"I can sketch things," I say vaguely.

"He's being very modest," Emily says. "He was telling me earlier about the magnificent portraits that he does."

"There is an artistic strain in the family," Harriet says. "Manfred got none of it, but his mother was very good with a brush. And of course Emily is at it constantly. Did you see Emily's paintings at home, Ramsay?"

"He doesn't like them very much," Emily says with a cutting sort of cheerfulness, and I feel myself unbalanced with embarrassment. "He's very discriminating. Although he did tell me he knew nothing about it as well. Landscapes, I mean."

"Forgive me. Forgive me!" I say, throwing my hands up in mock despair, which causes patrons at other tables to look at us. I stand quickly. "Shall we go to Raemaekers?" I say, but more as a command than a question. What these women need, I realize, is some leadership. And even as I begin to leave I wonder if they will follow.

I turn back, of course, too late to help Aunt Harriet out of her chair, and catch Margaret laughing at me as one would a puppy too easy to fool with a feint of the hand and a distracting look in the eye.

◈

At the gallery we step into a darkened, gloomy space, with only a few people left so near to closing time. It is the end of a beautiful afternoon, and I should have listened to Aunt Harriet and strolled through the gardens. But instead I am standing here looking at Mother Britannia with trident, in white Roman robes, kissing the head of a crazed-looking young soldier with raised rifle. "My son, go and fight for your motherland!" she says.

He looks like cannon fodder if anybody ever did.

"*Gott Mit Uns*," reads the necklace hanging from the German devil in another picture, drooling beside the nailed feet of Christ. And there are the Widows of Belgium, kneeling in black in a church, while in the sketch beside them an enormous skeleton is harvesting men with a scythe as if cutting wheat.

Daffodils would be fine. The smell of green grass. To watch the barges on the river, cast an eye over colourful dresses and hats.

A gloomy young man in a *pickelhaube* crouches in a trench, the walls too beautifully straight and clean, even for the Germans. Bombs are bursting overhead, the trench is crowded with huddled soldiers, a single body lies on the parados. "We have gained a good bit," Fritz writes in his letter. "Our cemeteries now extend as far as the sea."

"He doesn't pull his punches," Margaret whispers to me. It's that kind of gallery, the whispering kind, everyone tiptoeing around as if in church. I read a large board that explains that Louis Raemaekers has come to England from Holland, where his cartoons angered the Germans to the point of threatening the Dutch neutrality. But here is a picture called "Muddle Through": Mother England being accosted by the brutish Hun, while three young men in fashionable civilian garb hurry off to some pressing appointment. And here is "London Inside the Savoy," with handsome men in black tie waltzing with beautiful women, while "London Outside the Savoy" is a sidewalk pressed with saluting khaki, the only exceptions being an elderly man, a woman, and a newspaper boy.

"He really has captured the enormity of it all," Aunt Harriet says to me. She is standing in front of a drawing called "Europe, 1916." It's a beautiful woman, again in torn Roman garb, one breast bared, tied to a gun wheel with arms outstretched. The caption reads, "Am I not yet sufficiently civilized?"

"That's a British punishment," I say carelessly.

"No, clearly it's the Germans," Aunt Harriet says. "They're the ones trying to 'civilize' Europe with their marauding *Kultur*, their 'might makes right' philosophies of the superman and such."

"But the punishment in the picture," I say, "that's the British Field Punishment Number One, being tied up in the crucifixion position for hours. It doesn't have to be a gun wheel, it could be anything fixed. A post or a tree. I haven't heard of the Germans doing that to their men."

"I'm sure they just shoot them," Harriet says. "The ones who don't follow orders like drones."

We move on. In "Easter, 1915" the Germans and the Turks are mocking a bound Christ, trying to place a German helmet on his bowed head. In "Thrown to the Swine" the body of the martyred nurse Edith Cavell is being devoured by enormous, monocled German pigs. In the next cartoon a battleship of a peace woman proclaims that she and the other mothers will march in white before their sons, but the unimpressed soldier replies that he'd rather have armoured plating, thank you.

And there are "The Prisoners," three sad buggers sitting on crates with their backs against a shack wall, barbed wire hemming them in.

"The press keeps reporting that the Germans barely feed their prisoners," Harriet says. "It wouldn't surprise me, somehow. Our German prisoners are positively coddled. It's a shocking thing. And the Germans are forcing ours to engage in vital war work. The men, I mean. Not the officers, of course."

"No. Of course not," I say.

"We have been sending parcels off to the Red Cross," she says, "this group of Lady Templeton's. Chocolate and fruitcakes and tea and coffee. It seems so little, compared to what you men have had to shoulder. Your parents must be very proud of you."

"My mother is furious," I say.

"Well, I suppose she doesn't have roots in the conflict, coming from South America. And now three of her sons are in danger. But your father must be proud. I'm sure he was champing at the bit to get into the heat of it himself!"

I look at her. Clearly she doesn't know my father at all well.

"He didn't say much," I tell her.

Margaret and Emily approach and the three of us look at the unhappy prisoners. "Ramsay has been telling me that his father is against the war," Harriet says to her daughters.

"Not completely," I say, trying to defend him. "But he was very silent about it. Will was the first to join, and they had words, but in private, over a five-mile hike one afternoon. Then Thomas joined and little was said. When I signed up he said, 'I expected as much,' and that was about it. Now I've heard Alex is aching to join but Father forbids it, and Rufus of course is too young."

"Well, those Crome boys can be exceedingly silent. You wouldn't know it from Manfred, of course," Harriet says. "But I'll wager your father is quietly proud of the way you three have stepped forward."

About a minute later, as I am reading the small print on a drawing entitled, "Mon fils, Belgium 1914," a woman in black steps forward and smacks me with a small bag filled with white flour. "Shirker!" she hisses.

"Oh, bugger me!" I say, then look at Margaret, whose face fills with shock, then hilarity.

"Why aren't you at the Front doing your duty?" the woman snaps. She is in her mid-fifties perhaps, her face sagging, her arms thin as sticks. Part of the flour has stuck to the hem of her dress, but most of it is on my shoulder and trousers.

"Because he's home on leave, you silly woman!" Margaret says, stepping up between us and shouting the woman down, as if I can't defend myself.

"Well, he should be proud enough to wear the King's uniform," the woman snarls, and marches off self-righteously.

"If I were a man and thought I was defending the likes of you," Margaret jeers after her, "I'd want to bury my uniform as well, you old pudding-brain!"

"Margaret, that's enough!" Harriet says, just as the woman clangs the door shut. Harriet and Emily brush away at my clothes – at Uncle Manfred's clothes – while Margaret huffs at the door in continued concentration, as if the dragon lady might be back.

The small knot of others still left in the gallery look on in startled amusement.

"A simple white feather would have sufficed," I say, trying to laugh it off.

"'Pudding-brain,'" Emily says. "That's very good."

"Well, at least I said *something*," Margaret says.

They are still fussing at my clothes, trying to get me cleaned up, when I glance at "The Shirkers," two men lounging on a riverbank with fishing poles and happy-go-lucky expressions, while on the road behind them a blur of soldiers marches past.

What would I give to carelessly go fishing again? It looks like heaven, where those shirkers have feathered their bed. Except for the tramp of feet behind them. *Goddamn the noise!* I can hear them saying.

◈

They have done their best with hankies and such, but the residue of flour is still quite noticeable on my clothes. Harriet suggests that we go home but I insist we carry on to the theatre as planned. "I don't mind a few odd stares," I say. "Unless you ladies are ashamed to be seen with me."

"Margaret will bite the head off anyone who comments," Emily says. "She of the barbed tongue."

"Anyway, Uncle Manfred will be waiting for us with the tickets," I say.

I buy us a cab ride to the Criterion. It is not far but the traffic is a slow procession of poorly mixing motor cars, cabs, omnibuses and horse carriages. And the driver is having a bit of trouble with his gears, lurches us forward only to brake again, lurch and brake, barely quicker than a walking pace, even with women in the group.

"There has been no planning," Harriet says. "London is a complete mess. One system is larded over another and nothing works well at all. Sometimes I think the whole place should be levelled and they should start again at scratch. The way some of the North American cities are laid out. A beautiful grid. Wouldn't that be lovely?"

"We'd keep St. Paul's," Margaret says.

"And the Abbey," says Emily, immediately, and then the three of them start chiming in one after the other: "And London Bridge . . . and the Tower . . . And the Monument . . . and Piccadilly . . . and St. Margaret's . . . and Buckingham Palace . . . and Lambeth . . . and Hyde Park." This spontaneous, female singsong, like birds clattering in a tree. Margaret says, "With the

Serpentine full of water, not drained like it is now." When I look at her she explains, "Zeppelin targets! They want to disguise the city for the protection of all."

Manfred is waiting for us at the theatre door. "What happened to you, man?" he says as I usher his women out of the cab. "Some Canadian snowstorm find you out in the wilds of London?"

"It was a mad woman with a bag of flour," Emily says. "But Margaret scorched her righteously. Good thing it wasn't Henry Boulton standing there in civilian dress. Margaret would have digested the woman whole."

Margaret gives her sister a dark look.

"A white-feather lady?" Manfred says dubiously. "I thought they were a myth."

"It was a white-*flour* lady," Margaret says. "And I do believe she thinks she's winning the war for us."

Manfred tells us, in his breathless way, that he was unable to get a stall, so we'll have to put up with the dress circle, if that's all right. Margaret whispers in my ear, "He has *never* been able to get us a stall. He just wants you to think that he's rich." She holds my arm, briefly, and there it is again, a pulse of warmth and good feeling. I lower my head in some confusion, follow the others through the doors and into a tiny lobby. It is a strange theatre, stairs leading us *down* rather than up. It takes me a moment to realize that the whole thing is underground. The tiles too along the walls are dazzling and unusual, weird figures and theatrical masks in bright squares. There is a gleam and opulence that makes me feel shabby, especially in my soiled outfit, not even evening dress. How I long for my uniform, to blend in with the other soldiers crowding the place. For a time

I'm acutely aware of the white stain on my clothes, but in fact hardly anyone notices.

"I think Father chose this theatre because it's the safest place during an air raid," Margaret says to me. "One certainly doesn't have the feeling of being underground, though."

We find our seats. I gaze, somewhat slack-jawed, at the circular ceiling, the ornate plasterwork, the crystal chandelier in the centre. I am seated between Margaret and Emily, with a thin pillar partially blocking my view. I could lean towards either, I suppose, but am naturally drawn to Margaret's side to look down on the stage. The smoke in the room has already begun to accumulate, and I long to light up, but restrain myself for the women's sake.

A day and a half ago I was trudging in mud and filth, yet here I am surrounded by young women, by beauty and splendour and sophistication, in a comfortable seat, waiting to be entertained.

Manfred leans across Aunt Harriet and Emily to speak to me. "I heard the actress who plays the bit of fluff, the floozy, is a real knockout. Thought you might appreciate a feast for the eyes, Ramsay."

"And what are we, the dog's breakfast?" Margaret says sharply.

"What's that?" Manfred says, and Harriet elbows him back into his seat.

I take a moment to appreciate the buzz of hundreds of conversations, the latecomers hurrying for their spots, the ushers in their quiet efficiency, the rustle of clothing, whispers to the ladies still wearing their hats, the muffled laughter, settling in.

A gentleman leads his party straight across to where we're sitting, looks at his tickets in bafflement, apologizes, then withdraws, only to return in a minute with an angry-looking old usher. "Excuse me, sir, may I have a look at your tickets?" he says to me. Even as I stammer out something Margaret is referring him to Uncle Manfred, who sputters and exclaims before producing the stubs. We are in the wrong seats, and must retreat back up the cramped semicircular row, then up two more rows and along, bothering everyone in the process.

"You could have *looked at* the tickets," Harriet says in a low, angry voice.

"But, my dear, I *did* look at them. It was an honest mistake. Anyone could have –"

"But you *did*, and you do more often than anyone I know!"

The lights begin to go down before we are in our seats. "Bloody hell!" some soldier says to me. "Stay off my toecaps!" I glance down at his pimpled adolescent face. A private who looks all of fifteen. With a quick thrust of the palm I could flatten his nose. I almost do it. I am that angry all of a sudden.

"What is it, Chalmers? Oh!" says someone down on the stage, and then I'm in my seat with Margaret on my right this time, and the pimple-face beside me. I can see us at each other's throats in a minute, wrestling, flailing, punching. I imagine female screams, bodies flying off the balcony onto the crowd below.

"Telegram, madam."

"Thank you."

I turn my attention to the stage. There is the brightness of a drawing room, and a beautiful woman in fine clothes opening an envelope, a butler standing in attendance with a silver tray in his hand.

"Bloody civilians," the soldier says, almost spitting the words right at me. The girl he is with says, "Richard!" in a whisper so loud half the section turns its head towards us.

More telegrams are arriving. Without even getting up I could stamp on his other toecap, I am thinking. He'd turn to me and I'd knock him through till next week.

Slowly I settle into watching the play. At least there's no pillar to contend with in the new seat. The beautiful, aristocratic woman in the fine clothes is Pamela. Her slick-haired husband, John, slouches in wearing evening dress and Pamela hides behind the curtains. John makes a strange face in the mirror, and holds a vase to his forehead, which gets a laugh. When he leaves, Pamela goes through his coat and finds a pearl necklace in his pocket. Then John comes back, half-changed into his morning outfit, and the two commence a tense, nervous exchange. Pamela has come home early from visiting her mother in Folkestone. "Did you sleep at a – at your mother's last night?" John asks.

"Where did *you* sleep?" she asks him.

When he claims to have slept at home, she says, "I slept at home, too. Strange we didn't meet."

Then John twists on the rope while trying to explain that in fact he *wanted* to sleep at home but had misplaced his latchkey, so stayed with his friend Tully next door, after they had both come back from the opera.

She asks him to name the opera and he squirms delightfully. I can see the red on his scalp from all the way up here. He mutters something about a girl and a sewing machine – no, no, a spinning wheel, two long plaits, Marguerite . . . Finally he blurts, "*Faust!*" and we explode in laughter.

Pamela stays angry but cool. She is beautiful and rich, and supports him, we find out. He doesn't even work in the City any longer, since it costs her more to maintain his office than he actually earns in profits.

And then more telegrams arrive. There are six in all, from various of John's friends, in response to a query sent out by Pamela. Each claims John spent the night with him. "I can explain everything," John whines, to which Pamela replies, "I believe you could explain the Tower of London away, but you can't have slept in six different beds in one night, unless you were a sleepwalker."

Another explosion of laughter. John is like one of those dancing figures in "London Inside the Savoy," magically protected from the resolute grimness outside. His worst worry is getting his hapless friend Tully to corroborate his story. And here he is, long-faced Tully, with drooping moustache, stumbling in his explanation to Pamela, while John dances a mad charade behind her back to try to get Tully to say the right things. And the laughter is choking my breath, the action seems so ridiculous, so bright and madcap.

And Manfred was right about the girl, too – Fluffie, a dazzling blonde in a diaphanous, feathery gown, with blood-red lips and an outrageous hat. She is so feminine Tully breaks out in a nervous sweat. The necklace is hers, or rather is borrowed from the Rajah of Changpoor, and is worth five hundred pounds, and so John must get it back from Pamela, to whom he's given it as a gift to avoid disaster. But he decides instead to buy another one, using five hundred pounds he will raise by claiming a back injury in a motor-bus accident. It goes from one frantic episode to another, with Fluffie pretending to be Pamela, and Tully pretending to be John, and then John pretending to be

Tully, until even Pamela is trying to deceive the bus company, and Tully is in a dress, and his enormous Aunt Hannah is pulled to her undergarments by John, who thinks she's Tully, and the Rajah of Changpoor is demanding his necklace, and the only way out is to have everything forgiven, because it is a gay world, with Tully and Fluffie kissing as the curtain descends.

Even the idiot beside me has forgotten about his toecaps by the end. We stand and applaud. We cheer and holler until Fluffie and Tully come out and kiss again, and bow and wave, and John and Pamela, and the others, the beautiful, charmed people who are funny and talented and live by their wits, by art and luck. Then the curtain descends again but we won't let them go. Some of the soldiers now below us are climbing onto the stage. Drunk – anybody can see it – three of them are weaving and lurching, and when Fluffie comes out again they grab for her.

Tully steps in front of her – he doesn't look such a limp rag any more – and grips an arm. In a second they're wrestling. Fluffie screams, John and the motor-bus-company inspector pull her back behind the curtain, but drunken others follow. We stand staring in disbelief – only I *can* believe it, all too well. I can imagine a battalion of soldiers tearing this place apart in muddled rioting. I look to the jerk beside me, half expect him to take a swipe at my jaw just for the hell of it. He's looking as if he expects the same from me. Then there are whistles, and a swarm of red hats – the military police – takes over the stage.

In short order the fighting is contained, the drunkest are led away. We are filing out now, a crowd again, not a mob. The din of conversation is deafening.

"Oh, Margaret's got something more to write about!" Emily says behind us.

"Dear sister," Margaret says, clenching her jaw and turning around. For a brief moment the two lock eyes, and then we are swept in the current of people up the gleaming stairs, out of the smoky gloom and back up to the Strand, where a number of theatres are emptying at the same time. It's a dark rush of taxis and motor buses, the streets unlit, though several searchlights scan the clouds for signs of the invader.

We eat at a small restaurant some blocks away, a quick meal of thin soup, light meats, and a strange pudding of mashed potatoes, oatmeal, turnips, and what looks like the ends of any spare food the cook might have had hanging around the pantry. Talk of the play swirls around me. Emily, especially, is a whiz at remembering favourite lines, and every so often I am conscious of her exclaiming, "We never count John as anybody," or, "They say I have a bigger bump of tact than Lloyd George," and the others dissolve into laughter. Except for Margaret, who tends to look down at her food, and stays very quiet.

"Have you got a headache, dear?" Aunt Harriet asks her. "It has been a long day."

"It's not from the day, Mother," she says. "But from the show."

"What could you possibly have to object to?" Emily blurts. "It was a perfectly harmless bit of brilliance."

"Yes, it was," Margaret says distractedly. Then slowly, as if sorting through her thoughts as she goes along: "What I object to is how deeply in the sand we are sticking our heads."

"Oh, dear," Manfred says, in a comically dismissive way, and Margaret looks off, her face full of the effort of remaining silent.

It's too much. The day has been too long. I fall asleep against Uncle Manfred in the taxicab home, am vaguely aware of the chill of the night air, the ghostly gloom of the semicircle of houses on Stokebridge Street, of dragging myself up the stairs and collapsing half-clothed into bed.

◈

It is a wretched night. The bed is too soft for comfort, too warm to get used to. I thrash and turn, kick out, pound the pillow into this shape and that. The silence of the house is unnerving – it is almost as if I need a reassuring rumble of bombs to relax, or the clatter of train wheels, blast of a foghorn, some sharp rock poking into my back.

I throw blankets on the floor, curl into a corner, and from here I can feel the house breathe. It is not a bad place. The floorboards slant away slightly towards the door. It's nothing compared to some of the slopes I've slept on in past months. There is the whine of something outside the window, a branch worrying the glass in the wind.

Over and over I'm stepping into the soldier in the theatre, driving my palm up the underside of his nose. I can feel his slimy blood and bits of his teeth in my hand, and the red caps are coming, coming for me. It's hard to run with everyone there. Margaret stands up suddenly and says, "What are you doing?" I trip over someone's legs, fall forward into the mud, and when I stand Margaret says, "Bully for you! I'm not going to clean you up this time!"

She has an arm missing, and now that I look closer skin is hanging from her cheek, and her dress is burned black in places.

I try to put the mud on her wounds, but she won't have it. "It isn't for me," she says. "You can give it to Emily. She needs it more than me."

But Emily isn't there. It's Margaret by the banks of the Chemainus River, with the dawn sun rising behind her. Margaret taking off her Belgian-style dress, turning away slowly to walk into the water. Reaching down with her hand and scooping the water up to her face – healed now, Margaret whole, as striking as anyone could be, Margaret in the sun with bare breasts and a calm sort of wildness, like a deer looking up, still as moss.

◈

"Oh God, what time is it?" I say, before I'm really awake. It is light, and I am in an awkward position on the floor, twisted onto my shoulder with one leg under the bed and my head jammed onto a section of moulding.

"Don't rush yourself, Ramsay." Margaret's voice in the hall. I stand awkwardly, look towards the shut door.

"Are you going somewhere?" I ask.

"Off to church!" she says. "We forgot entirely about the day-light savings."

"The what?" I ask.

"The clocks have all been turned ahead an hour. It's quarter past ten."

"What for?"

"To make us all terribly more efficient!" she says. "Never mind. Get your rest. We'll be back by noon. Miffy has left a nice breakfast."

I hear her feet descending the stairs, and begin casting off the clothes that I have slept in. My uniform is hanging in the corner of the room, looking much finer than it did when I arrived. I slip into the bathroom quickly, shirtless but wearing Uncle

Manfred's trousers, and I shave my face. Done in a minute without a nick. Here is one skill I can thank the army for. Back to the bedroom, and in a trice I am kitted out and ready. I rattle down the stairs and find them knotted in the tiny front entrance of the house, waiting for Emily to choose her hat.

"Hurry up!" Uncle Manfred says. "We're late as it is!" And then when he sees me he says, "Not too early for Lord Faunterloy?"

"Go back to bed, dear," Aunt Harriet says to me. "It's only church. Nobody expects an exhausted –"

"All present and accounted for," I say, and snap a salute, in the course of which I whack my elbow on the wall, then pretend it doesn't hurt.

"This blasted daylight savings," Manfred says. "Whoever heard of such a thing? Now we're all going to be late!"

Emily finally settles for something in yellow. Outside she takes my arm and says, "Did you sleep well, dear cousin?"

"Yes, fine," I say.

"I thought your father was godless," Margaret says behind me. Her parents immediately turn and make shushing noises, but she continues. "Didn't you always say that your brother is godless?" Margaret says to Uncle Manfred.

"Margaret!" he sputters.

"My father is no supporter of organized religion," I say.

"And yet you yourself are a churchgoer?" Margaret says. "Enough to miss breakfast!"

"My mother took us," I say. I mean to finish the thought – *once or twice, when she could manage it,* but somehow the words don't escape my lips. Instead I say, "My father has seen what many missionaries are doing in poorer parts of the world. And he doesn't exactly approve."

"He doesn't approve of bringing Christianity to savages and improving the lower races?" Margaret asks – for sport, possibly. She seems in a dazzling, dangerous mood.

"Progress, yes," I say. "Bringing Christianity to savages, no."

It is another magnificent morning, sparkling and warm as a daydream.

"My father has a very scientific mind," I say. "And he is a fair man, on his own terms. He always drilled it into me that a gentleman does not discuss religion in mixed company."

"Quite right," says Harriet.

"So you cannot discuss religion with a woman?" Margaret asks. "But you could with my father?"

"I think he meant mixed in the sense of believers and abstainers," I say.

"What a diplomat," Manfred says. "You should go into politics."

"Ah, another thing that should not be discussed!" I say, laughing.

It is a morning for church bells, for strolling on the sidewalks under large, leafy trees. I salute a major walking with his family group in another direction – he returns the compliment quite late. A minute later a captain gives me an irritated glance when I'm slow to get my arm up to acknowledge him.

We come upon the church sooner than I expect. It is an old, brown, mouldering pile of stones and ivy that looks like it has grown and then slumped here over centuries. We enter in a hurry, occupy a row near the back, although several others shuffle in even later than us, no doubt also fooled by the clock-switching.

Almost immediately my inexperience is exposed: I stay seated on the bench while the others kneel on the cushioned rail to pray. Then when I kneel they are standing already, and when I stand I reach for the wrong book.

"It's this one," Emily says, sharing hers, and I mumble through a hymn that everyone else belts out with robust confidence.

Margaret looks around while she sings, not at me but scanning the congregation, and then her gaze settles on somewhere to the front and the right. She is in a subdued, dark-blue dress with richly shadowed folds – almost a metallic lustre in this morning light. I can't help but notice the womanly shape beneath it, the whiteness of her throat and fingers, the steady, intelligent gaze at something of interest up there.

I have a sudden memory of my father standing on the porch of the Brown House. "Intelligence *is* the great beauty," he said, and I turned to see what he was looking at: my mother coming up the walk in her yellow summer dress, her skin so dark and beautiful. The two of them were locked in a gaze far beyond my ability to understand. He said the words without looking at me. But he knew I could hear, that I'd remember.

We are up and down, intoning and singing, listening, praying according to some set pattern I fail to divine. Emily sees right away I am lost and spends half the time giggling at me, and the other half trying to keep me in step. But Margaret gazes away throughout, lost in some other thought.

The minister is decrepit, bowed like a wounded man under the weight of his robes. His bald pate shines with the light of the stained glass, of the candles and the gleam of sweat. He wears mutton-chop sideburns in the fashion of long ago – a harmless looking fluffy white fur – but has a voice that fills the church with thunderous, rumbling passion.

"I am taking up the words," he says, "of our dear Bishop of London. They bear repeating. 'To save the freedom of the world, to save liberty,' he said, 'to save the honour of women and the innocence of children, everyone who loves freedom and honour, everyone who puts principle before ease and life itself before mere living, is banded in a great crusade – we cannot deny it – to kill Germans, to kill them not for the sake of killing, but to save the world, to kill the good as well as the bad, to kill the young men as well as the old, to kill those who have shown kindness to our wounded as well as those fiends who crucified the Canadian sergeant, who superintended the Armenian massacres, who sank the *Lusitania*, and who turned the machine guns on the civilians of Aerschot and Louvain; and to kill them lest the civilization of the world itself be killed.'"

The minister pauses. His watery eyes roam over the congregation. "Was the Bishop of London misrepresenting Christianity when he said those words in Westminster Abbey?" he continues. "He's a passionate man. He's been to the Front, he's seen what the Hun is capable of. Yet how is it that a Christian can kill and not be doomed to eternal damnation? What about the sixth commandment: 'Thou shalt not kill'? Did our dear Lord and Saviour Jesus Christ not entreat us in the Sermon on the Mount to turn the other cheek? Did he not say, 'They who take the sword shall perish by the sword'? Yet he also said, 'He that has no sword let him sell his garments and buy one.'

"Clearly, the writers of the Bible and the founders of the church believed that one day, when the world is entirely Christian, then there will be no more need for armaments, for dreadnoughts, for machine guns and bayonets. Then shall the swords be turned into ploughshares. But until that day has come, it is every Christian man's duty to smash the foe, to defend his women and children, to safeguard our civilization."

His old fists are clenched red, and for some reason – my uniform, no doubt – he fixes me with his eye, settles on delivering his sermon directly to me.

"And yet the Germans consider themselves Christian," he says. " '*Gott mit uns!*' they cry, even while they sink civilian liners and bomb hospitals, boil bodies and bayonet children, even while they shoot nurses and invade helpless countries with whom they have concluded treaties of peace and protection. '*Gott mit uns!*' " The minister's voice is now shrill, a mocking, scratchy German.

"They are the Antichrist hiding behind the cloak of Christianity," he says slowly, with great gravity. "They are pagans. They subscribe to the Prussian creed: War is good. The absence of war is a thwarting of the natural order. Those trying to abolish war are both foolish and immoral, for how will the mighty and powerful win out otherwise? And under the Prussian creed war must be as ruthless as possible. Our enemies believe the sight of suffering hardens the belly and propels one towards the right.

"Has Christianity failed us?" the minister asks, his voice rising. "Why, some of you may ask, why are we suffering these trials now? Why, after nearly two thousand years of Christianity, are we locked in this mortal struggle for our souls, our existence? Has God let us down?"

An uncomfortable silence. I look hard at my fingernails – cracked, some of them, shattered but tough, like claws – and he continues to settle his gaze hard at me. "Let us shine a little light on ourselves," he says. "Why is God punishing us with this war? Well, think of the drink bill in this country – an increase of eight millions over the first half of last year. Under trial and hardship have we sought refuge in the shield of the Lord, or have we fled to other diversions? How much effort have *you*," he says (blessedly scanning the room again now, not focusing on me), "put into bringing the gospel to the drinking establishments, the dark, drug-infested alleys of Soho? How many of you have sent every spare penny to the Public Morality Council to support their good work? Have you done all you could to bring the light of Christ, our Saviour, to everyone you know who is depressed, discouraged, distraught, rudderless because of this conflagration? And if you have for the past day, the past week, the past year, what about the last five years, the last decade?

"Before you give up on Christianity, before you lose hope in the Lord our God, ask yourselves," he booms, "what have *you* done, what is your part in this struggle for the soul of mankind?" The question hangs in the air, the hot, still, suffocating air. Then the minister says, "Let us pray for those dear sons and brothers, husbands and fathers of our congregation who have passed from us in the last few weeks." And he turns to a sheet, reads off seven or eight names, while we sit in a subdued hush broken once with a heart-rending sob from a man just two rows ahead of us, who holds his head in his shaking hands.

We sing:

Father, who art alone
  Our helper and our stay,
O hear us, as we plead
  For loved ones far away,
And shield with Thine almighty hand
Our wanderers by sea and land.

Guard them from every harm
When dangers shall assail,
And teach them that Thy power
Can never, never fail;
We cannot with our loved ones be,
But trust them, Father, unto Thee.

Christ is in stained glass, looking at me in a fractured way, through sunlight and torment. There is an odd moment under his gaze, as if I feel the beginnings of an understanding of some sort. It's nothing I can put in words, more like a yearning ache in the gut. I look him in the eye and I think, "Poor bugger."

◈

As we shuffle out of the church, Uncle Manfred, who has shaken hands with many of his neighbours, mutters to me, "Sometimes goes overboard, old Fowler, but he means well." And then we are at the door and he is introducing me to the minister.

"I thought I recognized a front-line man," the Reverend Fowler says to me. He has puffy lips and spidery red drink lines on his face. He works my hand up and down like a pump. "You are doing God's work, young man," he says. "Remember that, for every Hun you bayonet. This is a righteous, righteous war."

"Yes. Thank you," I mumble.

"I was talking to the Bishop of London just the other week," he says. I am conscious of the press of people behind us wanting to get out the door. "He is most upset at the poor church attendance by the fighting man. He was telling me that in a camp of five thousand you might get twenty at a Sunday service. It's a shocking state of affairs. I hope that *you* –" he starts to say, and I free my hand suddenly.

"Thank you for your words," I say, stepping off. "Thank you."

And then I am outside striding and breathing again.

Emily catches me by the end of the walk and once more takes my arm. We turn to wait for the others. I try to see where Margaret has gone, spy her eventually standing with a tall, pale fellow in civilian clothes.

"That's Mr. Henry Boulton," Emily says, when she sees where I'm looking.

My first thought is, *No, not for Margaret.* He's bent and slouching, his hands are bony, and he's sporting a furry little brown moustache that looks like a smudge of dirt on his upper lip.

"Do you want me to introduce you?" Emily asks.

"I suppose," I say.

I hate the way Margaret gazes up at him, how close to his arm she is standing. Emily makes the introductions and I take his proffered hand – wet, limp – and he says, "Pleased, sir," in the most formal, ridiculous way, even clicking his heels slightly as if mocking me in my military demeanour. Then his expression changes and suddenly I'm aware that I'm inflicting pain on the poor sod. I let him go and he flexes his clerical fingers – long, pale noodles – in an exaggerated way, while Margaret shoots me one of her biting looks.

"It's a beautiful day," I say grimly.

Boulton sneezes badly, wipes himself with a handkerchief, and then sneezes again.

"You haven't been taking care of yourself," Margaret says.

"Ramsay, dear," Aunt Harriet says, coming upon us – and then she sees Boulton and says, "Ah, Mr. Boulton," and returns her attention to me. "You must be starving. That was quite a long service to last through on no breakfast. Are you well, Mr. Boulton?" she asks, turning back to him. "Have you two met? How is your mother?"

"Harriet!" Uncle Manfred says behind her. "Are you trying to engage in eight conversations at once?"

"Well, I'm not among the slow-witted," she fires back. "But now that *you're* here . . ." And she turns to Boulton. "Will you join us for a spot of lunch, Mr. Boulton, or do you have to return to your duties?"

"I would be honoured to take up your invitation, Mrs. Crome."

He sneezes again and Margaret says, "You haven't been gargling!"

"I have. I *have*," Boulton says.

"Miffy managed to find rabbit at market last night," Harriet says. "So we are feasting today. The food at the restaurant last night was *awful*. I had nightmares about odd things being done to oatmeal in the name of economy. Shall we go?" she asks, and takes Boulton's arm, at which Margaret is perturbed for a moment. Then she is with her father, and Emily and I follow. I am hungry, quite suddenly, and in a bit of a state, when Emily says, "Are you *listening* to me?"

"What? Sorry!" I say.

"I asked whose portrait would you paint from this morning?"

"Whose portrait?"

"From the whole congregation," she says, "was there someone whose portrait you'd like to paint?"

"Does someone want a portrait?" I ask impatiently. What I'm longing for, I'm thinking, is time alone. Why did I rush off to join these people in their church? I could have lounged in bed, gone out for a long hike without having to see or speak to a soul.

"No, no," she says. "It's hypothetical. Yesterday you said you love to paint portraits. I was wondering if there was someone in the congregation whose face you found interesting. I did notice you eyeing everything, as if to memorize it all for later use."

I look at her, this young thing who notices too much. "Well," I say, "the minister had a memorable face."

"The minister! I rather thought you were looking for pretty girls."

"That's some other artist," I say.

"Will you do mine?" she asks, squeezing my arm and leaning against me so suddenly I step a half-pace to the side to keep my balance. "Please. Oh *please!*"

Margaret turns back to see what the commotion is.

"Ramsay is going to do my portrait!" Emily announces. Then she says to me, "I have the brushes and the oils, I even have some spare canvas, if you could stretch it properly."

"Good for you, Ramsay!" Harriet calls back. "Perhaps you could do one of Margaret as well?"

"There's no need," Margaret says quickly, looking at Henry, or rather the back of Henry's head, for he hasn't turned round with the conversation at all, but seems fixated on some tree looming high above us. "We can save Cousin Ramsay's skills for the great beauty in the family," Margaret says.

Boulton sneezes three times in a row, and says, "Oh, dear." Aunt Harriet pats his thin back and says, "You've been working too hard, Mr. Boulton," and I think, *What am I doing here? How did I get mixed up with these people?*

◈

At luncheon, the promised rabbit is a single spare, stringy specimen for the six of us. We fill out the meal with potatoes, which
Emily assures me are getting rare, and cabbage, and the ubiqui-
tous brown sauce, with fresh bread that saves it. I find myself
cutting piece after piece of the bread, slathering each in margarine, and downing them like a hungry dog.

"I can see you have a bit of the endless belt to you," Uncle
Manfred says to me. "Pass him some more bread. Miffy, is
there another loaf? Ramsay is eating enough for the whole
British army."

"I'm sorry. I'm sorry!" I say, stopping in mid-chew. The others
seem horrified with Manfred for mentioning anything, except
for Boulton, who looks at me more in amazement than distaste.

"The rumour around the ministry is that food rationing will
only be a matter of time," he says.

"*Food rationing!*" Harriet says.

"Don't be surprised if they issue ration books soon for
certain foodstuffs. And we'll all have to register with particular
stores and stick to them."

"T.W.O." Emily says, without looking up. Margaret lets her
knife clatter against the plate and I look again from one sister
to the other. Emily leans towards me and whispers, "The
Worried One."

Harriet says, "It's not Mr. Boulton's fault he happens to know
depressing things before the rest of us."

"It looks like there'll be no Bank Holiday this year," Boulton
continues. "Just thinking about depressing things. It's not
official, of course." Then he asks me about conditions at the
Front. "It's so helpful for me to know what the Tommies are up
against," he says.

"Cousin Ramsay is Canadian," Margaret says. "I don't think he thinks of himself as a Tommy. Do you, Ramsay?"

"If you wanted to know about front-line conditions," Manfred declares, "you could always sign a certain piece of paper and find out for yourself!"

His remark is greeted with an awkward silence. Manfred cuts a square of bread in a studied way and pushes it through the brown sauce with his fork. It's hard to know what to say. Boulton is looking at a spot on the tablecloth a few inches north of his own plate. Margaret and Harriet are glaring at Manfred. And Emily is looking everywhere, taking it all in.

"Conditions are pretty grim at the Front," I say finally. "We're still suffering from a lack of ammunition. I know at the Salient it seems like there are three German shells for every one of ours. The Canadian rifles are garbage – it's a scandal that we're still using them." Then to Margaret I say, "The French and Belgian civilians consider us Tommies. That's probably what matters most. But strictly speaking I guess we're Canucks."

"Do you see much of the locals?" Margaret asks.

"Well, the girls aren't known for wearing bathing dresses," I say, which brings a howl of laughter from Manfred and Emily, and a reddening on Margaret's face.

"I'm trying to get transferred to Explosives," Boulton blurts out, changing the direction of the conversation. "I've been offered a post but Kingsley won't let me go, the rotter. It seems I'm too valued, or something. I'm working from nine in the morning till eight at night, pushing papers from one office to another, it seems. I'd like so much to make a real contribution for a change."

"Mr. Boulton is working in recruiting right now," Margaret

explains, her cheeks still red from my bathing-dresses remark. *Careful*, her eyes seem to be saying.

"We're seeing great changes, of course, with the Military Service Act," Boulton says. "I think the big voluntary-service push was spent anyway. But Kingsley has made his own empire in our office: he doesn't want to let anyone go." Boulton directs his remarks to me. "Kingsley was in the Ministry of Education," he says. "Our former head, Webster, had given up a huge salary in the railways to manage us. Then Kingsley came in, and he brought along a platoon of fellows from Education. Now it's as if we have two armed camps in the office. One group won't speak to the other. Kingsley and Webster can agree on nothing, and nothing gets done unless they agree. It's frightful. We have pitched battles over the most insignificant issues, and then long frigid stretches when no one is talking to anyone else."

"All the more reason to push the desk aside and go fight the Hun yourself!" Manfred asserts. "Any young man with blood in his veins would –" He stops when he sees the way Margaret and Harriet are looking at him.

"Actually I have . . . I have taken a first step," Boulton says, haltingly.

"Oh, Henry!" Margaret says.

"It's nothing serious," Boulton says, with false levity now. "I was required to register anyway under the Act. My medical is on Tuesday. I'm certain the doctors will take one listen of my chest and then send me on sanatorium leave for the next several years."

Margaret tightens her jaw, says nothing.

"I have filled out my form w3236," Henry continues. "That states I am employed by the ministry and have my certificate, and am exempt under exception six of the schedule to the Act.

That *should* settle it. But strange things are happening. If for some reason I am still wanted, I'm thinking perhaps of joining the air service. Of course, that might require some technical knowledge –"

"*Hnnn!*" Manfred snorts.

"I know you think I am cowardly, Mr. Crome," Boulton says, with a quiet, even passion. "But I feel it would be a waste of my talents, such as they are, to strap me with a rifle and march me through the mud. My apologies, Private," he says to me. "But in all honesty, I don't think I'd last twenty minutes at the Front." He sneezes again.

"Of all the people I've seen at the Front," I say quietly, "almost no one is a natural soldier."

"But you've lived in the wilds of Canada," Margaret says. "You haven't grown up breathing the filth of London air. You're strong and fit and you probably already knew how to shoot a rifle before you joined up. Poor Mr. Boulton has been of precarious health since he was a youth. And besides, he has been educated . . ." She stops herself. "Not that you haven't been educated," she says. "Of course you have schools in Canada."

And my father lined our house with books, I think, even while I realize she is defending this Boulton like a lioness defending a cub.

"Young men from around the Empire have answered the call," Manfred says, and as the conversation rolls on I look at Margaret and think of Father that day years ago by the wharf, when he was home and we were skipping stones into an ocean so calm it looked like polished glass. "Never marry your cousin," he said to me, out of the blue, one of those fatherly pronouncements on life. "That's what did in our family. Generation after generation of inbreeding. Weakens the blood and addles the mind." And so I imagined them, the English Cromes, pale, sickly, half-grown mutants. I never thought I would meet them.

Marry my cousin? Perish the thought.

◈

At Boulton's suggestion, and then Harriet's insistence, we go for a walk, we young ones, while Harriet presumably harangues Manfred at home over his behaviour. All the way along Emily has made sharp little remarks about Boulton and Margaret, who are strolling ahead of us, arm in arm at last.

"You're very hard on them," I say at one point.

"I have had to chaperone them for months," she snaps back. "If they don't get engaged soon I shall scream."

It has turned into an almost uncomfortably hot afternoon. After quite a bit of apparently aimless wandering we make it to a tall, eccentric, boarded-up house, the walls of which are bursting with strange, fussy, carved columns and busts and angels and frolicking cherubs. Boulton takes it upon himself to explain that the building, known as the Gingerbread Castle, was the obsession of a Dr. John Samuel Phené. "He died just a few years ago at ninety," Boulton says, "and the estate was never finished. There's some question about what to do with it. There's a real movement to have it torn down." Boulton further explains that Phené was trying to reconstruct the family ancestral home at Savenay, on the Loire. "He never lived in it," Boulton says, "but died just across the street there, at number 32."

"I think the work of true eccentrics should be valued above almost anything else," Margaret says. "Most of the best things in London were built by eccentrics."

Emily rolls her eyes in my direction and we continue along, Boulton lecturing us on the famous old Chelsea China, which in days past was apparently manufactured on nearby Lawrence Street. We make it to the river, bordered by a fine park, the Chelsea Embankment, and spend a few moments listening to Boulton expound about the Albert Bridge, spidery with suspension cables. "It's generally considered the most beautiful of all the London bridges," he says. "Perhaps not from here, but from more of a distance you get a better sense of the fine lines. It was designed by Ordish, of course, after the Franz Josef Bridge in Prague. When was it opened?" he asks himself, and Margaret, Emily, and I stand in suspense while Boulton casts about in his memory. "I believe it was 1873," he says finally, "about the same time the extension of the Embankment was completed. Just before, actually," he says.

I look down the river to another bridge and see beyond it a series of huge, smoke-belching chimneys which Boulton, as he follows my gaze, explains belong to the generating station at Lots Road. "It's the largest in the world. That one station supplies all the electrical-current requirements for the most important underground railways in the city. Now, over here," he says, and points in the opposite direction, "you see the rail bridge past the Chelsea Bridge. That's Grosvenor, which leads to Victoria Station, I daresay where you arrived."

"I was dead to the world at the time," I say. "Asleep, I mean," when Margaret gives me a strange look.

We walk on, and the lectures continue about Thomas Carlyle's house and other famous residences along Cheyne Walk, a terrace of red-brick mansions overlooking the river. We stand for a moment staring at "the Queen's house," number 16, where Charles II's neglected wife, Catherine of Braganza, lived, and later on, Dante Gabriel Rossetti. "There was a white bull in the garden," Boulton says, "and a raccoon and a kangaroo, and a peacock that died under the sofa." We continue our walk along the river, look out at a park across the water, and Boulton asks if we would like to see a garden of some type – I don't catch the name immediately.

"It's not exactly open to the public," Boulton says. "And it is Sunday. But I do get admittance, from time to time, as an amateur botanist of sorts, and I think I could talk you in with me."

"He's done it before," Margaret says.

"With you?" Emily quips.

Margaret remains enigmatic.

We stroll, it turns out, to the Chelsea Physic Garden, a beautiful property not too far away. Boulton is good on his word, and after private conferral with a stern-looking man – I recognize a born quartermaster when I see one – we are all allowed in. "They're somewhat sticky," Boulton says to me in an undertone when we are safely through the gate. "This is strictly a research facility. There was a bit of a row when they wouldn't admit convalescing officers from the hospital next door." He doesn't finish the thought, but his meaning is plain: *I have some standing around here.*

"Mother will be angry she didn't come with us," Emily says at the sight of the flower beds, the spring colours, the lush surroundings.

Boulton goes on about the huge old cedars of Lebanon that used to guard the river entrance. "*Cedrus montis libani,*" he says, pointing back at emptiness. "The first four were brought here in the 1680s. Two were planted in the centre of the garden, and of course that was untenable – they left no room for anything else. They were cut down in 1771, I believe. And the Chelsea cedars by the gate – that's what they were called, the Chelsea cedars – were eventually killed as a result of the London smoke and the arrival of the Embankment. You see, the river used to come much closer to the garden walls, and the trees would drink twice a day with the tides.

"Curiously," Boulton says – and I note Margaret looking up at him as if she could never get enough of his prattle – "the trees would have been done for anyway. As the London population encroaches, the water use has increased significantly, and the Thames water has turned much saltier. So those trees would have choked on the salt if they hadn't died of thirst."

Boulton leads us to the centre of the garden, where a tall, solemn-looking fellow in a wig and eighteenth-century britches looks out on a pedestal towards an artistic mound of rocks and plants. "This of course is Sir Hans Sloane," Boulton says. "The garden had much earlier been the property of Sir Thomas More. It was Sloane who deeded it to the Apothecaries' Society, in perpetuity, as long as they took care of it and continued to use it for research. It's not run by the Apothecaries any more, of course, but by the Trustees of the London Parochial Charities. You'll remember that Sloane was also essentially the founder of the British Museum. It was his collection –"

"Dear," Margaret says, gently, but finally with an edge as well, "perhaps we could just enjoy the garden."

"Of course!" he says quickly. "I did mention that you are

students of mine, so the appearance of a lecture is not to be unexpected."

"Not to be unexpected," Emily whispers to me as we separate from the other two and wander into the rockpile part of the garden – various plants peeking out of an assembly of what looks like lava, and old bricks, chalk, and flint. "Mr. Boulton is a dedicated collector of fairly useless facts. I don't know how Margaret can stand him sometimes. He was going on and on the other day about string."

"About string?"

"Yes! There was some sort of new discovery about the Romans having used a particular plant to make string. Not rope – they used different plants for rope – but string. And then he had this look of the most simplistic wonder on his face and he said, 'Someone really ought to do a volume on the history of string.' Margaret just encourages him. In the middle of the worst war known to mankind!"

She is clearly looking for an ally in her derision of Boulton, and I mumble a few things.

We catch up to the others standing under a gnarled, ancient specimen held up by four iron crutches, which Boulton happily tells us is "*Gingko biloba* – the maidenhair. You see, it is possible to have something other than a plane tree thrive in London's squalid atmosphere."

"We have redwoods on Vancouver Island," I say, "hundreds of feet high. You could drive a train through the centre of the trunk of some of them."

"In the primeval forest certainly!" Boulton says. "But this is filthy London. Think of the smoke and stench a tree must put up with, the congestion, the stiff clay. It seems like the entire city is convinced the only thing fit for survival here is the plane tree." He points over at a spotty-trunked beast in the distance, the upper limbs stunted horribly, with thick tufts of leaves sprouting from the amputated ends. "Look what they have to do to keep from having its limbs break through windows and buildings! It's prune and reprune. Madness! I've never seen anything so ugly. And it needn't be so."

"Mr. Boulton is doing a study of the trees of London," Margaret says with some pride.

"Not a study, actually. Just some preliminary poking about. Perhaps it will be a monograph of some type," he says, with a slight stammer. "I'm not qualified at all. I just happen to have an amateur's interest."

"You know every tree in the city, practically," Margaret says. "I've seen your notes, Henry. They could fill a trunk."

"When did you see Mr. Boulton's notes?" Emily asks, with a telling cock of the head. "I don't believe *I* was there."

"It must have been some other time, dear sister," Margaret says.

"It's the grime and the filth and the bad soil that interests me," Boulton says. He motions about him. "I suppose anything could grow in a nice garden space like this. But what about the streets of London proper, or the East End, with all the smoke belching from factories, and God knows what's in the water? Wedged into a solid clay with a few square feet of street frontage, omnibuses and motor cars puffing past day and night, and tall buildings blocking any light not already choked off by smoke and fog. Of course, the plane does well, it's so robust, and smooth-leafed, and sheds its bark – harder for the impurities to gain a foothold. But I've seen cotoneaster thirty feet high in Kensington Gardens, and the one here in the Physic Garden is healthy too. The grain is so tough they've been making golf clubs from it. Did you know that?"

He seems quite lost in the subject, his eyes shining, face animated, and alive in a way he wasn't at lunch.

"There's a mulberry at Mildmay Park," he continues, "whose trunk is over six feet in girth. It's thirty-five feet high, and, quite extraordinary for a mulberry, the branches spread a full sixty feet. That's where the American Declaration of Independence was first read in this country, under the Mildmay mulberry."

"The Mildmay mulberry," I say, rolling the words.

"I know," he says immediately, "it's ridiculous to know about such things. Useless knowledge now. But one day we will be at peace again."

"And you will write your book," Margaret says. "You must."

She looks at me and I say, grudgingly, "Yes," as much for Margaret's sake as for Henry's.

"There's a Canadian woman at my boarding house," Boulton says, as we fall into a stroll again. "Her son is in the fighting and she came over to be closer to him. She's from Toronto. Do you know it?"

"I've passed through it on the train," I say.

"She was fine while he was in training. He would come into town on weekends, or whenever he could get leave. But once he was sent to France she began to get hysterical. She would weep if the post were silent a few days. This Friday past she got a telegram stating that he has been wounded gravely. She went completely mad – began overturning furniture, tearing the curtains from the windows, ripping the hair from her head. It took several of the burlier chaps in the house to subdue her, and tie her into her bed with sheets until the doctor came to sedate her. Even this morning she was in a fury of panic and worry. She begged me to arrange it so that she could go to the field hospital and visit her boy – as if I had any influence in the matter.

"Then, just as I was leaving this morning another telegram arrived for her. We hadn't the courage to give it to her. I think it will push her completely over the edge."

"You must show her the telegram," Margaret says indignantly. "Perhaps summon the doctor at the same time, but you *must* tell her."

"Yes. I suppose," Boulton says.

We wander past various species of trees and flowers, upon which Boulton is only too happy to expound. I watch the way Margaret is with him, so hovering and protective, and unusually silent, unless it is to come to his aid. And the sweat trickles down my skin under my uniform, the sun baking us. The world slows to a drowsy pace as we pause to look at daffodils and rhododendrons, at daisies and Dutch tulips and lumbering trees planted by Henry VIII or some such figure – Boulton knows them all. And I think: it really is for the woman to choose. If she wants to be bored the rest of her life by a droning amateur botanist, that is her choice. Why should it worry me?

I am going back to the fields of France and Belgium, where all the trees are shattered stumps, and the air is choked with smoke and fire a million times blacker than London on its worst winter's day, and the stench of bodies makes the factory smell like apple blossoms, and the gas hangs low in trenches and turns them into swamps of death. And this garden, this pleasant chat, this sleepy, sunny afternoon, is all a dream.

◈

The rest of the day slips past, and I retire early after dinner, then sleep in late – in the bed this time, though not sleeping so much as staring drowsily at the ceiling, listening while the family begins their week. When the sounds of the house die down, and it seems safe enough, I cleanse myself and slip downstairs, and devour more pieces of the housekeeper's fine bread and margarine, with soothing sips of tea, while I pore over the morning paper, blessedly left behind for me.

There were large air battles on the Western Front over the weekend. The Allies shot down seventeen German planes, and lost ten themselves. There is a long, disturbing report on the deportation of Armenians from Turkey. Russian troops arriving in Trebizond found Armenian houses plundered and in ruins, with most of the population of the town, some ten thousand people, apparently exterminated. There was hope that a few hundred might be found hiding in villages. Similarly, another town called Erzum, where thirty-five thousand people used to live, is now empty. According to the report, after the people had been expelled from their houses last summer they were forced to live in the streets for several days while officials extracted taxation owing, even though they were leaving all property behind. All this was done with the approval of the German consul. "Among the spoils which fell to the Turks," the article states, "were several Armenian girls, and a share in this living booty was conceded to the Germans."

I look at the advertisement for J.W. Benson's luminous Active Service silver watch, which is visible at night, and can be had for three pounds, three shillings.

Another article tells of a seventeen-year-old girl burned to death riding an omnibus in the Strand. Her clothing caught fire, apparently from a dropped match, and the light summer material went up in flames in seconds. I think of the conductress I met my first morning – was it only Saturday? – and what she would look like with bits of clothing cooked into her flesh. The screaming of the passengers and the smell of it. I know too well.

I take a few extra slices of bread, then steal away from the house without having spoken to anyone. I make my way down to the river along streets becoming somewhat familiar, and spend the day on foot: along Cheyne Walk and the Chelsea Embankment, past the Royal Chelsea Hospital, with scarlet-clad veterans smoking, lounging on the park benches, staring off into space. Past gardens and bridges, wharves, sailing skiffs, barges, businesses. Past Westminster and Cleopatra's Needle, losing the river sometimes and gaining it back again. I wander for a while along ugly streets – it's Monday now, the city is back to work, everyone has a place to hurry to, a job to do in some small room of a large building in this warren of lanes and alleys.

I lunch on my borrowed bread leaning against a sorry brown brick wall hours away from where I started out. If I had brought a pencil and paper, I think, I could write a letter to mother saying, *Here I am in the heart of old London, safe from the fighting.*

I push on, obeying some obscure compulsion to keep walking. I have money in my pocket: I could take a taxi, or step onto any omnibus, or even take the Tube, if I could find it and knew where

I wanted to go. But I have no idea. I just want to be moving, to feel the blood in my limbs doing what it's supposed to do in a healthy young man.

Who might not be healthy for too much longer, and so I am walking for the sake of it, for being able to do it. I come within sight of what must be the Tower of London, and then push farther, the buildings getting bleaker. No parks now, no grass, hardly any trees even, except for stunted, pruned, tortured planes that I notice everywhere now, thanks to Boulton. All trunk with hardly any room for limb and leaf.

Military trees, I decide. Strong legs and chests, not much up top, hacked to a regulation appearance.

Soon enough, I come upon the block-and-tackle chaos of the dockyards. The wharves seem to be swarming with men of military age, but in sweaty civilian work clothes, with rolled-up sleeves and relaxed, grimy faces pulling cargo from boat after boat, or lounging around in quiet groups, smoking, chatting. Like men at the Front, I suppose, men at rest, with ropy muscles and lazy eyes. Look too hard in the wrong direction and someone will find something for you to do. The air is overstuffed with the smell of spices and burlap, of smoke from the steamers, of unwashed bodies, of coal and resin and water-soaked wood.

I happen upon, quite by accident, a sign that seems familiar: "THE PROSPECT OF WHITBY." My hand is on the heavy door before I remember where I've heard the name. This is the place Bill Kelsie mentioned when we met him in Trafalgar Square. It's too much to expect that he will be here. I step into the old tavern – darkness even in the mid-afternoon, a lungful of heavy smoke, a sense of lethargy and age. Men have been drinking here for hundreds of years, I think. The plank floor, the long bar. I step farther in – towards the river, it turns out; I can see it through the back windows – scan the place for Bill Kelsie, or anyone else I might recognize.

"Over here. Over here!" someone urges, at the far end of the L-shaped room. A group of Canadian soldiers is sitting in smoke in a booth by a big window. "You look like you could use a drink," one of them says, a sergeant from the Princess Pats.

I nod to them and order a pint at the bar along with a round for the table.

"What's that?" the barkeep says.

So I repeat myself, slowly, and he says, "What, you want to get arrested? No treating! You buy your own drinks, now."

So I bring my pint back to the table and apologize to the lads. The Princess Pats sergeant explains that the government earwigs figured out that men drink more when they buy rounds, so they passed a law against it.

"How'd you like to spend your time dreaming up shit like that?" he asks.

"Sounds pretty cushy to me," I say, and tip my glass to them. The ale slides down my throat and I glory for a moment in its warm familiarity – so good to be out of the henhouse for a while and back among my own kind.

They have all been into the thick of it: the sergeant is a machine-gunner, and there's also a scout for the 42nd, a sniper for the RCRs, a skinny cook for some outfit from Winnipeg I haven't heard of before, and one or two others who seem to know about mud and chatts and rum rations. The others in the pub, from what I can tell, are all still on training. These trench rats in the back could tell just from looking at me where I've come from. An extra shade in the eyes, maybe. A certain hunch to the shoulders and shudder in the step.

"Our number one got hit about four o'clock in the bloody morning," the sergeant says. "He goes down and he says to his number two, 'Jesus-cunt, Bill,' he says, 'I've been hit!'

The sergeant looks at me in dead seriousness, then winks once.

"So number two says, 'Casey,' he says. 'Where'd they get you?'

" 'I can't say,' Casey says.

" 'Why not?'

" 'It's in a bloody unmentionable place,' Casey says. 'But I'll tell you, Bill, I can give you a clue.'

" 'What's that?'

" 'Bill,' he says, 'I'm never gonna have children.'

"And after a while we drag Casey to the new set-up. He's bleeding pretty bad, but Fritz is pounding and there was no way the stretcher-bearers could get in. Poor buggered Casey, he knows he's had it. He says, 'Bill,' he says, 'I want you to grant me a last request.'

" 'What's that?' our number two says.

" 'Bill, my Maggie moved to London to be near me. She's a great girl, but she falls apart without a man to look after her needs. You know what I mean. The old in-and-out.' And Casey pushes his finger in and out of the Vickers barrel to show him."

The sergeant pushes an index finger through a circle of his other fingers, in and out.

" 'Do you think you could do that for me?'

" 'Well, Casey,' Bill says, 'anything for a buddy.'

" 'There is a hitch,' he says. And his breath is going quicker now, he won't last too much longer. 'She likes a gentleman to enter from the rear.' "

The sergeant stops to light a cigarette, inhales deeply, closes his eyes for a moment. He's balding and square-built, with a broken nose badly healed and jagged teeth.

"'Enter from the rear? All right, Casey, I'll remember that.' Then old Casey, he pegs out, and Bill gets some leave, and the first thing he does when he gets off the train at Victoria is hop in a cab to the address of Casey's widow. And this beautiful young woman in black opens the door. 'Yes?' she says. Her eyes are moist with sorrow.

"Bill says, 'I was with your husband, ma'am, when he died, and I just wanted to say, ma'am – here he remembered to take off his hat" (and the sergeant takes off his own, places it next to his heart) – "'I just wanted to say what a brave man he was. We was in the German trench, ma'am, fightin' them Huns at close range, and old Casey, he already had three of them stuck to his bayonet. But he just didn't have room for the fourth. I swear to God he should'a got the VC, ma'am – not that I do swear to God normally, you understand.'

"And the widow, she lowers her eyes and says, 'Yes, Colonel, I do understand.'

"Then old Bill, who's a corporal, says, 'There was one other thing, ma'am, that Casey asked me to do.'

"'Yes, Colonel,' she says, and looks straight at him again through her veil.

"But old Bill, he can't bloody well say the words. He hums and he haws, and gets blister red. Finally, he says, 'Ma'am, your husband asked me to perform a service for you.'"

"'What kind of service?' she asks innocently.

"And he starts stammering some more and sweating and kicking the door sill. 'It was sort of a last request.'

"'Yes, Colonel?'

"'It involves going through the back door, ma'am.'

"As soon as he says it she goes white, and shuts the door in his face."

The sergeant takes a slow, long pull of his beer, drains the glass, puts it down on the table.

"So Bill stands there, and he scratches his head. And then he figures it out. He was standing at the front door. So he goes around to the street and finds his way to the back lane and comes to the rear door, and knocks as loud as he can."

"Last call!" the barkeep yells, and the sergeant looks over in irritation. "Closing in five minutes!" the barkeep says.

"How can we be fighting for a buggered civilization that closes the pubs in the middle of the afternoon?" the sergeant asks.

I take a deep drink of my own pint, wipe my mouth, and someone asks the sergeant to go on with the story.

"Well," he says, "old Bill knocks on the back door as loud as he can, but there's no answer. He waits a minute, knocks again. Finally, he shakes his head and is just about to leave when a woman's voice says, 'It's open, Colonel.'

"So Bill pushes the door open and there's the beautiful Maggie draped over the back of a chair. She's got her dress hiked up and her arse in the clouds, naked as God made her, two gorgeous full-moon globes staring our Bill in the face."

The sergeant pauses.

"So Bill slides over to her," the sergeant says. "He looks her over. Then he pulls her up on her feet and turns her around and says, 'You'll catch your death of cold, ma'am.'

"She says, 'You *were* with my husband when he died?'

"'Yes, ma'am.'

"'And my husband did send you with his last request?'

"'Yes, ma'am,' he says. 'Now where's this gun barrel that needs cleaning out, anyway?'"

We straggle out after the sergeant – Langstrom is his name – into the back streets, because he knows of a place, and there's nothing better to do. It's a motley route march up one blind alley and down another, and after a while some of the men drop out, which is probably wise. I am thinking of it myself, because I'm hungry now, and a bit fuzzy from downing my pint too fast, and because this seems sad and pointless. But we come to an apartment of sorts and Langstrom, though drunk, is suddenly sure. He pushes the door open without using the knocker, and we are four soldiers up a dark, filthy flight of stairs and around a corner to another door. This time Langstrom does knock – three times, then once, then twice – and we wait.

"Any of you bleeders have money?" he asks suddenly, looking at me especially.

"Some," I say.

The other two are slower to answer, and Langstrom snarls, "Because you have to have money to be here. Piss off if you're broke!"

"How much?" the skinny cook from Winnipeg asks.

"What, you thinking of saving some for when you get to heaven?" Langstrom snaps. Then the door opens and a tired, droop-shouldered woman in a flouncy crepe dress – like Fluffie from the play, I think, but ages older and ground down – pokes her head out of the smoke.

"You gentlemen here for a good time?" she asks, her voice unmarked by the slightest degree of enthusiasm.

It's a pound each just to step through the door. Inside, heavy curtains are drawn across every window, and the place is lit by the dimmest of electric lights. Candles in a dugout burn brighter. The furniture is broken down and stained. A half-dozen other soldiers, in various states of inebriation, are lounging, drinking, talking in low voices. There doesn't seem to be anywhere to sit. We stand awkwardly, looking around. There might be another room in the back, I think, eyeing a door in the gloom.

"What can I get you?" the ancient hostess asks.

"Last time I was here there were women," Langstrom says. Even he is subdued, now that we're inside.

"No women here today," the hostess says, without irony. "We have gin and whisky."

"Any rum?" our fourth man asks.

"We have gin, we have whisky, we have the door," she says.

Langstrom looks like he wants the door, but is suddenly too weak to get there. So we order. Langstrom swings a huge pair of sleeping legs off a chesterfield and plunks himself down. The man – a captain, for Christ's sake – opens his eyes briefly, but takes no offence. A few others make room for me and Winnipeg and Rum man.

Our glamorous hostess comes with the drinks. The whisky tastes like kerosene. I almost spit out the first mouthful, but persevere. Then I light a cigarette and wonder idly if my throat will explode into flame. And I think of the letter home to Mother. *Dear Mrs. Crome. We regret to inform you of the death of your son. The exact circumstances of his passing remain unclear, as you can understand in the chaos of battle. But please rest assured that he died a valiant and heroic death, instantaneous and without pain.*

A terrible silence descends and we all look to Langstrom for some kind of commentary or joke. But instead he says in a sad, low, drunken voice, "A friend of mine got hit by shrapnel from a coal-box." Slumped in the broken-down chesterfield he looks like a bit of a frog swallowed up in moss and mud. "Peterson. Bloody fearless Peterson. One minute he's eating his Maconachies – there's nothing worse than cold Maconachies – and the next thing he's twenty feet away stuck in a mudbank. I run over to him. He's just this body, now. His head has been driven into the side of the bank. And I start pulling and pulling."

"Oh, Jesus," someone says behind us, "shut him up."

But Langstrom continues. "So I'm pulling him, and parts are coming off," he says. His glass is almost empty already. He stares at it a moment, in some amazement. "I have his hand, but it's not attached to anything else. I'm pulling and yelling. It feels like I'm standing knee-deep in blood. Then I feel something squishy, like wet rubber. I pull and pull. More of it comes out. I don't know how long I'm pulling before I realize it's his intestine. Then I start pushing it all back in. But it won't go, of course. It's this horrible rope out of coil."

He drains the rest of his whisky. I look at my glass too and see somehow that it's empty as well. So I order more. No rule against buying rounds here.

Langstrom says, "Then I smell something. I've almost got the body out. I'm still thinking, Jesus, he might be alive. If I can just stuff enough of him back together and get him on a stretcher. But this smell comes over me and I look at my hands. And it's

Maconachies. Little bits of bloody half-digested turnip and carrots and greasy gravy. It's bloody Maconachies from his guts."

◈

We stay too long. Some of the others buy rounds and I try the gin, but it tastes the same as the whisky. Every so often Langstrom starts awake and says, "What's the fucking time?" but can't seem to get out of the chesterfield. It's one of those deep-draw shell-holes with its own gravity. You can feel the weight of the mud, the grip of the vacuum like the arms of a corpse hardened around your waist.

I say a few things about Reese and Snug, blather on like a fool. At one point I realize we are all either sleeping or blathering. Winnipeg is going on about some buddy who lost both feet to gangrene. Rum man – his face looks like a soaked sponge – lost his girl to a bank clerk in Windsor. Langstrom is dead to the world. Other groups have come in, full of spit, but soon enough are pulled down into this ghoulish drunkenness.

There are women now too. I notice them in a sort of fog. A woman in a reddish swirl, with black hair and bloody lips. From where I am, lost, she can't see me. I mean to tell Langstrom, but he isn't here any more. And as I look around none of the others are either. Snug is, though. I see him stagger through holding a huge glass. Only it isn't beer. He stops, towering above me, and says, very clearly, "If you drink your own piss, they can't get you."

Reese is with the woman. It's Cynthia Elaine Whyte. She is pressing him against the door frame, trying to get his body to stay up all on its own. But he's like a huge sack of water. If you push on one side he collapses on the other. I mean to get up and help. Not because I want to do her. It would just be the proper thing.

I try to stand but my legs are water too, like Reese's. So I loll my head instead and say, "Miss Whyte!" In a strange way she looks a great deal like Margaret.

It's wonderful just to say her name.

She turns to me and Reese collapses to the floor and I tell her it's all right, he's just drunk. "These things happen with soldiers," I say.

◈

These things happen. You are wandering around in the dark by the docks and river water sucks and surges black and grey. You've been wandering so long you can't remember a time when you weren't stumbling around. And then you go down an old set of stairs and sit there by the dark water hugging your knees.

A body floats by. It could be any body. It's not particularly alarming. Bodies have been floating by forever. In this river. In *all* rivers. Bodies float by. As they do in India. Father said. That one time, at the kitchen table in the Brown House, he talked about bodies floating down the Ganges. He saw them.

It's what bodies do.

Only this isn't a body, it's a sack of something. (It could be a body in a sack.) It's floating in the black grey water and I'm going to have to get home somehow.

Molasses in the head. I stand, stay still, listening to the quiet shadows. All the pubs are closed. It must be very late. I need to hail a cab and tell the driver the address.

I'll remember it in a minute.

I'll just walk a bit. The blood will come back to my brain and then I'll remember. Down this way. Feet tired in these hard boots. But travelling feet. They keep going no matter what. Past bloody fatigue. When the legs are more ache than muscle, the sinews feel worn to dust, these feet will keep going. On cobblestone and mud, hard dirt, planks, over rocks, bodies, wire, sludge, roasted flesh. Long past imagination.

It's just a matter of following the river. Of letting the eyes adjust and the head clear. Of pausing sometimes to give the stomach a chance to sort out its battles. And pissing a long stream into a back lane of the world's greatest city, as if it were just another trench latrine.

I pass the organized chaos of dock workers unloading a ship, lit by a great arc lamp suspended above: sweaty, swarthy men heaving and grunting, disappearing into shadows and then reappearing again. Later on, by the glow and heat of a smith's station, I pause to watch a man shoe a docile horse. He turns to me and I stare like the beast he's working on.

Most of the night is blackness. No streetlights, no gas lamps, no windows lit. In the distance narrow searchlights sweep the bottoms of the clouds for Zeppelins, pale white ghostly impotent fingers.

I think of Uncle Manfred's Zeppelin contraption.

In one back alley a soldier and a collection of clothes – a woman, I suppose, although it's hard to see in the shadows – huddle and shake together standing up as if they have become one feverish animal. I stare too long, my mind still muddled and uncomprehending. When I do move off finally – his cap has fallen to the street, her hair is a dark bush in a windstorm – they haven't noticed me.

I feel like an irrelevant ghost. I move off but hear their moans and grunts from far down the lane.

◈

"Good God, man! It's four o'clock in the morning!" Uncle Manfred says, standing at the door in a dressing gown with slippers. "Where did you get yourself to?"

He is blocking the passage and it seems I will not be let in until I give a full accounting. But it's hard to know what to say.

"I got a bit lost," I blurt.

"*Lost?*" he says incredulously. There are noises on the stairs and then Aunt Harriet is beside him, also in a dressing gown.

"Ramsay! We were worried sick!" she says. "Where did you go?"

"I did an awful lot of walking," I manage to say.

"Have you been drinking?" Harriet asks. Then, without waiting for an answer, she says, "Manfred, he's been drinking!"

I slump for a second against the door frame. Not from the drink but from fatigue.

"Oh, Manfred, he's been *drinking!*" Harriet says again, and then Manfred has my arm. For a second I feel he might toss me out into the night again. But instead he helps me inside. My head is clear now. I mean to tell them, but don't quite somehow.

Margaret is standing at the top of the stairs, in her nightgown, an electric light shining behind her so strongly I can see the shadow of her legs through the fabric. "Is he all right?" she says, looking directly at me, but talking as if I cannot hear.

Emily comes into the hall yawning and pulling her dressing gown around her. "Oh, Ramsay," she says. "Did somebody beat you up?"

"Just the bottle, I imagine," Manfred says roughly. "Go back to bed! He's had a bit of a night of it, that's all."

"He *reeks*," Margaret says as we pass by her at the top of the stairs. "Perhaps you should clean him up," she says to her father.

"I am marching this soldier to bed," he says. "He can clean himself in the morning."

Sheets and covers and soft pillow. My boots on the floor, like parts of my feet pulled off.

If I'd found a taxi I would have taken it.

For a moment it seems I am going to vomit on the nice bed, but the nausea passes. I turn onto my stomach and listen to them talking in the hall. It's like a conversation overheard in a foreign language, with only a few words and phrases recognizable. *Drink! Sick as a dog! Smells like a distillery!*

This falling sensation. Sleep, finally. Unquestioning sleep. Relief.

Today is Tuesday. I've only got until Friday.

If I sleep from now until then, I won't have to explain a thing.

◈

In the morning I try to rouse myself from bed but find the walls reeling, my skin burning. I make it to the bathroom but cannot seem to run the bathwater. It takes too much energy and will. I stumble back to bed and sleep until the hours turn grey.

Aunt Harriet brings me tea, takes my temperature, and wraps me in warm blankets even though fires seem to have overtaken me from within. I sweat rivers into my bedclothes – somehow I am in pyjamas – and Harriet plies me with water and sweetened cocoa and ever more tea. I wake up in the afternoon to the sight of a pillar of chilly sunshine slanting through the window and the feeling of ice in my bones. I reach for all the blankets I have thrown off and distinctly hear Margaret's voice in the hallway say, "Well, it's his *own fault!*"

This fierce winter clattering my teeth.

Later, Uncle Manfred half carries me to the bath and lowers me into water just shy of boiling, and even then it takes some minutes for the ice to retreat. I lie still, shivering in steaming water, and then it is as if some great switch is thrown in my internal engine. What was frozen is now racing with steam, and my mind scalds itself with remorse and recriminations. How could I have been such an idiot last night? I call for my uncle and he helps me out of the bath, towels down my shaking body. By the time I'm in bed again I'm shivering with cold once more and the voice in the hallway is Margaret's again.

"Surely we need to call Dr. Prestwick!" she says.

"He is already on his way, dear," says Manfred.

If the doctor comes I do not see him. There is instead dismal sleep and more woolly hours. Margaret appears in my door sometime in the gloom of the evening, her face marked with concern. She stands forever in the shadows looking at me until I think she is another dream. Finally, I say, "Come in, please," mainly to see if she is real or not.

"I didn't want to wake you," she says, closing the door softly behind her. She puts a cool hand on my forehead. "Your fever is subsiding."

"I feel a bit better." I sit up without blacking out or embarrassing myself.

"You were wretched to go off on your own without telling

anyone," she says sternly. "We were all worried about you. And now look what's happened."

"I'm afraid I lost track of the time," I say weakly.

She shifts a small chair from the corner and sits near me. I consider reaching for her hand but can only imagine her pulling away.

"It's an awful thing to drink so much," she says. "So many of the soldiers become drunken disgraces. Like those men at the play the other night. That could have turned into absolute chaos. I thought perhaps you would be different."

"Did you?" I ask.

"Quite stupidly, it appears now," she says. She gets up suddenly. "Anyway, I just wanted to make certain that you're feeling better."

"You've certainly seen to that," I say sharply, and then, when I see her pained reaction, I say, "Stay, please," and reach out for her. "You can quote me the Bishop of London if you want. I'll take my punishment like a man."

"Oh, hang the Bishop of London!" she replies. She has, at least, taken her hand from the door. "But the drink problem is terribly –"

"Yes, all right, we'll hang the Bishop of London," I interrupt. "You be judge. I'll be executioner. And if he asks for a final drink –"

"You don't take me seriously," she says. "You think I'm an empty-brained female."

"No," I say.

"Then what *do* you think? Do you think public drunkenness is the right of every man who puts on a uniform and has the misfortune to be stationed in the worst of it? What kind of ideals are you fighting for? Or is it just naked victory you want, the right to participate in the carnage and when at home reel about in a state of oblivion?"

"I haven't thought of it," I say quickly.

"Why not? At times you seem to be thoughtful. What gives you the right to flout the rules and expectations of a society you profess to be fighting for? To pollute your mind and body, and endanger yourself –"

"Margaret."

"– and those around you, and to frighten us into thinking perhaps you'd fallen prey to some sort of –"

"Enough!" I say urgently. To my surprise she stops speaking. I look at her for some time.

"I hadn't thought about it," I say slowly. And then: "Sometimes a soldier drinks so that he doesn't have to think about things."

Margaret nods her head so slightly in the shadows. There is a pause, in which I can't for the life of me think of what further to say, though I don't want her to leave. At last, she says, "We'll give him mother's milk." And then at my blank look she explains. "The Bishop of London. When we hang him." A trace of a smile. I pat the chair beside me and am uncertain until she returns to it.

"My Tuesday has been a loss," I say and reach out again and this time successfully take her hand. It is such a small movement in the gloom but feels like an electrical switch has been pulled. "Tell me about your Tuesday."

She seems unsure, ready to leave again, and I am surprised when she says, "I will for a minute. And then you must get your rest." I look at her exquisitely stormy face, and think of the living corpse of a hostess in the private whisky bar – or whatever it was we were drinking. "I did some writing today," she says. "And spent quite a bit of the afternoon at the church making up care packages for prisoners. It's hard to know what to send. But they're frightfully short of things like tea and sugar, warm clothing, canned fruits – any food, really. We can only trust that the Germans will let the food through."

"Books?" I say.

"Sometimes, yes; we've heard they're awfully keen on anything we can send for entertainment."

We are still holding hands and I have been looking at her too intently. I should stop. I should let her go and retreat to my own addled dreams.

Instead, I ask her what she was writing.

"Oh, it's nothing," she says, blushing – I can see her even in the shadows.

"What are you writing, Margaret?" I press, though my voice is barely more than a whisper. I have a sense that anything sudden, or loud, or ungentle in the least way will burst the moment.

"I keep track of a few . . . observations," she says.

"Will you read some to me?"

"No. No, I couldn't." She looks away and in a second is going to find a reason to leave. So I say the only thing I can think of.

"Wasn't Mr. Boulton going to have his medical today?"

"Yes," she says quickly.

"How did it go?"

"He did telephone," she says quietly. "And he passed – unexpectedly, and quite unaccountably. His health is fragile. But he said this doctor is known for passing any man who can stand up unaided. Mr. Boulton didn't seem too concerned."

"No?"

Margaret looks at me thoughtfully, the corners of her mouth crimped, as if cutting off something she might want to say. "He should still get an exemption for his work in the ministry. But he says he will do whatever his country asks of him. And I know I must sound very selfish, but I think sometimes a country asks too much, and without reason. I'm afraid I seem to be quite in the minority with such thoughts these days." She smiles with a sudden fierceness. "I would not be too upset if your illness were serious enough to keep you out of the firing line a few extra days. Good for you for drinking yourself sick. I can see a certain method in your madness."

"And what would that be? I would very much like to know."

"Perhaps mad situations call for mad reactions."

"Sometimes a drink is just a drink," I say. Then I press her to read to me.

She runs through a list of possibilities – Kipling, Wells, Tennyson, Conan Doyle. "We have Norman Angell's book on the impossibility of war in Europe. Have you read it? It's brilliant," she says dryly. "The commercial interests would never stand for a protracted war. He proved it beyond a doubt."

"Read to me something of yours," I say.

"Father loves Dickens," she replies. "We have everything the man wrote."

"Something of yours."

She lets go of my hand and leaves me, and I am fairly certain she will return with some volume. But in a few minutes she is back with a thick notebook through which she begins to leaf. "I just write scattered thoughts," she says.

She flips and reads silently, flips again, can't seem to decide.

"Anything," I say finally. "What you're looking at right now."

So she reads, "Knitting circles can be like a buzzing hive of distracted conversation, as the ladies mutter to themselves to keep track of their knitting while talking to others at the same time. This afternoon Mrs. Witton asked if we'd heard of a young Major Parsley who got married. His regiment was to be off at six the following morning, so he took unauthorized leave – *miss one* – she said . . . and we all broke into laughter. 'No, no!' Miss Atkins said, '*knit two together!*' And after that we were laughing too hard to hear the rest of the story or get anything done."

Margaret flips the page quickly, then shuts the book.

"Read some more. Please," I say.

She sighs, and presently I hear her soft voice say, "The newspaper today had an interesting account of some of the unusual careers which have sprung up because of the war. One man makes his living running errands and buying breakfast for soldiers who have been locked up overnight on a drunk." She looks up from the page and asks me, "You weren't locked up, were you? No, I suppose not." She continues. "Another man stands in front of public houses and takes care of children whose parents have gone in together for a drink. He keeps little things in his pocket for the children's amusement: coloured chalk, nails, glass beads, and their favourite, putty. And yet another has become an official congratulator. He hangs about the registry offices in Covent Garden, and when a new bride and groom leave he opens the car door for them. The poor groom is normally so addled with happiness he tips lavishly anyone and everyone."

She closes the book again quickly and says, "It's nothing that anyone else would find the least bit interesting."

"A congratulator," I say. "That's what I should do as my bit for the war effort."

"Yes. It would be a fine job," Margaret says.

"Congratulations!" I say. "There, how was that?"

"More effusive."

"*Congratulations!*" I say again.

"Much better. Much better!" Margaret says.

"We could congratulate couples together."

"We'd get flowers from Covent Garden, and shower them with petals. And you could do quick portraits as the happy couple sat for a few minutes. *Can* you do quick portraits?"

"I'd need a pencil and some paper," I say.

"Yes. You would," she says.

We pause and I find we are staring at one another in the gloom. Then she says, "Would you do me?"

Her voice is carefully neutral, apparently lighthearted.

"All right," I say.

She rises and leaves, and in a minute has returned with a pencil and a rough sheet of paper, and a tray to balance across my knees. She sits still, mostly in shadows, and I look at her deeply for a while. My hand begins to move on its own – just the first traces of the line of her cheeks, her tight, firm chin, her small, feminine, but slightly hooked nose, the lips thin and cool, eyes pensive, almost too willing to return my gaze.

I fuss over the shading, slow myself down so that I can look at her longer. Take that, Henry Boulton, I think. You with your infernal trees and your damned luck. You will probably stay the rest of the war in your clerkship in London, and marry Margaret, and mutter on about clay soils and pruned planes and the history of string, and never have an inkling of the depth of your good fortune.

When I hand over the paper, reluctantly, Margaret studies it as if reading a newspaper report of commanding interest. Finally she rolls it up and says, "May I keep it?"

"Yes, of course."

I try to think of what light, glib comment might hold her by my bed a little longer. But words have evaporated. Yet she doesn't leave as I expect. She seems content to sit and look at me in some sort of understanding silence.

Finally, she says, "You have a talent, Cousin Ramsay."

"Thank you, Cousin Margaret."

"Some woman will be very lucky," she says. And perhaps there's meant to be more, but she thinks better of it. "I've monopolized far too much of your time. Forgive me," she says, rising. "Get your sleep."

"If I stay up later I stand a better chance of getting really ill," I say.

"Yes. And Lord Kitchener and all the rest would curse me for keeping you from your duty." She is almost out the door but turns back and leans over me, I suppose to kiss my cheek or forehead. But I turn my head and catch her lips – too suddenly. She gasps and pulls back and slaps my face.

Not a bad smack. Not as hard as she could have.

I should apologize but stay silent. And she should leave, but stands instead for too long a time, slightly out of reach. She is breathing hard, as if she has just run across a field. I have the feeling that if I got out of bed and pulled her to me she would not resist. But it is not my place. I have declared myself already and my face is stinging for it.

She looks at me far too long for mere anger, the portrait still rolled in her hand. This is how I should have drawn her, I think.

Finally, there is a noise downstairs and she leaves, closing the door behind her.

◈

"This Roger Casement is arguing he can't get a fair trial in England because he's already been branded a traitor by the press," Uncle Manfred says when I come down to breakfast. He barely glances up from his newspaper. "Are you all right, then? Somewhat recovered?"

"Somewhat," I say.

It is just the men at the table. There are empty places where the women have already eaten, I surmise. The silver tea set, a plate of cold toast, an opened jar of marmalade.

"What does he expect, riding a German submarine back to Ireland to start an uprising? Ten ships sunk yesterday, by the way. British, French, Norwegian, Italian, Danish, Swedish, Greek. Shocking. Do you want porridge?"

"No. No, thank you," I say, pouring some tea.

"The French are holding on to their gains at Douaumont, north of Verdun. They've taken more than three hundred prisoners." He puts the paper down for a moment and looks at me. "I don't see how the Germans can keep losing men at this rate and still field an army. In every single engagement they seem to be bleeding like hemophiliacs."

"The accounts might be exaggerated," I say.

"Yes. I suppose," he says soberly. "Keep up morale on the home front. Did you sleep all right?"

"Yes. Fine." I reach for some dry toast.

"You're looking awfully pale. I suppose it's that germ you caught. Knocked you right out."

"Yes."

"Look at this," he says, flipping a page. "Our daily average expenditure for the war is 4,820,000 pounds. Can you imagine? Asquith yesterday moved a vote of credit for another three hundred million pounds. Who's going to pay for all this? My Lord. The national debt is now, can you believe this, over two thousand million pounds!"

"I can't imagine it," I say. I reach for a section of the paper – a special on Empire Day, as it turns out. My eye skips down the page.

The general demeanour of our people may have given the impression in the Dominions and in India that we in this country take the rally of the Empire to our aid wholly for granted. No impression could be more misleading . . .

"I suppose, when you're facing the end of civilization, a few *thousand million* pounds is the least of your worries," Manfred says.

I refocus on the article.

We are beginning to see that things Imperial cannot go on as they are. The troops of the Dominions are with ours in many theatres of war. The utter devotion of their peoples to our cause is matched by the spirit which keeps them from criticizing the men in this country who are responsible for the higher command. We feel that they have criticisms to make, but are too great-hearted to say anything about them while there is the least chance of their doing mischief.

Margaret, Emily, and Aunt Harriet come down the stairs. I hear them first, then catch a glimpse of them in the hallway, dressed for out-of-doors. Margaret sees me and glances away quickly. But Harriet hurries towards me. "How are you feeling, dear?" she says. "Your appetite has come back?"

"Yes, thanks," I say, rising. Manfred, still seated, looks at me with some perturbation, then returns to the page.

"Don't get up!" Harriet says. "We are on our way to the church this morning. There was a piece in the paper about our prisoners in Germany. Did you see it? Shocking treatment!" She rummages amidst the pages on the table, then takes Manfred's section from his hand. "Excuse me, dear," she says. Then she reads, "One hundred and fifty British sergeants have been sent from Sennelager to Minden for compulsory work. At Döberlitz a Scotsman became mad and was placed in a barbed-wire enclosure, from which he endeavoured in his frenzy to escape and was shot dead. A Frenchman also went mad and committed suicide by throwing himself on a 'live' electric wire." She gives the paper back to Manfred. "Mr. Tennant said in the House of Commons that if it had not been for the parcels of food sent to the men from this country many of them would have starved."

"So you are going to send them some more food," Manfred says. "Good for you. Will you be back for luncheon?"

"Would you like to come with us, Ramsay?" Harriet asks. "It would give everyone such a thrill to meet a soldier back from the Front."

"Give the poor lad a rest!" Manfred says. "He's just been

deathly ill, now you want to suffocate him with female attention. Let him spend the morning with me reading the newspaper and catching his breath."

"Actually, I think I would like to go," I say. "It wouldn't be too
strenuous, I imagine. And I'd like to get out."

Manfred looks at me like I'm the traitorous Roger Casement.

"Finish your toast, dear," Harriet says. "We can wait."

◈

As we are walking – slowly, to make allowance for my weakened
state, though in truth I am feeling much better – Aunt Harriet
tries to fill me in on the principal players in Lady Templeton's
Foundation: a Mrs. Campbell, who is also involved in the
Belgian Relief Fund, and a Mrs. Wainsmith, whose son is a
lieutenant colonel of some description, and of course Lady
Templeton herself, who is so involved in charity work she is
rarely seen. "And when she does appear she is like a humming-
bird, wings beating a hundred times a second just to stay aloft,"
Harriet says.

Margaret, walking ahead of us with Emily, looks back at that
remark, and I catch her eye briefly, but can't read her expression.

Perhaps it was a mistake to come.

"Will you paint my portrait today?" Emily presses. "You said
that you would."

"Yes, of course I will," I say, a little too sharply.

"I hope you're not going to disappoint me. When do you have
to leave?" she asks.

"My train goes Friday evening."

"That's so soon. You must be getting anxious!"

"It's ages off, actually," I say. "Days away. I try not to think of it."

Lady Templeton's Prisoner Relief Foundation works out of the basement of the church we went to on Sunday. It is a gloomy, dampish room lit by weak electric lights that hum and crackle. There are no Mrs. Campbells, Wainsmiths, or Lady Templetons present when we arrive, just a jumble of tinned and packaged goods, stacks of cardboard, rolls of string, piles of light wooden crates, straw for packing, clumps of knitted things, and chocolate bars and cigarettes, bars of soap, packages of tea and sugar. Aunt Harriet sets me up in my own corner, and I work in silence while the three women exchange chit-chat over their parcels.

It's good to do something with my hands again. After a while Harriet says to me, "You *are* an efficient worker! Your pile is even larger than what the three of us have been able to put together. Isn't that marvellous. Look, girls!"

"Perhaps he should stay here for the duration of the war," Margaret says dryly. "His example could spur on the other charity workers."

"It's a relief, actually, to turn my mind to something," I manage to say. "You know, at home we were taught that if you were going to work —"

"Yes, yes. Quite right," Harriet says quickly. I am uncertain for a moment if, despite her praise, I have somehow blundered by working too silently and too hard. But her attention is turned elsewhere. "Now who is this coming down the stairs?"

It is a Mrs. Ogylvie, who smells of lavender, and who is introduced as the mother of four sons serving the war effort: one is supervising canteen cooks in Scotland, another inspects telephone equipment before it is shipped to the Front, a third writes dispatches for the War Office, and the last is in charge of pay distribution for an entire battalion.

"It is so noble of you to devote your time to others in your off hours," Mrs. Ogylvie says, her gloved hand a damp rag in my fingers, "when you could be enjoying yourself with all that London has to offer!"

"Our dear cousin has not neglected his revelries," Margaret says. "But you're right, Mrs. Ogylvie, it is rather selfless of him to devote himself to a cause this morning."

"You must tell me what the conditions are like," Mrs. Ogylvie says. "Have you seen fierce fighting?"

"Nothing too fierce," I find myself saying, looking over at Margaret.

"And the mud I hear is frightful," Mrs. Ogylvie says. "My Richard was washed in it some time ago when he toured near the Front with General Haig. He said you could hardly hold yourself upright sometimes. But the men were *all* in good spirits!"

"Yes," I say quietly. "Good spirits."

"Such daily heroism," she says. "It is a privilege just to be part of it, isn't it? To be asked by England."

"Indeed it is, Mrs. Ogylvie," Harriet says. "Of course, our Ramsay has come all the way from Canada. His father is my husband's brother. I'm afraid we thought we'd lost George to the Dominions forever, but now three of his sons are fighting for us."

"How marvellous!" Mrs. Ogylvie effuses. I find myself looking away in embarrassment.

"Which is why we *must* get some more work done," Aunt Harriet says, "or I'm afraid we might look back with regret on our own misspent efforts. Except for our Ramsay, of course, who has shown us the way with his industry. Ramsay, why don't you have a rest, and we'll just plod along . . ."

I refuse, of course, and find myself packaging parcels with a stupid intensity, merely to keep up appearances with the ladies. Whenever they look over and exclaim at my progress it just gets worse, until I am steaming like a one-man factory.

Margaret slides beside me finally and says in a quiet voice, "It's all right. You don't have to win the war all by yourself."

"I'm sorry. I apologize," I say.

"Don't *apologize*," she says. "Just relax. Join in the conversation."

"For last night," I say.

"Don't apologize," she says.

◈

Margaret, Emily, and I go to a West End variety show in the afternoon. The air in the theatre is thick with smoke, and right off it's clear that most of the khakied crowd has spilled over from the just-closed pubs. The chairman is an implacable, older gentleman in a white suit with a thick, snowy moustache and pale eyes. He introduces the man on the pianoforte as "the finest musical talent unfit for combat." About himself he says, "I come from a very distinguished family. Perhaps you don't know that. My grandfather was a peer. Yes, yes it's true. Had terrible kidney problems, he did."

The opening act comes on in a pink dress and a huge flowered hat with parasol, an aging, red-haired woman with one eye lower than the other. She sings a Scots medley, including "I Belong to Glasgow" and "Loch Lomond," which gets everyone singing, even Margaret. There is drunken applause, and after she leaves the chairman comments, "That's the cheapest round of Scotch I've found," and the laughter is like an explosion of giddiness.

"My nephew," the chairman says, waving his hand to quieten us down, "my nephew went to sign up the other day." Some of the men applaud again and the chairman nods approvingly, until the whole place is thundering. "Yes, yes, it's true, my nephew went to sign up the other day," the chairman repeats, his voice booming above the din. "He's all of thirteen years old. But when they asked him his age he said he was *sixteen*." The chairman waits for the noise to subside. "He said he was *sixteen*," he repeats. "And the examining officer looked at him very sternly. He said, 'Son, do you know where boys go who tell lies?'

" 'To the Front, sir.' "

The floor jumps with laughter.

The next act is a chimney sweep with soiled face and filthy clothes, and a black brush he twirls and pokes. He sings about pushing his brush up a certain madam's chimney, and wriggling it gently about. "*Try to be slick, but don't go too quick, You may find you can't get it out.*"

The soldiers are all crazy with hilarity. I look over at Margaret and find her grinning gamely.

When the song is over the chairman tells us about his great-uncle, who just got married at the age of ninety. "His bride was a lovely young thing only eighteen years old. It was a fairy-tale wedding, I tell you, absolutely Grimm!" After the laughter he says, "He died on the honeymoon, I'm afraid. He had a stroke . . . and then he had a stroke. It took a week to wipe the smile off his face. Poor man. And a fortnight to get the coffin lid shut."

Screams of laughter. I can't help it, it seems unbearably funny. Emily is blushing badly and Margaret's smile has turned rigid.

"Did they cut off his pecker, then, guv?" someone yells drunkenly from the back.

The chairman retorts, "That side of the family is of *German* extraction, you see, so they hid the offending member with a *pickelhaube!*"

Gales of laughter; men weeping on one another, it seems so funny.

"Do you want to go?" I ask Margaret.

Emily immediately says, "Not on my account!"

So we stay to watch a comic dwarf stage a mock David-and-Goliath battle with a monocled giant in jackboots and *pickelhaube* who stops every few seconds to click his heels, and is outwitted at every turn by an adversary who runs between his legs, takes calculated tea breaks, smashes him on the nose with an umbrella, then runs up his back and rides him around like an enraged donkey. We watch an elderly man in blackface sing and blow bubbles while juggling lit torches, and a handsome officer in uniform serenade a beauty in the park, with bright-green cardboard bushes in the background. Then an elderly man in stripes comes on and plays the banjo at breakneck speed.

"Is there anyone here from out of town?" the chairman asks, after the banjo player has retired. Hundreds of hands shoot up in the smoke. He chooses someone in the gloom and asks, "Where are you from, then, sergeant?"

"I'm from Ottawa," the sergeant says. I crane my neck to see who it might be.

"From Ottawa! Did you know, I only recently learned that Ottawa is *not* a new kitchen appliance. But good for you. I say, good for you for coming to the aid of the Empire! Did you know that today is Empire Day? Is there anybody else here from the Dominions?"

Countless hands, including my own.

"We are so grateful you haven't rebelled yet. I say, is there anyone here from the United States? No? I'm not surprised no one would own up. I did meet an American . . . listen to me, quiet down there or the show will go on forever! That's better. I was saying, I did meet an American. A very solid young fellow, dressed in the uniform of the Black Watch. He'd crossed the ocean to defend freedom, you see. And I asked him, when are your compatriots going to join you? Wasn't the *Lusitania* enough? And he said, '*Lusitania*? I just joined up for the pay.'"

Another gale of laughter, and then we watch a contortionist do unbelievable things on a tightrope, and we sing, with drunken gusto, "Covent Garden in the Morning" and "Tipperary" and "Mademoiselle from Armenteers," with half the audience singing "Ain't been kissed in forty years" and the other half insisting on the cruder version. And then the chairman sings "Dear Old Pals," and soon enough it is over. We are spilling onto the streets in the late afternoon. I feel like it's been an all-day smoker.

"That was awful," Margaret says on the omnibus back to Chelsea.

"It was. It was dreadful. Dreadfully funny," I say.

"It was sick, sad, and pathetic," Margaret says.

"It wasn't that bad," Emily says.

"We are *delusional*," Margaret says. "Can't you see that? When I leave a show like that these days I feel paper-thin, emptied of all purpose and semblance of moral fibre."

"Spare me the moral fibre," Emily says. Then, to me: "How are you on moral fibre?"

"Very thin. Thin at the best of times," I say.

"I believe that," Margaret snaps.

"What are you two on about? Have you been fighting?" Emily asks.

Margaret looks out the window immediately, and I shrug my shoulders, and the bus lurches on.

◈

"How was the show?" Manfred asks at dinner – a stringy roast of beef, but real meat, thank God, with rich gravy and almost enough potatoes to satisfy.

"It was regrettable," Margaret says.

"It got us through the afternoon, at any rate," I chip in. "Most of the crowd seemed to enjoy it."

"It kept them from rioting in the streets, I suppose," Margaret says.

Manfred and Harriet exchange looks. Emily studies her plate with a slight grin on her face.

"How do you feel about women in the war effort, Ramsay?" Manfred asks me suddenly. "Do you think they're making a contribution? Should we be asking even more of them?"

"Father," Margaret says sharply.

"*What?*"

The two lock eyes for a stern moment, and then Margaret says, "You are baiting me."

"I simply asked our young Ramsay what his opinion is. Surely at a civilized dinner we can discuss the great issues of the day."

"You know I have strong opinions about the subjugation of

women in our society. You simply asked Ramsay to take a few steps into barbed wire, so that you could tell us all how letting women out of the parlour is a disaster in the making. How children will be neglected and men will take even more to drink and women will get rough hands and callused minds and poor Ramsay will open and close his mouth like a fish out of water and you will all think it the grandest sort of joke and I will be left –"

She pauses to take a breath.

"There! Even now you're laughing at me," she says, and throws her napkin on the table. But instead of rising she stays still long enough for me to say, "My father does that, too. He knows exactly what to say at the dinner table to fuel a complete row."

"Your father!" Manfred blurts. "I almost completely forgot. Your father telephoned me today. He wants to meet with you first thing tomorrow morning."

"Father is in London?" I feel my face burn with the thought of it.

"Yes. Apparently. We spoke for all of about twelve seconds. He said, 'Manfred, is Ramsay with you?' I said, '*George*, is that you?' He said, 'Tell him to meet me tomorrow at seven-thirty sharp at Elephant and Castle station.' I said, 'Seven-thirty in the morning?' and he said, 'Of course!' and he hung up."

"But what's he doing in London?"

"I haven't the faintest idea. But it was George all right."

Harriet says, "Perhaps you should go with Ramsay in the morning to see your brother."

"He won't have a word for me," Manfred says. "He obviously wants to talk to his son."

"I thought perhaps you could show your nephew the way to Elephant and Castle, dear," Harriet says.

"Oh, that," Manfred says. "You could find Elephant and Castle, couldn't you, Ramsay? It's just a matter of taking the Tube."

"If someone points the way," I say.

"But how did he know you were here, Ramsay?" Harriet asks. "Did you write to him? He surely wouldn't have had time to receive correspondence – not if he's been travelling himself."

"My father works in mysterious ways," I say, shaking my head. "I did get a strange letter from him the day my leave came through. He said that I should look you up if I got a chance to go to London. It was quite the coincidence."

"I should like to meet him," Margaret says suddenly. "Would you mind terribly if I went with you? I could show you the route. Elephant and Castle is across the river. We'd have to change lines."

"That would be delightful," I say. "I'm sure my father would enjoy meeting you."

"Settled, then," Margaret says, and as I turn back to my plate I catch a fleeting look of annoyance on Emily's face.

"I *will* do your portrait," I say to her. "When I get back."

◈

I sleep fitfully, thinking of Father, of what he could possibly be doing here, and what he wants of me. I doze and start awake and doze again and turn on the light every half-hour or so through-out the night to make certain I don't oversleep. I think of him in the landing of the Brown House, looking over the array of kit and luggage I had assembled. I came thundering down, my mind split a thousand different ways, and he raised his head and fixed me with his eye, the saddest look I had ever seen.

"How could you do this to your mother?" he asked quietly.

I stopped before reaching the bottom step, tried to think what I could possibly say. Will and Thomas had left months ago. At any rate, it all seemed unreal. They were still in training, their letters full of a sense of hopelessness of ever getting into the thick of it.

"Never mind," Father said dismissively. "'Twas ever thus. I did it to my own mother." Then he turned his back and stepped over my gear, walked away as he always does.

I stare at the darkness, finally get up in gloom, am downstairs shaved, cleaned, in uniform, and scraping up my own toast and tea even before the help has arisen.

Father! Just the thought of him here has me in a state.

The news of the day is not good. An editorial makes fun of Falkenhayn for butting heads against the Verdun wall for three months, but I don't have to read too much further to see that Douaumont has fallen to the Germans, and that fighting has reached "a fury for which even the Battle of Verdun itself has no precedent."

The Honour Roll lists 247 recent Canadian losses. I check through the fine print closely, and there they are: Reese, 166699, J., and Jackwell, 116101, P. Privates both, so rank is not listed. Reese and Snug, officially counted now among the glorious dead. I look for Ferguson and Gryphon but don't see them listed. Then my tea spills, soaking the paper and the table. I rise cursing, retreat to the kitchen to find a cloth. When I get back to the table Miffy is on the scene. She takes the cloth from me and rescues what she can of the newspaper.

"I'm sorry," I say, my hands still shaking.

I think about stepping out right away. It will be an hour at least before Margaret is ready. I could just leave word that I've gone on my own . . .

"There, sit back down again, sir, right as anything!" Miffy says. "Did you want heggs this mornings?"

"Heggs?"

"Yes. Heggs! Bought just yesterday!"

I sit down again, have the "heggs," which are wonderful, and try to calm myself. Reese would go with Margaret, I think. He would say, "Two more days in London with a beautiful, intelligent woman? Paradise!"

Margaret comes down much earlier than I expected. She looks lovely and fresh in a simple dark dress. "You're up early," she says, then gazes at the sodden newspaper. "Is it raining?"

"It's raining tea, I'm afraid," I say.

"Father won't be happy," she says. "He lives for his newspaper. Perhaps we should leave a little early and avoid the storm."

We are out the door at six-thirty. It isn't raining, but the glorious sun of the last few days is not in evidence now. It's cool and gloomy, and for the first time I feel the weight of the city air, which seems heavy with smoke and fog. I light a cigarette and that clears things a bit. But almost immediately, Margaret says, "Would you mind?"

"Of course not," I say and throw the cigarette away.

"No. I meant could I have one, too?" she asks.

I halt on the sidewalk and look at her.

"What? You smoke?"

"I do sometimes. I'm sorry. I shouldn't on the street, I know, but no one's about, and there's no other place for me. Are you shocked?"

"I just . . . I never imagined," I say, and light up again quickly, one for her and another for me. "I suppose two on a match is all right," I say.

She takes a deep lungful and we continue.

"You are full of surprises," I say.

We walk several blocks, then Margaret shepherds me into the Tube station – South Kensington – and we purchase our tickets, then pass the wicket, walk down the stairs and onto the main platform, which is already pressed with people. "I don't know what the city would do without the Underground," Margaret says. "People would take all day to get to work, and by the time they got there they'd have to turn around again. It's made quite a difference getting the horses off the streets. I remember when I was little, even, the filth of it. Here, now, wait for the people to clear the doors."

She seems to think I've never been on a train before. But it's just that, a train in a tunnel, not so much a novelty after all.

"The Tube is very democratizing," Margaret says to me quietly, as we chug and rock between stations. "You can literally rub shoulders with all classes. Although of course the very wealthy tend to have their own vehicles or take cabs. But the streets are so slow. And the Underground is a perfect shelter for a Zeppelin raid."

"Have you been in one? During a raid, I mean," I say.

"No. But some of my friends have. One poor woman went quite mad for a time. She was screaming and howling, apparently, just couldn't calm down. But most people take it well,

considering there are enemy craft overhead, and the bombs
are getting nastier with every raid. Does one get used to it, I
wonder? Bombardments?"

"Only somewhat," I say, thinking of the crowd of us in the
dugout, with men crying and shitting themselves, the whole
world turned to thunder and wrecked nerves.

We change trains at Charing Cross, then take a moving staircase – now here is a novelty, I think – and then a lift down into
the bowels of the earth. We board another train on the Baker
Street and Waterloo Railway – Bakerloo, it's called. As we hurtle,
apparently, underneath the Thames River, Margaret says, "I
have something to ask you."

"Yes?"

"I wonder if you wouldn't mind lunching with me this
afternoon."

"Why should I mind?"

"I have made plans to meet with Henry – with Mr. Boulton –
during his luncheon break, and I'm hoping that you might . . .
have a word with him."

She does not look me in the eye as she makes her request,
and I realize that her coming with me this morning has all
been a ruse to enable her to keep her appointment with her
young man.

"A word?"

"He seems . . . he seems resigned to . . . to joining up and going
to the Front. He's even talking about not taking a commission.
He thinks what *you've* done, settling as a private, is an extraordinarily brave and honest thing. And it is, I know it is," she
says hastily. "But we have talked of this before, and now you've

met Henry. You know he isn't soldier material. But I think he needs to hear that from someone like you. He looks up to you tremendously, with all your experience . . ."

"He might well make a good soldier. Certainly a better soldier than an officer," I say, somewhat bitterly. "An officer should know what warfare's about, have a sense of the trenches and the men, a grasp of strategy and logistics and a thousand other things. A soldier follows orders, and there is training – he wouldn't be sent right away."

She sets her jaw in her formidable way, exhales once loudly, as if I have elbowed her in the stomach.

"You do love him," I say, and look down at my boots.

"Whatever my feelings for Mr. Boulton, I cannot imagine him contributing one iota to an Allied victory in the mud. His nerves would collapse miles away from the shooting. You don't want him anywhere near a weapon. But he is at the point of just giving up his clerkship and doing whatever the powers tell him to do. The powers will not even realize what has been lost. But I will. I will know all too well."

We ride along under the river, although I can't see anything. I have to take her word for it.

"I'll talk with him," I say.

◆

At Elephant and Castle we are on lifts again, and moving staircases bring us back to the surface. For just a moment I get a hallucinatory sense of the city having given itself over completely to some great growing machine, of the crowds of tiny workers entering and serving the machine, feeding it with fuel and money, with themselves, rushing to work in their bowler hats, clutching umbrellas, faces grey, eyes down, taking care not to be crushed in the path of the huge pistons, the trains, ships, buses, buildings of the machine. Our quiet queues, unquestioning acceptance of orders – we are all at war, it seems to me. The workers here or the bleeders over there.

Although Margaret and I are early, Father is waiting already. He does not stand out in the crowd, seems smaller even than I remember: a wizened man in a dark suit. But his eyes are their usual black blaze. They latch on to me from a hundred feet away and do not let me go.

His hand is as strong and sure as ever, though he is greyer, leaner than he has been. It's unbelievable to see him here, to be here myself. Father! My heart pounds as it always does, the rare times he appears.

"Father, I would like you to meet Uncle Manfred's daughter Margaret. Margaret, this is your Uncle George."

"I am so pleased to meet you, sir," Margaret says. "I have heard so much about you."

Father eyes her strangely, as if she were an apparition he can't quite believe. Finally, looking at me, he says, "I haven't much time. Can we talk in private?"

"Yes, please excuse me," Margaret says. "I'll take a walk in the neighbourhood."

"You shouldn't be out on your own!" I say.

"It's quite all right, Ramsay," she says. "This is London, and times are changing. So nice to meet you, Uncle George," she says.

Father does not return her gaze and she leaves us uncertainly, half frowning. For a moment I mean to abandon Father and go with her.

"That was bloody rude of you," I say instead.

The commuting crowd swirls around us as we stand in the middle of the station. Father says, "I can see the army has taught you how to swear, and to disrespect your elders. Can you unlearn these things, I wonder?"

"Margaret is your niece, whom you've never met!"

"She's your cousin. She's just the reason why I left in the first place." And when he sees that I don't understand, he says, "All right, you care for her, that's obvious. But there's nothing here for the likes of us. It's too crowded with eldest sons sitting on their wealth. So we will have to make do with the rest of the world."

"You asked me to stay with them!" I say in exasperation. "And Margaret kindly offered to guide me here so I wouldn't be late."

Father glances at his pocket watch, then looks me up and down. "Don't they feed you any better in the army?" he says. "At any rate, you still have your limbs, and most of your faculties, apparently. I wanted to tell you that I am working on your transfer. They need mechanics for the aeroplanes here in England, and I'm arranging for you to take the course. But there have been some delays. So for God's sake keep your head down in the next few weeks and you may yet get through this alive."

I feel myself blanch with the shock of his words. But I manage to say, "How can you possibly arrange these things? Did you see to my leave as well? You're not even in the military!"

"But I know some of the men who are pulling the levers," he says. "Do you understand what I've just told you?"

"I will not accept a transfer," I say. "I will not accept your meddling. It was my decision to fight in the first place and I mean to see it through. What kind of man would allow his father to –?"

"Don't talk to me about being a man!" he explodes. Crowds now are rushing by us, but we are alone in this private struggle. "You are a stripling boy and you have no idea of the forces you are dealing with!"

"I have a damn sight better idea than you have. Where do you think I've been the last months? Lying on the beach? I've seen friends twisted to hell and I will not shirk away at the first underhanded, corrupt manoeuvring out of my sworn –"

His face is red, his fists doubled, as if ready to strike me.

"– duty," I say, the wind fleeing my sail.

"You listen to me," Father says. "You know *nothing*. A shilling, threepence a shell. That's the royalty British firms are paying German Krupp on fuses. A million marks of Krupp money has been invested in British stocks of munitions firms." When he sees my blank look, he says, "Do you know about General Alderson? Have you kept any of your wits about you? Alderson is being removed from the Canadian command so that Sam Hughes's cronies and relatives can continue to supply you with hopeless weapons. That's the tip of the iceberg, believe me. *Thousands of millions* are being spent, not to stop this war but to prolong it. You know the men who are fighting, and they are poor sods, and may be your friends, but I know the men perpetuating this disgrace. They can waste their own sons if they want, but I will not let them waste mine."

"It's not that simple," I say.

"Don't give me any backchat. If other men want to send their sons off to slaughter for dubious reasons, then so be it, but you and I do not have to be part of the generalized insanity." He pauses, as if bringing on new ammunition. "I know what it's like," he says slowly, with terrible intensity, "to be a young man. You think the right direction has got to be whatever your father tells you *not* to do. Well, use your brain. Think it through. Be your own man for once."

He looks at his watch again. "Write to your mother," he says. "And keep your head down. Or by God you will be heartbreaking fertilizer."

His eyes are as darkly blazing as I've ever seen and I have to tell myself for a moment, *This is Father showing concern.*

At that he strides away, disappears into the bowels of the station.

◈

"What's happened?" Margaret asks sometime later. I am sitting on a bench outside the station, looking at my hands. "You've gone white," she says.

She puts her cool fingers on my cheek for no reason at all, as far as I can see.

"My father has a way about him."

"Well, he's every bit the charmer I'd been led to expect," she says, and sits beside me. Noisy, filthy traffic passes by just feet away, and the workaday crowds now are substantial, many of the commuters young women, indeed, walking on their own. "What did he say to you?" she asks.

"He told me to write to my mother."

"Is that all?"

I sit very still, my mind in disorder.

"What else did he say?" Margaret asks.

"Nothing. Nothing at all."

◈

We have the morning ahead of us, and I have no heart to descend back into the Underground. So we enter the curving, confusing tunnel system for pedestrians to cross the road at this enormously busy traffic hub, and finally emerge on the surface again to stroll together down a long avenue, while Margaret pumps me for information about my father. For the most part I have to tell her that I don't know – what he is doing here, what projects he might be working on, what news there is of my brothers, my mother. "We're an odd family," I say at one point, as if that might explain it.

"How on earth does your mother cope with such an exasperating man?"

"He is not there to exasperate her all that often," I say. And then, because that has left the wrong impression, I say, "He loves her in a way that I can barely comprehend."

"I'm sure it's very difficult to comprehend anything he does," Margaret says.

"He wrote her a poem," I say. "Years ago. And he made all of us boys memorize it. He said, 'Learn this poem, and you might have the beginnings of an understanding of what it is to love a woman.'"

"Your father said that?"

"Yes."

"Well, then, let's hear it," Margaret says.

So I recite:

Espérance qui m'accompagne
A travers bois, pré et montagne
Depuis qu'ensemble nous allons
Ai-je jamais trouvé le chemin long?

A travers bois, pré et montagne
A ton côté pressant le pas
Espérance qui m'accompagne
Marchons toujours n'arrivons pas.

"You have a lovely accent," Margaret says. "Do you speak French?"

"Just those words. Drilled into me," I say.

And we walk in mind-churning silence, come across a small garden near the river and linger there. Father is overreacting, I think. Independence is everything for him. That's the real reason he left home so early – he couldn't wait to get away, to make his own mark. And he wants his sons to be free men as well, just as long as they follow his example and obey his every command.

On the bridge across the river we pause to look through gathering mist at the ships, the lighters, at the spired Houses of Parliament, at what Margaret tells me is Lambeth Palace on the side we have just left.

I look at her gentle, knowing, beautiful face, feel suddenly overwhelmed with tenderness towards her. And she is looking at me as if . . . as if she will expire if I do not hold her immediately. Then we are kissing. I can't say who started it. But there are hoots from passersby, and some man says, "On, Jack, at it!" and I don't care, I crush her towards me until I can't breathe.

We separate finally, and she looks at me, wild now, lost, near tears. "That *mustn't* happen again," she says finally, and hurries on ahead of me.

◈

We meet Boulton on the street in front of his office building, the Hotel Metropole. He spills out with the cascade of other workers, elderly men, many of them, and short-skirted young women by the dozen. He is carrying red and white carnations for Margaret. When he sees me his disappointment is evident, but only for a moment.

"I could not pass by these this morning when I walked through Covent Garden," he says. Margaret, resolutely avoiding my gaze, beams up at him and brings the flowers close for smelling.

"I'm afraid they won't last until I get them home," she says.

"Well, then, let them die," Boulton says theatrically. "We are in an age of wasted youth." Then he turns to me and says, "Hello, old man. How has London been treating you? I'm insanely jealous that you get to spend so much time with Margaret."

"Henry!" Margaret says.

"What?" he says, again in a theatrical, almost mocking way. "We are in a time of war. Passions are worn on the sleeve!"

The two exchange glances – some sort of question and response passes between them – and then we are walking to a luncheon restaurant packed with noontime workers. It is so crowded we have to stand squashed at the door for a time, waiting to get in.

"Are there no other places to eat?" Margaret asks.

"There are, but most days for one shilling here you can get roast lamb, potatoes, chocolate mould and cream. It's worth the queue."

Margaret asks him how his work is going and he says, "Incessant insanity. I always have two or three people waiting for me. Telephones are constantly clanging. Kingsley and Webster are either not talking or are at one another's throats. And to top it all off, we can no longer get a decent cup of tea. We used to have a male messenger who could carry up a tray of five teas at a time, but now we have these female replacements who only serve tea to the bosses."

"The hardships of war," I say.

"Yes, yes, I know," he says with some irritation. "I have absolutely nothing to complain about. But it doesn't stop me, does it?"

We eventually make our way to a small corner table hardly big enough to support Margaret's carnations, which stick out for their extravagance amidst the drab clothing of most of the diners. She eventually places them under the table to make room. The meal is served very quickly – steak and kidney pie today, low on the steak, but delicious nonetheless. The din of other conversations cloaks the awkwardness of the situation. At last, Margaret says to Boulton, "What has happened with the desperate Canadian woman in your boarding house? Was there more news of her son?"

"Oh, yes," Boulton says. "She's in France now, I imagine. Left the other day. The second telegram said her boy was making progress, and she immediately set about visiting him in hospital. I don't think a battery of howitzers could stop her from going to his bedside."

We chew on that for a while, and I watch the two of them, think what an old married couple they will make. She will pour herself into the frustrating work of furthering his career, until finally, with relief, the children will come along and distract her.

Or perhaps I am being unfair. But I can't see starlight here.

Margaret excuses herself from the table, gives me a knowing look, and heads off, I suppose to find a ladies' room. We stand awkwardly in the crowded space, sit again once she has moved away. It is my cue, and so I ask Boulton about registration.

"It will be a relief," he says quickly. "I am sick and tired of having the whole world think I'm doing nothing for the war effort. Every time I look at your uniform I am green with envy. I'd trade with you in a minute."

I look at him, a touch of gravy on his twitchy moustache.

"I know. I know," he says. "Margaret has probably brought you here to talk some sense into me. She did, didn't she?" I look as noncommittal as I can, yet he immediately says, "I knew it. She is a brick. I love every idea in her silly little head. But really, she ought to know what an agony it is for me. I can't stand it any more, the disrespect, the implied cowardice in my lack of uniform. And with what's coming up, the war will probably end before I can even get in it."

"What's that?" I ask.

"Nothing," he says quickly, then looks dartingly at the nearby tables, and lowers his voice. "The French need relief at Verdun," he says. "The situation is quite desperate. Rumours of revolt, and packing it in. We all know the French."

"So our forces are coming to their aid?"

"By attacking elsewhere, apparently. Nothing is official, of course. But probably at the Somme. There's an extraordinary effort to mass munitions as they've never been massed before. We're going to bomb the Germans into oblivion. But tell no one this. My career would be in ruins if it got out. It's still somewhat uncertain anyway."

He stares nervously at his plate. I glance over to see if Margaret is returning, but she is giving us plenty of time for our conversation.

"Whatever is coming up," I say carefully, "you mustn't lose sight of the fact that your talents are probably best employed elsewhere, not on the battlefield. Don't be too quick to join. There are lots of us who have nothing better to do with our lives. And Margaret loves you. The war will be over someday and people will forget who fought and who didn't."

"You're about the worst liar I've ever come across," he says, only partly smiling. "It's all right for you, you'll either be part of the great victory or you'll die a hero."

And you're about the worst fool I've ever met, I almost say.

"I wonder," I say, trying to sound nonchalant. "Have you heard anything about a royalty being paid on Krupp fuses? Somebody mentioned to me a figure, what was it? A shilling, threepence a shell. Which adds up, I suppose, when shells are being fired off by the –"

"Yes, yes," he says dismissively. "There's been talk of that type of thing. Some sort of theoretical debt, at least, is accumulating. And I've no doubt huge fortunes are being amassed by a number of the wrong sorts. It's inevitable, I suppose, in any large war. Still, it gives one pause when it comes to offering one's life."

Margaret is heading back now, so I say nothing about Alderson and the damned Ross rifle. I try to avoid her questioning gaze. As we seat her she says, "This restaurant might have a cheap hot meal, but they are going to have to learn to accommodate women. The facilities are frightful. I shall say no more." She smooths her napkin on her lap, takes a small bite of her food, and says, "What have you boys been talking about?"

"The progress of the war," Boulton says. "What else can one talk about?"

The chocolate mould is fine for dessert, and then Boulton must hurry back to his files, his pressing issues, his clanging telephones. I pay for the three of us – I expect a wrestling match, but Boulton gives no struggle whatsoever, as if, as a soldier, I am wealthy beyond imagining and so of course would pick up the tab. As we head to the door, and before we say our goodbyes, Margaret slips a letter into his pocket. It is done without an exchange of glances, and I only happen to catch it out of the corner of my eye.

"You're off soon, I imagine?" Boulton says to me – somewhat hopefully, it seems.

"Tomorrow evening."

"I get so depressed seeing people off," he says. "I don't know how any of us can stand it. When my turn comes," he says to Margaret, with an effort at lightheartedness, "don't bother seeing me off at the station."

"I might be too busy, anyway," she says.

"Do you see that?" he says to me. "Your cousin cuts me to the quick. She is the personification of cruel womanhood! I suppose you two are going to go saunter about the park now?"

I look at Margaret, standing with her carnations. She says, "I'm afraid I have to get back. But maybe Ramsay will want to saunter for a while."

"Right then," Boulton says, and grasps my hand suddenly.

"Bayonet a few Germans for me, will you, old boy?" Margaret looks at him oddly, and he leaves without saying his goodbyes to her.

We begin walking, I'm not sure where.

"What did he say?" she presses. "You told him not to be such a fool."

"Not in those words, exactly."

"Well?" She stops and looks in my face with the most naked of expressions.

"He said that he envies me. Which just goes to prove what an idiot he is."

◈

Margaret says several times that she must return, reminds me also that I promised to paint Emily's portrait. But we end up walking in St. James's Park instead, where military buildings have been erected on dried lake bed, an effort to mask the city from the Zeppelins, apparently.

"The war is swallowing everything," Margaret says to me. "It's like a great omnivorous beast from which nothing is safe. It affects what we eat, what we talk about, what we work at, what we dream at night, our first thoughts in the morning. I'm sick of it. *Sick of it!*" she cries.

Large numbers of off-duty soldiers are lounging on the grass looking like indolent sheep – trainees, obviously, innocent of the Front. They turn at Margaret's outburst, watch her expressive face, probably think the carnations are from me, that we are lovers somehow coming off the rails.

"We'll win it," I say quietly. "We're going to win it soon."

"People have been saying that for nearly two years!" she says.

"We're coming to a big push, I think."

"What we've seen to date has not been a big push?"

"For the Germans it has. But they haven't yet felt the kind of attack that we can mount. There's real reason to hope. I think maybe by Christmas . . ."

"*No more!*" she says. "I don't want to hear another word about the war this afternoon. Can we manage that? Even if it means utter silence?"

And so silence it is. We leg it through the various green places – fine stretches of parkland, most littered with soldiers with nothing to do – the flower beds looking somewhat neglected, some turned to vegetable patches, and too many trees (if Boulton were here he would lecture us on the many, many trees; but at least it would not be war talk). I can't for the life of me think of what to say, and Margaret is lost in her own troubled thoughts. At any thick spot in the shrubbery I long to pull her aside and kiss – just kiss, for ages, for the entire afternoon. No need for words at all.

Yet I cannot summon the strength, or find the moment, or the one or two short words to make it happen.

We walk as if on route march, doggedly on, burdened beyond reason, not sure where we're going or why, but simply going, each step a lesson in tired misery . . . but nothing that cannot be endured. I keep thinking: tomorrow night I will return to the nightmare. This is my last full day in London, and I am with a beautiful woman I could easily love, I might already love. Why not be in love? Why not make the most of this peaceful gloom, and put off till tomorrow the debts that are not due today?

But we walk and walk, and for fear of losing even this strained time together, I do not say a word.

◈

"Uh, your father, Uncle Manfred," I say somewhat awkwardly. We are seated on a bench now near a fine stand of trees – planes, I suppose – out of the sun but within reach of a pleasant breeze.

"Yes?" Margaret says, grateful, I think, finally, for some stab at conversation.

"I'm afraid I'm not really sure what he does."

"You mean for a living?"

"Yes."

"He doesn't do anything," she says, with a hint of derision in her voice – I'm not sure if it's for him or me. "There's family money, of course. Not a great deal, but enough, I'm told. He manages that, but doesn't spend much time at it. 'Let well enough alone' is one of his great mottos. And the rest of us live off him."

"Family money," I say, and wonder for a moment at the strangeness of it. "I suppose that's what gave my father his push out the door. Not being the eldest son, and all."

"He's a lucky man, to have done such extraordinary things," she says. "You can tell that my father usually doesn't have enough to do. A part of him is absolutely dying to sign up for this wretched war. Of course, at the first sign of unpleasantness –" She shifts in her thoughts. "What does a soldier think about in the worst of it?"

"I thought we weren't going to talk about the war?" I say.

"And that hasn't turned out to be terribly successful, has it?"

I am quietly stung with her rebuke, can't help thinking of Boulton and his endless facts and novelties. What wouldn't I give now for a fraction of his gift for polite conversation?

"In the worst of it," I say, "you're hoping against hope you won't panic too badly."

"Yes. What else?"

I smile grimly and look away. "It isn't . . . something that one can simply chat about."

"You mean to a woman?" she presses. "If I were a man, some-body you trusted –"

I find myself nodding, if only to be agreeable.

"Then don't think of me as a woman. Think of me as that lieutenant friend of yours we met in Trafalgar on Saturday. I haven't been in battle yet but I'm going to be, and now I'm asking: what is it like, the worst of it? What goes through one's head? How does the body react?"

I gaze at my hands for a time, find myself breathing harder than I should be, just sitting here. She is bearing down, and finally I force myself to look at her.

"I somehow can't think of you as Bill Kelsie," I say.

"Ramsay!" she pleads. "How else am I to know – or any of us, for that matter – what we're asking you men to do?"

I squirm on the bench. "I'm not sure I can explain it."

"Of course you can!"

"It's like nothing, really – I mean nothing can prepare you for it. Certainly not our training. When shells are falling one on top of the other, and it's so loud your brain is scrambled, and the boundaries between bodies – I mean, you see things you never would, and that you'll never, ever forget."

I'm blathering, and she's listening as if it were some speech

from an important pulpit. I look around for any means of
rescue. "I wonder . . . I wonder what sort of trees those are?" I
say, pointing.

"*Trees?*" she says incredulously.

"It's a fine thing to be able to talk about trees," I say quietly,
then slip back into painful silence, which she allows for a time.

"What do you think of Germans?" she asks, switching
directions.

"Of Germans?"

"Yes! Our mortal enemies! Have you met any?"

"I've seen their work," I say coldly.

"Yes, I suppose you have," she allows. She is thoughtful for
a moment, then she says, "I remember we went on a trip to
Germany when I was very little, and I loved every last bit of it.
The people were so kind, especially to me. Wherever we stayed
they brought me treats, wonderful sweetmeats and candies, and
there was one man – I forget where – he insisted that I ride his
horse. It was more of a pony, really. I remember him helping me
up, and calling back to his wife in German, and the whole family
came out. They invited us in for a meal."

"I have seen their work," I say again grimly. That puts a stop
to her reminiscences, and I feel badly. I should have let her talk
on. "Of course a lot of Germans can't help the leaders they've
been stuck with," I say.

"And some of our leaders are no great wonders either," she
replies. A smile at last, and something we can agree on. I fill her
ear about the disgraceful Ross rifle, and then the peculiar shovel
we were forced to train with. "Our minister, Sam Hughes,
dreamed it up, and patented it in his secretary's name, then had
his father produce it," I say. "It was supposed to be a shield and

a trenching tool at the same time, but it wasn't big enough for a shield, and the metal didn't stop bullets, and it had a hole in it as well, so it was awful as a shovel. That's the kind of equipment they're foisting on us all the time. And men are dying in the thousands because of these mistakes!"

"Surely it's time to put a stop to it," she says.

"Exactly! We need the right equipment, proper leadership, a decent chance to do the job right!"

Her eyes narrow. "That's not quite what I meant," she says.

"Oh," I say. "You want to sue for peace? Beg the Kaiser for terms that will allow him to get away with everything he's been up to because he knows we haven't the stomach for a real –"

"What did your father want to say to you?" she asks suddenly, cutting me off.

"Nothing important," I say.

"He came all the way to London in wartime to tell you nothing important?"

I stare again at the damn trees, then stand suddenly.

"We aren't going to agree on certain things," I say. Then, as an afterthought, I add, "My father and I."

"What things?"

I look at my watch. "Perhaps I need to get you back."

"Ramsay, what things?" she says. She stands, takes hold of my hand and pulls me so that I must look at her. I stay in her gaze too long, feel myself crumbling.

"Why do you want to be Bill Kelsie?" I ask her.

"Don't avoid the question!"

"You do," I say, "you want to be, or at least be like, a man. Why? What is it you would do that is barred to you now? I don't think you want to go and fight, which is what you would have to do, certainly, if you weren't protected by your sex. Why are you yearning to look into things that are not your burden?"

"Because it is my burden. It's inescapable, it's everybody's burden," she says. "And because I want to understand. Is it such a horrible thing for a woman to want?"

It is horrible, to stand here so close, and feel such burning and ache, and yet not have the slightest inkling of how to proceed. She looks at me again as she did on the bridge, as if she wants me to gather her in my arms and drink deeply of whatever it is she is offering.

Instead, we march rapidly, in mounting silence, out of the park. How I want to stop and kiss her again for as long as it takes to stop time completely, force the present moment to outlast whatever is to come. But I have no words to make it happen, no courage to try.

◈

At the stop we continue to stew painfully, then climb aboard the omnibus almost as strangers. Margaret takes a seat by the window and looks out with resolved indifference, Henry's carnations protectively taking the space beside her. I'm of half a mind simply to head up the stairs to the second level. Then I notice the conductress on the steps – it's Miss Laughton, the same girl who was so friendly to me the morning I arrived in London. I look away quickly, in fear that she might recognize me and call something out loud, which would surely broil my entrails forever as far as Margaret's good graces were concerned.

I take the seat next to Margaret, and we ride in a tense silence for several minutes. Finally, and extraordinarily, I see a familiar figure walking by himself on the King's Road. "Hey, Johnson!" I yell out the window, and his head jerks round comically. The bus rolls to a halt shortly after and I make a quick decision, leave Margaret looking surprised and abandoned. "It's Johnson," I say. "From my platoon. I'll see you later!"

As I hurry by her, Miss Laughton looks me full in the face without the slightest hint of recognition.

Then I am out the doors and on solid ground, and the air, dirty as it is, fills my lungs, as if it is the first time I've really been able to breathe all afternoon.

"It *is* you!" I say.

Johnson nearly breaks into a run when he sees me. "Crome! You bleeding bugger! Fancy meeting you here!"

We clasp hands and speak at fifty miles an hour.

"Reese pegged out," he says. "In the hospital."

"Yes," I say, "I saw the notice in the paper."

"In the paper?"

"In *The Times*."

"The bloody *Times*," he says, shaking his head at the wonder of it. "Williams pegged out too," he says.

"Not Williams!"

"The tiniest little buggering piece of shrapnel you can imagine. Lodged in his throat. We thought he was choking on his rations. Hardly looked like more than a rat bite."

I am so happy to see him. Johnson cleaned up, washed, shaved, standing here in London. He appears almost human, his face a bit jowly, most of the haunted look chased from the eyes. I ask how long he has been here and he says he just arrived last night and is staying in soldiers' lodgings near the station. He asks and I tell him when I'm leaving.

"Well, we'd better get drinking!" he says.

So I pull him across the street and we catch another bus on the fly, and like the old London hand I have become I point out the sights as we pass them. "That's Sloane Square," I say. "Named after the man whose collection started the British Museum."

"You don't say," Johnson says. Then, after a pause, he says, "The British what?" and it seems like the funniest thing, we laugh like we're already drunk.

We get off near the theatres but follow some of the others to Soho to a proper British pub packed with servicemen, with shavings on the floor, dark wood panelling, smoke to the ceiling, the smell of sweat and the rumble of conversation. I tell him about the no-treating law, and we swear to not let it hold us back. I ask about the new sergeant, since Williams is gone, and he tells me it's a decent guy named Shipley. "His leg went napoo a few months ago. But now he's all better, and assigned to us." Then Johnson says – nearly yelling, because of the din – "Where is bloody Perley Street? Any idea?"

"What's on Perley Street?" I ask.

"Cynthia Elaine Whyte. She's this girl Reese was engaged to. I saw him in hospital just before he went. He asked me to bring her this letter." He pats his breast pocket. "On bloody Perley Street, wherever that is."

"I don't think they were engaged," I say. "He told me he'd never met her. They just corresponded."

"Maybe they got engaged through the mail," Johnson says. "What do I know? I just have to find Perley Street."

It turns out to be a more difficult assignment than might be expected for two crack soldiers like ourselves. The several pints of beer do not help, particularly, although it is all strictly legal since we buy our own. We ask a number of times where the hell we might find Perley Street, but as just about everyone we ask is a soldier from out of town, the results are deemed un-bloody-satisfactory.

"Have you had any skirt since you've been here?" Johnson asks. We are standing on the street now, wrestling with a map he has bought from a little tourist shop.

"Me?"

"I think this Cynthia Elaine Whyte is a nice piece of tart. Reese described her to me. He told me to take her to Hyde Park in the evening."

The streets are a tiny web of spider lines, the writing of the street names too delicate to focus on. Every few seconds a whoosh of wind rattles the map like a sail and Johnson loses his place.

"She'll probably be overcome with grief," Johnson says, bright-eyed. "She'll need emotional support." So I start telling him the joke about the machine-gunners and the in-and-out, only it's so funny I start laughing when I get the guy to the lady's back gate, and then can hardly go on.

"There it is! Shit, I saw it! Perley Street!" Johnson screams.

We hail a cab, being wealthy, futureless buggers, and the drive takes forever. I try to finish my story but I barely get my machine-gunner in the door before I'm a laughing ruin again. The driver keeps looking back over his shoulder to see if I'm all right. But I'm having a hard time breathing, my eyes are running tears, and Johnson is a wreck just watching me.

"'So where . . . where's this gun that needs cleaning?'" I say finally, and for once we both *stop* laughing, until that too is painfully funny.

I pay the driver a full pound, don't wait for change, and we

get out in a neighbourhood quite rundown compared to
Stokebridge Street. But the houses look strangely similar, though
made of older brick, more worn around the edges.

Johnson takes the letter out of his pocket and squints to read
the address. "Seventeen," he says finally. "Old Reese wasn't
writing too good. Seventeen Perley."

I put my hand on the latch of the wrought-iron gate and say,
"Pearly gates," which is shatteringly hilarious. Johnson staggers
on the sidewalk and holds himself, as if to keep his centre from
exploding. I maintain my feet but only by grasping the gate and
propping myself up.

"Pearly . . . pearly," Johnson blubbers.

Some kid stops to look at us, then runs off.

"P-p-p-pearly Gates," Johnson says.

We lean against one another to make it up the walkway.

"Get control of yourself, soldier," I grumble, but sputter on
the last word. Tears flood down. I look away, concentrate on
breathing in and out.

"In-and-out," I say, and we explode again, fall into one
another against the doorway.

"Look. _Look._" Johnson isn't looking at me at all, but at his
bootcaps. "_Straighten up,_" he commands.

He seizes the knocker and raps several times. Then he stands
back, squares his shoulders, and whispers, "Do I ever have to
take a piss."

"Hold on to it, Private," I snarl. "Suck it up."

Nobody comes to the door.

I grab the knocker and rap louder.

"I can't bloody well hold it," Johnson says. "It's all this
laughing."

"I think it's the *beer*, myself," I say.

Nobody comes to the door. "Just put the letter through the slot," I say.

"I wanted to *see* her," Johnson says. "How the hell am I going to get a skirt in London?"

"Like everybody else," I say. "You're going to have to pay for it."

I rap again but it's no use, the house sounds empty as a tomb. I turn to leave and there's Johnson with his fly open, watering the shrubs on the side of the walkway.

"Jesus, Johnson!" I say.

"In a second," he says.

But he isn't done in a second. He isn't done in a minute. The amazing Johnson keeps up a prodigious arc that threatens to flood the little front garden.

"Come on!" I say.

"In a *minute!*"

Soon I can't stand it, and I join him. My arc is nothing compared to his, but I cross streams with him anyway. Then we are fighting, sprinkling one another's boots, and the door opens.

"What are you doing?" comes a female voice.

Johnson, stream only now beginning to slacken, turns to her, a full-frontal idiot. She screams and slams the door, just misses getting sprayed – a mousetrap of a woman with a sharp overbite, a skinny face.

We are arranging our kit, running towards the gate, when Johnson suddenly remembers the letter. He scampers back as if under fire, thrusts it through the door, then we're sprinting down the lane, some dog barking at our backs but not chasing.

◈

Nighttime now, and we are standing, sober, more or less, in line with a crowd of other poor sods, in a dark Soho alley, where the rats in the moonlight remind me of the Front, and the lads are quietly smoking as if waiting for some lieutenant to remember that we haven't been assigned anything to do.

It's dark as a forest except for the tips of our cigarettes, which burn slightly brighter with each restful inhalation, and the city searchlights, which scan the skies from time to time with their pale, strange beams.

"Did you ever go to that place in Pop?" Johnson says.

In Poperinghe. I tell him no, not yet.

"A real stinkhole," Johnson says. "Lineup a mile long. Never seen so many desperate fuckers. You should go on your way back."

"Wouldn't miss it for the world," I say.

A bottle of bitter whisky is making its way down the line. I take my turn – a slight nip – and pass it on to Johnson, who stands the thing bottom to the stars and then, when he relents finally, exhales noisily.

"No wonder you piss like a horse," I say.

He passes the bottle to the fellow behind us and says, "This guy here" – meaning me – "he saved my life."

"Bloody wonderful," the soldier says.

"I fell off the duckboards and he stayed to fish me out. Some lieutenant was going to order him to leave me behind but Ram claimed I was a major. Do you remember that?"

My brain feels shrivelled, like a slowly rotting egg.

"What was that guy's name?" Johnson asks. "Bentshit?"

"That's it," I say softly. "Lieutenant Bentshit. Why don't we just be quiet for a minute and contemplate the coming ambrosia?"

"The coming what?" Johnson says.

"Just the coming," the guy behind says, and some men chuckle lifelessly.

We stand like bloody cattle. To a man I'd say we are cold and tired and we just want what we want. It's better not to talk about it.

Some kid comes out the door, maybe sixteen years old, lost in his uniform. "How was it, sonny?" someone asks, and he grins like an oaf.

"Unbelievable!" he says. He stumbles along the lane and then gets in line again at the back.

"A glutton for punishment," somebody mutters.

For the longest time there's no movement at all. Conversation dies. I lean against the brick wall and try to remember what a naked woman looks like. There were those Belgian women in the river, and I have seen French pictures. Reese had a collection. I wonder what happened to it? Hopefully not sent home to the next of kin with his registration tags and his shaving kit. There was one picture in particular – she looked like a Greek statue. Her head in a scarf, eyes closed, shoulders pulled back, and a long necklace curving down between her breasts, the left pulled slightly higher than the right. Her hand on the small of her back, and the soft darkness between her legs. No matter how bad the whore looks, I'm thinking – and I've heard of them being old bags of flesh, disease-ridden ghouls – no matter how bad, I can think of that beautiful picture. And maybe I won't make a complete fool of myself.

"Jesus-fuck, it's cold," Johnson mutters.

We shuffle forward a few steps.

I start to sing softly, in honour of Reese:

We're here because we're here because
we're here because we're here . . .

A soldier comes running up the alley with a gang behind him. "Conshies!" he yells out when he gets close enough. "Come on! Bloody buggered conshies!"

It's a toss-up suddenly about what to do, because I can see in a minute the lineup is going to decrease substantially. But it's no contest really; the whole tide of us follows along, and by the time we have rounded the corner and sprinted down several more blocks we are a mob of forty or fifty men, yelling and running like boys out to meet a rival gang in an open-field fist fight. But this is night, and London, and the darkness, the searchlights high above give everything a strange air.

A bunch of the lads burst into a meeting hall. I'm happy to stay outside and watch, but Johnson ploughs forward and I have a sudden thought that he might get a chair broken over his head, and I've already saved him once, it would be a shame to have him die stupidly. So after a pause I run in as well and find pandemonium: a big banner in the front, half torn down, "PEACE BETWEEN" something, it says, the rest of it gone; a tweedy man standing on a platform, yelling out some speech, and women cowering in the corners, soldiers pushing over chairs and thumping whoever they can among the men. Johnson overturns a table and looks like he's going to kill someone, so I tackle him from behind and yell, "Johnson! Johnson!" right in his ear, which stuns him.

And then I see Margaret just a few steps away from the podium, arguing with a drunken soldier.

I get hit in the back and fall forward, slam into something and then the floor. So I roll and take someone else down, and crawl away, and look to see where Margaret has gone. It's hard to get my bearings. The room is chaos. Something hits my arm and I whirl, punch a soldier in the back, push my way over a few steps.

Whistles now and screams, and soldiers fighting soldiers, the sudden smell of blood.

I stagger to the front, to where I saw her, and a bomb goes off some distance away. Someone smashes me with an umbrella, and I turn to see a fat, elderly woman in black yelling obscenities just inches from my face. So I shove her back and have a strange thought, that she might have been the whore waiting for me a few blocks away.

Another explosion and we stop, suddenly, the whole room, and instantly people are yelling, "Zeppelins! Zeppelins!"

Margaret is wandering dazed at the far end of the stage. I push over some chairs, run to her as another few bombs fall, but not close, fairly distant thunder.

"Ramsay!"

She has blood on her cheek, and her dress is torn at the sleeve, her face sheet-white.

"Where's the nearest shelter?" I yell at her.

"I don't know!" she yells, and throws herself at me. "What are you doing here?" she blurts in my arms.

"It doesn't matter," I say hastily, and disentangle myself.

Most of the crowd – suddenly sober, chastened – is heading down to the basement of the building. The bombs are falling nowhere near us but Margaret clings to me and I let her. On the dark stairs a few people hold candles. We are strangely civil and helpful to one another, after the scene of just a few moments ago, the soldiers holding the arms of the ladies, the men in civilian clothes saying soothing things. The basement is unlit, except for the few candles, and we huddle on the clammy floor listening to the dull thud-thudding of the defensive guns.

In the Salient this would be a quiet night, I think, but here some of the women are weeping.

I sit in the darkness with my arms around Margaret, saying, "It's all right, it's all right," more or less in time with the guns.

"Why are you here?" she asks again. "Did Henry tell you where we were going to be?"

"It doesn't matter," I say. "It's all right."

"Henry!" she calls out suddenly. "Is Henry Boulton here?"

A few voices in the shadows and darkness repeat the question.

She calls again and soon it seems apparent that Henry is not here.

"Did he come with you?" I ask. "Did he drag you to this infernal meeting?"

"I dragged him!" Margaret says. "But I lost sight of him in the melee when the soldiers came in." And then she says, "*You* were with the soldiers!"

"I can't believe you are part of this bunch of conshies," I say.

"Quiet down! Do you want to start another fight?" A stern voice, somewhere in the darkness.

"What are your parents going to think?" I whisper to her harshly.

"You've been drinking again," she counters. "You're an alcoholic savage!"

"Shhhh!"

Screaming whistles, the clang of bells from up above.

She pushes me aside and wraps her arms around her own knees. "I need to find Henry," she says.

"He probably left the building with the others," I say. "He's probably in a Tube shelter."

"I'm going to look for him," she says.

"No you're not." She starts to rise but I pull her down by the back of her dress.

"You can't stop me! Take your hand off me!" she whispers fiercely.

"I have a duty to your parents to make sure you're safe."

"You're a drunkard and a lout who beats up women," she says. "And you abandoned me on the bus, anyway."

"And you told me that London was fine for a woman alone."

We boil in silence for a time, until I finally say, "I'll go look for him."

No reply. I glance over but can barely see her in the gloom. Her head is turned away. It is as if she is trying to keep as great a distance as the small space will allow.

I stand unsteadily, grope along the wall a few steps. "Thank you," she says bitterly in the darkness.

I climb the steps until I find the door, and then I am through and along a small passage and back into the half-lit chaos of the assembly room: a scattering of chairs, a broken chandelier, the sad, drooping banner. "Henry!" I call sharply. There is all manner of clanging and shouting from the street – there must have been a hit not too far away. Maybe one of the early bombs. "Henry Boulton!" I call.

He's not here, as I thought. I contemplate simply leaving the building. I've no doubt the danger has passed – if this thunderstorm can even be called danger. But Margaret will need escorting home. Henry has deserted her – naturally, in his cowardice, I think. Getting her involved in these fool-headed movements, then running off the moment –

"What do you want?" someone says. A voice from the back of the stage.

"Henry, come out here!" I say sharply. "Let's go down to the basement. For God's sake!"

"My leg is . . . rather painful," he says.

So I head back to the darkened area behind the stage where Boulton is sitting very still on a chair with his hat on his lap.

"Come on! Get up!" I say. "Margaret's waiting for you."

"I don't believe I can," he says calmly. "Something has happened to my knee."

His right leg does have a strange bend to it. I kneel and feel it gently from the ankle to the knee and down again.

"I think it must be broken," he says, wincing.

"What were you thinking?" I say. "Going to a conshies' meeting when you work for the Ministry of Munitions!"

"It was Margaret's idea," he says sadly – and I see the helpless look on his face, his eyes like a cow's. All for the bloody love of Margaret.

"Where's your backbone, man?" I bark at him, pulling him up – and not gently, either. And then I think: he's got his Blighty, the lucky bastard. And he didn't even have to leave town.

And my backbone is still on that bus, I think – where if I'd stayed any longer she probably would have convinced me to come to the meeting too. Anything to be with her.

◈

There are motorized ambulances in the street. The female driver of one of them nearly runs us over. I have to step back quickly, and Boulton leaning on my shoulder almost takes me down before Margaret gets the driver to stop. I load Boulton and Margaret, then stand on the back as the crazed driver tries to finish us all off on the way to the hospital. After one stomach-churning corner Margaret calls to her to slow down before we have an accident.

Margaret's concern is certainly not on my account, even though one slip of the hand and I will be thrown.

At the hospital I help unload the groaning Boulton, then leave it to Margaret to see to him indoors. I sit alone in the night on the front steps, smoking, watching the slow, now fruitless crawl of the searchlights across the clouded night sky.

I must wait to see Margaret home, I think. But then I can pack my kit quickly and be on my way, change my ticket at Victoria for an earlier train. Maybe in Poperinghe there will be a few extra hours to get properly drunk and join another of those long, hopeful lineups where men like me belong.

I close my eyes to think of Reese's picture, the naked statue lady with the necklace, the fine breasts of white-marble flesh. But instead I see Margaret with blood on her face, Margaret on the bridge, her eyes imploring me to embrace her.

I fall asleep for a moment, I suppose, and am woken with a nudge to find Margaret sitting on the steps beside me.

"Do you have a cigarette?" she says.

"They're not for ladies," I say.

She looks at me wickedly. *You're all right, Margaret*, I think.

I light one for her. "They stunt your growth, you know."

"Yes. I'm sure they do," she says.

"I'm trying to picture you with five children," I say. "All young Henrys, trooping in a field of daisies, bending over with their magnifying glasses, while their father tells them about the local pollen. You have a picnic basket on your arm and a wide, flouncy hat that you have to tie on in the wind. And there's a big hairy dog with a long wet tongue and flappy ears who loves to lie on your lap, though he's five feet long. You let him curl up by your toes in front of the fire at night, and he doesn't smell too bad as long as you feed him fresh meat."

I stop to smoke, feel for her hand beside me. She squeezes once and tries to let go, but I hang on to her.

"That dog is me, Margaret, after the war, when I've been properly planted and have come back in another form, atoning for my many sins. Be nice to the dog after the war."

"Shhhh. Don't talk like that," she says. And then: "You *want* to go back. I know that you do. It will be a great relief to get away from here."

"Don't talk nonsense," I say.

"To get away from me. I saw your face, Ramsay Crome, when you stepped off that bus to go to your chum. You looked freed from a prison term of indefinite years. And there you were elbow-deep in the crowd of soldiers who couldn't stand the idea, the *idea* that some of us want to put an end to the senseless slaughter. *Don't talk!*" she says as I turn to defend myself. "You and the rest of you, you *wanted* this war, and the very notion of peace pales beside it. And because of you we are doomed ever to be fighting it."

"You couldn't be more wrong," I say.

"I could be. I could be a damn sight more wrong than I am," she says. And when she sees the shock on my face she says, "I'm sorry for my tongue – no, I'm *not* bloody sorry."

"I am dreading the return," I say quietly. "In some ways I wish . . . I wish I had never taken leave. I wouldn't trade this week for the world, of course, but –"

"Just let's be quiet," she says, blowing out a cloud of smoke.

"No. You must understand. Tomorrow . . . tonight . . . I'm going to get on a train that will take me into the pit of hell. And I can't even claim ignorance because I've already been there and now I must return with the full knowledge . . ."

"What did your father come all the way to London to say to you?" she asks suddenly. When I don't answer, she says, "He has found a way out of the war for you and you won't take it."

"How do you know?" I ask, startled.

"Because he called me on the telephone late this afternoon. He asked specifically to speak with me, and said that I must talk sense into you about your transfer. I said I didn't know what he was talking about, and he said, 'Ramsay will not accept a transfer out of the firing line.' *Why won't you take it?*"

My God, what won't my father stoop to? I look at her in astonishment, then in an effort to stay calm I turn my gaze away, watch the pale, ghostly searchlights exposing the underside of the clouds from which the Zeppelins have long gone.

"He had a lot of nerve telling you about this matter," I say finally, measuring my words. "It's none of your business. But he knows that I care for you and so thought you could influence me. Can't you see? He's meddling up and down over this. A man has to choose his own path, he can't be forever –"

"You are choosing to die! To throw your life away!"

"In defence of my country! In defence of *you*, and your sister, and this bloody city, and everything that we believe . . ."

"You have done your bit!" she says. "Can't you see that? Let others replace you now in the most dangerous roles."

"Others like Henry?"

And now it is her turn to be silent.

"There are no others," I say. "At least not enough of them. We're running out of volunteers. These men who have to be compelled to defend their families, what kind of men are they? It will take months, years to condition them to fight in the trenches. In the meantime, the Germans will simply overrun us. They are hardened soldiers, and they don't mean to lose, any more than we mean to lose. We cannot give up our nerve. Those Zeppelin bombs are not going to stop falling at night just because some well-meaning women in an assembly hall want peace. The Germans want peace, too – on terms that they dictate. And then they'll feel free to start the war again whenever it's to their advantage. We can talk around this all night but there it is."

There it is. We finish our cigarettes and it is time for me to escort my cousin home, to call for a cab and ride along black-ened streets at an unholy hour and maybe steal a kiss – no, it will be more angry silence, frayed nerves, exhausted impatience. I have no heart for it but there it is.

"You are an exasperating man," she says, not rising.

"I need to see you home."

"You are self-centred and quite stupid about some things."

"Your family will be worried. Did you get a chance to call your father? What did you tell them you were doing tonight?"

"Be quiet," she says, rising finally and pushing me into the shadows beside the hospital door. She pulls against my neck and kisses me hard, with her eyes wide open, biting my lip almost in anger.

"I am not going to kiss you tomorrow when you get on your damned train," she says.

When I lean down for more she pushes me away and announces that we really must get home.

◈

"Thank God! Thank God!" Manfred says, rushing from the doorway and down the walk even before the driver stops. I fumble in the dark for the money, do not make it around in time to open the door on Margaret's side.

"We're quite all right, Father," she says, stepping out on her own.

"That's it, no more evening dramaticals," he declares. "Ramsay, what a spot of luck you happened along!"

"Yes," I say uncertainly.

"Is Miss Liddell all right?" he asks me. "Did she get home safely? Perhaps we should telephone her family?"

"It's quite all right, Father," Margaret says. "As I said on the phone, we were very safe. No need to bother the Liddells. But Mr. Boulton, who was with us, has injured his knee falling on some steps. Hello, Mother," she says to Harriet, who is standing in the doorway in pale silence. She bursts into tears when Margaret approaches, and the two hug ferociously on the doorstep.

"Not quite like Ypres, I suppose," Manfred says to me, "but an infernal, blasted business all the same."

Miffy has made tea and Harriet presses it upon us, but I beg off, pleading exhaustion. I head up the stairs quickly, turn into the bathroom, accomplish my ablutions without glimpsing my face in the mirror. Then I dart into my room, close the door. In darkness I strip down, slip between the sheets, clench closed my eyes. It's my last night in London and I just want it to speed by in a slide of oblivion. But my mind is whirling. *You want to go back there*, Margaret says to me, over and over. *I saw that look on your face.* And Johnson is pissing again like a firehose. Where's Johnson now? I wonder. Wandering drunk in some dark part of London.

You want to go back there.

How could she misunderstand me so completely? And why should I care?

I'll get up in a few hours and pack my kit, leave before dawn, catch an early train. I compose a note in my head: *Thank you so much for your hospitality. I hope I have not been too much of a bother. For me it has been a pleasant stay and I know . . .*

I turn and pull the pillow over my head, grimly hold myself still so sleep can come. And the house slowly subsides into night: I hear Manfred and Harriet trudge up the stairs and down the hall, then Margaret, whose step is lighter, and who pauses, I think, outside my door, but then moves on. The crack of hallway light under the door falls dark, ages crawl by, and then finally I hear Uncle Manfred's snores, fancy I can feel the sighing breath of the others succumbing to sleep.

You want to go back, Margaret says in my head, again and again.

It's better not to think, not to have the time. That's why the army keeps a man so occupied, why these leaves are such a bad idea. They throw everything open again to corrosive question and debate.

You know the men who are fighting, my father says, *but I know the men perpetuating this disgrace.*

It's a terrible thing. I should never have come here.

I hold myself as still as stone, but instead of sleep I am tasting her soft mouth, pressing myself against her body . . . which is the same as the statue girl in the picture, the same smooth lines, womanly skin which I will never feel, not now. This is my last night, my last chance, and now that the house has eased into darkness and calm I think: what if I just crept out of my room and down the hallway? She is sharing with Emily – of course, it can't work. But that doesn't stop my wretched mind. What if I stepped silent as a scout in No-Man's Land, and slipped through the crack in the door, deposited myself burning beside her? She would gasp but I'd put my hand on her mouth until she realized who it was, and in a moment we'd be kissing again, she'd slide herself under so softly . . .

I hear a noise down the hall.

It's nothing. The breathing of the night. My whole body is taut as a pole.

Another noise, I can't believe it. A footstep outside my door.

I stop breathing, turn entirely into straining ears. She is standing there like the other night, I can hear her soft breathing, mean to invite her in, but I don't trust my voice to be gentle enough.

Then I see the handle turning. The door sticks, makes a jarring little noise that sounds through the house like a gunshot and she pauses. I expect footsteps, lights, sleepy, puzzled questions.

The door stays still until the house proves silent, and then it resumes opening again. I hurriedly close my eyes, hear two steps towards the bed and the door sighing shut behind her. Then her hand is on my sheet and I grasp it, pull too suddenly, she half collapses against me and I am lost in the disorder of her dangling hair. Then she is fighting further onto the bed and I have to push her quickly to keep her away.

"Emily!" I hiss, and she glares at me in the darkness, wild as any animal. "What are you doing?"

No words, just heaving, crazed breath.

"*Get out of here now!*" I try to keep my voice from carrying too far, but it has enough command in it to hammer in some sense. She turns quickly, flees back down the hall. I expect Manfred next, in his dressing gown, demanding explanations. I lie as if smacked awake, waiting for his angry steps . . . but there is nothing but strained calm, the exaggerated stillness of a household stretched to breaking.

That's torn it, I think, and turn over in a fit of helpless anger.

◆

There is no sleep, but no rising in the morning either, until I hear that the household has shaken slowly awake, has cleaned, clothed, and fed itself and headed out the door. It takes bloody well forever, and I lie feigning dreams, nursing an overfilled bladder until there seems the least chance of encountering anyone. Then I am about my business quickly, and don't even linger over my last civilized bath.

I pack up my razor and brushes, my drawers, mess kit, canteen, whale oil, spare shirt, my socks and towel and underwear, roll up my greatcoat.

You want to go, she said, and she's bloody well right. I can't stand the strain of this civilian life any more. Give me straightforward bombs and barbed wire, things that I might understand. Not the machinations of sisters. . . .

I make my bed up, snapping the sheets tight, and hang my wet towel on the door, leave my gear leaning against the bed. Then I lightfoot it down the stairs to nip a late piece of toast . . . and Harriet catches me standing over the table with my mouth full.

"You don't have to leave yet, do you, Ramsay?" she says, and by instinct I shake my head and tell her no, no, not till later. "You just have that look about you," she says, "as if you're heading out the door."

"Not yet, no," I say. "I'm preparing kit and writing last letters and –"

"We all had a terribly slow start this morning," she says. "Because of last night, of course. The girls have gone to visit Mr. Boulton in the hospital. We are so glad and grateful that you were there last night, Ramsay, during the worst danger. A coincidence, I gather, but nonetheless –"

"I happened upon them," I say vaguely.

"At the theatrical," she says.

"I suppose that's what it was."

She looks at me for an uncomfortable moment as I am standing, chewing, guilty.

"We are so glad that you came, Ramsay. It has been a very memorable visit."

"Yes. Thank you for having me," I say.

◆

Dear Mrs. Jackwell, I write.

I am a member of the 7th Pioneers in your son's platoon, and I was there by his side when Peter – Snug, we called him – died. I have been meaning to write you for some time to express my condolences and to tell you that there was no man in the company who was more of a gentleman or a hero than your son.

Not a day passes now when I don't think of him or what his friendship meant to so many of us.

The commanding officer has probably written to tell you of the circumstances of Peter's death. I am not sure there is much that I can add. We were under deadly fire from a German sniper who had installed himself behind our lines. One man had already been killed when Peter insisted on being the first over the top to flush out the enemy. His actions helped us to pinpoint the sniper and direct fire his way, but not before Peter was hit.

I can tell you that he died quickly and in great peace, and that in the year that I knew him he talked often of you and the others of the family.

I am not much for writing these types of letters, so please excuse me if I haven't found the right words. Perhaps I can end by telling you how Peter got his nickname. Early on in the days when the battalion was first forming, we spent some difficult nights training in the rain. But Peter never complained, in fact, he always seemed in better spirits than the rest of us. He had a knack for finding the driest spot, and an uncanny ability to fall asleep in almost any circumstance. One time I found him tucked in an old wooden barrel out of

*the storm, sleeping like a baby, so I called him Snug and the
name stuck.*

*My deepest sympathies to you and your family. We all
miss him terribly.*

Yours sincerely,

Ramsay Crome (Pte.)

◈

The girls are late getting back, and when we eat it is mid-
afternoon. Neither Margaret nor Emily will meet my eye. It
makes me wonder, in terrible discomfort, what, if anything,
they have said to one another.

"So Mr. Boulton is going to survive?" Manfred says, chewing
his cabbage roll.

"He was very pale and almost disoriented," Emily says. "He
looked like he was still in shock, poor fellow."

"Well, one night's wrecked sleep and I'm in ruins, too," Manfred
allows. "I think I'm going to need to nap this afternoon. My
dear?" he says, arching his eyebrows across the table at Harriet.

"No doubt a nap would do us all good," Harriet says. "What
time do you need to be at the station, Ramsay?"

"Actually," I say, "I was thinking of getting an early start of it.
No need to see me off. I'm sure that if I caught a cab shortly I
could hop on an early train. There will probably be delays in the
transportation along the way."

For the first time during the meal Margaret looks at me, a
knowing, disappointed, accusatory glare.

"You haven't done my portrait yet!" Emily blurts. "You *promised*, Ramsay."

"He's *itching* to get back," Margaret says.

"Well, if there are going to be delays –" Manfred says.

"Be quiet, darling," Harriet says. Then to me: "No need to rush back, Ramsay. The war will still be going when you get there."

"Of course it will," I say.

◈

Emily has said nothing of last night, and so I will say nothing either, and just get myself through the rest of this day. She has left a ringlet of light reddish hair falling across her cheek, has rouged her lips for the occasion, and worn too frilly an outfit. I find I don't want to deal with it. It has to start for me with a line somewhere – the curve of her bottom, perhaps. I have her turn slightly and support herself with her hand on the small of her back.

"If you raised your other hand," I say. "Just up by your cheek."

A dull, grey, tiresome light is coming through the bedroom window. I've left the door open, want no repeat of last evening's near disaster.

"An awful shame about Henry," she says, retreating to her old theme, and I shush her.

"Models do not speak," I say.

"I've never been able to understand what Margaret sees in him," she says.

She has a pointy, thinnish nose, and has tarted up her cheeks badly. I try being true to them but then mute them. Eyes looking slightly away. There is a small twist to the back.

Very light on the jawline.

One breast higher than the other. Quite full, I should think. I decide to give her a necklace.

"Will you write to me?" Emily asks.

"I'll write to all of you," I say.

"But I want you to write to *me* in particular," she says. "I'll send you the most lovely letters. Perfumed if you like."

The line of her belly, and her legs.

"Could you lift your right leg slightly?" I ask.

"What, like this?"

"Relax. Just like that."

"I can't hold this for very long," she says.

It is hard to capture a sense of her skin, to make it look as soft as falling asleep on a feather bed. (I'm going to miss the bed, I think.)

"When can I look?" she says.

"Stay still!" And she is startled back into her position – or not quite. The twist is gone from her back, and I can see more of her eyes now.

I touch up her lips, return the colour to her cheeks. And just a hint of soft darkness down there.

"Promise me you will not look until I have gone," I say.

"Why not?"

Because it's a ragged sort of soldier who leaves unexploded bombs behind. But this is a ragged sort of war and I just want to be out of here and away.

❖

I leap from the cab at Victoria Station, stumble once with the weight of my haversack, rifle, and Aunt Harriet's going-away basket of preserves and chocolate and other supplies. I step into a puddle before gaining the kerb. The rest of the family is content to wait until the vehicle has fully halted.

The rain is a steady, soaking wash, a full brigade of grey clouds settling on us in a strong imitation of forever.

"Please, I don't need you to wait on the platform," I say. "It's good of you to come this far. But I have to check in with the transport officer, I'm sure it's going to take a while."

"Right then," Manfred says, and turns to the cabbie, presumably to hire him for the ride back. But Harriet says, "Nonsense," with the assurance of a commander.

A major walks by, a luggage-loaded batman behind him, and I salute. Emily says, "We're going to see you off, and that's that!"

So it's into the seething cauldron of the station. I find myself walking too fast, have to slow myself to allow them to keep up with me. A muted Margaret gazes at the big clock and asks me what time I arrive at Folkestone.

"I don't know," I say. "Whenever we get there."

I find the RTO's office almost too quickly, and the validation of my papers is surprisingly smooth. But the gate is a mess of sobbing women, burdened, subdued soldiers, older men standing hard-jawed and silent in the steam and smoke. We're early but the train is already waiting, and I haven't the heart or stomach to face much more of this.

"We got you a little present," Margaret says. "We were going to buy you an armoured vest. We thought it would be the best thing, and went all the way up to Southampton Row to get it. But it turned out we could barely lift it between us, and I've heard so many stories of soldiers throwing away things in the Channel trying to lighten their kit. So we bought you these puttees instead."

"Thank you. You've been most thoughtful," I say, taking the small package wrapped in brown paper.

"They're Lupton's," Emily says. "Apparently the best made."

No doubt far better than anything else I wear, I think, but I keep my mouth shut. Margaret looks weary, and Emily is near to tears, and so I must go. I turn to Manfred and ask him if he tested his Zeppelin-finder listening device last night in the raid.

"Do you know, I completely forgot!" he says, grasping my hand in farewell. "But our gunners could have used it. We seem to be utterly helpless beneath those airships."

I let go of Manfred's hand. "Thank you for taking care of me this week," I say to them all. "I will think of you all."

"Thank you for looking after our Margaret last night," Manfred says. "It's a good thing you were there, or who knows what fool sort of trouble she might have got involved in."

I look towards Margaret and she smiles sadly for me.

"You just come back and visit us on your next leave," Manfred says with a forced jollity.

A large contingent of soldiers marches towards us on the platform, and I have my excuse.

"I think I'd better get on now and save my seat," I say. "Thank you again. Thank you!"

And I kiss Aunt Harriet and embrace Emily – her tears wet my cheek – and she whispers, "I had to look. I'll never show anyone, but it's beautiful. Thank you."

Margaret offers her hand in a polite goodbye.

"Be good to your dog after the war," I say, and go to kiss her cheek, which she allows. It is only when I pull back that I feel the note in my hand.

"God bless you, Ramsay, dear," Harriet says. "Keep safe."

"Right then," Manfred says brusquely. "Is that enough?"

"It's enough," I say quietly and turn with pack and rifle and basket, eyes swimming, to step onto the train. It's a smoky, crowded, soldierly place. I work my way back, find an empty compartment, sit by the window.

The others have turned to go but Margaret is still looking. She finds my face and we watch each other from behind glass, her raincoat pulled round her shoulders, her face so white and small.

The soldiers from the large contingent swarm by her and onto the car, and soon the compartment is full of us, young, healthy, doomed men whose leaves are now over, who sit muted and subdued.

Manfred comes back for his daughter, and now Emily is there again too, and they won't leave while I am looking. So I pull my face from the window and close my eyes and try to think of nothing.

Sometime out of London, with a beery corporal asleep on my shoulder, and two other men playing a silent, tense game of cards in the seat across from me, I unclench my fist and read the note from Margaret. *It is enough, perhaps, to write about his hands*, it says.

Some of the nails are cracked, the skin is split and bruised in places, but they do not look like a soldier's hands. When I held them in my own cold fingers I thought, they are not meant for killing. The dark purple veins are engorged from difficult labour. The long, tapered, slender fingers are not

*meant to wrap round the throat of any enemy, to choke the
breath of any mortal soul.*

I do not believe in murder.

But I do believe in those hands.

*I have watched them sketch in darkness – a shade, an
aspect, an emotion come to life in a few quick strokes.*

*I have felt them race my pulse and warm the deepest
imaginings, long for them even now that they are being taken
so far away.*

What was he thinking when he kissed me? I have no idea.

*I cannot say I know too well the man behind the dark,
haunted eyes. But I believe in those hands, would kiss them
now if I could.*

Unsigned. The script thin and scratchy in places, not as
rounded and full as I expected. I smooth the paper as much as I
can, then refold it and slip it in my pocket, turn to look out the
window. In the night's darkness I see mostly my own bleak
reflection.

THREE

We bump and lurch, stop for ages without explanation in the middle of the dark nowhere, arrive finally at Folkestone close to dawn. I make certain my name is in for the next troopship passage and then spend hours pacing the heights, looking out to sea, facing the wind. I fancy I can hear the rumble of battle in the distance, but it is very faint, a mere rumour of thunder. The waves, however, are formidable, grey rollers incessantly pounding the shore, the wind blowing like a constant, chilling, accumulating blast that must be fought.

At the empty bandstand I pause, wonder for a moment why the wind has not yet lifted off the roof and sent it rolling down the road like an errant wheel. It's ridiculous to think of musicians sitting here in straw hats and gay red-and-white striped jackets, tinkling some brassy tune. In this wind the hats would have blown to town, it would be work just to hang on to the instruments, and the dresses of the ladies in the audience would have flown over their heads.

Thoroughly chilled, I walk down the hill to the little town and finally find a small tea shop willing to serve me at this ridiculously early hour.

"You've been over before, then?" the owner says, a bit of a rooster with a beaked nose, eyes that look safely fifty or more.

I tell him I was at Ypres and he nods. "And now you're going back," he says.

I sit at a small table by the window and watch the wind bend huge, rigid trees as if they were saplings, and I think of Boulton with his fortunate wound.

Dear Mother, I write in pencil on a battered piece of stationery that has weathered far too much at the bottom of my pack. *I have passed a fine week in London, but now am on my way back into the heat of it for a while.*

The heat of it! If only, I think, and wrap my hands around the tea mug for a little bit of warmth. (I imagine Margaret, no doubt sitting for hours by Boulton's bedside, stroking his ink-stained hands.)

I did see Father briefly in London, but he didn't explain what his business was. I trust you know more of the details. There wasn't even time to inquire about Will and Thomas, so please write to me their news.

I sip the tea steadily but begin to feel my teeth clattering together, a terrible chill like the night I was sick. A good stiff drink will put me right, I think, and for a moment I feel nostalgic for a shot of rum in the trench after a long cold night.

Please don't worry about me, I write, my hand shaking badly. *You must know that by now with all my experience I have a good idea of what to do and how to stay out of trouble.*

I smoke my last cigarette, but borrow another from the shop

owner and then finish the pot of tea. From where I'm sitting I can see the sun climbing higher in the morning sky, and a grey corner of slashing waves punishing the pier where the ferry boat will arrive. I have the strange sense that I could just continue to sit here, smoking and drinking tea, trying to warm up. That the boat could arrive, unload, refuel, reload, and leave without me.

◈

The departure is delayed several hours, and a gnawing sense of dread slowly begins to take hold. I just want to get it over with, but time has turned leaden.

In an effort to stay out of the wind, I spend far too long at the garden gate of a hideous hospital. It is not just the blind and the amputees, the shells of men in wheelchairs, the bandaged wrecks, but the men whose nerves have been shattered – they are the hardest to watch, and the most difficult to turn away from. I stare at one who walks lurching like a child's wildly spasmodic toy, his back perfectly straight, torso bobbing up and down with the violence of a recoiling gun. Another bounces like a spring, his arms straight at his sides as if fastened there. Yet another smashes his forehead methodically against a stone wall until blood runs down his face and a nurse arrives to pull him away.

I stand and stare until a legless man on a wooden platform with tiny wheels and blocks in his hands squeaks past me on the other side of the gate. "What yer starin' at, guv'nor?" he asks.

"Nothing," I shiver, shocked somehow even to be addressed, and move away.

◈

We sail finally at mid-morning, when the wind seems to be at its worst. For a while I stand on the howling deck and scan the waves for signs of mines or U-boats. The spray chills me even further but it feels real, somehow, and therefore tolerable.

Below decks, I am drawn into a smoky game of pontoon. There are three others to begin with: a Welshman with tired eyes, an Aussie with twin dragon tattoos on his forearms, and an ashen-faced, unshaven Highlander who looks like he'd slit the throat of his grandmother for a chance at a drink.

We have agreed on a pound-maximum, shilling-minimum game. The Scot deals me a king and I bet a pound right off. The Welshman and the Aussie are in for a shilling each. Then the Scot turns up a ten of hearts in front of me. The Welshman gets a nine and eyes my ten, the Aussie a pitiful three.

The Scot deals himself the ace of spades, uncovers his jack, and takes double stakes from each of us.

It's only money.

In the next round the Scot pontoons again against my nine-teen, and five-cards it after that, then wins with a royal of triple sevens. I am beginning to see the lay of the land, and should walk away, but I'm down nearly five pounds by now. I bet stupidly with a jack facing but only a six below. The Welshman and Aussie both crash out and leave, and the Scot wins again with nineteen.

Now there's no shortage of men happy to take the empty places. We're the centre of a large crowd, all of us watching the Scot's quick hands.

With every win his eyes turn more filtered and remote. He is like a man sitting on an unexploded shell, knowing that the slightest movement could set things off. So he becomes more sober and silent, and slides his winnings into his pocket with great delicacy.

We all overextend and he wins again. I force myself to walk away while I still have some slight weight to my wallet.

It doesn't matter, I think. It's only money. And I'm going to die anyway.

◈

I'm going to die.

The thought seizes hold and won't let me go. This is what Snug felt so suddenly, I realize now. That nothing matters. Whatever I do, there is no escape. A shell is going to rip me to bloody bits, or a sniper will ventilate my brain, or I will become one of those men back in hospital whose bodies jackknife and jerk in mad explosions of movement, who wander around muttering and spitting, who cannot keep themselves still for a corseted old biddy to shave and clean their faces and hold the hospital pan under their tired organs.

These are the cards I am being dealt, these sixes and nines against aces and kings. How the hell have I held out so long? That is the miracle, it occurs to me. That I've survived thus far in such a rigged game.

Back on the rolling deck, by the lifeboats, I try to find a sunny spot out of the wind. But there is no such place. Everywhere it is chilly and dull, and the men crammed together in huddles of three and four all look green to the gills and disgusted.

I'm going to die and there is no way out. Not even my father's transfer can save me. I realize it now. That would be weeks away and I'm going to peg out in the next few days at the most, maybe the minute I set foot back at the Front.

It might even happen now. A torpedo might already be on its way. I can't see it spitting through the water, but that doesn't matter. Nothing I do will make the slightest bit of difference.

These are the cards I've been dealt.

I pace the deck, swing my arms, jump up and down self-consciously. My heart is racing but I'm stone winter cold. "Windy bastard!" I say out loud. Then I turn to the wind itself and yell out, "You're a windy bastard!" Two muffled men drinking surreptitiously from a bottle look up to see what I'm on about.

"You're a windy bloody bastard!" I yell.

◆

"We had one guy who wouldn't go out of his tent without his lucky nail scissors."

The voice is a detached one in the stench of a cattle car rolling somewhere north of Boulogne. I have my eyes closed and am trying unsuccessfully not to listen.

"They were a silver pair given to him by his grandmother just before he sailed. They'd been with his grandfather in the Crimea and he'd made it through without a scratch. This fella was a scout, but with those scissors it was like he had a magic ring around him. He'd be out there in No-Man's Land in the dead of night, bombs falling left of him, right of him. Miracle Jones we called him. Lucky scissors!"

Another voice pipes up, says he has a silk scarf his girl friend gave him. He ties it around his left knee whenever his battalion gets called into action. Another voice says he repeats the twenty-third Psalm once every hour to himself, and it hasn't served him wrong yet.

"My best buddy died drinking plonk in an *estaminet* miles from the firing," another voice says. "A single shell – nothing else fell within a thousand yards. And it didn't even go off. He was sitting at the table talking to three or four of us, and all of a sudden this thing comes screaming through the roof and takes him, and him only. I tell you, when it's got your name on it . . ."

There's nothing you can do. All the voices in the dark agree. You can carry your silver scissors, your lucky scarves, say every Psalm in the book, but when it's your time, that's it. Pray for a clean, quick death.

"That guy with the scissors," the first voice says, "we found him one morning trailing guts for a hundred feet. He'd been shot through the belly with a dumdum and lived most of the night. When I saw him he was still alive. He offered me his lucky scissors and I refused. There wasn't a man in the company would touch them after that."

◈

The train pulls into Poperinghe well after dark. My legs are liquid, my head feels clenched in a vise that has slowly been tightening all the way up the French countryside. What was a whisper in Folkestone and a rumble in Boulogne has turned into a ceaseless, angry, volcanic roar in the not-too-distant gloom, and I am seized with the feeling that the earth itself is splitting open along a jagged, roiling seam whose irresistible gravity is pulling us all closer to oblivion.

I feel like a ghost already.

Dozens of the men sprint from the train to be the first with their paperwork to claim their due – hot food and a place for the night. But ghosts neither eat nor sleep, so there is no hurry. My papers are processed near the end by a weary, irritated lieutenant who shunts me into a back office with several others. There we drop our drawers for short-arms inspection by a bullheaded, cold-fingered doctor who asks the same question of all of us: "Did you have carnal relations at any time while you were on leave?"

"Just fifty or sixty times," one man says.

"About every hour," says another.

"Whenever I wasn't drinking," says someone else.

"Not bloody likely," I tell him, my teeth clattering, and not just from the cold.

I'm terrified to be back here.

We are all herded into another room for washing and application of noxious cleansing agents, whether we have admitted to carnal relations or not. Then I am in another lineup. I stand stupid and exhausted, like a pack mule in full weight, and shuffle forward in the greyness of the night, until finally I am at the front, the last one left in a nearly empty room.

"Name and number," grumbles the officer, and for a moment I fail to respond. It's as if he is asking something novel and unknown.

"Name and number!" he repeats.

"Crome, R.H.," I say, coming to my senses. "Private, 430776." I hand him my papers and he studies them as if certain in the conviction that I am a German spy.

"Your leave commenced the nineteenth?"

"I suppose so, sir."

"Well, did it or didn't it?"

"To be honest, sir, I can't remember," I say.

"Oh, it was one of *those* leaves, was it, Crome?" he asks wearily. "Your *form* indicates you commenced leave May nineteenth. Do you have any reason to suspect the form might be in error?"

"No, sir."

"You went to London?"

"Yes, sir."

"And did you spend a single moment there sober, Private Crome?"

"No, sir. I don't believe I did, sir," I say stiffly.

"Have you got your billet?" he asks finally, stamping papers furiously.

"Yes," I say in a daze. I haven't actually, was under the vague impression that this lineup was to procure billets. But I can't admit that now.

"Right. You will report to your company headquarters tomorrow morning at nine-thirty sharp under your own transport. Sign here."

I sign, stare for a moment at the alarming slant of my own hand.

"Done," he says, rising sharply. "Dismissed!"

I manage to straighten up.

"What are you waiting for?" he barks.

"Nothing. Nothing, sir," I say.

"Then be on your way, soldier!"

◈

I am on my way. Step after step down the dark, cobblestoned streets of soldier-squashed Poperinghe, across the square where crowds of men are milling under the shadows of the walls and spires of these old, old buildings, or spilling out of loud cafés, or moving en masse to some other location. I keep my eyes open, wander along the back lanes, try not to trip over drunken louts or fall into darkened doorways. Eventually I make it to the back of the longest lineup.

"How much is it?" I ask the next fellow, who tells me an absurd figure, which turns out to be in francs.

"Do they take pounds?" I ask.

"One and eight," he says, which sounds all right until I check my wallet. I have all of four shillings left.

"Does anybody have some extra cash?" I call out, to a near-universal chorus of "Bugger off!"

"Thanks, lads," I say bitterly. "Thanks for all your help."

"Anytime, arse-head!" someone says. I scan the shadows for his face. Silence, then the bastard says, "What's your problem, then. Lost your dick?"

He's leaning against the wall, a head taller than me and fat as a cook. When he sees me looking murders at him, he takes his hands out of his pockets and straightens up.

"Come on at it, then, if you want a beating," he says. Some of the others jeer and in a moment we are surrounded in a tight circle. I leave my pack and rifle and get hit on the side of the jaw, step back once in shock, get hit again in the ribs and bend over.

I clench for a smash but it doesn't come, the idiot, and that is the end of him. I am fists, elbows, knees pounding at him regardless of the cost, because blood doesn't concern me, I'm dead already. He's so large he can step out of the way once and then again, but I catch him in the gut, then the neck and the side of the head, and he goes down like a cathedral in a heap of dust and whimpering.

Soon I'm being pulled off him and for a moment it seems like I will be separated limb from limb in the desperate darkness of this bitter town. But then there are whistles and running boots, and we scatter like rats. I'm lucky to be able to move at all, almost abandon my kit and rifle but think better of it, and dash crazed through too many confusing, winding streets. I run long past hearing anyone after me, stop only when my lungs feel gassed and torn, and a man in a doorway yells, "Here!" in such a clear, crisp tone it sounds like an order. "What's the problem?" he says.

I'm too winded even to talk, and he pulls me inside a crowded, rollicking place, shuts the door behind us.

"Been fighting someone besides Germans?"

In the light I see he's a major. Down the smoky hallway an officer is pounding badly on the piano, just part of the cacophony of lusty singing and a hundred different loud conversations.

"No, sir," I say.

"There are no ranks here, man," he says. And then, after seeing my blank stare: "Talbot House. All the beds are taken, but you can stay till things cool down, if that's what you want. Let me register you."

I stand in full pack while he brings the book.

"Are you just back from leave, then?" he says.

"Do I look like it?"

"Let me find a place for your gear. You do know there's no drinking here."

That's fine, I think. I'm quite drunk already on fear and stupidity. I sign the register and follow him past dozens of men talking and smoking, captains and sergeants, privates and lieutenants. Up the stairs and into the middle of an even larger crowd.

"Or did you want peace and quiet?" the major asks.

"It doesn't matter," I say. "I don't know what I want."

"Then we'd better keep going," he says. I follow him up much narrower, steeper stairs, and we emerge in an attic room that is . . . a chapel, with red carpet and flowers, an A-frame roof, white-painted walls, and, at the front, shell-casing urns, candles, rough wooden crosses, what looks like a carpenter's bench for an altar. There's a scattering of men here, but it's silent except for the muted roar from downstairs.

"Leave your things at the back here. And you can just be quiet a moment, if you like, or I can sit with you."

"Quiet," I manage to say.

He helps me off with my pack and takes my rifle. I sit on a bench near the back and catch my breath.

"Take all the time you need," he says, but he doesn't leave. He sits a few feet away from me, immediately closes his eyes and bows his head. I do the same, out of politeness, I suppose, and in a moment I'm bawling like a baby, awful, shuddering, clenching tears and gasps. I hold my face in my hands and fight to get control.

"Our Father," he says beside me, "who art in Heaven, hallowed be Thy name."

"Shut up," I manage to say.

He goes quiet immediately, and I fight for my breath, my faculties.

"This has nothing to do with the father," I say.

"Shhhh," he says, and puts a hand on my shoulder.

"It has nothing to do with God either," I say bitterly. "God is a joke. God has gone fishing in some other part of the universe."

My eyes are blurry with tears and I want to hit someone very badly. If he argues with me, if he gives me any bunkum about God or religion or –

"It's all right," he says, and simply sits in silence with his hand on my shoulder for who knows how long, until the shuddering has stopped.

There are about a half-dozen others, hunched silent men alone in this attic room, eyes away from one another. Besides the muffled roar from below, there is the constant boiling of the war outside, not too many miles off, and even the occasional shell landing, I suppose, somewhere in town. It is peaceful here, though, as if we were in a warm cave far underground.

"I'll leave you, then," he says softly, "unless there's something you want to talk about."

"No."

So he goes and I sit staring at my knees, then at my hands, then at the altar and the other men, the candles, the crosses and urns, at a suspended brass chandelier I didn't notice before. Without thinking I take Margaret's note out of my pocket and read it through again. *It is enough, perhaps, to write about his hands . . .*

I think of her on the platform, of her biting kiss that night outside the hospital, of our grim march through the park on what should have been a romantic day together. I think of her contriving to have me speak with Henry – Henry, who's now out of it anyway, whether he likes it or not. I think of her sitting so still in the darkness, of the line of her cheek and how soft her hair would feel in my hands – of just locking eyes with her.

I know nothing of God, but the thought of Margaret fills this little room.

This kind of blasphemy is sure to get me killed, sitting here in the chapel thinking such thoughts. But they are the thoughts I think, and if they are not good enough for God then damn my soul to hell.

Sometime later the room begins to fill up. A crowd of men comes up the narrow stairs one by one as if spilling out a chute through barbed wire. There's room for perhaps thirty sitting, but more and more arrive, until three times that are standing and the air begins to disappear. Apparently a service is about to begin, so quietly I take up my gear, squeeze my way down the stairs against the flow.

I look for the major on the way out, meaning to grasp his hand. But he is nowhere to be seen and in the end I do not linger.

◆

Midnight now, and as I have no billet, but must report in the morning, I let my feet take me down the narrow, poplar-lined road back to perdition. It is dark and rutted, but hardly lonely: the road is clogged with a long, lumbering, mud-choked supply line of gear-grinding trucks, horse-drawn limbers and gun carriages, and slogging men on foot . . . most going in the wrong direction, away from the Salient.

"Heading for the Somme," one lad says to me on his way by, when I ask. "I feel like a lucky bastard to be away from here."

The arc of battle stretches ahead of me, with the dark, brooding ruins of Ypres smoking in the distance.

Better to keep my eyes down. I plod along, boots squelching in the roadside mud (and what fine boots these have become, now that my feet have adjusted through the pain). We are rank, sweating, filthy, unwashed men and beasts, silent except for the tired tramp of feet, the machinery of our breathing, the occasional fart or grunt or muttered curse aimed at nothing in particular. Silent, that is, compared to the explosions beyond, which are so constant they hardly count as noise.

The road is far too small to accommodate us. More and more I am squeezed to the side by passing trucks and field guns heading away from the line of fire. I expect the shaking, the cold, the fear of some hours ago to return and reclaim me. But step follows step, breath turns to breath, and while my pack and rifle grow heavier, my heart stays slow and calm.

Then for no reason at all I look up at just the right instant to glimpse a brilliant star flare illuminating the night sky. I watch for several more paces as shells explode across the horizon, and then I find myself standing in a field some steps off without being aware of having consciously decided to leave the road. I gaze dumbfounded at the distant splashes of deepest blues and scarlet reds and angry orange balls of flame, of yellow streaking flares and sudden riots of green, purple, blinding white, and then seconds of profound darkness broken again and again by more explosions of colour.

For the briefest moment I suffer the confusion that God is trying to get my attention by this awesome display. But of course there is no God, no God anywhere, unless the darkness itself is God, the unmarked palette of the night sky. The rest of the work is ours completely, our damnation increasing with every blast.

I stand rooted, almost, in the face of this demonstration, suddenly weakened with hunger and despair. How can I go on? How can anyone? Why not be done with it, lie down here and sink peacefully back into the earth? Wouldn't that be better than walking, fully conscious, into the blast?

I stand staring, shaken, an unnoticed scarecrow in a deserted field not far from the true fields of agony and death.

But in the end it is only a moment in a loose collection of moments, a sliding to the side in order to move forward. Soon enough, and under my own steam, I am walking again towards my doom, part of the huge, slogging effort which seems to be moving in two directions at once, like a great slithering beast that cannot make up its mind.

A shell lands screaming in the field, hitting perhaps the exact spot where I'd been standing a few minutes ago. It causes a ripple in the body of the beast, nothing more. I glance back anxiously, try to see what, if anything, was obliterated.

It occurs to me that that was the shell with my name on it. I was supposed to die in that blast, standing alone in the field marvelling at the great bloody buggered universe.

But here I am instead, my feet still moving forward, leaving my ghost to haunt at the shell-hole meant for me.

"Sure is pretty if you don't think about it too much," I say to the guy next to me, who doesn't know what the hell I'm talking about.

◈

"Jesus, Crome, you look worse than the day you left!" Binks says when I finally find the lads, sometime after dawn, in a half-collapsed farmhouse just short of the outskirts of bombed-out Ypres. It smells intoxicatingly of sausages and baked beans.

"What did you do, spend the whole time in Piccadilly fighting Germans?"

Some new guy is handling the pan over a low fire. A dozen others are sprawled in cots or beds of blankets and filthy hay, looking like they've been out all night on hard duty.

"Somebody had to do it," I say. "What have you guys been up to?"

"The usual shit," Binks says. "Williams pegged out."

"I heard," I say.

"Poor bugger. You heard about General Alderson?"

"What about him?"

"He's out now, gone to his reward in England. He was blamed for St. Eloi, but it's really the rifles, of course. Everyone knows that. Sam Hughes got him in the end. We're Byng's boys now, I heard. What's his name?"

"Sir Julian," someone says sarcastically. "A man with a brilliant record. He retreated from the Dardanelles without too many losses."

"And we're stuck with the Maggie Ross," Binks says bitterly. "It makes a good club, anyway."

Someone asks me if anything happened in London and I stand staring at him blankly for a moment, thinking Father was right about Alderson. Maybe right about everything. We're being led by incompetents only too happy to waste our lives in the mud.

The question is repeated and I say, "Nothing happened in London. A great glorious nothing. I saw Johnson, for God's sake. And we had Zeppelins one night."

"Zeppelins!" Binks says.

The guy at the pan is handing out the sausages and beans now so I whip out my mess kit. I ask how the last stint went.

"Not bad," Binks says. "Laying rails, for the most part."

"God, we need it," I say. "The roads are awful. If we ever had to get somewhere quickly . . ."

"Yeah, well, Fritz found our co-ordinates early," Binks says, "and had a hard-on for burying that line. Bloody relief to get out of there finally. Not quite Zeppelin-watching in London."

I almost burn my tongue on breakfast, it's so hot, and I'm so hungry. I scrounge some water and then attack my food again. I can't remember eating anything as good.

"Where the hell did you get sausages?" I ask the new guy. He smiles a bit like Reese.

"I had to do a little trading around," he says.

"He traded an Iron Cross for these sausages," Binks says.

The new guy shrugs his shoulders. "I heard the Kaiser's giving the Cross to anyone who successfully takes a shit. Anyway, you can't eat an Iron Cross. But sausages . . ."

"You can eat and then shit them out later on to collect your medal," Binks says, half-chewed sausages and beans slurping out the corner of his mouth while he talks. He turns to me. "Bet you missed this kind of sophisticated conversation when you were back in Blighty," he says.

"Every hour of every day," I say, thrusting my mess tin forward. I am eager for more of this soldierly fare, for anything, in fact, that will pull my thoughts away from argument and doubt about what the hell we are doing here, and who these distant gods are, gambling so recklessly with our bodies and minds.

◆

The new guy is Phil Livesay, who we call Lives, because he has such a way. It's Lives who finds the goose for us to roast at dinner, and the bedding for us to sleep on, hidden beneath the floorboards of another farmhouse down the way. Hundreds of soldiers must have combed through that place in the last few months, before Lives turned up that cache. And it's Lives who trades silver candlesticks for a bucket of real, honest-to-God oranges, Lives who hears first that the Ross rifle is bound for the trash heap after all, Lives who, increasingly, fills the void left by Snug and Reese and the others.

We work behind the lines for some days, and the memory of London turns weak and pale. I think vaguely of writing to Margaret, but everything I commit to paper in idle moments seems false and unimportant. Finally, a perfumed letter on rose-coloured paper arrives from Emily. She tells me how "boring" the house is since I have left, asks if I will be able to come back on my next leave in August, mistakenly thinking I get leave every four months, like an officer.

Margaret and Mr. Boulton have become officially engaged, she writes. *He is limping now with a cane and has taken on the air of the walking wounded. Margaret says to give you her kindest regards, by the way. She says to say she hopes you will be sensible. Whatever could she mean by that?*

That is all from Margaret.

I do scratch a few inconsequential lines in reply, but they remain mired in the bottom of my pack, along with my new puttees, which are too good for the muddy conditions I must work in. I'll save them for the next time I'm on parade.

The pullout for the Somme continues but we are not to be part of it, staying behind to hang on to this grim grey soup in

Flanders. Over a smoky dinner of our old reliable, bully beef, Lives reports a rumour he heard from someone in an *estaminet* in Vlamertinge that the Germans have been pushing out T-sap trenches near Mount Sorrel, and are probably going to try to join them up to make a new advanced front. Mount Sorrel is one of the few places we have a slight elevation advantage.

"They've been running out T-saps the last three weeks," Miller says. "Nothing new there."

"All kinds of railway activity in the rear, though," Lives says. "I talked to a corporal who saw the air photos."

"Fritz likes playing with trains," Miller says.

"Trains carry a lot of shells," I say. "This war might be won with trains."

One evening Sergeant Shipley, a decent man it turns out, pear-shaped with heavy jowls who looks like he should be stamping papers in a bank somewhere, gives us news of our new assignment. We're to head forward again and build up the reserve trenches in Sanctuary Wood. "We're moving out within the hour," he says, detailing the equipment and materials to be brought up, the order of formation, the assignments once we're in place. "Except for Crome," he says, stopping in mid-thought. "You're wanted at battalion headquarters about something. Colonel Murchison."

"Did you murder somebody, Crome?" Lives pipes up. I think immediately of that idiot I hit in Poperinghe. But he wasn't dead. Last I saw he was running to get away from the military police. No, it must be my father's transfer, I think, with a rush of blood to my face.

"I know what it probably is," I say. "I don't need to report."

Everybody is looking at me now, Shipley suddenly near anger.

"You've been ordered to report, soldier," he says coldly. "There is no question of choice. Do you understand that?"

"Yes, Sergeant," I say. "But I'll catch you up when I'm through."

"Sergeant, I'd be happy to report for Private Crome if he'd rather go on ahead in my place," Lives says, and then several others chime in that they'll volunteer for me, too.

"Maybe he got leave again, the lucky bugger," someone else says.

When I walk out they are busy once more with the preparations, stuffing their sacks, cleaning their rifles one last time, writing the brief notes to relatives we're required to pen whenever heading into danger.

"I'll catch you up," I say, but Lives, Miller, Binks, and the others, they're all engrossed in their tasks, and nobody looks my way.

◈

At battalion headquarters – a battle-scarred farmhouse a couple of muddy miles off – Colonel Murchison is not expected back until morning, and the orderly sergeant has no idea what the matter is about. "But if you were ordered to see Colonel Murchison then you'll just have to wait to see him. And I suggest you straighten up your uniform, soldier, before morning!"

I don't want to see Colonel Murchison. I don't want to straighten up my uniform, or spend the night here if I can help it.

"I think I know what this is all about, Sergeant," I say. "It's a mistaken request for a transfer. I'm happy to sign off now and say that I refuse all –"

"Are you still here, Crome?" the sergeant asks.

"I can sign a piece of paper, a form – you must have a form –"
I say it as quickly, as manfully as I can, to get my refusal over and
done with, before I am too tempted and muddled.

"And I told you to report in the morning. Would you rather
spend the night in the stockade?"

I step out fuming, look towards the dull darkness of Ypres
and the lens of battle beyond. The lads will be heading out the
Lille Gate by now, I think. There's not as much action as some
other nights, so it's a good time for moving forward. But I'm
stuck here.

I wander in disgust, find a deserted, private ruin where I sit
and clench my knees to my chest like a child. But I'm not a child,
I'm a soldier, and this is a long night with too much time to
think. I'd rather be doing almost anything else – digging a
latrine, hauling corrugated iron, polishing my bloody buttons.

Shouting at my father.

My father and his meddling, his disdain for anything I choose
on my own. This is not his war – fine, let him stay out of it. Let
him stay out of my affairs. He thinks he's right, he might well be
right, but damn him.

I had set my nerve. This, this is the worst, this waiting.

I almost believe he has arranged it all to happen this way. But
if he has, he is driving me in directions he cannot approve of,
into the arms of Margaret, who would happily see me pulled out
of this war as well, even if she doesn't mean to have me. I can
imagine frantic, fruitless trips to London on my days off, more
long, depressing walks in lonely parks, terrible arguments and
stolen, ragged moments of passion that would tear at the both
of us. I can feel the ache of my body for her even here. Would it
be any better if I were close to her, or would it be far worse?

Could I ever win her in this state I'm in? And if I did, could she ever forgive me?

I root through my pack, pull out a pencil and pad of paper, and make a quick rough sketch, with hard lines and dark shading, of an empty-eyed, grinning skull, teeth smashed in on one side, a sorry cigarette poking out of the other. Below I show a blackened, bony hand, and on the other side of the paper, and then four more sheets, I write:

Dearest Margaret,

You asked me once, and so I'll try to tell you, even this is not the worst of it. This is a sketch of "Fritz-boy," whose charming face graces the sandbagged wall of one of the many communications trenches leading to the forward lines. It's not much of a trench at that – even a short man like me must bend nearly double to traverse it safely. But it's considered very bad form to pass him by without shaking hands, and terrible luck to either snatch his cigarette away or light it for him. I can't say how long he's been there, but everyone knows of him, and half the men here think they've felt him squeezing their hand in return.

If you'd asked me a few weeks ago I would have said that the worst of it, for me at least, was in my very first week up the line, uncovering a rank, decomposing body of someone I knew. It was Charles Turner, or Mr. Turner – sir – as I'd always known him, the grade-school teacher who taught me how to grip a pencil and write the alphabet. He had a strong hand for whipping the backside of any boy who made trouble – used to brag, in a way, of having built up his muscles disciplining Crome lads. He was the man who set up an apple on a plate at the front of the room and explained to us in meticulous detail about shading and dimension, and then, before he could finish, realized I hadn't been listening and ripped the paper from under my arm. He was furious with any sort of disobedience, usually, but in this case he paused to look at what I'd produced, and had the grace to show the class, and say, "There's what I mean. Do it like young Crome!"

I had no idea he had enlisted. Though strong and fit, he must have been fifty when the war broke out. And here he was, a worm-eaten, bloated corpse coming out of the mud of the very first trench I was set to dig. I had his pay book in my hand, and I couldn't hold it still.

Everyone here has a story like that. When it's your teacher, your friend, even some chap who always managed to get your nose out of joint somehow – when it's someone you know whose guts have been shredded and whose bones have been exposed to sun and rain, then the war becomes something else. It's not a theory, or an exercise, or even something most of us can talk about rationally. We are here for each other, because of each other. When a man's been dragged down screaming into the fire, he cannot help but emerge, if he is to emerge at all, part hound of hell.

Ask me now and I'd say that the very worst of it, dearest Margaret, is being granted a reprieve, a temporary glimpse at life as it ought to be. The hardest thing has been meeting you and then having to leave you behind. I know you think I might have some sort of choice in the matter of how I continue to serve this conflagration. I wish to God I did. I would

*tell you not to marry Boulton, and would turn the earth over
to be with you, for you are as fine and kind and wise and
beautiful a woman as I have ever known, and I would count
myself the most fortunate man alive if I could spend my days
with you – even days banished to the harsh weather outside
your good graces. For surely such times could not last long in
a heart like yours.*

*But I have seen too many friends perish in this struggle,
have had both feet plunged into the pit and now the chains of
hell have hauled me back. And the worst of it, as far as I can
tell, is that I was freed for a time.*

*You asked what I was thinking when I kissed you. I was
thinking nothing, nothing at all, and you'll have to believe
me, dearest Margaret, only love could have brought such
blessed peace.*

◈

In a dream I'm walking slowly down the hall. It's so dark, my
toes must feel for the edge of the carpet, the slight depression
where one door leads to the wrong room and the other . . . the
other is a black barrier with no handle, no entrance. I have to
stand, still as death, have to stop my heart, calm my blood, and
wait for her to open it.

No breathing, no looking. It's for her to decide. Against my
will my toes curl into the floorboards – no carpet here, but the
creaky wood of an ancient house. The noise of it surges inside
me. I've ruined my chances, I realize, so pound on the door. The
darkness falls off, there's a mist rising from the river, and the
grass is as wet as if it had rained.

"It looks cool but it's warm," she says, standing straight, her skin so white in the shadows. I try not to stare at the fall of her breasts, her hair on her bare shoulders, the softness of her legs. She steps out a pace or two, the water already at her knees, and turns her backside to me, face to the sun now. I start walking hard to reach her, strain with the buttons of my uniform. She's farther away than she seems. But if I run it takes longer, so I head into the water as soon as I'm free of clothes, stroke hard and kick to cover the distance.

It is warm, like the bath we never get but long for after a filthy, hard march.

She rises from water red with blood, smiles to see me groggy after my swim, staggering on the soft bottom as I try to stand.

"I thought you'd be quicker," she says.

She steps closer and pulls my head towards hers and I taste the saltiness of the blood.

"It's just a small wound," she says.

I see it for a second on her neck, press my thumb on it.

"That's not what I want you for," she says.

We are on the grass now, spongy and warm, like a blanket spread out in the sun, and she pulls me on top of her. Her breasts are soft as pillows, and she closes her eyes, laces me inside her arms and legs.

"You would leave this?" she whispers.

We're soaked now from sweat and blood, and I can breathe out but not in as the lacing tightens, tightens, as if we are both inside a corset meant for one.

"You would leave this?" she whispers, again and again.

◆

Colonel Murchison is not there at seven-thirty in the morning. I have had an open-air breakfast of lame tea, thick porridge, and an alleged biscuit, at the battalion "mess," a filthy, drooping tent under cover of some half-broken trees. I have gone back for my kit, have shaved and washed, have blackened and brushed down my boots, have even donned the new puttees from Emily and Margaret.

I take a seat on a rough bench and wait for His Eminence to appear. It's a sunny morning, the firing in the distance constant. It picked up blazingly in the night, then seemed to die back. I hope the men got through.

A few birds persist in singing outside and the bog of Flanders oozes perceptibly – a great, sighing undertone that is usually drowned out by the din of artillery. And so I think either the bog has grown or the shelling is a little light this morning.

But Colonel Murchison does not arrive until mid-morning, and it is a stomach-churning time of doubt and uncertainty, the arguments whirling endlessly round and round my tired brain. Surely I've done enough, I think. I should save myself. The generals will spend my life as carelessly as throwing a cigarette into the wind. But then I see Snug lying in the gloom, I see Reese's body leaking life and spirit. Then I hear my father's voice, clear as a whipsaw: *For God's sake, be your own man for once in your life.*

Murchison is tall and strained-looking, with grey hair but a young face, dark bags lining the undersides of his eyes. I come to my feet uncertainly, like a schoolboy who has arrived for an examination with theorems and formulae swimming drunkenly in his head.

"Crome," he says, "who the hell do you know in the Ministry of Munitions?"

"I beg your pardon, sir?" I stammer.

"I won't stand for this," he says, livid. "This backroom string-pulling. Do you understand?"

I look at him blankly.

"Don't pretend you have no idea what's going on. Norman Webster, one of the key men at the ministry in London, has personally directed that you be transferred immediately to the Royal Flying Corps for engine technician training. What the hell could Norman Webster care about you, Private Crome? Except I find out that you have just returned from leave in London. So don't stand there and tell me you haven't a clue what's behind all this!"

Margaret and my father have joined forces, I realize angrily, and dragged Henry into it as well to get him to use his contacts.

"*Well?*"

"I, uh . . . I was in London, it's true. But . . ."

"Do you know how often I've had to deal with this sort of thing recently? I tell you, Crome, I won't stand for it!"

"I refuse the transfer, sir," I say quickly. "Of course I do. I never put in for it and I don't want it."

I'm sorry, Margaret. I'm sorry, Father.

"I beg your pardon?"

"It must be a mistake, sir," I say. And then, after some thought, "Permission to rejoin my platoon, sir. They've gone forward, and I should be with them."

"Do I understand you correctly, Private?"

"Whatever you want me to sign, sir," I say with a veneer of certitude, though my heart is racing off the rails.

What have I done? In an instant the matter is settled, yet the relief I expect does not materialize. Instead, I feel a squeezing of the chest that threatens to drive out all breath, a dizziness similar to what hit me at Westminster. But there is no Margaret here to catch me. I force myself to feign fitness, to go through with the signing and wait for dismissal. Then I stagger out, stand leaning against a post with my head down and eyes closed.

What an awful thing, this cowardice, I think.

Colonel Murchison leaves his office, strides past me, turns suddenly. "Are you all right, Crome?"

I pull myself straight.

"Yes, sir."

"You're looking pale, Private. Have you got the wind up?"

"It's nothing, sir."

"All right," he says doubtfully. "You report to the duty officer for now. We'll see about having you rejoin your mates tonight."

"Thank you, sir," I manage to say.

I spend the day on garbage detail, covered in flies and smelling of creosote. My partner, Adams, is a slack-jawed slouch with a black eye from fighting. I am wrestling an ungainly wooden limber down a rutted, pocked track while he leans on one side, allegedly helping. At one point he says angrily, "What are you whistling about?"

I stop and look at him.

"You've been whistling all bloody day," he says.

"Have I?" And I mean to tell him, it forces me to breathe.

"I've murdered people for less," he says.

I believe he has. He waves wildly at the flies then kicks the wooden wheel of the limber so hard I think he might break it. But the beast just shrugs a bit then settles back, unharmed.

It is an odd moment, the pitiless sunlight reflecting off the rotting pile of tins and food and broken helmets, of smashed cartons and other junk nearly overflowing this creaky limber, the flies and Adams's black eye, almost purple, actually, his haunted, craven look, and the mud on my new puttees, the feel of the grain of the wood of the handles in my hands.

I love it dearly, I think. This sorry, limping life of mine.

"Jesus-bugger these flies!" Adams says, and then, "What are you staring at?"

For once I have the sense to keep my mouth shut.

◆

Under cover of darkness I move forward with a reserve unit heading to Sanctuary Wood. It's a grim, sober group, silent on its feet, focused, and I try to fit in. I hear myself noisily panting like a dog, am filled with a dreadful sense of unreality, that I am an actor in a play with no idea what I'm supposed to say or do. But I follow along like the charlatan I am and we pass soundlessly through the Lille Gate, slip by Shrapnel Corner, and up the road past Zillebeke without incident. The German guns are almost silent in this sector, a strange bit of luck for us that makes me think of the Scot on the boat who, in this disordered universe, might be twisted in the slime somewhere right now, whatever his winnings at pontoon.

We hurry forward into the labyrinth of trenches with unexpected ease, as if it were a training exercise from all those months ago in Shorncliffe. When I get to the right section of the reserve position I find Lives, Binks, and the rest swarming the trench like worker ants, taking advantage of the quietness of the German guns.

"Bless my buggered soul!" Lives says when he sees me. "Look who decided to join us!" I smile with relief to see them, feel as though I have finally burst through the surface of the water after remaining too long below.

"What did the colonel want?" Binks asks. "A game of tennis?"

"Golf, actually," I say giddily. I unload my gear and then grab a shovel. "He needed some pointers on the use of the niblick."

"Quiet down there!" comes a stern voice – Shipley, somewhere in darkness along the way. "Who's that, Crome?"

And the news travels in spurts of whispers.

"Crome's here."

"Crome came back."

"Crome just arrived, finally!"

I tear into the work like a whirlwind, at last unreasonably relieved to be back where I'm supposed to be, among the damned. The night is so quiet, and even the mud is drier than it has been in the past, though the roots of the shattered trees give us problems. We are deepening a dugout and progress is slow, but I don't mind somehow. For a time at least it feels extraordinary to be here – to be young and strong and to test muscles and limbs against the elements, to have everything in life focused on the point of this shovel, to be told what to do and not have to decide.

We work through the night, hours of sweat and hard breathing, and it's quiet almost till dawn, when the Germans open up again as if to remind us there's a war on after all. But by that time the dugout is nearly done, the supports and beams in place.

Shipley brings the rum round and we sit dripping and filthy and strangely happy, each one of us, it seems to me, in our fine new digs, big enough for all twelve in our section. I tell the lads about the no-treating law in the pubs of London, and Lives pipes up, "Well, no point in us going there! My round after this!"

"Come on, Sergeant," Miller says to Shipley, who has the rum jar tucked under his arm, and pours with the solemnity of a born barkeep. "What about another round? We won't tell! It's been diluted more than usual anyway!"

"You're bloody right you won't tell," Shipley says. "Toss it back now, lads. There's going to be an inspection in half an hour." To our blank, disbelieving stares he adds, "General Mercer and Brigadier Williams are coming through. I just heard. Byng's men come to have a look at us. I want you all polished to the points of your noses. You can sleep later. Snap to it!"

It's unbelievable, an inspection in the trenches, with bloody generals to top it off! We are sour at a stroke, are still sitting and grousing some minutes later when the lieutenant pokes his head in the dugout. "What are you doing?" he says, staring at us. I suppose we look every bit a band of filthy-faced, rum-slowed, exhausted men who've spent the night digging out this cave and who aren't in a hurry to leave it.

"They're going to be here in twenty minutes!" he nearly screams. "A major general and a brigadier!"

Why not advertise to the Germans? I think. Get a megaphone?

"On your feet! Look smart! Scrape the mud from your clothes at least!"

We rouse ourselves and he leaves. Lives says, shaking his head, "Let's not be a disgrace," and then it's all right. Someone brings a bucket of water and we wash ourselves, after a fashion.

I use my bayonet to scrape clean my boots and puttees, now as filthy and worn as everything else I own. Miller has a stiff brush and goes around scrubbing everybody's back. I even manage to shave without cutting myself too badly. Soon enough Shipley herds us all out of the dugout and we line up at attention along the trench walls.

"What about breakfast?" Binks mutters.

"After Mercer and Williams are gone!" Shipley says. "Now look smart!"

It's a clear, cool, bright morning, wet with dew, will be as pretty a day as God makes, I think. But the smell of the place hits me anew – the reek of the bog, and the decomposing bodies just beyond our gaze. The light breezes are full of their gases, the soil is mulched with their flesh and juice.

Twenty minutes stretches into half an hour and we're still standing here, waiting.

"Maybe the generals are off playing croquet," Lives mutters. Shipley gives him a look, that's all. My stomach starts to rumble rudely. Shells fall not too far away and I can't believe we're standing here, waiting like this, for a couple of bloody generals who want to see what life is like at the Front. Any closer with those shells, I think, and I'm going back in the dugout. They can inspect me down there just as easily.

But the shelling moves on after a bit of return fire from our own guns. I'm surprised there's any left, given the pullout for the Somme.

After forty minutes, Mercer and Williams show up finally and we stiffen like statues. I focus my eyes straight ahead on a small point on the parados. If the Germans moved now, I think, they could round us up in a minute like toy soldiers.

The delegation gets to our section of the trench and out of the corner of my eye I can see, besides the generals, a lieutenant-colonel and two captains – a nice little clump of target. They move along briskly, stop to talk to Lives a few feet away from me.

"And what's your name, Private?" one of the gods asks.

"Livesay, P.W.," he says. Like some schoolboy in form.

"And where are you from, soldier?"

"Vancouver, sir! British Columbia," he says stiffly.

"Very good," the general says, as if anyone had a choice where they were born.

They walk by me quickly. Someone says, "We'd best get a move on, sirs, if we're going to keep schedule," and then it's over. They're on their way even farther up the line.

The lads bring tea, and something brown and mushy and mildly warm, which is labelled breakfast, and we lounge around in the dugout kidding Lives about his stiff response. "*Vancouver, sir!*" Binks says, shoulders to his ears, eyes popping, standing straight as a board, the top of his head rammed against the roof of our cave. "*British Columbia!*"

"*Very good!*" Lives shoots right back, in a good imitation of the voice of the general. "*Do you play tennis, Private?*"

"*No, sir. Not here, sir!*" Binks says.

"*Well, why not?*"

"*Sorry to say, General, sir, most of the courts have been blown to horse manure, and we lose a lot of balls in the mud, sir!*"

Seconds later a shell lands close enough to shake the timbers above us and bring glops of mud dropping on our heads.

"Oh shit!" Lives says, wiping the filth from his shoulder and neck.

More shells, some closer, some farther away. We huddle suddenly stunned and shaken – too much in the old moment, the joking over breakfast, to respond to this latest insult. Two, three, four nearly simultaneous explosions send more raining mud and I yell to Lives, "I turned down a transfer to be here for this!"

It's meant to be funny, but he looks at me like I'm a lunatic.

Some minutes later a rending blast brings half the dugout crashing down. One second Lives is crouched beside me, and the next his body is buried in rubble and mud with only a shin and boot sticking out. I'm blown back towards the doorway but return to the kicking boot, clawing at the dirt with my hands to dig him free. I look around for help but there's no one left. They've all disappeared under the soil. I pull myself out of the dugout to go for help, but can't find the trench. Everything has changed, is folded under now or been shattered into rubble and shell-holes.

"Hang on in there!" I cry, and somehow my hand finds a spade, and I hack and grope my way back under into the blackness. The shells keep falling all around. With half an ear I'm listening for our artillery's response – that normally quiets them down. The buckled remnants of the dugout won't hold much longer. I work furiously, following Lives's leg by touch up to the knee and hip, trying not to imagine that that's all I'm going to find, a detached limb.

But for the longest time I find nothing else of him, and my common sense tells me he can't survive this long without breathing. But I keep shovelling. His leg is moving still – it might be him, I think, or it might be just the jerk of the explosions, which are raining down in unleashed madness.

I find his other leg, try to keep the point of my spade from straying too close to where the rest of him must be. I imagine it slicing his backbone, cracking his neck. It's an agony of effort, the air now fleeing: I'm gasping but still force the spade forward. Then I throw it aside and pull and pull as hard as I can. Hardly anything to grip – he's slippery and impossible, but I work farther and farther until my arms are engulfed and my hands seem to be around something solid. Then I brace myself and pull and twist. He's too large, and it takes far too long, but at last he comes jerking out, slimed like an immense calf born of a shuddering, collapsed heifer. He's choking, spitting, coughing. I thrust my fingers in his mouth to pull out the clods of mud.

"Ah, Jesus, ah!" he says. "I thought I was gone."

I hack some more in the darkness at the jumbled wall of mud, broken timbers, slime, and old roots.

"Where's the bloody door?" he says.

"I'm trying to get the others out!" I yell at him.

"There's no bloody door!" Lives screams back.

He's dazed, panicking. I turn to show him the door, but it's gone, I can't feel it anywhere.

The explosions follow one on top of the other, and the earth starts to push against me, to grab at my knees and hips. We both now dig frantically towards where the door must be, Lives with his hands, I with the spade. I kick hard to keep my legs free.

But it's no use. The earth closes in. It grabs my waist and squeezes out the breath, and soon I can only jab with the spade, the tappings of a child.

"Lives!" I say, and get a mouthful of mud. I gasp and close my eyes, try to breathe, but my body now is in a vise and I'm being pulled down, compacted into a smaller and smaller space.

I hold my breath and try to think of one pure thing. It's Margaret in the bedroom door in the darkness, with my sketch rolled in her hand, looking at me. Looking.

The darkness turns completely black, and try as I might I can't hold her there.

Then everything bursts apart in a flash of mud and sky, and I am suddenly released from bondage to the other extreme, molecules blown to the very limits of their tolerance. I feel it all in extraordinary detail and slowness: my skin stretching like a great envelope under pressure, my body twisting and turning over onto itself, the sudden gasping freedom, the sense that one more ounce of pressure and everything will fly apart in bits of flesh scattering in all directions.

I am aware of the sun shining above me despite the smoke and ruin, the world writhing all around.

◈

Ages later I am able to focus on a single small thing, the way my breath starts a tiny channel of water and mud sliding beside my cheek, which is planted in the wet soil. And the mud in my left eye, in my ears, has made the world more bearable: the crashing of explosions has diminished; I can't see farther than the safe few feet around me.

I keep my face in the soil, in a hole that seems made for me. A space that is warm and comfortable, with a certain sucking strength. For the first time in ages I think of the Frenchman I shovelled into those sandbags. I can see now how he would have crawled down, down, yearning for rest and peace.

The shelling is much weaker than before, farther away. Our artillery must have responded finally, I think, the gears in my brain slowly turning again. Someone would have realized that the generals were up here with us, and rained down ten times what the Germans sent, and that's why it's so quiet. We've all had enough for now.

There's a funny huffing noise, like a burning wind. Please, not gas, I think. My mask is on my chest, buried deep in the mud, and it would take an enormous effort to pull myself out, to extricate it and put it on.

I wipe some of the mud from my face instead, and there's Lives beside me. Lives! With a silly grin and a bad scar . . . and no body. I move in a sudden spasm of panic, grab the thing by the hair and hurl it down the side of the shell-hole. It bounces and rolls like a rock and skids to the bottom, where water is already starting to collect.

I don't see any trace of the rest of him. Or of anybody else, for that matter.

I try to weld my eyes shut, to press myself down into the earth, but it's no good. Everything is upset now. I'm aware at once of a throbbing in my whole body, as if my skin has been scraped raw and I am bleeding from every pore. I shift with great reluctance, check myself, but all I see is a man of mud.

And something flickering in the distance, a flash of bright orange. With some effort I peer out at the world, expect bombs, smoke, explosions, but all that is clearing, subsiding wreckage after a storm. Instead, a few hundred yards off, I see waves of bucket-headed men in grey moving slowly, in formation, with packs, rifles at the ready. And then another orange flicker over there. I turn but miss it, catch another to the right – flame-throwers, my God. They are scorching the earth ahead of them, these quiet, slow grey men walking towards me.

I look round for a weapon – a rifle, a bayonet, a spade to bash in heads if necessary. But there's nothing but an awful sea of mud.

Where's our artillery? They must be able to see the German advance by now. There's sporadic shelling, some return fire down the line, but nothing to stop the slow grey waves, the awful bursts of the flame-throwers.

Then I spot a Lewis gun in a battered emplacement three shell-holes over, abandoned and pointing the wrong way, for God's sake. It looks too far to get to, and probably isn't functioning; that's why it was abandoned. But I'm moving towards it anyway, a sliding, sloshing, groping sort of slither over the rim of one hole and falling down the next. I expect a bullet in the back any second, think absurdly of the body armour Margaret and Emily almost got me, how if I were wearing it now . . . I wouldn't have the strength to pull myself out of the slime.

Down to the bottom of the second hole, and then I have no purchase. I can't climb out, but scramble madly, churning my legs to nowhere like a motor car sunk to the axles. Minutes go by. It's awful, the side of the hole starts to give way and fall towards me like the dugout did before.

I'm not going to be buried again.

Better to die on my feet than to disappear here under the soil without struggle. I have the absurd thought that Margaret should know where I was and what I was trying to do when Ypres fell and the Germans broke through the line.

Somehow my hand catches a bit of root and I'm able to pull myself up, am insanely upright on top of the shell-hole before sense takes hold again and I hurl myself down in the third. No time to glimpse anything. I struggle over a mound of bodies at the bottom of this hole, step on faces and arms, helmets, hands, kick and pull wildly until I am on my back heaving beside the Lewis gun.

They must be almost on top of me. I hear the roar of the flame-thrower somewhere close, pull myself to examine the gun. It is mud-splattered but all right, I think. The gunner is probably this paste of body parts smeared down the far side of the emplacement, now buzzing madly with flies. An ammunition pan is already loaded so I turn the gun, apply my shoulder, have to squint over broken sandbags to see where I'm aiming. I pull the trigger without thinking, waste a burst and bring a host of shots my way, slashing at the few sandbags left around me.

In a fit I let loose again, scrambling around to sweep the gun barrel on its stand from the left to the right and back again, firing like a madman without aim, at where I'm guessing the enemy might be. The noise fills the world, and soon enough my little spot is blanketed in a cloud of gun smoke. I blast until the pan goes empty, then stare out in shock at a desolate country-side littered with grey-clad bodies.

There is a pause before the return fire, and I scramble about looking for another loaded pan. Something buried a few feet away turns out to be a helmet brim. Something else is a rum jar, and then I pull up a mess kit and a grenade lands beside my hand, in such a way that I'm able to pick it up immediately and throw it back, and duck my head before it blows.

There is another pan in mud-covered canvas sacking upon

which the Lewis gun is resting. I take the gun down, tear open the sacking, pull out the second pan – why aren't there any more? – then wrestle the gun back into place, all the time looking wildly for any other bombs, as if I might be able to catch them all and hurl them back. I spend far too long getting rid of the old pan and inserting the new, and when I settle my shoulder behind the gun again my heart is pounding through my brain.

The grey soldiers are still coming. I try to aim before firing this time, watch as a man spins violently, as if drilling himself into the earth, and another falls straight back and disappears down a shell-hole. Bullets rip at me from the side and from behind, even, as parts of the German advance sweep past me. My angle of fire is restricted – to aim to the side I'd have to knock down part of the barrier that's protecting me.

Protecting me! Ridiculous. I'm not going to live through this battle.

That seems clear enough as I stand and hoist the gun on top of the sandbags – at least it isn't a bloody monster Vickers, I think – and fire into the smoke on the left side. I'm completely exposed now from the back and expect to be hit any second. But I force myself to count to ten before whirling and firing in the same way on the right.

A German makes it to within a dozen feet before the Lewis gun turns his body into a sputtering mess.

I dive down again and shoulder the gun back into its original place. Once more I fire madly, empty the pan before I can think. It doesn't matter. Minutes later, while I'm crawling away, a shell hits the side of the emplacement and sends a shower of earth skyward, and me rolling, rolling down to the bottom, where I belong.

More shells, falling faster, and not German ones either. Soon enough I realize they are coming from behind our lines. The rattle of machine guns sends a curtain of bullets overhead, makes me hug the earth again, want to burrow down into safety. I'm waiting for the Germans to find me, for some lad with blond hair to skewer me with a bayonet and have done with it. But we must have all gone to ground.

Nothing else to do. The only thing left, I realize, is to continue to breathe, but in every other respect to do my utmost to resemble a corpse.

◈

I rot and shiver in the mud for who knows how long. There are no redeeming final thoughts: the God of this disaster abandons me; I fail to conjure any image resembling Margaret, or anyone else I could remotely love. There are no final words for my mother or brothers or any of the lads – who are dead now ahead of me, their ghosts perhaps looking on, taking ghoulish bets, no doubt. After all, I hurled Lives's head down the side of a shell-hole.

If I make it to nightfall, I think without much hope or energy or faith, I might be able to crawl back behind our lines, wherever those might be.

I try to keep my muscles from seizing, my strength from leaching too quickly into the soil.

Espérance qui m'accompagne
A travers bois, pré et montagne . . .

"It is not my time," I say out loud, but it's a little voice, weak and hollow.

It takes the longest time to wake, and even then it is to darkness and disorientation. I feel my body welded into the soil, my clothes heavy as clay and rock. I stand and lurch, fall almost immediately, groan with the effort of rising again.

"You've been drinking," Margaret says bitterly.

"A man does," I say. I mean there are certain things. But she knows already. "Dearest Margaret," I say.

"Shut up and keep your head down," she says. Somehow she's talking in my father's voice.

"*Dearest Margaret,*" I say. "I wrote you a letter. But I didn't send it, did I?"

"Be quiet! Keep your damn fool head down!"

"I wrote you a letter," I say again. "Where did it go?" It's the censors, I think. They would never have passed it anyway.

The sidewalk spins and slams me on the side, I go bouncity-bounce, all the way down, but get up right away – out of the puddle, where the other bums are, sleeping it off. So I find my own bed.

Enormous noise for this time of night. A circus of some sort, with bright lights. I look for a long time at the skyline. Margaret says something and I tell her to be careful, the sidewalk is not in order.

"It's the Zeppelins," she says.

"Zeppelins!" It seems ludicrously funny. I laugh and laugh.

I would move if my arms didn't weigh a thousand pounds each and weren't planted in the ground. I would roll over and find where she is and pull her against me. She couldn't object to that.

"Darling, I'm going to have to ask you for a favour," she says.

"What's that?"

"I'm going to need you to come with me."

"Yes, of course," I say. But I don't move. I can't, I'm nailed here – like that sergeant on the barn, I think, except it's more a feeling of having soaked sandbags for limbs.

"Ramsay," she says, "darling –" I do like the sound of it, when she says it. And she seems to know that, so she repeats it. "Darling, I think I need you to show me the way. Would you mind terribly?"

Of course she doesn't know her way around. She's never been out here. And I would show her, I would! If the earth wasn't holding me down, I'd be the first one up and at it.

Terribly noisy all of a sudden, and the awful stench of factories and effort. It's no place at all for Margaret.

"Ramsay, come on!" she says.

"You go ahead," I mumble.

She is at my shoulders now, digging her hands under my armpits.

"Come on, Ramsay!" she says right in my ear, a touch of lead.

"Well, I can't –"

She's pulling and lifting. She isn't strong enough, for God's sake; she's a feeble woman and I mean to tell her, but I have to turn around to do that because of the noise and smoke, and by then of course I'm on my feet.

"It's this way, I think, darling," she says, softening her voice.

"I don't think so," I say, and point the right direction. She doesn't know this area at all, and here she is trying to tell me –

"If you must," she says. "But take my arm, please, dear."

She waits where she is, and so I must stagger towards her, before the drink has worn off, and at this ungodly hour. When I get there she clamps to me like a steel spring and heads us in precisely the direction she'd meant to go all along.

I stop her finally, close to a great mound of rubble.

"Enough!" I say and lean over to catch my breath. She glances about wildly as if an omnibus were about to run us over. I ease myself down, knowing exactly where I am, thank you, and stretch out.

"Fine, darling," she says. "I suppose this will be all right."

I close my eyes but don't sleep because of her chatter.

"I'm just sorry that we've come all this way," she says. "The train will be getting in soon but we haven't settled anything, have we?"

"I thought it was settled," I say idly. It's so nice to hear her voice, though I'm not sure what she's talking about.

"Did you?" she says. "And what did you think we'd decided?"

The roar of trains going by, several of them stacked on the same track. They're going to collide some time, I think. Bloody bad planning.

"After the war," I say slowly, figuring it all out despite the noise and confusion, "when you've married Boulton, I'm going to be –"

"Yes, dear – my dog, you said."

"Still in love with you," I say, though the wind erases nearly every word.

Daylight now, and I've been chasing her for ages, without water, without a bite of meat. When I look left I catch a glimpse of her right, and when I look right, there she is left, and the world has turned to the worst sort of boggy swamp. I'm on all fours, of course, and that helps, but it's hard to keep my snout above mud.

She's hardly gotten her dress dirty; it isn't fair the way she knows where to step. Every so often she turns and calls me, impatiently, as if I'm hopeless, will never catch her up.

I've lost her, I think. She'll never have me back in the house like this.

I stop and wait, try to gather my strength. Maybe if I were on two legs . . .

But I can't rise. I've forgotten how. In my rush to become a dog – even Margaret's shaggy beast – I've completely forgotten the most basic things. And my poor tangled coat is loaded down in mud, I'll never . . .

She starts pulling at my collar.

"Ramsay, come on, boy!" she says, but it takes all her strength to lift my head. "Come on!"

She yanks so hard I have to rise, but when I turn to see she isn't there.

She isn't there.

My beautiful Margaret has left me standing on two slender legs in the middle of a storm.

"Get down! Get down, you damn fool!"

Not Margaret's voice. Not Margaret at all. It's so bright, suddenly. I sink to my knees, and the earth erupts all around in flying clods of dirt and awful rushing noises, some kind of accident, locomotives hurtling into one another, but on and on and on.

It takes forever for my mind to clear.

"This way if you can!"

He's an odd sort of Englishman, dressed in the wrong uniform.

"Down! Dammit, man, down!"

My body is so slow to follow commands.

"Where are you from?" the soldier yells across the mud to me, his head barely visible. So I tell him. And he says, "Have I got that right? Vancouver Island?"

"Yes! Yes!" I tell him.

"Well, man, did you ever fish the Chemainus River?" he yells.

"The Chemainus?"

"Yes!"

We are screaming at each other across the noise of explosions.

"I fished there as a boy!" I yell.

"Well, if you stay down, and work your way towards me," he says, "you just might live to fish the Chemainus River again!"

I fight my way towards him, burrowing, almost, in the torn soil, pulling and struggling every awful foot. Then I'm over and safe, a puddled little pile of weakness at the feet of a man in the wrong uniform. He thrusts his hand into mine – a warm, strong, dry hand – and says, "Baron Frederich von Leiden. I spent years on Vancouver Island, fishing the Chemainus River. There is no place on God's earth more beautiful."

To which I find I cannot say anything.

"Look at you! You're exhausted," he says.

"Water," I manage to say, and he instantly offers some of his, which I drink with abandon. Then I tell him I'm starving and he shakes his head sadly.

ALAN CUMYN

"They told us the British weren't feeding their men," he says.
"But I didn't believe it." He has a hunk of cheese right in his
pocket. I gobble it down, and then some more of his water. "How
long were you out there?" he asks.

I shake my head dumbly.

"I watched you weave around shell after shell," he says in
amazement. "I've never seen such a thing. You wouldn't be a
priest by any chance?"

I have some more water.

"You're right, not many priests out here," he says. "But we've
captured three or four of your generals. Your officers probably
didn't tell you that. Won't be very long now till the war is over."

I close my eyes, numb to the thought of it.

◈

Later, a strange light – a kerosene lamp, and I am in a dugout
like I've never seen before, with ceiling, walls, and floor all concrete, a built-in shelf lined with dark bottles of wine and tins of
food. On a small table sits a silent phonograph and beside it my
baron, bent over something – a letter – his tunic draped on the
back of his chair.

"Awake, are you?" he says, noticing me. He sounds more
British in his accent than Uncle Manfred. And the noise outside is fearsome, the ground shuddering with each successive
explosion. I look to the ceiling with worry but everything
seems secure.

"I had to drag you in here," the baron says. "No sense trying
to go anywhere just now. Do you want any food?" He follows the
largeness of my eyes, and in short order I am at the table tucking

in to a fine plate of German meat and black bread and downing it with Belgian wine. He watches me with some satisfaction as I gorge myself. Slowly, I come to realize he has cleaned me up, washed the mud off my face and hands.

"I remember a particular salmon," he says. "I fought him for forty minutes on the fly. He was the size of a man's leg, almost, and when I finally danced him into the net, he leapt up one last time and bit me on the arm, then twisted free and swam off. You don't believe me?" He rolls up the sleeve of his undershirt and shows me a small red scar on his bicep. "Only in the Chemainus River!"

My eyes find his letter on the table. "I am writing to my wife," he says. He roots through his pockets, produces a creased photograph of a young woman perhaps half his age, in a simple dress, looking away, with an aureole of whitish blond hair surrounding her head. "Here she is," he says with enthusiasm. "This is my Felice."

I swallow hard, nearly choke with the desperate pull of my hunger.

"How is that for someone to dream about?" he asks. "But when I am actually at home with her . . ." And here he shakes his head almost in an exaggeration of ruefulness. "We fight like rats, and I cannot wait to be back here, so that she will act properly, in my mind. Women! They have never understood a good war."

He shakes his head again, drunkenly I see now, gazes at his lovely wife. "Not that I understand this good war, either," he says.

He finishes his mug of wine, and pours more for me, and a terrible explosion sends a shower of dust down from the ceiling. We're alone here, I think. I should be able to spring at him, overpower him, choke him on the floor. But it seems ridiculous.

He's too large, my limbs are spent, and besides, the war raging out there with such anger, that's for other people now. I drain my mug, tip it towards him for a splash more.

"I am in love with a woman I will never marry," I say soberly, and raise my mug. "But I think she has somehow saved my life. Or the thought of her has, at least."

"Then yours is the luck of the ages," says the baron, smiling.

In time the cannonade outside lulls and he pushes himself back from the table, shakes his large head like a black bear ridding itself of flies.

"Come on, then. I will see you to safety myself." He helps me to my feet, and out of the fine concrete dugout we climb. Other German soldiers scramble up and down the trench, with hardly a glance at me, since I am with the baron. But he stops three, four soldiers in a row, and in a torrent of German that seems unnatural, considering how well he speaks English, he tells them, so I gather, of my exploits in staggering from shell to shell unhit through the worst of it. Every few breaths he smiles at me, nudges my shoulder, pantomimes my miraculous passage with a drunken zigzag of the hand. I am shocked that they look so much like my own fellows, these pale, ragged, weary German soldiers, their eyes full of admiration and longing for fortune as profound as mine.

The trench is deep and wide, dry, higher than the tallest man's head: a fine German fortification, not just a ditch in the mud. For a time it seems to me I'm dreaming again, will wake up any minute to find myself – where? Back in London, in that fussy, gentle room? In the dugout with the lads? Or in a tent with my brothers sleeping on the banks of the sweet Chemainus?

One step follows another, past wounded men now, and

exhausted soldiers and other prisoners, wretched, laid out some of them, barely alive. I cannot focus on anything except the large, rounded back of this Baron von Leiden, who walks slowly, as a baron would, I suppose, in no particular hurry to get us out of harm's way.

In time we are on a muddy track with crowds of others heading away from the battle. There's a shocking number of prisoners, it seems to me, many of them carrying stretchers, or lending a shoulder to a lame man. Their eyes are down, heads lowered in defeat and exhaustion. We tread like tired animals with hardly a German guard to poke us or bark out directions.

By the side of the road is the corpse of a fallen, fly-coated Highlander, his kilt torn to shreds and smeared in aging, blackened blood. I can see in a moment where a thousand German soldiers heading away from the Front have had bayonet sport with the body. My baron shakes his head in disgust, and mutters to me as we pass, "Do you know, you can make men do anything."

I look back for a moment at where we've come, and see columns of black smoke rising in the distance, and forlorn groups of fellow prisoners limping dully, and the same sort of shattered trees, demolished farmhouses, busted carts, broken machines, and mangled bodies that line the route away from our side of the fighting as well. It seems to me the saddest thing I've ever seen, this death and despair so equally divided on either side. For a strange moment I imagine there are no sides at all, that we're fighting ourselves, that the corpse that comes with victory will be our own.

It starts to rain again in thick, cruel, relentless Flanders fashion. By a half-smashed farmhouse, walls open to the world, the baron hands me over to a squad of mounted lancers, looking like medieval knights. Their horses are black beasts sick with the disgrace of this pedestrian duty. They restlessly tap their iron-clad hooves on the slippery cobblestones, their muscular flanks glistening in the wet. *What sort of war is this?* they snort, looking at me as if I'm personally to blame.

No more words from my baron. He shakes my hand with stiff formality, steps back and bows briefly, then is on his way. "Thank you," I say to him, too late for hearing.

I scan the faces of the other prisoners straggling in, but they all seem to be strangers. We are bandaged, muddy, dispirited men, our clothes torn, faces either blank or stricken, eyes raw with terror or dull as stone. No one has the heart to speak, and too soon a platoon of us is collected here, and once again we are stumble-marching along, the enormous horses now in front of us and behind, their riders spit-polished and miserable, faces hard, the rain running rivers down their helmets.

"Uhlans," someone mutters to me.

I hear a commotion behind and turn to see in the rear a wounded fellow, his arm in a blood-blackened sling, on his knees by the side of the road, scrabbling with his good arm at some papers in the mud. One of the Uhlan guards looms above him, prodding him with a lance. Like the others I watch dumbly for a moment, as if spectators at some sporting event. The soldier persists in reaching for the papers – letters, I realize, utterly soiled. Suddenly the Uhlan runs him through the shoulder and the man falls over, lies in agony on his back.

I am by his side without realizing the effort of several strides. "Back away, bastard!" I yell at the helmeted fool perched so high above me, his lance now raised to the level of my throat. I ignore him, turn to the poor sod whose life is draining fast into the broken ground. He convulses, his hand clutched around one of the letters, the ink running like blood. Then I feel the point of the lance on my own shoulder and turn in anger, have both hands on the damn thing before I know what I'm doing.

"Private! Release that lance immediately!"

A bloody English captain has raised his finger – I nearly laugh, it's as if he's pointing a pistol at me.

"*Now!*" he yells, and I don't move. For a second I imagine the Uhlan spurring his horse forward, running me through.

But he doesn't, and when I let go of the lance the captain pushes me away from the wounded man and the angry guard.

"It's finished," he says to me. I turn back, see the pages scattered, the dullness glossing the eyes of the newly dead. "You've done your worst. Now it's a matter of staying alive. That's your duty." Then, loud enough for the others to hear as well, he says, "Your duty is to stay alive!"

Step by step. My weary legs. It seems too much to comprehend. But the war *is* finished, I think. It really is for me. And Margaret, and all I love, is over there behind me, on the other side of the great, stinking conflagration. By my own design, it occurs to me, a conclusion so sickening and absurd it is almost funny. A man with a black eye and half an ear missing catches the expression on my face, looks at me for a moment like I am the devil's fool.

"I am!" I say to him crazily, and it becomes a stubborn little refrain in my mind. "I am, I am."

I keep on bloody walking, for there is no choice in the matter. We have all done our very worst, and yet here we are, the devil's fools, sentenced to survive. Step after step, and on the interminable march my beautiful new boots, my stolen boots that took me to London and then back again, start to fall apart and flap in the rain, the soles separating into layers of rot in this most lost and wretched season of our lives.

ACKNOWLEDGEMENTS

The author gratefully acknowledges the financial support of the Canada Council for the Arts, the Ontario Arts Council, and the City of Ottawa arts funding program in the preparation of this manuscript. Thanks too to my wife, Suzanne Evans, whose research interests dovetailed with mine for this project, and whose love and support have meant everything for many years; to Frances Itani, for her invaluable advice and encouragement in the beginning; to Bruce Cherry of Back-Roads Touring of London, for sharing his extraordinary knowledge of that old city and of the battlefields, cemeteries, and museums of the Western Front, and for his help in reviewing an early version of this manuscript; to Norm Christie of CEF Books for his helpful advice on research issues, and for reviewing the manuscript in the later stages; to Carol Reid, Phil White, and Eric Fernberg of the Canadian War Museum and to the staff of the National Archives in Ottawa and of the Imperial War Museum in London for so enthusiastically sharing the wealth of their historical treasures.

This is a work of fiction and, except for references to public figures, the names, characters, places, and incidents are the product of the author's imagination, and their resemblance, if any, to real-life counterparts is entirely coincidental. However, I have pulled upon some strands of family history and mythology, and in following them up am most grateful for access to family papers shared by Joan Matthews and Barbara Fraser, and for Philip Arthur Cumyn's memoir and family history, *The Sun Always Shines*. The poem "Espérance" was written by my great-grandfather, George Louis Cumine, and the letter of condolence read by Ramsay in the butcher's house upon arrival in London borrows heavily from the letter written to my family upon the death of my great-uncle Claude Cox.

I consulted too many published works to name here, but among the most valuable were Sandra Gwyn's *Tapestry of War*, Will R. Bird's *Ghosts Have Warm Hands: The Letters of Agar Adamson*, George Coppard's *With a Machine Gun to Cambrai: The Journal of Private Fraser 1914-1918*, William Boyd's *With a Field Ambulance at Ypres*, Mrs. Peel's *How We Lived Then: 1914-1918*, *Chronicle of Youth: Vera Brittain's War Diary 1913-1917*, C. Sheridan Jones's *London in War-time*, John Bignell's *Chelsea Seen from Its Earliest Days*, A. Rawlinson's *The Defence of London 1915-1918*, Michael MacDonagh's *In London During the Great War*, Albert Marrin's *The Last Crusade: The Church of England in the First World War*, Norm Christie's *The Canadians at Mount Sorrel June 2nd-14th, 1916*, and *Songs and Slang of the British Soldier 1914-1918*, edited by John Brophy and Eric Partridge.

Finally, I must thank my publisher Ellen Seligman and assistant editor Jennifer Lambert for their skilled guiding hands, and my agent, Ellen Levine, for her help in seeing it whole.